The Lost Daughter

R.P.G. Colley

Novels by R.P.G. Colley:

https://rupertcolley.com

The Lost Daughter

Rupertcolley.com

'A baby is God's opinion that the world should go on.'

Carl Sandburg (1878 – 1967)

PART ONE

Chapter 1

And so the moment is almost upon us – the moment I've been dreading for weeks, months, perhaps even the last twenty years. I look across the round table at my daughter, my baby, now all grown up and on the threshold of adulthood, talking excitedly about the halls of residence, about the other students she's already met. 'The halls have even got a cleaner who comes in twice a week,' says Tessa, between mouthfuls of noodles.

It's all a little odd, a bit surreal even. Sitting here in this huge restaurant in Leeds next to Barry, my ex-husband, in this chain restaurant that seems to serve nothing but noodles, every variation you can think of, trying to remain civil for the sake of our daughter. A television installed high on the wall in the corner of the restaurant is showing a football match. I can see Barry trying his best to ignore it while craning his neck when he thinks I'm not looking. I sip my wine, a large glass of red. I sensed Barry's disapproval as I ordered it but boy, I need it.

'So when do your lectures start?' asks Barry. I must've told him this already half a dozen times but I hold my tongue. Tessa tells him in unnecessary details the comings and goings of her first year timetable. Barry cocks his head to one side listening, trying his best to show he's interested.

Tessa tries to eat and talk at the same time, everything so quickly, as if she is fighting against a deadline, while I pick at my food. She's a girl in a hurry, and why shouldn't she be? Her future beckons. I notice her glance to her right at a table full of boys, good-looking young chaps, all of them, but even a beauty such as my daughter can't divert them from their interest in the football. On our other side sit an elderly couple, silently hunched up over their bowls, concentrating. The elderly couple aside, I think Barry and I must be the oldest people here. This is a restaurant for youngsters; the place is teeming with them, talking loudly, laughing, enjoying the easy food, the loud music, the garish colours.

Tessa stabs at her noodles. 'I don't think I can eat all this.'

'Don't talk so much, then.' Did that sound as curt as I fear?

'She's excited, Liz.'

'Yes, I'm sorry.' I flash her a smile. 'Of course you are, darling.'

'Oh, and the college bar do half-price cocktails all night on a Tuesday.'

'Careful how you go, though, Tess,' I say, immediately regretting it.

'Please, Mum, spare me the last-minute lectures, hey?' She reaches out for my hand.

'I'm sorry.' Her soft fingers rest on the back of my hand.

'I wish I went to uni,' says Barry.

'You never went to university, did you, Mum?'

Why did she say that, I wonder; she knows full well I didn't. Barry throws me a sideways glance; he knows the matter has always been a little chip on my shoulder. Did I see a trace of a smile on his face? I hope not.

'My mother... she wasn't keen,' I say. 'It was a different time then, especially where we lived.'

Barry laughs. 'Oh, come on, Liz, it was hardly the Stone Age.'

We've had this conversation before; I will not rise to the bait.

A cheer erupts from the table of boys. They all take to their feet, standing on tiptoe, trying to see the television. They high five each other and, one by one, return to their seats with smiles on their faces. I see the elderly couple shaking their heads. This is no way to behave in a restaurant. I realise I envy them. They don't talk, but I can sense their ease with one another, an ease built on forty, fifty years of companionship, of togetherness. Perhaps they've just seen off a grandchild to university.

Barry, too, is grinning.

'Who's playing?' asks Tessa.

'England versus Germany,' says Barry. 'Amazingly, it's two-one to us.'

England v Germany. A cold shiver trembles through me. Those hated words, the memory, oh, so long ago, but vivid still. I was only eleven years old, but no one ever had cheered England on as much as me – and I have no interest in football whatsoever; indeed, I hate it.

Tessa's phone lights up on the table. 'Oo,' she says. 'That's Gabbie.' She reads the text, her fork loaded with noodles poised mid-air. 'She's waiting for me. I'd better be going.' She places her fork on her plate. She pulls on her blouse. 'How do I look?'

'Beautiful,' says Barry with a smile.

He's right, of course; she does look beautiful, her long

eyelashes framing her almond eyes, her Cupid lips, the little upturned nose, the fresh complexion. Too much makeup for my liking but that's a battle I lost long ago. Still, she is beautiful. She is my daughter, and she is leaving me.

She checks the contents of her handbag, checks her phone again. 'Well,' she says with a satisfied sigh, 'I guess this is it.'

We all rise. Barry offers to walk her back up to the halls.

'No,' she says, firmly. 'You stay finish your lunch. I'll be fine.'

I smile away my disappointment. 'If you're sure, love.' My eyes are pricking but I mustn't cry, must not; it'd be unfair on her.

Tessa smiles but there is a flicker of hesitation. This really is it. My baby is leaving. 'Thanks for driving, Dad.'

The two embrace. 'Anytime, sweetheart.'

She plants a kiss on his cheek. 'You need to trim your moustache, Dad,' she whispers into his ear.

'Mum.' She holds her arms out for me. I hug her, my only child, now taller than me, now a woman in her own right. Her arms wrap around me, and I breathe in that familiar smell, lavender and coconut, but more than that, I breathe in her very essence, my only child, my girl.

'Give me a call tonight, yes?' I ask.

'Sure.'

'Promise?'

She kisses me. 'Promise.'

'Good luck, love,' says Barry with a wink.

Tessa winks back at him. 'Thanks, Dad.' She looks at us both, her estranged parents, reunited for the day for her benefit. 'Thanks for the lunch. Bye bye.'

'Bye, love,' says Barry.

'Goodbye, my darling.'

And with that, Tessa swings around and jauntily walks through the restaurant, checking her phone, and out. I fight the urge to take Barry's hand. We watch her from inside as she waits at the pedestrian crossing, then crosses the high street bathed in late afternoon sun, and walk briskly up the hill, hugging the shops on her right. We watch as she disappears into the crowds, getting smaller and smaller, but we can still see her, just about. I will her to stop, turn around and come back to me. *Don't leave me, Tessa, don't go*. And then she turns a corner, and she is gone and something inside of me dies.

Barry and I sit back down. I feel so heavy. I finish my wine and immediately want to order another but I can't face Barry's sanctimonious telling off. I so hoped she'd find a university within East Anglia, closer to home, so that she could carry on living at home. But no, she was set on this course in this city.

Barry sighs. 'Twenty years. Gone.' He clicks his fingers. 'Just like that.'

The elderly couple at our neighbouring table have paid their bill and are now standing up and gathering their coats and bags. As they make their leave, the woman winks at me, an acknowledgement of some sort.

Meanwhile, the boys at the next table cheer and shout again, thumping the air. Barry jumps up, craning his neck. 'Oh my God, we've scored again. It's three-one! Three-one, Liz – against Germany. Bloody unbelievable.'

'Yes, Barry. Unbelievable.'

Barry remains on his feet, unable to take his eyes off the screen, while the memory returns to me… Then, as if to reinforce the unwelcomed intrusion into my mind, one of the boys, facing the television, throws out his arm, and shouts *Sieg Heil*. My heart runs cold. Barry throws me a worried glance.

'It's OK, Liz, ignore it.'

'It's not OK, how dare–'

'No, Liz, not now, not here. Leave it.'

He's right. I sit on my anger, breathing deeply, trying to calm myself. The boy can be no more than seventeen, a respectable-looking boy, totally unaware of the effect he's had on me. I must hold myself together. *Don't let it overwhelm you, Liz,* I say to myself. I poke my fork at the now cold noodles. 'I need to go.'

'What? Now?' says Barry, who is now standing watching the football. 'It's almost finished. Ten minutes plus injury time. This is the best match–'

'Please, Barry, I need to get home.'

His eyes flit from me to the television screen and back again. With an exaggerated sigh, he sits back down. 'OK, perhaps it's for the best. I'll get the bill.'

Chapter 2

We drive the hundred and sixty miles home mostly in silence. England have just beaten Germany five-one, and Barry is happy. The fact that our only daughter has left home for university seems to have had no affect on him. 'Never thought I'd live to see the day,' he says to himself, shaking his head with obvious wonderment.

'Why? She's an intelligent girl. You know that.'

'No, I mean…' He glances over at me, not sure whether I'm teasing him or not. Silence, he decides, is the best option here. He weaves the car through the traffic, swearing occasionally at other drivers. He turns on the car radio, and the first item on the news is the damn football. He turns the knob and finds a classical music station playing a Beethoven piano concerto. Barry taps out the rhythm on the steering wheel. Beethoven – bloody German.

After several miles in silence, Barry brings up the subject I always dread. 'So…' Even that, the elongated 'Sooo' is enough to alert me. 'So how's it going with the house sale?'

'I'm still clearing it out, Barry.'

'Have you had it valued yet?'

'No.'

'Jeez, Liz. What you playing at? I thought we'd agreed–'

'It doesn't seem right. She's not even dead yet.'

'You know why, Liz; we've talked about this a hundred

times. You know why.' I can see him trying to contain his annoyance. Trying to rein it in. 'This week, right? Just phone the sodding estate agents and make an appointment. It ain't that hard, is it?'

'No.' Oh, but it is, it's bloody hard.

Barry drives me to my front door. He parks up, and we sit in the car for a moment. The sun has petered away but the day is still warm. I live on a long, quiet street in an outer Norwich suburb. We watch a group of boys playing football ahead of us. I wonder whether I should invite my former husband in for a cup of tea. I want to, desperate not to face an empty house so soon.

He sighs. 'Look, Liz, you need to lighten up a bit. She's only gone to uni, not to the moon.'

But it is more than that. He'd left me less than a year before. My life, as I knew it, had collapsed around me. I dread to think what I would have done without Tessa. And he tells me I need to 'lighten up a bit'. I don't respond, don't know how to without breaking down.

After a while, he says, 'Look, I'd better go. I promised the boys I'd take them out for pizza tonight.'

'Oh. OK. That'll be nice.'

'Hmm.'

His boys, his new family. Having left me, Barry shacked up with the woman he'd been having an affair with, a woman twenty years younger with two boys from a previous marriage. Barry had a ready-made new family. And tonight, he was taking them out for pizza.

'Thanks for dropping me off,' I say, opening the car door. 'Have a nice evening.'

'Sure. Hey, Liz.'

I pause, my feet on the pavement. 'Yes?'

'Look after yourself.'

I swallow. 'Yeah. Thanks.'

I find my front door key. I glance back as Barry cruises away, pausing while the boys stop their game of football and make room for him to pass.

I live in a large, three-bedroom, semi-detached 1930s house. A year ago, with the three of us, it was full of life. Now, returning, it's as if it's had its heart ripped out. My heart sinks to my stomach as I turn the key and step inside. Tabby, our unimaginatively named tabby cat, comes to greet me. So, you see, I'm not quite alone.

The first thing I do is go upstairs to Tessa's bedroom. I stand at the door and take in the familiar room that now feels so different. On her chest of drawers is a framed photo of the three of us, taken on a holiday when Tessa was thirteen. She grins at the camera, a brace on her teeth, the freckles on her shoulders picked out by the sun. We were a small family, just the three of us, but a happy one. That woman, that bitch, hadn't walked into our lives yet, hadn't stolen my husband and destroyed everything I held dear. Another photo shows Tessa with her grandmother, taken, I think, just two years ago on my mother's eighty-fourth birthday. I've never liked the picture; there was something false about my mother's smile; it sort of summed her up.

Opening the wardrobe, I rummage through her clothes, the ones left behind. I pull open her drawers and spy a red cosy jumper she always wore on cold, snuggly nights. I sit down on Tessa's bed and bury my head in it, breathing in the familiar, reassuring smell of my daughter. Oh, Tessa, you've no idea how much I'm going to miss you.

Having fed the cat, having eaten a passable microwave meal, having put the TV on, I finally put my feet up and relax.

I watch the news. President Bush and Prime Minister Blair are talking; protesters are demonstrating against the rise of petrol prices, and, of course, the good news is that England beat Germany five-one away from home. Perhaps I'll have a bath; perhaps I'll play loud music; perhaps I'll dance; perhaps I'll walk around naked. I can do anything I want now, no one to admonish me, no fussy husband, no daughter too wise beyond her years. Just me and the cat. I am free. Free. But all I do is watch the TV and, from the corner of my eye, keep a constant check on my charging phone, willing it to light up, to ring. She said she'd ring. It's past ten o'clock now and still she hasn't rung. I could ring her. Surely it's my prerogative as a mother but I can't bring myself to intrude on her first night away from home. She'll ring me when she needs to, when she's ready. Tabby settles down on my lap, purring.

Two hours later, I go to bed. She never phoned.

Chapter 3

My eighty-six-year-old mother lives in Woodlands View, a plush care home, has done for over a year already. Only a twenty-minute drive away, I usually go to visit twice a week, one evening after work and, if I can face it, every Sunday. I feel guilty even about that – is it enough? Should I visit more often? But I work full time still. I get tired, and visiting Mother is always a draining affair. My mother had lived alone in an old damp cottage in a small village called Waverly on the East Anglian coast. Today, we'd call it 'downsizing'. My overriding impression of the second home was of living somewhere constantly buffeted by wind and lashing rain, whatever time of year. My mother has been a widow some forty years. It's a long time to be alone, but she never once considered finding someone new, at least not to my knowledge. It isn't out of loyalty to my father, I'm sure. My mother has no loyalty to anyone – except perhaps herself.

We'd visit just once a month, the three of us. It was never something we looked forward to. Tessa, once she got to the age of fifteen, refused to go. 'It's so boring,' she'd said, 'and she's so horrible.'

'Tessa, how–'

'She's got a point though,' said Barry.

'Yes, but this is her grandmother we're talking about.'

'Yeah, a bad-tempered, bitter old witch.'

'Barry, you…' I didn't know what to say, to either of them. But he was right; she was embittered. The dementia had only exacerbated it.

The care home is two large Edwardian houses merged into one. It accommodates about fifteen residents. It's a Tuesday evening; the ground is still wet after an earlier downpour, and the air smells fresh. I press the buzzer next to the front door and the door swings open. I walk in and breathe in the familiar smell of disinfectant and canteen-like food. One of the carers greets me as she passes. I walk through to the lounge area. A number of residents, mostly female, sit round the perimeter, some vaguely watching the mounted television set that is permanently switched on, all day, every day. Mother isn't here. I walk through to the conservatory and find her sitting alone in an armchair staring out into the garden, watching a robin pecking at a bird feeder swinging from a low branch of the elm tree.

'Hello, Mum.'

'Hmm? Who's that?'

'Your daughter.' I pull up a hardback chair and sit next to her. 'How are you today?' She pulls her shawl tighter; she smells of carbolic soap. 'Have you had your lunch?'

'Oh yes.' She proceeds to tell me in great detail what she ate for lunch. Anyone listening would have thought she'd eaten at the Ritz. It's all nonsense, of course.

'Barry and I took Tessa to her university over the weekend. She was awfully excited.'

'Tessa?'

'Your granddaughter.'

'How old is she now?'

My mother often asks about people's ages. If I ask her how old she is, the answer varies from twenty-five to sixty depending on where she is in the recesses of her memory that particular moment. She is never older than sixty.

A carer with a swirly tattoo around her wrist pops in and offers me a tea. I thank her but say no. I won't be staying long; I rarely do.

And so I proceed to tell my mother all about our last day with Tessa: the halls of residence, our meal of noodles, the football game, saying goodbye, returning home to an empty house. At least I missed my daughter. I can still remember when I left Waverly so many years back, suitcase in hand, mackintosh tightened. I asked my mother for a lift to the local railway station. I was catching a train to my new life and new job in London. She refused, saying she had too much to do. So I called a taxi. I remember sitting in the living room, eyeing the china figurines she kept on the mantelpiece, horrible little things: little Victorian boys in dungarees or rosy-cheeked girls in dirndls. On this, my last day at home, I had to fight the urge to smash them, every single last one of them. Oh, what satisfaction to stamp my heel into their pinched, nasty little faces and grind them into dust. Instead, I sat there, picking at my cuticles while keeping an eye out for the taxi, hoping my mother would join me on this momentous occasion of my leaving. My heart sank when I heard the vacuum cleaner come on upstairs. Did she really have to do this now? The taxi arrived and I gathered my things. I paused at the front door and called up the stairs. 'Mum, I'm off now. Mum? Mummy?' No answer. I wanted to run upstairs and shake her, tell her that despite everything she was still my mother and that I loved her. The deep whirring sound of the vacuum cleaner seemed to intensify. The taxi driver beeped his horn. 'Mummy? I've got to go now. Mummy…' I gave up; what was the point. I got into the back of the taxi, and as it drew away from the cottage, I looked out the rear window, peering upwards. I saw her briefly at her bedroom window looking down at the car. She saw me and then drew away, closing the curtains. And I hated her.

I carry on talking while my mother waits for another bird to appear and take its turn at the feeder. 'I imagine she's made lots of new friends already. You know what she's like, never shy in coming forward, our Tess. As far as I can tell, she's got wall-to-wall parties this week. Lectures don't start in earnest until next week. She's probably having a whale of a time.'

'*Wo ist das Rotkehlchen?*' she says. Where is that robin?

This is a recent development, this speaking in German, my mother's mother tongue. The total avoidance of what I'd been talking about though – that is not new. I tell myself, it's not her fault; the illness is to blame. I hope if I tell myself this often enough I may actually come to believe it.

'I remembered something the other day. Do you remember when I was about eleven, I was interested in that football game, Mummy? England against Germany. West Germany, I suppose they were back then. Do you remember?' Of course she won't remember. Even without the illness she probably wouldn't remember.

Another resident wanders in holding a cup and saucer. Mr Charlton stoops, wears a beige jacket and a tie. He looks dapper. He dresses the same every day. He looks like he's got an important meeting to go to. But he hasn't. He simply walks around the care home all day, taking delight in seeing things or people for what he thinks is the first time when, of course, he has seen them a thousand times already. 'Aha, Mrs Marsh, there you are,' he says to my mother as if he'd been genuinely looking for her. The cup tilts on the saucer. 'Soon be time for tea. I hope you're hungry.'

'*Geh weg von mir, du alter dummkopf,*' says my mother. Get away from me, you old fool.

'Hello, Mr Charlton,' I say to him.

'Hello there. And you are…?'

'I'm Mrs Marsh's daughter. Nice to meet you.'

Satisfied with this, he about-turns and ambles back the way he came, cup and saucer at a precarious angle.

My mother points outside. '*Ah, er ist zurück.*'

'Who's back? Oh, Mr Robin. Of course.'

'We have a bird table in the garden. I put breadcrumbs on it every day.'

I've heard this several times, this inconsequential reference back to her childhood said in the present tense. On days when she's especially confused, she'll talk about her parents as if they were still alive and she a small girl back in 1920s Germany.

'You like the birds, don't you, Mummy?' I look at my phone, hoping for a text from Tessa. There isn't. 'Well, Mummy,' I say, standing up. 'I'd better be going. Lovely to see you again.' I reach down to kiss her cheek but she jerks her head away. I straighten up and tell myself not to feel hurt; what did I expect? 'I'll come by Sunday as usual, if that's OK.'

'*Er wird fett und isst immer.*'

I look out at the robin. 'Yes, you're right,' I say. 'He will get fat.'

I sit in my car, a little rust-coloured Peugeot, and sigh. Why did I bother? Who benefits from my visits? Was it just to show the staff I was a caring, loving daughter? But we keep going, don't we? I pull out my phone and text Tessa: *Your granny sends you her love.* She'll see through the falsehood, I know. But we do these things, don't we? The little inventions we hide behind, doing the things that are expected of us. That

17

layer of gloss we paint over everything so we can present ourselves to the world as the people we'd like to be, should be.

My phone pings. *Thanks. Send her my love back. xx.*

I turn on the ignition, and it hits me that the whole time I was with her, my mother never looked at me. Not once.

Another text: *I'll call you later. xx.*

I smile to myself; at last, I've got something to look forward to.

Chapter 4

Today, being a Saturday, I force myself to return to my mother's old home in Waverly. It's a fine day but showing early signs of autumn. I've made myself some sandwiches and filled a thermos flask with my homemade tomato soup. I'm about to leave, unlocking the car, when I see a familiar car draw up. It's Shelley's but Barry is driving, about the only time in Barry's life these days that he's in the driving seat. I smile inwardly at my little *jeu de mots*. Shelley is in the car with him and, sitting in the back seat, her boys. Barry parks quickly and awkwardly, his back end sticking out too much. He jumps out, looking every inch like a man in a hurry. 'Hiya, Liz. You off out?'

'Mum's.'

That stops him. 'Oh, right. Good. You must be almost finished. She didn't have much after all.'

'No.'

'That charity shop must love you. Anyway, can't stop. Just wanted to grab my trunks. We're going swimming. Do you mind?'

I want to say I do, very much, in fact, especially as it means he'll be in *my* bedroom. We're not divorced yet, just separated, and he still has a front-door key and thinks he has every right to pop into the house anytime he wants. I almost steel myself to say something but he's already let himself in. I smile weakly at Shelley, sitting in her car, wondering whether I should wait for Barry to come back out or whether to get in the car and drive off. But then first one boy, then the other, emerges from Shelley's car.

'Hi, Auntie Elizabeth,' they both say, almost in unison.

'Oh, hi, Dylan, hi, Jake.' It amuses me that they call me *Auntie*. I wonder whose idea that was.

Shelley shouts at them from within the car. 'Get back in here, will ya.' Then, perhaps aware of sounding like an old fishwife, she also gets out of the car, emerging like the Queen of Sheba. 'Good morning, Liz,' she says, running her hand over her hair.

'Hi.'

'We're off swimming. Family swim Saturday mornings.'

'Barry said.' The image of Shelley in a bikini flashes through my mind, and a little surge of hatred rises within me.

'How's your mum?'

'Hmm? Yeah, great, yeah. She's good, considering, you know.'

'Yes, of course.' Of course, what she really wants to know is have I put my mother's house on the market yet. 'And I hear Tessa's enjoying herself.'

'Is she? I mean, yes, she is. Oh, here's Barry. Did you find them?'

'Sure did.' He waves his trunks up in the air, unnecessarily, looking rather absurd. I remember them – they're not his swimming shorts but his trunks, budgie smugglers, I think Tessa called them. He's put on weight since being with Shelley, and the image of his belly hanging over those skimpy little things is too much to bear. 'Best be off,' he says, signalling at the boys to get back in the car. He turns to me and hesitates and I'm not sure why. 'See ya,' is all he says.

'Yeah. Bye. Bye, Shelley. Dylan, Jake, have fun.'

'We will,' says Shelley, a little too smoothly, a slight narrowing of her eyes.

'Work hard,' says Barry, manoeuvring himself into the car.

'What?'

'At your mum's.'

'Oh yes. Of course.' I force out a feeble little laugh, a titter.

It is only as they drive away, I realise why Barry had hesitated – he was about to kiss me on the cheek, like he always used to. I'm not going to read anything into it. But the thought catches me short. I'd have given anything for that kiss.

*

Two hours later, I am at the cottage. It has begun raining, reflecting the mood I always feel when visiting my (second) childhood home. Standing outside, I breathe in the familiar smell of the air scented with brine. It is a mild day but whatever the temperature outside, it's always chilly inside the cottage. I open all the curtains and let the light in, open a couple of windows to try to rid the musty smell. The place sounds echoey, stripped already of so many things – pieces of small furniture and the books. I make myself a cup of tea and sit down, preparing myself for the task ahead. I have, as Barry said, already cleared much of it, boxed it up and delivered it to the Oxfam shop in Waverly itself. I was pleased to see that those horrible little figurines, so beloved by my mother, have already sold. I'd already got rid of all the knick-knacks, the horse brasses, the kitchen stuff, old paintings, the record player and radio, and a hundred other things. There wasn't much. All that is left, in essence, are the big items and the paperwork, and surely the latter won't take long to sort out. At some point I will need to ring a house-clearance firm and get rid of the beds, the white goods and such like.

I lug a few box files down to the living room and pile them up on the dining table, causing a little explosion of dust. The table is one of those that pull out for when we had lots of guests. We never did. I don't remember a single time. I sit in the deep silence and open the first box. Bank statements. Hundreds of them, going back years, the most recent on top. I don't need to look at them; I already know the state of my mother's financial affairs having become her power of attorney a while back. The next box consists of bills – nothing but bills, and again, going back years. I hope to find some evidence of my existence, of my childhood – school reports, perhaps, a certificate or two. I definitely remember winning a couple of things – a spelling test here, a hundred-yard dash there and especially winning the first-prize certificate for my essay on the suffragettes. Then finally I find a box of vaguely interesting stuff – namely birth certificates and my parents' marriage certificate.

I decide to have my soup and sandwiches. As I eat, sitting on the old settee, I cast my eyes about the place. I don't want to sell the house, yet I'm not sure why that should be. I have no real affection for the place. Indeed, once I'd turned eighteen, and once Tom had gone, I couldn't wait to leave. But I know I can't put it off any longer. I need the money in order to pay for my mother's care home. And Barry wants his share. That was surely the worst mistake I made – allowing my mother to leave the house to both me *and* Barry in her will.

It is time to get back to work. I come across a large buff envelope. I pick it up, run my finger along the brittle dryness of it. My mouth goes dry; my heartbeat quickens a notch. There is nothing outwardly wrong with this envelope but it is as if my subconscious is already warning me. There is no writing on the front, but it is open; the passing of time has

22

unglued it. Inside is a piece of card, about the size of a modern sheet of A5. My eyes pop on seeing the hated letterhead – the German eagle, its massive claws clutching on to a wreath, within which is emblazoned the swastika. My insides hollow out. 'German bitch, German bitch'. How could they have called me that? I was only a kid; I swear the scar from that relentless taunting could still be traced in the folds of my heart. What was this piece of card doing amongst my mother's paperwork? The writing is in German, written in thick, black Gothic script, dated the first of December 1944, two months after my birth, and containing the number fifty and two scribbles – signatures perhaps? Just holding it feels wrong; as if I risk being caught out somehow. The cottage is colder somehow. I want to close the windows but I can't move. I can't read German but it looks like a receipt, although there is no sum of money involved. It is almost like a modern-day delivery note. It looks like an address. Yes, that is it – two signatures, the date and an address somewhere in a place called Baden-Württemberg. I gaze at this sheet of paper for a while and wonder why it was quivering so much, as if it's taken on a life of its own. But no, I realise my hand is shaking.

Somehow I know with utmost certainty that these few words on this old piece of card concern me and that it is something I need to know about.

Chapter 5

Sunday morning, and that piece of card is still bothering me. I know the date, two months after I was born, is significant somehow.

A couple of months before Tessa left for university, I'd bought a computer and Tessa had set it up for me, and connected me to the internet. She taught me how to use it, sitting patiently while I tried to get my head round this wonderful new technology. While I wait for the modem to connect, my front doorbell rings. Tabby disappears under the settee, as is her habit whenever a visitor comes by. 'Mind if I drop by?'

'Yes, Barry, if you must. Come in.'

He plonks himself on the settee with a heavy sigh, sitting immediately above Tabby. He reaches over to the low table and grabs my TV guide and starts flipping through it. 'I've heard a rumour that your kettle's not working,' he says with a chortle.

Barry's one of these people who thinks a joke remains funny no matter how many times you've said it before.

'What brings you here, Barry?'

'Oh, you know, just passing.'

'Shelley kicked you out?'

'Don't be daft. Two sugars, in case you forgot.'

But I must be daft; that's exactly what I am, allowing my

former husband to waltz in anytime he wants, whenever he feels like a break from his much-younger partner and the boys. I drop a tea bag into a mug and watch the kettle boil. Why couldn't he have found himself a woman who lived the other side of the county rather than shacking up with one just five minutes away? Barry seems to think that we have slipped seamlessly from husband and wife into old friends. I've had no say in this; my consent was never asked for. He simply assumed. So here I am making him a cup of tea while he's sprawled on my settee reading my magazine in my house. I can't decide whether to mention the certificate to him or not. He speaks no German, has always proudly stated he can speak not a single word of any foreign language, and that his command of English is suspect – another joke that's been recycled more times than a child's hand-me-downs. But I need to talk about it. Who else is there? Certainly not my mother.

'Heard from Tessa?' he shouts through.

'She rang last night. She's loving it.'

'That's good.'

That's all he needs to know. He won't be interested in the details, her new friends, the city, the accommodation, the lectures, the lecturers.

'Here, your tea.' I am tempted to spill it on him, especially when I realise I've made it for him in his favourite mug, one decorated with puffins. I am my own worst enemy.

'Thanks, love.'

He takes a sip of his tea and sighs with a *that hits the spot* satisfaction. 'You always make the best tea.'

How gratifying.

'How's Shelley?' I ask. *Has she broken her leg? Got any infectious diseases? Or is it just a broken fingernail?*

'She wants me to put up glass shelves in the bathroom

now.' He says the word *now* with great emphasis as if eliciting my sympathy.

Oh, so that's why you're here. I knew there had to be a reason. I will say this for Shelley – she has turned Barry, a man who'd never used a drill in his life before, into quite the DIY man about the house. More than I ever managed. But obviously there are many things Shelley is better at than me. Except, perhaps, making tea. Actually, I know for a fact that she's a terrible cook. The thought of Barry smiling through gritted teeth at yet another burnt or undercooked offering tickles me no end. Poor Barry. More sympathy.

After a string of dead-end jobs, Barry worked as an estate agent for a while, working Tuesday to Saturdays and was well paid for his efforts. He lost his job and now works occasionally at whatever he can get his hands on. He used to like the occasional game of tennis with one of his mates, a drink at the pub, a night out at the cinema, the usual stuff. All that is gone now. Now, it's *take the boys here; take the boys there.* My God, I hope she's worth it, Barry; for your sake, I really do.

'How's your mother?' he asks.

'She's… she's OK.'

'What? What is it? Why did you hesitate?'

'Stay put a minute.'

I go to the bureau and retrieve the certificate. 'I found this yesterday,' I say, passing it to him. 'Amongst her things.'

Taking his reading glasses from his inside pocket, he squints at it. 'What is it?'

'That's it. I've no idea.'

'It's quite creepy, isn't it, what with that swastika and all. Number fifty. Nineteen forty-four, the year you were born. Have you tried looking it up on the internet?'

'I was just about to. Come, you can help me.'

Barry pulls up a chair and we sit together at my recently impoverished computer desk. 'Shelley's got one of these computers,' he says. 'Hers looks a lot newer though.' There's a surprise.

I click on a button that brings up Google, something Tessa told me was better than Ask Jeeves, the search engine I had been using, and from there type in the address as written on the certificate. We wait a while before the search results load.

'There,' says Barry. 'Click on that first one.'

I drum my fingers on the mouse as we wait.

'Oh,' says Barry. 'It's a hotel. Look at it, it's huge. Looks lovely.'

The picture shows a large building with several thatched roofs at different levels, massive chimneys, arched windows, stone steps, situated on a vast expanse of grass and surrounded by a pine forest. The website tells us that Hotel Cavalier, in the heart of Baden-Württemberg, is a four-star hotel renowned for its luxury and cuisine.

'Wouldn't mind a couple of nights there,' says Barry. We click through the whole website, not that it takes long, and look at the pictures of the main bedrooms, the dining suite, the bar, the grounds. 'So, there you are, love, nothing to worry yourself about; it's just a hotel.'

I click back to the home page and, inching forward, peer at the picture. Something about it is drawing me in, intriguing me.

'Liz?'

'No. It couldn't have been a hotel then, not back in forty-four. It was used as something else.'

'But what?'

'I don't know. But I want to find out.'

'Do you? Why?'
'No, more than that. I *need* to find out.'

Chapter 6
September 1943

It'd been a long journey all the way from Berlin. During peacetime, it would have taken about five hours but now, with so many unscheduled stops and hold-ups, it'd taken double that. The train's heating had broken down, and Hannah kept her coat on the whole journey. Occasionally, she had the compartment to herself. Making sure no one was loitering in the corridor, she had a cigarette. It was a risky endeavour – she knew full well what people thought of women smoking in public, especially one as young as her.

At last, the train pulled into the railway station one stop before the terminus at Weinberg. Night had just fallen, the last wisps of daylight disappearing over the horizon. Hannah yawned and stretched, gathered her suitcase and jumped off the train. The cold breeze bit into her. She wandered through the departure hut, such as it was, and out into the square behind the station. She saw a bent old man with a large feather in his hat leaning against a cart, smoking, the pony snorting. He caught her eye. 'Fraulein Schiffer?' he said, his voice gruff.

'Yes. Hello.'

'Hurry up; I'm freezing my balls off here,' he said, throwing his cigarette away.

She climbed up onto the trap and took her place behind him. He didn't offer to take her case, nor did he introduce himself. He didn't welcome her to the town nor ask after her journey. Hannah wasn't accustomed to such poor manners, but it mattered not, she thought; she was too cold and hungry to care. She wanted to ask how long the ride to the school took because she was starving. The sandwiches and homemade cake her mother packed for her were far from enough and disappeared a long time ago. But she couldn't. She pulled her hat down and tightened her scarf as the pony and trap clattered through the village. The place was deserted but she saw the occasional light behind the small windows of small houses. She wondered whether people here were subject to the same miniscule rations as Berlin. She was always hungry but this was the worst; it'd given her a headache.

They passed through the village and followed a path that meandered through vast fields, acres of nothingness in the gloom of early evening. An old scarecrow kept guard over a field and watched her pass. She stuffed her gloved hands deep into her coat. Despite the cold, Hannah succumbed to her fatigue, lulled by the gentle clunking rhythm of the wheels on the rough road. The sharp cackle of crows in a lonesome tree jerked her awake. By the time the school came into view, her legs were shaking with cold, her stomach seized with hunger. The school was isolated, a good kilometre from the nearest village. A large swastika banner hung above the main entrance. Smoke from the chimney obscured the slither of the moon.

The driver brought the pony to a halt. He didn't move, didn't speak. Hannah took her suitcase and clambered down. 'Thank you,' she said.

The driver snapped his reins and the pony responded. Hannah watched them disappear around the bend.

The school was four storeys high, arched windows and, on the first floor, a balcony. It was surrounded by meadows and, squinting in the gloom, Hannah could see the forest of pine trees in the distance. But it wasn't a school any more, having been requisitioned as a care home for evacuated children with a capacity, according to Hannah's Maiden leader in Berlin, for just forty kids.

Something was odd, not quite right somehow. It took a few seconds to realise what it was – the silence. Just listen to it, the utter stillness of the place, broken only by a soft, cold breeze and the faint, gentle bubble of a stream. My word, she thought, she'd never heard such silence. The air was so sharp, so fresh. She breathed it in, felt it filling her lungs.

So this was home now, she said to herself. She had her father to thank. He'd pulled numerous strings to get his seventeen-year-old daughter away from the bombs and danger. They needed a Maiden's leader out here in the countryside to help look after a group of evacuee girls. Saying goodbye to her parents at the Berlin station was perhaps the hardest thing she'd experienced. Just a few hours ago, but already it seemed like an age since the three of them stood on platform two in that awkward hinterland of not wanting to leave while wishing she could get on the train and slam the door shut and get going. 'It'll be just for a few months,' said her father loudly. 'Just until we win the war.'

'Well, that'll take forever, won't it?'

'Hannah,' he said, lowering his voice. 'Mind your tongue. You never know who's listening.'

The main door to the school opened, a shaft of orange light throwing out. Two silhouettes appeared and began walking towards her. 'Are you Hannah?' called out one.

'Yes.'

The two women, about Hannah's age, maybe a little older, drew up and each shook her hand and told her to come into the warmth. Like Hannah, both wore the uniforms of Maiden leaders. Once inside, they introduced themselves. The taller one, with blonde braids, introduced herself as Angela and the shorter, darker girl as Ella. 'The girls are having their dinner,' said Angela. Hannah's mouth salivated with the thought; she could hear them, the hushed rumble of voices coming from an adjoining hall. 'You must be hungry?'

'Yes, a little.'

'Would you like to see your room first or–'

'I'd rather eat first,' she snapped, then reddened.

'Ah, here's Jan,' said Ella. 'Jan, over here. Hurry up.' The man called Jan picked up his pace and hastened over. He was young, not much older than Hannah; his hair was dark, a shadow of a beard. 'This is Fraulein Schiffer.'

The man nodded.

'Take this suitcase up to room forty-two.'

Hannah caught his eye and was taken aback by his startling good looks, the deep mournfulness of his dark brown eyes. He took Hannah's case and made haste with it.

'That's our errand boy,' said Angela. 'You're not to speak to him unless you need something done.'

'He's quite dishy, don't you think?' said Ella.

Hannah wasn't sure how to respond.

'No, he's not,' snapped Angela. 'Don't be ridiculous; he's just a Pole.'

'He's not even called Jan,' said Ella in a conspiratorial tone. 'We don't know his real name so we just call him that.'

'Seriously, don't speak to him,' said Angela. 'Right, shall we eat?'

'That'd… that'd be nice,' said Hannah, trying to maintain her composure, while, inside, her stomach screamed in hunger.

Chapter 7

The alarm clock rang. Seven a.m. On opening her eyes, it took Hannah a few seconds to remember where she was. Her room was tiny, consisting only of her narrow bed, a wardrobe and a small table and chair. Hitler's portrait hung over her bed and, on the opposite wall, a photograph of the school, dated 1920. She switched on the electric fire and, sitting cross-legged, shivered in front of it, trying to warm herself up before changing into her uniform for the day. Checking the time, she decided she had just about enough time to have a cigarette. Opening the window as far as it could go, she leant out and lit up. The heat that had been slowly built up from the little fire vanished immediately. But that was the choice she had to make – warmth or nicotine. Finishing her cigarette, she was about to close the window when she saw the Polish labourer pushing a wheelbarrow full of leaves across the lawn. He looked up. Their eyes met. He stopped for just a second. She waved at him but then froze, remembering she shouldn't. What if someone saw? Quickly, she withdrew, quietly and firmly shutting and locking the window behind her.

She came down to a deserted dining hall. The places had been laid on a pair of long tables, chairs either side, a sideboard loaded with bread and ham. Another portrait of Hitler, this one enormous, hung over the fireplace. Angela and Ella appeared together, their polished shoes clacking on the wooden floor as they approached.

'Good morning,' said Hannah. 'Is there anything you want me to do?'

'No,' said Angela. 'There are staff who'll do it all.'

'They all used to work here when it was still a proper school,' added Ella.

'All we have to do is make sure the children eat and behave themselves.'

'But they always do,' said Ella. 'They're good girls.'

The dining hall soon filled with forty uniformed girls, aged from thirteen to fifteen, filing in twos and threes. As each of them passed the three leaders, they paused, bellowed, 'Heil Hitler' and moved on.

Once settled, Angela stood at the head of the two tables in front of the fireplace. 'Good morning, girls.'

'Good morning, miss,' came the uniform reply.

'Let us bow our heads.' She waited a few moments, silence descending. 'O, Lord, we give thee thanks for having brought us together under the guidance and love of our beloved Führer.' She looked up at the girls with a benevolent smile. 'Tuck in, girls.'

*

Forty girls and three leaders stood outside in a circle on the drive in front of the former school. The morning was bright but the cold sharp. Angela and Ella took their places at the centre of the circle, next to the flagpole, ropes in hand. 'We salute you, our dear Führer,' shouted Ella. Forty girls with backs straight and heads held up high threw out their arms and shouted, 'Heil Hitler.' Between them, the two leaders hoisted up the national flag. Once hoisted, they stepped back and led the rendition of the national anthem and the Horst Wessel song. Their cold breaths floated through the air, their voices echoing around the grounds. It was, thought Hannah, all very solemn.

Once done, Angela dismissed the girls. Time, she told Hannah, for their ablutions and tidying of their rooms.

'Do you do this every morning?' asked Hannah, stamping her feet against the cold. 'This flag stuff?'

'*This flag stuff?*' said Angela.

'Sorry, I didn't mean it like that, I…'

'If you mean do we raise the flag and salute our Führer every morning, then yes, of course.'

'Come rain or shine,' added Ella.

*

That night, after the girls had gone to bed, Angela, Ella and Hannah sat down in the warm cosiness of Angela's bedroom, the biggest in the school and the only one with a log fire. They kicked off their shoes and loosened their neckties. Dinner hadn't been easy for Hannah; trying to stuff as much food in as possible, while remaining polite and hoping no one would notice. Now, post dinner, she lay back in one of Angela's armchairs and stifled a yawn. She hoped her hosts were smokers. She wouldn't dare light a cigarette until they had. They didn't but they did have the second best – wine.

'We borrow it from the cellar,' said Ella with a mischievous grin. 'There's loads down there.'

'Borrow it?'

Ella giggled, shushing Hannah.

Their glasses full, they asked Hannah about life in the capital. They knew about the bombs. There were reports daily on the radio. 'Those English are barbarians, bombing our cities.'

'We need more logs,' said Ella. 'I'll get Jan to bring some up.'

'I'll go,' said Hannah with indecent haste, such was the eagerness to have a quick cigarette. 'Where will I find him?'

Ella looked at her watch. 'At this time, in his hut out the back. Go through the kitchen and outside. You'll find it.'

Hannah checked her pocket for her packet of cigarettes and a box of matches. She found the kitchen. A couple of orderlies still washing up pointed the way out.

She saw the hut, a real woodcutters' hut with a corrugated roof, built on stilts, a feeble light in its window. A four-rung stepladder led to the door. Hannah hesitated; it didn't feel right, somehow, disturbing him here. So, instead, she smoked half a cigarette. *He's just a Pole*, she reminded herself, repeating Angela's words. Fortified after her cigarette, she approached and, standing at the bottom of the steps, called out. 'Hello? Anyone at home?'

The door opened straight away, his head peering round. On seeing her, he came out but remained on the top step.

'Hi, yes. Erm, we wondered, where c-could I get some logs, please. For the fire.'

He jumped down and with a nod of his head, told her to follow him. He wore only a cardigan over a shirt but if he felt the cold, he wasn't showing it. Wrapping her arms around herself, she had to skip to keep up with his long strides as he followed a path leading to the outbuildings behind the house. *He's just a Pole* yet some deep, ingrained need to be polite manifested itself. 'Have you been working here long?' she asked.

He made no answer. Maybe he didn't hear. They reached a small barn. Hannah followed him in. Jan switched on a light and there in front of her a stack of neatly cut logs. 'Oh, that's great. Thank you.' Hannah went to pick up a log but he held up his hand.

'Here, let me,' he said in a surprisingly gentle voice.

'No, it's all right. I can manage perfectly well, thank you.'

He shrugged in a 'suit yourself' manner. She scooped up three logs but they were heavier than she thought and one slipped her grasp and fell. Jan picked it up and placed it on top of the others. 'Thank you,' she said. He held her gaze for a moment, a second too long, and she averted her eyes. 'It's cold; I need to get back.'

'Here,' he said, removing his cardigan.

'No, don't do that. You'll only have that shirt. I'm fine, really.'

He nodded.

'But… thank you anyway.'

Chapter 8

Life within the former school soon became claustrophobic. The daily routine rarely changed. Breakfast, flag raising and anthems, then a morning of tedious things like singing Hitler Youth songs, or writing home or crafts, such as knitting or painting or drawing. One of Hannah's new jobs was to model. She would sit still for an hour while a dozen girls tried to draw her image. Afterwards, looking at their efforts, she couldn't help but feel that only one had come anywhere close to capturing her. She liked the way the artist had made her hair look wild, her eyes alert, her smile broad. Hannah peered at the name squiggled on the bottom right of the portrait. The artist's name was Greta.

Twice a week, Hannah had to walk the kilometre to the local village to pick up the post. On this, the first occasion, Ella joined her so that Hannah wouldn't get lost. The postmaster, according to Ella, had joined the Wehrmacht and was currently stationed in France. The postmistress, too busy running the post office to deliver, hadn't yet found a replacement. The sun shone but it didn't do anything to lessen the cold. Hannah breathed in the pine.

The village consisted of only a few businesses: rationing and the lack of menfolk had forced many to close down. There was one truck parked up but no other vehicles. Petrol rationing had seen to that. Swastika bunting stretched across the high street. Ella led Hannah to the post office and introduced her to the postmistress. The woman dumped a small cloth bag onto the counter.

'Any black borders?' asked Ella.

'Just the one,' said the woman.

'Black borders?' asked Hannah.

'Letters with black borders – means that some relative has died.' She sorted through the letters. 'Here it is. Oh dear, it's for little Greta.'

'Greta? The artist?'

'She is good at art. You'll have to give it to her in person and help her when she opens it.'

'Me?'

'It's your job now.'

'But I don't know Greta.'

'You soon will.'

Walking back to the home, Ella told Hannah what to say to the unfortunate Greta, how to tackle it and couch it in terms of a worthy and noble death. 'And she'll believe this?' she asked.

'Of course,' said Ella. 'They're all good little Nazis, aren't they?'

The girls were waiting for them in the dining hall when Ella and Hannah returned with their bag of post. Hannah was to learn the atmosphere was always the same – a mixture of excitement, hope and dread. It was the latter that tempered their excitement, that stilled their voices. They were all so desperately keen to receive a letter with news from home, but all dreaded that their letter may be a black-bordered one. Hannah had yet to know all their names so she left it to Ella to scan the girls' faces. They knew what she was doing and each one slunk back as Ella's eyes passed them. And then her attention stopped, and Greta turned white.

Hannah approached the girl, the letter in her hand. 'Greta?'

She nodded.

'Shall we sit away from the others? Come.'

Greta, like most of the others, wore her hair in pigtails with a central parting. Hannah reckoned she was thirteen. So young to lose a parent. They sat on a pair of comfortable armchairs at the far end of the hall, ignoring the bustle of relieved girls eager for their letters.

'Do you want me to read it first?' asked Hannah.

Greta shook her head. 'No, I'll read it.'

Hannah watched her as Greta's eyes moved left to right. She screwed up her face, her delicate frame slumped. '*Vati*,' she said quietly. *Father*.

Hannah reached for her hand. Greta allowed her to take it. How small, how clammy it felt. 'I'm so sorry, Greta.'

'He was killed somewhere in Russia.' She looked at the letter again. 'It says he died for the Fatherland and for the Führer.' Her hand dropped; the letter slipped out of her fingers. She looked up at Hannah. 'He's with God now, isn't he?'

'Yes, he is. He's with God.'

They sat in silence a while. The hall emptied, the lucky girls rushing off with their letters, the disappointed ones already resigned. There was always a next time.

'I wish I could go home.'

Hannah stroked the girl's hand. 'I know. I think we all do.'

'I don't know what to do now.'

'You carry on doing what you're doing, Greta. Learning how to be a good servant to the nation, just like your father was. Be true to your Fatherland; be true to yourself, and your father will be proud of you.'

Greta looked up at her, her sad eyes tinged with understanding.

Hannah continued, knowing Greta was absorbing her words. 'We all have to believe in the final outcome. If we didn't, what would be the point? We have to believe and we have to be true – to ourselves, to each other and to the Fatherland. We have to do as we see right and true. Truth, more than anything else in the world, is the most important thing. And we know who is the truest of them all.'

'The Führer.'

'Yes. The Führer.'

Chapter 9

Angela, Ella and Hannah sat in the dining hall, listening to the radio while the girls changed into their PE kits. 'Today Berlin suffered more grievous damage. But for their part, the enemy incurred heavy losses. Our brave fighter planes and anti-aircraft guns brought down fifty enemy planes. Despite these attacks, our German people stand strong; the morale of our people will not be broken.' Hannah's thoughts turned to her parents; she hoped to God they were OK. Ella placed her hand on Hannah's sleeve. The newscaster continued. 'On the Soviet front, our troops are engaged in an orderly disengagement and an honourable retreat.'

'Shit, we're being pulverised,' said Ella.

'Not one bit of it,' said Angela. 'You heard what he said. Orderly disengagement.'

Ella and Hannah exchanged knowing looks.

'Anyway,' said Angela. 'Our Führer knows what he's doing.' She turned the wireless off. 'He won't let us down.'

The highlight of the week, every Tuesday afternoon, was the visit of twenty or so Hitler Youth boys from a camp in the village itself, some two kilometres away. Accompanied by their leaders, they'd march over for another round of solemn flag raising and singing. Then, solemnity over, they'd play games – soccer or rounders. It cheered the girls up no end, meeting and flirting with the boys. Ella also flirted – evidently taken by one of the boys' leaders, a tall, blond boy called Hans, a young man totally committed to the National Socialist cause and the justice of the war. He seemed equally enamoured by Ella and they spent as much time as possible being next to each other, talking and laughing. But, much to Hannah's discomfort, Hans' comrade, Wolfram, had, it seemed, taken a shine to Hannah.

On this particular Tuesday afternoon, Hans, Wolfram and the boys were accompanied by Herr Müller, the area's Hitler Youth leader, a commanding man in his mid-forties, Hannah reckoned, with shaven hair, a large moustache and a silver-topped cane under his arm. Herr Müller and his young leaders stood together in line on the edge of the sprawling line while their charges played rounders – girls versus boys, a fixture that always brought out the competitive spirit. Hannah noticed Greta was bowling. Wolfram took his place next to Hannah. Leaning over, he whispered, 'You missing Berlin?'

Hannah shrugged. 'A little perhaps.'

'Hmm. What about your boyfriend? You missing him?'

'I don't–'

Herr Müller turned to Hannah. 'You seemed to have settled in well, miss.'

'Oh, yes, sir. Thank you.'

'Your parents are still in Berlin?'

'Yes, sir.'

'Remind me, what is it they do?'

Before Hannah had a chance to answer, the boys erupted in a loud explosion of cheers – one of their numbers had hit the rounder's ball so hard it had landed in the stream.

'Bravo, bravo,' said Herr Müller. 'We'll take that.'

None of the girls had moved: too unwilling, Hannah guessed, to get their feet wet in the freezing stream.

43

'Do we have another ball?' asked Hans.

'No,' said Ella. 'We lost that one too.'

Angela caught sight of Jan pushing his wheelbarrow. She called him over. 'Hey, Jan, fetch the ball, would you? It's gone in the stream,' she added, pointing vaguely in the direction the ball had gone.

Jan ran over towards the stream, watched by everyone, the children eager to resume their game.

'Damn it, man, hurry up, would you,' shouted Angela.

'Who's that ape, then?' asked Herr Müller.

'He's Polish. He was at the PoW camp but they've lent him out to us as our odd-job man.'

'What's taking him so long?' said Hans. 'The ball's bright red: can't be that hard.'

'He's too far to the right,' said Herr Müller.

They watched impatiently as Jan tried to find the ball, jabbing at the weeds with a stick. The children began a slow handclap.

'The stupid idiot,' said Herr Müller. 'I saw where it fell; I'll go.' He marched across the field, his boots leaving damp impressions in the grass, his cane tucked firmly under his arm.

'Hey, girls,' said Hans. 'Me and Wolfram are going to the inn in the village tonight, the Golden Angel. Fancy coming?'

'Oo, yeah,' said Ella.

'Absolutely not,' said Angela. 'We're to be up early tomorrow morning.'

'Oh, come off it, Ange,' said Ella. 'We have to be up early every morning. We deserve a bit of fun.'

'Good German girls do not drink.'

'Come on, there's no harm in a bit of fun,' said Wolfram. 'We'll meet you there at nine and promise to have you back for bedtime. What about it, Hannah?'

'Me? Well…'

Before she had a chance to finish her sentence, she heard Herr Müller's triumphant voice ringing out. 'Found it.' He held the red ball up in the air. The children cheered as he threw it back. Hannah could see Herr Müller berating Jan for not finding it and wasting his time. It took but a moment but Herr Müller whipped Jan across the side of his face with his cane. Hannah winced. Jan fell back, his hand grasping his cheek. Herr Müller turned and stormed back. By the time he'd reached them, the children had resumed their game.

'Want a job done, do it yourself,' said Herr Müller on reaching them. 'Bloody idiot.'

'Well done, sir,' said Angela.

'You have any more problems with that scum, you tell me, OK?'

'Sir.'

Hannah kept her eye on the game but spotted Hans and Ella talking; no doubt planning their rendezvous. Then, from the corner of her eye, she watched Jan walk briskly back towards his wheelbarrow, his hand still against his cheek. Then, taking his hand away to inspect it, she noticed the vivid gash of red on the side of his face.

*

An hour later, they were back indoors, enjoying half an hour's free time before the afternoon's craft session. Herr Müller, Hans, Wolfram and their boys, happy in their victory, had returned to their camp in the village. She lay on her bed, her thoughts full of Jan and his cut. No one would see to it; it could get infected. Deciding she had to do something, she crept down to the kitchen and pulled out the first aid kit from under the sink. She found a tub of antiseptic cream and a roll of plasters, and making sure the coast was clear, slipped outside.

Hannah knocked on the hut and waited. Jan appeared. Her mouth gaped open at the sight of the cut. It seemed so deep, so long. She held out the tub and a plaster. 'Thought you might need this,' she said.

He considered her for a moment, as if fearing a ruse. He jumped down the steps and took Hannah's offerings. 'Thank you,' he said.

'It's worse than I thought. He shouldn't have done that.'

He didn't answer but she could see by his eyes that he was touched. With a flicker of a smile, he returned to his hut, closing the door behind him.

*

'Come on, Hannah, it'll be fun.' Ella had invited herself into Hannah's room. The two of them now sat on Hannah's bed, legs pressed against each other. 'You know you want to.'

'You heard what Angela said.'

'"Good German girls don't drink",' said Ella, mimicking Angela. 'She won't know. We'll both say we're tired and want an early night. Then at half eight, we'll slip out. The boys will see us back and goody two-shoes Miss Angela won't know; she'll be tucked up in bed reading *Mein Kampf*. Come on, Hannah, please. We can wear make-up and drink a little and you can smoke as much as you want to.'

'Suppose.'

'And you know I like Hans, and that Wolfram…'

'What about him?'

'Oh, come on, don't say you didn't notice. Can't stop eyeing you up. He's nice.'

The thought of having a couple hours away from the

home, of being able to smoke and have a proper conversation did appeal. She was so stifled by the routine of this place, the same people, of Angela's righteousness. And Wolfram, well, he did seem quite nice. 'OK, you win. We'll go.'

Ella squealed. 'Yes! Thank you, Hannah, thank you. It'll be fun, you'll see.'

Chapter 10

Hannah had imagined the Golden Angel to be a large beer hall, packed to the rafters, filled with smoke and hearty voices. Instead, it was the smallest inn imaginable, a couple of oval-shaped tables at which old men with long whiskers drank their beer and played dominoes. Hans and Wolfram stood on seeing them, slightly unsteady on their feet, and beckoned the girls over. They bought them a small beer each and lit their cigarettes. They sat boy girl boy girl, Hannah at the end, next to Wolfram.

'We've already had a couple,' said Hans.

'You don't say?' said Ella.

'Oh, is it obvious?' said Wolfram.

'Not much of a place, is it?' said Ella.

'Maybe not,' said Hans. 'But we can still have fun, eh?'

'Yeah. Sure.'

'A toast,' said Wolfram. 'To our beloved Führer and for our final victory.'

Four dimpled glasses clinked. Hannah thought of Jan: hoped the cream and plaster were helping heal his cut.

Hannah noticed Hans' arm slide around Ella's shoulder. He leant in towards her and said something that made Ella laugh. 'So,' said Wolfram. 'What's it like in Berlin?'

'You mean between the constant bombing, the craters, the rubble, the lack of food and the freezing cold: spending most nights in air-raid shelters?'

'Well, yeah, but it'll come good in the end, won't it? The Führer won't let us down, you know that, doll.'

'Doll?'

'You still believe in victory, don't ya?'

Of course she didn't. No one did; not any more. 'Yes, of course I do, Wolfram. So where are you from?'

She tried to listen while Wolfram regaled her with his life story. At least it was warm here, and she could smoke without people commenting. The old boys were too engrossed in their game, and there was no one else to care. Wolfram talked continuously, pausing only to gulp his drink and smoke his cigarette. 'My brother got killed in North Africa two years back.'

'Oh, I'm sorry to hear that.'

'Ah, we didn't get on. Anyway, he was proud to die for his country.'

And you know that, do you? 'I'm sure he was.'

'Yeah. Cheers to my brother.' They clinked glasses again. 'Oh, I've finished. I'll get us another.'

'No, no, it's fine. We should be going soon.'

'What? Don't be daft; you've just got here. We've got the whole night in front of us.' He wiped his mouth with the back of his hand. 'Back in a minute.' He rose to his feet and had to pause a moment to steady himself. 'Don't go anywhere,' he said, wagging his finger.

Hans took the opportunity to stagger over and join his friend at the bar, the two men with their arms around each other, whispering and laughing.

'How's it going?' asked Ella. 'He definitely likes you.'

'Yeah but he's so dull. He's worse than Angela. Please, Ella, can we leave?'

'You're joking? No way, sister. Not now.' Ella hiccuped. 'Excuse me.' She laughed. 'Oh dear, give me a moment; I need the loo.'

Another hour passed, maybe two. Wolfram, emboldened by alcohol, clumsily draped his arm around Hannah, letting his hand droop precariously close to her breast. She tried to manoeuvre him away but with his weight pressing against her, found it impossible to dislodge him. 'And my sister, she's working as a nurse somewhere.'

'Oh, is she?'

'Yeah, a nurse. I forget where though.' Wolfram seemed to be talking to her chest.

Hannah folded her arms. 'You're sounding very slurred, Wolfram.'

'Hmm? Am I? So what?'

Finally, nearing eleven, it was time to leave the Golden Angel. The old men had packed up their dominoes and gone some time before, and the bar staff were eager to get home.

Hans and Ella led the way out, draped over each other, laughing loudly. Wolfram had difficulty standing and Hannah had to help him to his feet. 'You OK, Wolfram?'

'What? Yeah, yeah, I'm f-fine. Damn it, why's this room so wobbly?'

'Come, give me your arm.'

He fell on her with his full weight. 'Hell, Wolfram, you're heavy.'

'You're very beautiful, doll. Has anyone ever... Shit, I think I'm gonna be...' He lurched his way to the toilet, zigzagging around the tables, almost falling over a chair.

'He better not make a mess in there,' said the barman.

'Fine way for a leader to conduct himself,' said another.

'He'll be fine in a minute,' said Hannah with a weak smile.

'Sorry. He's just heard his brother's been killed fighting for the Führer. He's very upset; they were very close.'

'Oh. Right. OK, we'll let him off, then.'

'Thank you.' Hannah looked around. Hans and Ella were already outside. She hoped Ella was OK.

An age later, Wolfram re-emerged from the toilet, again wiping his mouth with his sleeve.

The barman looked over. 'Sorry to hear about your brother, young man.'

'Eh?'

'Come on, let's get out of here. Give me your arm.' There was no way, she thought, that Wolfram or Hans could accompany them home now, they'd have to make their own way back.

She pushed open the heavy inn door. The cold air hit her. Hopefully, she thought, it'd sober Wolfram up a little. But where were Hans and Ella? Outside, next to the door, was a wooden bench. 'Let me sit down a minute,' said Wolfram.

'No, Wolfram, it's too cold.'

'Just a tiny minute.'

It was then Hannah heard voices in the cold silence – a screech of some sort, a cry. Her heartbeat quickened. 'Ella? Ella, is that you?' She hurried around the corner of the inn and found herself on a wide path between the inn and shrubbery. She heard them first – Ella crying, Hans swearing under his breath. She saw their two silhouetted figures in the dark, their arms outstretched, thrashing, hands intertwined. A light came on from inside the inn, and then she saw it all – Hans, his trousers unbuckled to his hips, Ella crying, one hand to her face, the other trying to shake off Hans' grip. 'Get *off* me,' cried Ella. 'Get off. Leave me alone.'

'Ella, what's happening?'

51

Hans released her and went to pull his trousers up, lurching from left to right, still cursing but laughing at the same time. Ella rushed over to Hannah, her lipstick smudged, her eye make-up running. 'Hannah, thank God.' She hugged her friend and looked back at Hans staggering in the path, trying to stay upright. 'I hope he chokes,' said Ella, wiping her eyes.

'Your mouth? Ella, is that… Did he *hit* you?'

'Please, Hannah, let's get the hell out of here.'

Chapter 11

Hannah woke up early, and the full enormity of what happened the previous night hit her. Together, Ella and she had fumbled their way home. It seemed to have taken hours, and it was so damn cold. They'd followed the path through the forest, stumbling through the dark. The branches in the woods clawed at them, their shadows circled around them. Ella cried the whole way.

'Why did he hit you?'

'He… he didn't hit me,' said Ella. 'I fell.'

Hannah stopped in her tracks. Did she hear that right? 'You didn't fall. You know you didn't. Why are you lying?'

'I like him, right? Hans wouldn't hit me. Did you see him hit me?'

'Yes. Well, no, not exactly.'

'There you are, then. Shit, I'm so cold. How much farther?'

They arrived back at the home, exhausted and cold. They stole in, shushing each other, creeping up the stairs. Hannah tried to take Ella to bed, concerned for her friend, but Ella brushed her off.

Later, as she lay in bed, Hannah's thoughts turned to Jan. He didn't deserve to be hit like that. It was only a bloody rounders' ball, after all. She only hoped the cut had not become infected. She woke up, and Jan was still forefront in her mind. She wanted to go check on both of them – Ella and Jan.

She dressed quickly, splashing her face with cold water. She glanced out the window – the stream and pine forest beyond were invisible under the thick swirl of morning mist, the grass shining white with frost. She crept along the corridor, reaching Ella's room. She knocked gently, then, on receiving no response, a bit louder. 'Go away.'

'Ella, it's me, Hannah.'

'I said, go away.'

'Suit yourself,' Hannah said quietly.

The kitchen was already full of staff preparing the girls' breakfasts, the clatter of metal plates and cutlery, the smell of ham and coffee. No one took any notice of her as Hannah slipped by and out through the back door. The pathway to the hut had frozen over. She hoped Jan had a heater of some sort in there; he'd freeze without. She approached but stopped short upon seeing the padlock latching the door to the frame. Yes, it was locked. Yet, she could hear something inside, someone moving. 'Jan?' she called as loudly as she dared. 'Jan, are you in there?' The noise inside stopped. 'Jan, are you OK?' No answer. She would've looked through the window but, the hut having been built on stilts, it was too high.

She returned indoors, pleased to be out of the cold but puzzled. Nothing made sense – why had Jan's hut been padlocked? Why was Ella refusing to see her?

She made her way to the dining hall, bumping into Greta along the way. 'Hello, Greta, how's my favourite artist?'

Greta giggled. 'Fine, thanks.'

Hannah was surprised to find Angela already in the dining hall. The girls weren't due for breakfast for another twenty minutes.

'Good morning, Angela,' she said, trying to sound breezy.

Angela shot her a dismissive look. 'We're expecting Herr Müller straight after breakfast. We're meeting in my office.'

'Herr Müller? Why?'

'Well, naturally, he's in overall charge. We need to decide what to do after last night's unpleasantries.'

'Oh.'

'Yes, oh, indeed. Did I not warn both of you? Ella's told me all about it. I rang Herr Müller first thing and I can tell you, he's not happy. Now, if you'll excuse me.'

'Angela, can I ask, why is Jan's hut locked up?'

Angela's eyes narrowed as if she didn't understand the question. 'I would've thought that was fairly obvious under the circumstances.'

Hannah watched Angela pound out of the dining hall and down the corridor. 'Circumstances?' she said to herself. 'What circumstances?'

*

Angela's wood-panelled office hadn't been designed for meetings. Hannah squeezed along the bench and took her place next to Angela. Herr Müller at the opposite side of the table, his eyes boring into her. He placed his silver-topped cane on the table. No one said a word, no greeting while they awaited Ella. Müller tapped the end of his pencil on his pad of paper, occasionally glancing at his watch. Hannah watched the second hand tick by on the clock. Eventually, she broke the silence by offering to go fetch Ella.

'No need,' said Müller. 'Here she is.'

Ella looked as if she'd spent the whole night crying, her eyes puffed up and red. A purple bruise ran from the corner of her mouth across her cheek. Struggling into her place on the bench between Angela and Hannah, she apologised for her lateness, but Müller brushed her apologies aside. Ella threw a look at Hannah, a look that Hannah couldn't quite work out.

Angela placed her hand on Ella's. 'Have you had any breakfast, dear?'

Ella shook her head.

'I'll get some coffee.'

'I'm fine.'

Müller cleared his throat. 'In that case, let's get this over and done with. *Then* I'll decide what to do with him. So, in your own words, please, Ella, tell us what happened last night.'

Ella glanced from Müller to Hannah and back again. 'Well, I know we shouldn't have gone out, but we don't get much chance to... to meet boys our own age.' She coughed, her face quite red with embarrassment. 'So, Hannah and me, we walked to the village and we went to the Golden Angel. You see, we'd agreed to meet Hans and Wolfram there. And they bought us some drinks. I'm sorry.'

'We'll let that slip for now,' said Müller.

'And we got talking. Mainly me and Hans together and Hannah and Wolfram.'

'So you – what's the vernacular – paired off?'

'Hmm. Yes, sir. Paired off.'

'And you, Ella, paired off with Hans. Yes?'

'Yes.'

'And how were you getting on, the two of you?'

'Fine. Nice.'

Müller tapped the end of his pencil on his pad. Turning to Hannah, he asked, 'And what about you, Hannah? Were you getting on with Wolfram?'

'Yes, sir. He seems very nice.'

'Hmm. So what I don't understand is why two nice young

men, and I know they are very nice young men, why didn't they walk you home?'

Because, thought Hannah, they were so pissed, they could barely stand up. But how could she say that? Instead, Ella spoke. 'They did offer, sir, many times, but we said no. We knew they had early starts.'

'Well, perhaps, but no earlier than normal. Hans, by the way, is here.'

'Is he?' She tried to sit on her excitement. 'He's here now?'

'Yes. He's waiting for you in your dining hall. He heard about your ordeal last night and wanted to see if you were OK.'

'That's nice of him.'

'Indeed.'

Hannah stared at her friend, trying to understand her.

Herr Müller continued. 'And so you walked home alone, just the two of you?'

'Yes, sir.'

'But you know there's a PoW camp not far from here, did you really think it was safe?'

'Normally, it would be.'

Angela cleared her throat. 'And, sir, they are Maidens; they're not so defenceless.'

'Perhaps not when faced with a German boy. So carry on, Ella. You arrived back and…'

'We got to the house and I told Hannah I wanted one more…'

'Cigarette?'

'Yes, sir. Sorry.'

'What?' said Hannah.

'So Hannah went in, and I stayed outside for a few minutes longer and that's when it happened.'

'No,' said Hannah. 'Wait—'

Herr Müller put his hand up. 'This is Ella's story. Please be so kind as to let her finish. What exactly happened, Ella?'

Ella's eyes moistened. 'He just came out of nowhere. He pushed me against the house and... and...'

'He tried to force himself on you?' asked Angela.

Ella nodded, producing a handkerchief to dab her eyes.

Hannah turned to face her, her features creased with confusion.

Herr Müller continued. 'Now, Ella, think carefully. Did you know the man who attacked you?'

'Yes, sir, I did.'

'His name, Ella.'

Ella glanced at Hannah. Hannah shook her head. 'No, wait...'

'I don't know his name, sir, but we all call him Jan.'

Chapter 12

The name Jan hung in the air, reverberating. Hannah couldn't understand why would Ella do this? She glanced over at Angela and Herr Müller, the former nodding sagely, the latter writing up his notes. Ella sniffed and dabbed her handkerchief against her nose.

Herr Müller turned quite red. 'How dare he force himself upon a good German girl. A rape upon Ella is as good as a rape upon all of us, the whole nation.'

Hannah had to say something, had to tell them what really happened. Her throat went dry with the effort. She spluttered.

Herr Müller looked up from his notepad, his pencil poised above it. 'What is it? Did you want to add something, Hannah?'

'No. Yes. I mean, it wasn't like that.'

'I beg your pardon?'

'She – I mean, Ella's got it wrong. It happened outside the inn, not here, at the inn. It wasn't Jan who attacked you, Ella, you know that. It was–'

'Wait.' Herr Müller's voice boomed. 'What are you actually saying here, young lady?'

Angela leant forward to see her across Ella. 'I'd be very careful what you say, Hannah. Very careful.'

It was so hot in this small office now. The sweat spread up her back. Hannah turned to Ella. 'You tell them, Ella; tell them the truth.'

'I h-have already. I told you, it was Jan.'

'But it wasn't. I was there, remember? I saw him, it was Hans.'

Hannah sensed the sharp intakes of breath all around. Herr Müller's face positively turned purple. Pointing and jabbing his finger at her, he lowered his voice. 'Are you seriously suggesting that Ella here was attacked and almost violated by Hans?'

Ella placed her hand on Hannah's sleeve. 'It wasn't Hans, Hannah. We both had too much to drink, you especially. You're mistaken, honestly you are. I know what happened.'

'Exactly,' said Angela. 'Thank you, Ella. So, Herr Müller, what do you suggest we do now?'

'He's still locked up?'

'Yes.'

'No, no, this is not right.'

'Hannah, calm yourself.'

'Tell them, Ella. Tell them the truth.'

Herr Müller narrowed his eyes at her. 'Why are you so keen on defending a Pole anyway? Firstly, the Poles are our enemy and secondly, he doesn't matter, he's just… just a Slav, a subhuman.'

'Because a lie is still a lie.'

'I'm not lying, Hannah. How dare you?'

'I can't believe—'

'Enough!' Müller slammed his hand against the table. 'Silence. You…' he said, pointing at Hannah, 'are not to say another single word.' Turning to Angela, he continued. 'I've already alerted the Gestapo. They're sending a couple of officers over.' He stood up abruptly, pulling the creases out of his jacket. He picked his cane and slapped its end against his palm. 'But first, Angela, I'd like a word with the little bastard myself.'

'Of course, sir.'

Hannah shook her head, unable to force her voice out. He'd kill him, she was sure. Herr Müller noticed. 'And once I've finished with that piece of shit,' he shouted, 'you and I need words, young miss.'

Herr Müller stormed out of the office, slamming the door behind him. Angela rose to her feet.

'Angela, please, stop him.'

'Me? I have no authority over Herr Müller. I did warn you to be careful, Hannah. I knew you wouldn't listen. That's your problem – too headstrong.' She shook her head at Hannah's folly. 'You silly girl.' She checked the clock. 'I shall do the flag raising on my own. Ella, you may return to your room. Hannah, you stay here and wait for Herr Müller's return. Heil Hitler.'

Ella also made to leave, but Hannah grabbed her arm.

'Get off,' said Ella.

'Why, Ella? Why?'

Ella sniffed. 'You heard Herr Müller, it don't matter anyway; he's just a Pole.' She looked down at Hannah. 'A *subhuman*.'

'But if you let Hans get away with this, next time it could be worse. He attacked you, Ella. Who else gave you that bruise?'

Ella's fingertips went to her bruise as if she'd forgotten it was there. 'No, he loves me. I know it. And he's come all this way to see me, so if you don't mind…'

'Ella, wait…'

'Oh, and one other thing.'

'What?'

'Hans is Herr Müller's son.'

'His *son*?'

Ella left, a smile of satisfaction on her lips. Hannah sat by herself, the walls pressing in on her. There was nothing she could do. She buried her face in her arms.

*

Hannah waited half an hour, an hour. Finally, she heard footsteps approaching. But they weren't Herr Müller's footsteps. The door opened. It was Angela. 'Herr Müller has been called away. He'll be back in an hour by which time the men from the Gestapo will have arrived. You're to go to your room and stay there. On no account are you to leave your room unless I say. Is that understood?'

Hannah sighed. 'Yes, if you say so.'

'Off you go, then. Oh, and whilst you are there, you might as well pack.'

'Pack?'

'You don't think you'd be staying here after that little display earlier?'

'Will I be going home?'

'Home? Of course not.'

'So where, then?'

'That, Hannah, is for Herr Müller to decide.'

Chapter 13

Hannah paused at the dining hall door and watched as Angela made her way down the corridor towards the laundry room. She was about to head for her room when she heard a giggle. Squinting, she could see at the far end of the hall Ella sitting on Hans' lap, stroking his face. They hadn't seen her. And to think Angela thought her full of folly. Quickly, Hannah returned to Angela's office, closing the door behind her. She opened the key cabinet and ran her finger along all the keys hanging up on little hooks, a little label under each. Sure enough, there it was – key number eighteen, the key to the outdoor hut.

She half walked, half ran along the corridors, bumping into the occasional girl, through the kitchen and out. With trembling fingers, she slotted the key into the padlock and unlocked it. She opened the door, quietly calling out his name. 'Jan? Jan, it's me, Hannah.' She could hear him groaning, whimpering even. The hut was dark, just outlines, but it was the fetid air that hit her – the smell of dirty clothes and staleness. She ran her hand down the side of the wall next to the door and found a light switch. She saw him, lying in a foetal position on his bed. She ran to him, placing her hand on his shoulder. He looked up at her through squinting, swollen eyes. Her hand went to her mouth. 'Oh my God, what has he… what's he done to you.' He looked unrecognisable, his face bloodied and mushed. 'Oh, you poor man, you poor man. How could he?' She looked round for something to help clean him up. There was no basin or tap in here, just a cold tap outside. She noticed a small photograph pinned to the wooden wall – a shot of Jan with an attractive, dark-haired woman and a small girl of about three, maybe four years.

'Jan, listen, listen to me. You need to get out of here. The…' She could barely bring herself to say the word. 'They're coming to get you, the Gestapo, to take you away. They'll be here within the hour. You must get away from here.'

'No.'

She didn't expect that. 'But, Jan, can't you see. You must.'

'And where would I go, Hannah?' The way he said her name in his strange accent took her by surprise. 'How would I survive in the forest with no food, and in this terrible cold?' His voice seemed to shake, as if it were an echo she was hearing, not the voice itself.

'But if you stay here…'

'Help me sit up.'

She took his arm and helped ease him up. He sat on the edge of his bunk, shivering, his body jagged, broken. She shook her head.

'An hour, you say? Perhaps you're right. Perhaps I could survive.' He said it just at the moment Hannah realised he'd never make it, not in those woods, not in this cold. 'If you could perhaps find me a knife?' He didn't look up, his head remained still, his eyes fixed on the floor in front of him.

'A knife? Why would you–'

'If I am to survive, I'll need a sharp knife, very sharp. Could you find me one from the kitchen?'

'I'm not sure.'

'Please, do not worry. I'll not harm anyone with it. But out

64

there, in those woods…'

'I suppose.'

'Please. And a water bottle.'

The kitchen was still mercifully empty. Hannah opened and shut several drawers in quick succession before finding one full of kitchen knives, including several huge ones. They all looked sharp to her. It was a busy kitchen after all. They had to be. She picked one up and felt its weight in her hand. It looked large enough to easily cut through the flesh of a slaughtered rabbit or whatever. She heard the sound of an engine arriving outside. She ran to the huge kitchen window, scratching away the layer of frost on the inside. Her heartbeat quickened – it was *them* in their jeep, the Gestapo. From inside the home, she could hear doors opening and shutting. The girls had finished their morning ablutions and routines; they'd soon be swarming all over the place. Quickly, she grabbed a couple of bread rolls and a whole hunk of ham, and a small string bag to put everything in. She forgot the water bottle.

She ran for the back door, knife in her hand, when she heard her name being called from behind her. 'Fraulein Schiffer, are you modelling for us again?'

It was Greta with her little pigtails. 'What? No. Oh, actually, it's Tuesday, isn't it? Yes, I am, then. I'll be with you in five minutes. Two minutes.'

Greta glanced down at the flash of silver in Hannah's hand. Her eyes widened.

'Look, you go, Greta; I'll catch you up.'

'Yes, miss.'

Hannah darted back outside, knowing every second counted. She found Jan in his coat, a threadbare thing that would do nothing to keep out the piercing cold. 'They're here,' she said passing him the knife and the bag.

'Who?'

'The… the Gestapo.'

He swallowed; he seemed to shrink a little, the fear clear in his eyes.

He considered the knife a moment. 'Now, you must go. They can't find you here.'

'Will you…'

'Yes, I'll be fine. Please go now… quickly.'

She paused at the door of the hut and looked back at him.

He flashed her a smile, revealing his reddened, bloodied teeth. 'Thank you, Hannah.'

She tried to smile in return but found she couldn't.

*

Hannah rushed back through the kitchen, through the dining hall and along the corridor that led to the main entrance and the staircase. She found Angela, Ella and Hans waiting in the hallway, their backs straight, the chins held high. Behind them, unnoticed perhaps, a whole gaggle of girls, unusually silent. Hannah joined her colleagues just as Herr Müller burst into through the entrance followed by two huge Gestapo officers. Herr Müller, who usually seemed so authoritative and sure of himself, now looked positively small and diminished beside these two younger harder-looking men with their long coats and dark, narrow eyes. Everyone greeted each other with booming Heil Hitlers.

'Now, gentlemen,' said Herr Müller, 'this is the young lady I was telling you about.'

One of the Gestapo men stepped forward. 'It was you he attacked?'

Ella shrunk, her neck disappearing into her collar. 'Yes, sir,' she croaked. Hannah noticed Hans take her hand.

'We'll need you to identify him, then. And who are you?' he asked, turning to Hannah.

Hannah's stomach caved in. 'Hannah Schiffer, sir. Heil Hitler. Ella's companion.'

Herr Müller addressed Angela. 'Is the accused still locked up?'

'Yes, sir,' said Angela, swallowing.

'Take us to him,' said the main Gestapo man.

'Follow me, gentlemen,' said Herr Müller. 'This way.'

They all followed – the Gestapo men, Angela, Ella and Hans, and, behind them, Hannah, a solemn but determined procession, their boots echoing down the corridors. Hannah feared her heart would explode at any moment. Jan had barely five minutes to escape. Once they'd found him gone, the Gestapo officers would ring their headquarters, and a search party with dogs would be sent to hunt him down. There was no way he would have had enough of a head start. They would find him; they would tear him from limb from limb.

Herr Müller led the way through the kitchen to the hut, striding confidently in front. It was only as he approached the steps to the hut that he stopped. 'What the… why's it unlocked?' He turned to Angela, his face beetroot red. 'Why's it unlocked?' he bellowed.

Angela turned white.

One of the Gestapo officers, the one who'd spoken to Hannah, brushed Herr Müller aside and jumped up the steps, pushing the door open. Hannah heard him cry out. 'Oh, shit. Oh, the bastard.'

The second officer joined his colleague. Herr Müller glared at Angela. Ella and Hans reached for each other's hands, and Hannah's heart dared to hope. In that same order, one by one, they crowded into the hut. Hannah heard Ella gasp, saw Angela's legs give way, saw Hans pale.

'What's happened? Let me see; what's happened?' She forced her way through, almost falling forward as she edged herself forward. Her legs buckled. Jan was on the bunk, lying on his back; in his hand the photograph Hannah had seen earlier, and the kitchen knife sticking out of his chest.

*

The following few minutes passed in a blur. Angela broke down in tears as Herr Müller yelled at her, demanding to know why the hut had been unlocked; the Gestapo officers dragged Jan's body off the bunk, allowing it to fall in a heap on the floor where they proceeded to kick it. Hans urged Ella not to cry, that it wouldn't look good if the Gestapo men saw her like that. All the while, Hannah stood rooted to the spot, her mouth dry, her heart deadened as she watched them desecrating Jan's corpse. Her parents had warned her. Some of her friends had warned her in whispers that the regime was evil incarnate. She'd survived by adopting a hefty load of cynicism, while hoping they were wrong, but a part of her still believed, *wanted* to believe. After all, she'd grown up with it, had known nothing different, had been shaped by it, so how could it be wrong? But now in this cold ramshackle hut, with the mayhem swirling around her, the scales fell from her eyes like a veil floating and drifting away in the mist. She wanted to reach out for a friend, for a reassuring touch, but no, no one paid her any heed; she'd become invisible. Her misery was hers and hers alone, and the realisation left her shivering and desperate, and she knew with a fearful certainty that she'd never be the same again.

They stood outside the hut, the Gestapo men shouting at Herr Müller and, incredibly, Hannah felt sorry for him until he pointed directly at Angela, blaming her for the hut being unlocked. But Herr Müller's attempt to deflect the blame only made the Gestapo officers more incensed. Ella and Hans had quietly crept away, leaving Angela and Hannah, shivering in the cold, to witness Herr Müller's fall from grace.

Finally, they returned indoors. Tempers calmed. But Hannah knew no one was safe until they had left. They all stood in the hallway, the junior Gestapo man scribbling notes in a small pocket notebook. Various girls passed, as if on a dare, to see these frightful men for themselves. Hannah, desperate to get away, as Ella and Hans had done, knew to do so would only draw attention to herself, so she remained, conscious that she and Angela had gravitated towards each other, standing next to each other, their arms touching. They hadn't, however, looked at each other, but Hannah knew exactly how Angela felt, how far she'd fallen in just the last few minutes. Angela had played a game – playing the stern mistress acting in the name of the Führer. But now, faced with the real thing, with real power, she knew just how, in the scheme of things, insignificant she really was. She and her, Hannah and Angela, they'd become allies in weakness; for in the dictatorship of tyranny, they were merely foot soldiers.

The Gestapo men were about to leave; it was over. But it wasn't quite.

Greta ambled over to them, politely and nervously calling for their attention. That this tiny, earnest-looking girl should stop them amused the two men. The senior one bent down, the better to hear what little Greta had to say. Hannah watched with increasing horror, knowing what was happening, unable to prevent it. Greta was being true to herself, just as she'd told her, that truth, more than anything else in the world, was the most important thing. She watched with horrified detachment as Greta spoke in the ear of the Gestapo man and lifted her arm and pointed her finger at her – at Hannah. The Gestapo man's smile disappeared in an instant. He drew himself up as Greta finished her say and glared over at Hannah. Their eyes locked, and Hannah knew she was as good as dead.

He marched over towards her. In her befuddled mind, Hannah wondered how he was able to cover so much ground in so few steps. He stopped directly in front of her. She gazed up as this devil-like Adonis loomed over her and trembled.

'So you supplied him the knife.'

Hannah opened her mouth to respond but her brain hadn't told her what to say, whether to deny it or be damned and admit it. Her mind was simply a fog of incomprehension, devoid of thought.

'Well?'

She nodded, simply a hint of a nod, indiscernible to anyone except the one, single person who mattered, the man in front of her.

He slapped her so hard, and with such force, she feared her head might spin off.

Chapter 14
November 2001

I was no spring bride when I married my husband. We'd only known each other for a couple of years. I was thirty-three when we met, Barry two years younger. I was working in the housing department at Kent County Council; Barry was in insurance, neither exactly the most glamorous of occupations. It was the seventh of June 1977, the Queen's Silver Jubilee, and I, like much of the country, was celebrating at a street party. The whole road where I rented at the time had been sealed off, trestle tables covered in pristine white cloths and chairs tapering into the distance. The sun shone, thank God; we wore round Union Jack hats beneath red, white, and blue bunting and multicoloured balloons. Union Jack flags hung from every other bedroom window. Older women in aprons bustled around delivering tray after tray of food, mainly chicken drumsticks and sandwiches – mountains of sandwiches. We'd started with a crackly rendition of 'God Save the Queen' played over an old PA borrowed from the village hall. Then, with the volume turned down, a continual repertoire of pub singalongs. It was a marvellous occasion but for the fact I was miserable. I'd only been in Kent a few weeks and, as yet, knew no one. Everyone I worked with was much older than myself, my fellow tenant was a chain-smoking punk with dubious standards of self-hygiene and, frankly, I was lonely. So when a deliciously good-looking gentleman with long sideburns and fulsome moustache, balancing a paper plate of Indian food asked if he could take the vacant seat to my left, I couldn't have cared either way.

'Where did you get that?' I asked, pointing at his curry with undisguised envy.

'Aha,' he said. Leaning over, he whispered that Mr Guffour, owner of the local Indian takeaway, was giving out free servings, but one had to be in the know, he said, tapping the side of his nose, and in the right place at the right time. His name, he said, was Barry Swingle. And so we talked – about life in Kent, our jobs, where I came from, the usual stuff. He spoke quickly, enthusiastically, usually with his mouth full, which I found rather intolerable. Then, to add insult, he ceased eating halfway through his pile of curry to have a cigarette. He didn't think to ask if I minded. Then, half finished, he dropped the still-burning fag into a polystyrene cup, where it fizzled and burnt a hole. He then returned his attention to his lunch. He liked motorbikes, the odd flutter on the horses and darts. I looked around, hoping someone might come to my rescue, but no, I was truly stuck with this Barry Swingle. Yet, despite it all, there was something about him – his naïve enthusiasm for life, his perpetual optimism, his total lack of artifice, which I found endearing, so when, after half an hour or so, he invited me out for a drink, I found myself saying yes.

I only said yes because I was lonely, I told myself. Yet, I had a most enjoyable evening. Barry was kind, attentive, and he made me laugh so loud I thought I'd wet myself. No one had ever made me laugh like that. Not ever. We went out several times, and I realised that, despite my initial reservations, I liked him. I liked him a lot. He lived with his mother, and she welcomed me into her two-up, two-down terraced house as if I myself were royalty. I liked her immediately. Their respect and love for one another was evident, their playfulness and teasing heart-warming. She was the only person I ever heard calling Barry 'Barrington'. I so envied their relationship to the point it could, at times, reduce me to tears; I couldn't remember a single time sharing a joke, or any affection, with my mother. Barry's mother lavished me with food, praise and affection. I never knew it could be like this.

We went out for a couple of years. Barry's mother never minded me staying the night. She never minded that after a while my 'sleepovers', as she called them, as if I were a childhood friend of her son's, became more and more frequent. She tried not to mind when, three years after first meeting Barry, I fell pregnant.

Barry wept with joy when I told him.

But she did insist on one thing – that if Barrington and I were going to bring a child into this world, then we should be married.

In 1980, we watched Tessa Sanderson competing at the javelin at the Olympic Games. 'Hmm,' said Barry, stroking his chin. 'Tessa. Nice name that. What d'you think, Liz? If it's a girl? Tessa.'

Chapter 15

The heavens open as I dash from the car park into Woodlands View Care Home. As soon as I step inside, shaking out my umbrella, I could hear Elvis' dulcet singing through from the lounge area. 'He's back,' says the carer with the wrist tattoo as she passed.

'Can't keep away, can he?'

It's true – Elvis is a frequent visitor to the care home. There he is, strutting in the middle of the lounge, singing 'Blue Suede Shoes'. He always makes an effort, this gentleman from rural Kent, with his fake sideburns and dyed black hair, shaped carefully into a quiff, his white bejewelled jacket unbuttoned right down to his potbelly, its collar turned up, naturally, his hairy chest sporting a massive silver crucifix. His eye-wateringly tight white trousers are held up by a wide belt with the American eagle on its buckle. He shuffles around the shiny linoleum floor singing into his microphone attached to a tiny amplifier. He has a large ring on every one of his fingers. Well, it's one for the money. He sees me and winks. Well, that's something I can tell the grandkids – Elvis winked at me. Now go, cat, go.

One song segues into another, but for this one, 'Heartbreak Hotel', he takes the hand of one of the ladies and, pulling her up, clasps her tightly. The poor thing, she is barely half his height, her face nestled in the mass of chest hair. The residents sit around the perimeter, some singing along, tapping their feet in time. My mother is nowhere to be seen. No surprise there – she finds this sort of thing awfully common.

I sidle behind the chairs, hoping not to be noticed. 'Heartbreak Hotel' comes to an end, and Elvis pushes away his dancing partner and, with a curling lip, shouts over, 'Hey, pretty lady, where are you going?'

Oh good god, is he really speaking to me?

'You care for a dance with the King?' he asks in his American South accent tinged with East Kent.

Frankly, I'd rather stab knitting needles into my eyes. 'No, thank you,' I mouth, conscious of my glowing face.

I make it to the conservatory with the opening bars of 'Hound Dog' ringing in my ears. I close the door behind me, reducing Elvis to a muffle. Mother is sitting there, flipping through the pages of a glossy magazine. 'Hello, Mum.' She shoots me a glance as if I'd just stolen something from her. 'Well, they said you was high classed. Why aren't you joining in? Don't you like Elvis?'

'No, I do not. These people, they think this is music. This is not music.'

'They're just having fun, Mum. Everyone loves Elvis.' I pull up a chair and sit beside her. 'How are things anyway?'

She ignores me, rattling her magazine.

'You OK? Had your lunch yet?' No answer.

The conservatory door opens, and Elvis' voice blares in a moment until the door swings shut. It is the dapper Mr Charlton again with his beige jacket and tie. 'Mrs Marsh, don't you care for the singer?'

Mother ignores him. I flash him a weak smile. He stands, gazing out over the garden, rocking on his heels. Elvis has fallen silent. Maybe he's having a fag out the back with his groupies. Mr Charlton reminds my mother it'll soon be time for lunch, then exits.

I don't know how to approach this so I take the envelope from my handbag. My mother's short-term memory is, of course, shot, but she often remembers things from her childhood or when she was still a young woman. There's every chance she'd remember this. Opening the envelope, I pass her the certificate. 'Do you recognise this, Mum?'

'*Mein Gott.*'

Yes, she did recognise it. 'What is it, Mum?'

She turns her attention back to the garden. '*Wo ist das Rotkehlchen heute?*'

'I don't know where the robin is today.' Sod the robin. 'Mum, please, what is this? Is it important?'

Since developing her dementia, my mother's body language is that much easier to read; she has the subtlety sometimes of a small child. She sits now with her arms crossed high on her chest, her head back, a look of defiance written over her features.

'Mum? Please, I–'

'I don't know what this is. You and your silly questions. Always too many questions.'

'It's dated December 1944, during the war. You were twenty-nine at the time. I was born that October. What does this certificate mean, Mum?'

'I cannot remember.'

'You *must* remember; you were in Germany, for Pete's sake, you had a baby and most likely being bombed day and night, living in God knows what sort of conditions. You don't forget something like that.' I'm being too brusque with her, I know that, but I can't help myself. 'Please, Mum, just for once in your life, help me out here.'

She says nothing.

'OK, be like that. I shall go to Germany, then, and I shall find out for myself.' The thought of going to Germany by myself does not appeal. But if I have to, I will. I can hear the music starting up again, the opening bars to 'Suspicious Minds'.

'Ah, he's back,' says my mother.

'Who? Elvis?'

No, she doesn't mean Elvis. She means the robin, the blasted robin.

Chapter 16

My mobile rings just as I arrive home from work. Joy, it's Tessa. 'Hi, Mum. You all right?'

'Sure. How's it going, love?'

'Oh, it's brilliant, Mum.' She proceeds to tell me how it's brilliant. I settle on the settee, kicking off my shoes while anchoring my phone between my shoulder and jaw. Tabby comes to say hello. She jumps up on my lap, arching her back. So Tessa has settled into her new life, new friends, dazzled and excited by the lights of a new city, exploring its bars and clubs. The lectures are going well. She's enjoying it, but all along I sense an undercurrent in all this. She has something to tell me. It's almost as if she's trying to persuade herself what a great time she's having. Tabby headbutts me on the chin – which means she's hungry. Tessa tells me about the girls in the halls of residence, how they're all bonded, and what great fun they are.

'Well, that all sounds great, Tess. I'm so pleased.'

'I've met someone.'

Ah, so this is it! 'Oh?' I manage to stop myself from saying *So soon?*

'He's called Thomas. Tom.'

'Tom?'

'Yeah, he's nice, really nice. He's from Liverpool, so he speaks with a bit of a Scouse accent. You'd like him, Mum.'

Heck, I think, are we already at the meeting-the-parents stage? 'That's lovely, Tess. Mind how you go now.'

I hear the intake of breath at the other end. She knows exactly what I mean; I don't need to spell it out. We don't need to go through the 'condom conversation' again.

'I'll give you a ring next week, Mum. Love you. Bye.'

'Love you too.' But she's already rung off. I pull on Tabby's ears. Tom. It's a common enough name, but couldn't she have found someone with a different name? So now Tessa's got me thinking about Tom, my Tom, all those years ago. I feed Tabby then switch on my computer. I've decided to do something I've been tempted to do for months now but have never been brave enough to go through with it. I make myself a cup of tea while the computer stirs into life. Ready now, I sit at the keyboard, willing myself to start typing. My fingers are clammy all of a sudden. 'You're just looking,' I say aloud. 'There's no harm in just looking.' Steeling myself, I type in the web address: friendsreunited.co.uk. OK, so that was the easy bit. Their strapline sums it up – the place to find old friends and new. I login to my account, having registered months ago. Next, I type in the name of my old secondary school in Waverly. There it is. Then I type in his name – Tom Fletcher – and wait. It takes a few seconds but nothing comes back. I'm not sure whether to be disappointed or relieved. But wait. It wouldn't be 'Tom'. So, instead, I tap in Thomas Fletcher. I hold my breath as the little hourglass spins around. I hear the sound of the cat flap rattling. Tabby has finished her dinner and is now off out to explore. And there he is – no photo, thank God, nor any text outlining what he is up to. But he has filled in the basic details although, I notice, he's left the 'relationship' box empty. He works as a freelance graphic designer and lives... oh my, he's moved back to the area. He is no longer in Kent; he's living some twenty miles away. My heart pounds at the thought of Tom living so nearby. I start typing, not stopping to think. If I think, I'll hesitate and if I hesitate, I won't do it. *Hi, Tom. You might remember me – Liz Marsh (as was). I hope you're well. It's been a long time. Love…* No, I can't sign off with 'love', so instead I write 'best wishes'. Then, quickly, before I can change my mind, I click the send button. I fall back on the settee, taking deep breaths. I'd done it. I'd done it. If he answers, great; if he doesn't, so be it. In fact, thinking about it, I rather hope he doesn't answer. I've done what I can, I can do no more. I'm happy with that; he really doesn't need to answer. I puff out my cheeks. I really ought to do some dinner now, I'm starving. In fact, the more I think about it, the more I hope he doesn't respond.

The thing about living alone is that one has to think about things differently – even the smaller things. For example, having eaten my microwave lamb curry, do I wash up the plate or put it in the dishwasher? But by the time the dishwasher is full enough to warrant switching on, it could be a week or more. It's these small things that bring me up short. There were only the three of us but, looking back, I'm amazed at how much noise and how much space we took up. We were such a happy family unit until that bitch came along and turned Barry's head. Why are men so predictable. Why are they so weak?

I'm still thinking of Barry when my doorbell rings. I open the door to find my ex-husband standing there grinning widely. 'I've been thinking. Come the New Year, we should go to Germany.'

'What?'

'You going to let me in or what?'

I follow him into the living room.

'Mmm, smells nice. Curry for dinner, was it?' He stands, rocking on his heels, still looking pleased with himself.

'What do you mean *we* ought to go to Germany?'

'To that hotel. I've given it some thought. You're right. That certificate, or whatever it was, might hold the key to your life as a child in Germany. We could go, together, you and me. You got leave owing from work, haven't you? And I'm owed a few days, and it's quiet anyway come January.'

'But—'

'Don't worry – separate rooms and all that. But I reckon if you find something, you might need someone to talk to. You were born in *Ger-man-y* during the war, Liz.'

Why did he say Germany like that, as if it was some dreadful crime. Back in the 1950s, it almost was.

'You never know what you'll find there,' he says. 'You might find you're Himmler's daughter or something.'

'Don't you think Shelley might have something to say about this?'

'Shelley?' he says as if the thought has only just occurred to him. 'Oh, I'll square it with her; don't you worry about Shelley.'

I hear the cat flap again. Tabby's come back in. It's true; I don't want to go by myself. It's also true that I am worried about what I might find. Having Barry with me would help. I warm to the idea. And if he can 'square it' with Shelley, so be it. She isn't my concern. 'OK,' I say. 'You're right. We'll do it. We'll go to Germany.'

Chapter 17
January 2002

Today, early evening, I receive another call from Tessa. She's about to go for dinner with her new boyfriend, Tom. I can tell by the way she talks so quickly that she's nervous about it, telling me she can't decide what to wear. Should she wear *this* outfit, or did it look too conservative, too serious, or *that* outfit, but this one might be a 'tad too racy'. Oh, the dilemma. I know I'm not expected to say much; my role here is simply to listen and act as my daughter's sounding board. 'But, Tess, it depends more on where's he taking you.'

'Oh God, Mum, I looked it up on the net. It looks dead nice, and expensive, and all that.'

'Is he paying or are you going Dutch?'

'Going what? I don't know, Mum.'

'Have you got money on your card, just in case?'

'Just about. I might wear that necklace Dad bought me for Christmas.'

'Oh yes, that always looks nice.'

What I really want to ask is what does Tom want from this evening out with my daughter. I so want to tell her to be careful but can't face irking her. She tells me a little more about this Tom she's seeing. He's studying physics (that's good); he's into cooking (good), likes cats (very good), football (don't they all?), likes the occasional bet on the horses (that's not good), and his parents are well off by all accounts (aha!). 'And he's very good-looking,' she adds as if it were an afterthought.

'And what about college? How's that going?' I ask.

But Tess is too keyed up about tonight to think about anything else. I wish her luck and hope that the evening goes well.

I'm about to put my feet up and watch telly. But I'm too distracted by Tessa's mention of that necklace. I remember it well. Tess has no idea, but her necklace was the necklace that broke up a marriage. It was August two years ago, and I was having one of my occasional clear-outs at home. Trying on all my clothes, making sure they still fitted, deciding which ones to keep and which to send to the charity shop, refolding the ones to keep and re-stacking them in my drawers and the wardrobe. In the midst of this, I came across two thin velvety boxes at the bottom of Barry's underwear drawer. I knew immediately they were necklaces. Not the most subtle of places to hide something, I thought. I tried to resist the temptation to have a look. But, of course, I did. They were both similar, a 'job lot' I said to myself, laughing. But, to be fair to my husband, he'd chosen well. They were Art Deco-styled, both silver, one with a blue diamond-shaped pendant, the other with a round aquamarine gemstone. Not cheap, I thought, not cheap at all. I was impressed. We were two months away from my birthday. Barry, being a typical man, usually did his birthday shopping the day before, but it looked like he was ahead of the game for once. I guessed one was a Christmas present for Tessa, the other for me. I put them both back in their boxes and returned them to their hiding places. Good old Barry, how I loved him so.

My birthday came, and I opened my presents, eagerly anticipating my necklace. I got a book of nineteenth-century poems, a silk scarf, a book on feng-shui and a very nice, if a little garish, brooch in the shape of a bumblebee. But no necklace. I thanked Barry for his presents but asked whether he might have forgotten one. He looked hurt, of course. *Had I not done well with what I had* was the unspoken question. But no, he hadn't forgotten anything.

I was worried but told myself there was no need to panic. Perhaps he'd over-bought for me and so decided to hold the necklace back till Christmas. Christmas came and indeed Tessa did receive one of the necklaces as a present from her father; she got the diamond-shaped pendant. She was thrilled. More nice presents for me but still no necklace. Perhaps it was hidden beneath the Christmas tree. I looked – but no – nothing else. I risked asking the same question again, had he forgotten anything? I came across as the greediest wife on the planet, but still, I had to ask. And again, the same answer and the same expression – no, he hadn't forgotten anything.

So then I knew – that necklace had never been for me. It was intended as a present for another woman, for it wasn't the sort of present you gave to a colleague or a boss or one's sister. No, Barry, my husband of twenty years, was having an affair.

Once I knew, finding further evidence proved easy. It was 1999, and Barry had only just got his first mobile and hadn't got used to it yet. I don't think he knew where the 'delete' key was, so there it was – a whole series of texts between my husband and a woman whom I knew by name, a woman called Shelley. I only read a couple; I had no need to read more, no desire to. I was winded. I started looking for reasons. I soon came up with several reasons why I was to blame and why Barry was justified in sleeping with this woman called Shelley. Why do women always do that? We take the blame; it is always our fault.

I pour myself a glass of white wine from the fridge and settle down again on the settee. Tabby comes to see me. I stroke her a little roughly. 'It's just you and me now, Tabby. Just you and me.'

There is nothing I want to watch on TV so I decide to check Friends Reunited – just in case; you never know. I drink half a glass of wine while waiting for the modem to kick in and 'authenticate', whatever that means. I go to the site and log in. Oh, my heart skips a beat – there's a message in my inbox. I double click, and I see the name of Thomas Fletcher. I shake like a leaf as I click open the message. *Hello there, Liz. How great to hear from you. Do you still live in Waverley? Cos I've moved back not so far away. Fancy meeting up? I'd love to see you again. Look forward to hearing from you, Best, Tom.*

Oh. My. God.

Chapter 18

Today I visit my mother again.

'Mrs Swingle?'

Oh, now this is a rarity; it's Mrs Hale, the manager of the home, and her unexpected appearance invariably means something's wrong.

'Yes.'

'Oh, hello. I was told you might be visiting today. I'm pleased I caught you. I wonder before you go if I could have a word, please. No hurry though.'

'Sure. Nothing wrong, is there?'

'No, no, nothing urgent.'

'But what is it?'

Mrs Hale, a short, plump woman with curly hair and round glasses, looks awkward. She motions with her head that we should step aside into a small alcove. She starts with a heavy sigh. I'm not going to like this. 'Mrs Swingle, since your last visit, your mother has been rather abusive to the other residents.'

'*Abusive?*'

'Not physically, but… your mother's been shouting anti-Semitic abuse at, well, frankly, anyone who comes too close to her. Not the staff, just the residents.'

'What… what do you mean anti-Semitic abuse? Like what?'

'Well, she uses words and phrases I'd rather not repeat. And it gets worse, I'm afraid.'

Oh, I could do without this.

'Mrs Swingle, I know from our records that your mother was born in Germany in 1915. I don't know my history but I looked it up on Wikipedia. Now I know they say Wikipedia can't be trusted, but apparently your mother would have been a young woman at the time of *Adolf* Hitler.'

She emphasises the name Adolf as if I may get it confused with another Hitler. 'You're not going to tell me she's become a Nazi.'

A member of staff walks by. Mrs Hale waits until we're alone again. 'Yes, I'm afraid I am. The other residents are not too upset by any of this: most of them don't take any notice, but it's upsetting the staff.'

'But what can I do? I can speak to her, but that doesn't mean anything.'

'But if you could try. Who knows, she *may* listen to you.'

I want to say why should she? She's never listened to me ever, so why would she change her ways now? But I don't say it.

I find my mother in her bedroom on the second floor, humming to herself. She shares her tiny bedroom with another resident, a sweet woman called Ruby who never speaks. Fortunately, Mother is alone sitting on the edge of her bed.

'What's that you're humming, Mum?' I sit next to her.

She stops.

'So, apparently, you don't like the Jews now.'

She makes a *pft* sound and stares out of the window.

I ask how she is, whether she's had her lunch, whether she'd seen Elvis recently, the usual things. Then I tell her that Barry and I are going to Germany, to a town called Weinberg.

The name hits home. It happens occasionally, a name from her distant past and her eyes widen and she *remembers*. 'Do you remember Weinberg, Mum?'

'Weinberg? I met your father there.'

'Dad?'

'Nineteen forty-three. He was a handsome man in those days.' She smiles at the memory.

She doesn't mean Dad. Dad was in Germany only at the very end of the war in 1945 and after Germany's surrender. He couldn't have been there in 1943; no Brit was unless he was a spy or something, and I couldn't imagine my dad, the café owner, making a very good spy, not with his Norfolk accent. The thought makes me laugh. I knew, I'd always know, that Dad wasn't my *real* father. But he never mentioned it, and my mother certainly was never going to. No, she was referring to my biological father – we'd entered new territory and I knew I had to step cautiously.

'What was my father doing in Weinberg in 1943, Mum?'

'He was a handsome man but I knew he wasn't right for me.'

I wait, hoping she'll say something else. When she doesn't, I try prompting her. 'He wasn't right for you? Is that why you split up?'

'Hmm? They made him fight. Put him in a uniform and made him fight.'

'And he was killed. Was that it?'

She's thinking, her mind is taking her back. 'What happened to him, Mummy?'

She shrugs as if the answer is of no consequence and I want to scream at her.

'Please, Mummy, try to remember. I loved Dad with all my heart but the man you're talking about is my real father.'

I'm losing her by the second, I can tell. I show her the certificate again. 'Was this from Weinberg, Mum?'

This time she looks at it more carefully. I can almost see the cogs of her memory turning, trying to remember. 'I had to leave that place. I had to leave.'

I inch closer to her. 'Why, Mum? Why did you have to leave Weinberg? Was it because of my father?'

She concentrates; her brow furrows. It's almost as if, for the first time in her life, she wants to help me. But then she shakes her head and flaps her hands about and I know it's gone. I've lost it.

'Where are the robins today? Have you've seen the robins, Elizabeth?'

'No, Mum. I haven't seen the robins today.'

I stay a while longer, trying my best to smile, willing the anger to dissipate. I can't stay for long; I need air, I need to escape this room, to escape from my mother.

As I leave, I say, 'Mum, try to be nice to the other residents. Don't shout at them or call them names, hey?'

'Shout at them? I don't shout at them, Elizabeth. Why would I do that?'

'Goodbye, Mum. I love you.'

I stand to leave. By the time I've taken the five steps to Mum's bedroom door, she's starting humming again. I stop and listen, straining to catch the tune. I do. I recognise it. I walk back down the stairs and, on reaching the ground floor and the foyer, creep out, hoping not to be spotted by Mrs Hale. I make it to my little Peugeot, quickly slam the door shut and turn the ignition.

As I drive away, I realise I'm now humming that tune. And now I know what it is – it's 'Deutschlandlied', the German national anthem. I almost laugh. The older my mother gets, the more she regresses to her childhood. Another year or two and I might know everything.

It's only as I arrive home and about to get out of the car, I remember something else – two things in fact. My mother actually called me by my name, the first time in years, certainly since the dementia started taking hold. And, second, I told my mother I love her. The realisation stops me in my tracks. Where did that come from? I told my old bat of a mother that I loved her. Furthermore, I mean it; I really do.

Chapter 19

It wasn't being shoved so hard that I fell to the ground and scraped my knees that hurt, it wasn't so much the kick in the small of my back that hurt, it was the words, the cruel chant that cut into me. 'German bitch, German bitch.' First it was just Cerys Atkins, her mouth full of chewing gum rotating like a washing machine. Soon her friends joined the chant and, like wildfire, it quickly spread until in the time it took me to stagger to my feet, the whole playground had taken it up. *German bitch, German bitch, German bitch…* I stood there with nowhere to hide, pathetically exposed, with this surge of hate pressing down on me, five hundred pairs of eyes piercing me, five hundred voices pounding in my eardrums. I wanted to disappear, to die, but it was that sense of isolation, of being entirely without a friend, or even an ally, that truly made me crumble, that made my eyes water. Finally, a couple of the teachers brought the terror to an abrupt end by marching haphazardly around the playground shouting, 'Stop it, stop it this instant,' and slicing the air with their hands.

Another teacher, a rake-thin woman in tweed, Miss Barrett, came bounding over to me, a coffee cup in her hand. I knew by her expression that she felt no sympathy for me; indeed, I probably deserved it, that I had disturbed her hitherto quiet playground duty. 'Who started this, Marsh?' she barked at me. 'Tell me, who's the ringleader here?'

Instinctively, my eyes darted over towards Cerys, who immediately stepped back. Quickly, I tried to avert my eyes away from her but too late; Miss Barrett swung round, following my gaze. She saw the telltale expression on Cerys' face, a mixture of guilt and defiance. 'Atkins,' she said, marching up to her. 'Was it you?'

'What, miss?' said Cerys, her cheeks bulging with chewing gum.

'Don't you "what" me, Atkins. Did you start this loathsome chanting?'

'No, miss.' She said it with such conviction, such hurt, I almost believed her myself.

Miss Barrett spun round. 'Well, Marsh? Was it Atkins?'

I looked down and noticed the trickle of blood on my right knee. I shook my head, Cerys still visible in my peripheral vision, a leer on her face. 'No, miss.'

'So who was it, then?'

'Dunno, miss.'

She threw her arms in the air in exasperation, spilling much of her coffee. I truly had ruined her hour. She turned to face the whole playground of wide-eyed kids. 'Right, unless the foul-mouthed child who started this comes forward this instant, you're all be kept behind for an hour after school, every last one of you.' Her announcement was met with a wave of disgruntlement. Everyone knew it was Cerys Atkins, Miss Barrett included, but I knew this was an insufficient enough threat to force Cerys' hand; indeed, Cerys would be enjoying this because Miss Barrett had hoisted herself up by her own petard – why suffer alone, Cerys would think, when I can make everyone suffer. And, of course, no one stepped forward. Five hundred kids and not a sound beyond the cold East Anglian wind blowing in from the sea.

So by the time our detention had finished, it was almost half past four when I left school and headed for the bus stop. I walked alone along the familiar shadowy street of terraced houses, kicking away sheets of an old newspaper, avoiding dog shit, buttoning my coat, keen to get home. But I could see the outline of a group of girls ahead of me. I heard their raucous laughter. I recognised the voice of one, the loudest – Cerys Atkins. I stopped and pressed myself into a doorway. I was almost at the bus stop; there was no other way. I gripped the strap of my satchel and, taking a deep breath, walked on, head down. I walked quickly to the other side of the street, a car approaching. I reached the other side, but as the rumble of the car disappeared, I heard Cerys' voice calling out. 'Hey, look, it's our very own Kraut.'

Ignoring her, I pressed on, desperate to get away. But no, Cerys lumbered across the street towards me, her henchmen following. I'd been bullied for a long time, but it's not something one ever gets used to. I hated school. I was the hated German in their midst. The war may have ended eleven years earlier, but we English still hated the Germans. And I *was* English, except for the fact that I had a German mother with a strong German accent. But not a single atom of me identified with my German ancestry; I couldn't speak the language. I'd never been nor wanted to. No one ever went abroad anyway; to say one might go to Germany one might as well say you were planning on going to the moon. But anyway, these were pointless arguments when confronted, as I was now, by the likes of Cerys Atkins and her gang.

'Not so fast, Krauty.' Cerys put herself right in my path. 'So where are you going?' I looked up at her, her eyes mostly obscured by her wayward fringe, her hair gelled-up despite school rules that banned hair oils. The strange thing was – she was the cleverest amongst us: top of the class in maths, the sciences and French.

Keeping my head down, my eyes focused on the pavement, I tried stepping around her.

'I said, where you going, German girl?'

'I'm not German,' I said, the steely tone in my voice very different to my beating heart inside.

Cerys and her friends laughed.

'You hear that?' said one of the others, a lass I knew called Becky. 'I'm not German,' she said, mimicking a German accent. 'I'm not German. I'm not German. I'm...' The chant continued.

'Excuse me.'

Cerys shoved me. I fell back against the brick wall. 'So you got us kept in for an hour. All of us, the whole bloody school – all because of you. Well, ain't you gonna say sorry?'

'Sorry.'

She laughed as well she might, the cow. But she wasn't finished with me yet. 'Now, listen, you German bitch, England are playing West Germany tomorrow.'

I had no idea but I couldn't admit that. 'I know that already.'

Becky laughed again. 'She knows that already, Cerys.'

'Oh, so you're an expert on football now, are ya?'

'*Ve have vays of making you talk,*' said another of her gang.

'Now, listen here. England better win, right?'

My fingers gripped my satchel strap. 'I don't like football.'

'So what? It's more than just football, ain't it? We hate the Krauts, we do, and I'm telling you now, you little German cow, if West Germany win tomorrow, we'll make your life hell, got it?'

'Please, I gotta get home.'

'Oh, bless her,' said Becky. 'She's gotta get home, home to her German mummy.'

Folding her arms against her chest, Cerys stepped aside, allowing me to pass. 'Remember, if you Krauts win tomorrow…'

Chapter 20

I'd never been so invested in a football match. It was the first thing I asked my father about when I returned home that May afternoon from my school detention. Mum was dusting her horrible little china figurines.

'We're playing in Berlin,' Dad told me.

'Is it on the wireless?'

'Guess so.'

My mother popped her head in from the kitchen. 'Since when have you been so interested in the football?'

Maybe it was as a result of my brush with Cerys that tonight I really noticed just how strong my mother's accent was and her occasional odd use of words. We'd never talked about it. But tonight I was determined to. 'Do you ever wanna go back to Germany, Mum?'

She looked at me as if I'd just dropped the F-word. 'What did you say?'

'Well, you're German, aren't you?'

'Hey there,' said my father, lighting a cigarette. 'What's brought this on?'

'I'm not German,' said my mother. 'I am English since the day I married your father.'

'Hey? What?' I couldn't articulate my mother's odd turn of phrase except it showed just how *foreign* she was.

'I am as English as you are.'

'No you're not. You're not English at all; you're…' I was aware I was almost shouting at her. 'You're *German*.' I said the word as if it was the filthiest thing I'd ever said. And I meant it; I hated her German-ness, hated having a damn Kraut as my mother; why couldn't I have been born to a *normal* mother, an English mother? Why did I have to be so different? We stood, either side of our tiny living-cum-dining-cum-everything room, and glared at each other like a pair of gladiators sizing each other up pre-fight.

'Has someone upset you?' asked my father in his usual matter-of-fact voice, the eternal epitome of calmness.

'No. Yes.' A pause. 'NO!'

'Elizabeth, now wait a minute…'

But I had gone, storming out, slamming the door on my father and my sodding German mother. I flung myself onto my bed, hugged a pillow against my chest and with tears forming, stared up at James Dean. In truth, I knew nothing about James Dean, only that he was gorgeous and somehow dangerous, that he was everything that was exciting about this strange world I lived in, and yet, despite his cool exterior, there was something deeply vulnerable about him, something I couldn't put my finger on yet understood at some deep level nonetheless, and that I was in love with him. He and I – we were of the same skin, of the same mould. I understood him in the same way he understood me. We floated on a higher plane, he and I, one which the likes of Cerys Atkins, Becky and their dim, slow-witted friends, and the likes of my German mother could never understand. So why was it that Jimmy Dean, my soulmate, the most handsome man that ever lived, was dead while my German cow of a mother was still alive. Life truly was unfair.

*

Saturday is the day I go to ballet in the mornings and help Dad out in the café in the afternoon. To get from one to the other, I cut through Waverly Town Park. Often I see one of Dad's customers, Mr Watts, playing football with his son, eight-year-old Rory. I always say hello.

My father once had a 'proper job', as he called it, in a bakery when, a few years back, he lost it – why, he never said. He soon found another job, helping a friend out in a café, only one of two in all of Waverly. His friend retired and Dad bought the business, all of it, 'lock, stock, and barrel', as he said, several times. So now, Dad was the proud owner of *Arnie's café* in central Waverly, and Saturday afternoons was his busiest part of the week, and I helped in return for a wage far more than I needed or deserved. But that was Dad for you, generous to a fault when it came to his daughter. He also employed another 'Saturday girl', Betty, two years older than me. Betty was all right, but we were usually too busy to speak.

I loved working with my dad. I wore a white shirt and a little pinny, and spoke to adults as if I were also a grown-up. The work was hard, no doubt about it, running between tables, taking orders, rushing between the kitchen and the dining area, trying to get the orders right, trying to keep my father's customers happy. And I loved it. And I knew my dad liked having me around. It was our time together, our special time, him and me. Afterwards, once we'd finished, we'd catch a bus home together, me feeling six feet high, warmed by the sense of satisfaction that comes with a day's hard graft. Perhaps, a year or two earlier, we'd hold hands but I was too old for that now. He knew that, respected it, but it didn't diminish the warmth between us. We'd sit on the bus together, a good twenty-minute ride, and Dad would read his paper, smoking, tutting occasionally and shaking his head at the folly of the world miles away from our little haven in East Anglia while I gazed contentedly out of the window. Now that I was older, I would steal a glance at him, at his profile, and realise that even as an old man in his forties, James Dean couldn't hold a candle to my dad. So, how was it, I wondered, how was it he ended up married to a bitter old cow like my mother?

But this particular Saturday in May 1956 was different because tonight there was a football game I hardly understood except that its result somehow would impinge on my life. I was tense all day, couldn't concentrate at ballet and felt even worse at the café. I saw Mr Watts and Rory playing football in the park. 'I wanna be Duncan Edwards when I grow up,' Rory shouted over at me while his dad looked on proudly, the ball at his feet. Everyone was talking about damn football. At the café, I mixed up my orders, dropped a plate, spilt a cup of tea. Betty asked if I was OK and when I snapped back yes, she told me to buck up, then. Even my father, usually so calm, shouted at me. I'd happily be kicked every day of the week than have my father shout at me. So when I stood between tables in the middle of the café, cigarette smoke swirling around me, my bottom lip trembling, he stopped in his tracks, mortified.

'My God, Lizzy, what's the matter?'

'She looks a bit pale, Arnold,' said one of Father's customers. 'Reckon you're working her too hard, mate.'

'I'm f-fine,' I managed to stutter. 'Just fine.'

By the time Dad and I got home that Saturday afternoon, the football game had already started. Dad went straight to the wireless and turned it on.

'Your tea's ready whenever you're ready,' said Mum.

I couldn't eat a thing.

'So who you supporting, Mum?'

'Me?' She flicked the tea towel she was holding. 'Couldn't give two hoots.'

'But you're German, aren't you? You should be supporting Germany.' I realised I was almost shouting.

She held my gaze, wondering, perhaps, why I seemed so agitated. 'You don't tell me how to think, young lady. You mind that tongue of yours.'

'She was just asking, Babs,' said Dad. 'No big deal. Anyway, lovey, how was ballet?'

After much turning of knobs with his ear pressed against the grill, Dad finally found the station. A dismembered voice crackled over the airwaves.

'It's still nil-nil,' said Dad.

'What happens now?' I asked.

'Now? Well, we just wait until England score and then we'll cheer.'

'And what happens if West Germany score?'

'Then your mother will cheer.'

'No, she will not,' said my mother from the kitchen.

'But England will win, won't they, Dad?'

'I don't know, lovey. Let's hope so, eh? But West Germany are the world champions, and they are playing at home so it won't be easy. So, tell me, why this sudden interest?'

I thought of Cerys, her contorted features peering in front of me, the raw hatred in her eyes and my stomach twisted. I thought of Becky and her friends laughing at me, taunting me with their silly German accents. 'Nothing,' I said. 'Nothing at all.'

And so I sat with my father concentrating on the commentator's words. Every time the Germans attacked, my heart sped up as the dread seized me. Every time England attacked, the anticipation, the hope, was unbearable. I could hear my mother clanking things in the kitchen, unnecessarily loudly, I thought. Then, on the twenty-sixth minute, Duncan Edwards scored. I was seized by a happiness and relief I'd never experienced before. Oh, the jubilation. My father laughed at my outburst of joy and cheering. I thought of little Rory in the park wanting to be the next Duncan Edwards. By the time the game had finished over an hour later, I was drained. Drained but happy. England had won three-one.

Chapter 21

That Monday, I woke up with the usual knot of worry deep in my stomach, but at least England had won; thank the Lord for that. I forced my breakfast down and, ready for school, said goodbye to my parents. My father called me back. 'Hey you, ain't you forgetting something?'

'No, Dad. I'm too old to kiss you now.'

He faked hurt, his hand on his heart as if he'd been shot. 'Did you hear that, Barbara? Spurned by me very own daughter. To think of all the things I've done for her, Babs.' Mother didn't laugh; never saw Dad's funny side.

'Dad, you'd make an awful actor.'

'Oh. I thought I was doing all right. Fancied myself as a bit of a Laurence Olivier there.'

'Yes, Dad.'

'Go on, then, be off with you. Don't you worry about me. But if I get knocked over by a bus today, may you be consumed by guilt forever more.'

The bus I caught from the end of the lane into Waverly town itself delivered me to within a three-minute walk from school. I turned the corner, the school looming ahead of me, to see Cerys and her gang hanging around outside the school gates. My insides tightened. This didn't look good. But there were lots of kids passing. If I kept my head down and tailgated a group of girls, I might get away with it. Perhaps, I thought, now that England had won their stupid game of football, they might have lost interest in me. I huddled close to three girls.

One of them was saying how much she fancied Tom Fletcher, a boy I knew by sight in the same year as me. All the girls fancied Tom Fletcher, with his Elvis-like good looks and smooth talk. I was still thinking of him when I heard the singsong chant. 'Three one, three one, three one.'

Cerys stepped out, blocking my way. 'So how about that, eh, Krauty? Three bloody one to England. You sodding Krauts, you'll never beat us.'

'I'm as English as you are, Atkins.'

Cerys' friends laughed. I swallowed, bewildered by my own bravado.

'You're not bloody English,' she said, pushing me. My arms flailed like a pair of windmills. I tottered; I screeched; I fell, landing heavily on my coccyx, a bolt of pain shooting up my back.

The girls screeched with laughter. I lay on my back, my legs spread-eagled, a thumping on the bottom of my backbone. Cerys stepped on my hand. She leant over. 'My old man says if he ever saw your mum in the street, he'd spit at her.'

'Leave me alone,' I screeched, holding my hand under the armpit of my coat.

'You go back home to where you come from, you German bitch, we'll leave you alone.'

They started again… *German bitch, German bitch*… We were outside the school gates; no teacher would come to my aid this time. But another voice cut through the chanting, a voice I sort of recognised, a boy's voice. 'Hey, you lot, quit bugging her, will you?'

I propped myself up on an elbow. I heard Cerys speak in a different voice. 'Oh, hi, Fletch.'

'What the hell you doing, Cerys?'

'It ain't anything. It's nothing, really, Fletch.'

Tom Fletcher stood over me, looking down at me with his dark, James Dean eyes, half obscured by his fringe. Well, that was it, I thought, utter humiliation. I might as well die now. He reached his hand out. 'Come,' he said. 'I'll help you up.'

Did he... did he just say that? I took his hand, so warm and so much bigger than mine, and he hoisted me up. I felt like a ballerina and he my very own Rudolph Nureyev. 'Thank you,' I whispered.

'S'alright.'

He spun round. Cerys, Becky and the others slunk back as if face-to-face with a wild animal. 'You're pathetic, all of you.'

'We was just having fun,' said Cerys.

'Yeah, no harm in it,' said Becky.

Ignoring them, Tom turned to me. 'Come,' he said, with a jerk of his head. I followed him into school, my mind spinning, unsure whether to be grateful or mortified that the best-looking boy in the school found me in such an undignified heap on the pavement. Cerys and Becky shot me daggers with their eyes – everyone fancied Tom Fletcher.

We were near the school entrance. I was wondering how to thank him, what to say. I hadn't planned on saying what tumbled out of my mouth. 'I can look after myself, you know.'

He stopped and looked at me and I knew I'd hurt his feelings. 'It didn't look like it.'

'That? That was nothing. I can handle them.'

'Right. OK. Suit yourself.'

I watched him march off across the front yard and into school, his hands in his pockets, a slight shake of the head. My coccyx still hurt a bit, my hand, too, where Cerys Atkins had stamped on it, but it was nothing compared to the pain stabbing at my heart.

PART TWO

Chapter 22
October 1943

Bruno Spitzweg was going home at long last. He just wasn't sure what he was going home to. Would his home still be standing? Would his mother still be alive? And what about his brother? For months now, he'd clung on to the hope his little village deep in the Baden-Württemberg countryside was too small and insignificant to be of any interest to the Allied bombers. But it didn't necessarily mean anything. Nothing could be guaranteed.

The train carriage was packed. Every inch of space taken. He was lucky to have nabbed this seat next to the window and he wasn't giving it up for anyone. What a sight they made, the bedraggled remnants of a once-proud regiment, now decimated. And the noise. No one talked but the continual coughing, snoring, yawning, groaning, crying, farting; it never stopped. They'd been on the move for days, shoved from one train to another, their train kept waiting in the sidings while damaged tracks were repaired, or giving precedent to trains carrying troops going *to* war, not those coming back. The food was even more basic than on the front. What tea to be had ran out a day back; the toilets weren't fit for pigs. Sleep provided the only respite – but Bruno was used to that. Sleep had soon become one of the most valued commodities; it's astonishing what a desperate man would do for sleep. He'd slept much of the journey but he was still tired. His backside ached from sitting too long; he had pins and needles in his right leg, and his shoulder pulsed with a continual throb where the bullet had entered through his shoulder blade and exited near his collarbone.

God, he couldn't wait to get off this train, to rid himself of his stinking uniform, to have a bath, a shave, to feel *human*. Human. Less than human. He'd lost his humanity a long time ago; he knew that, knew he'd have to live with it for the rest of his life. The fact that they were all murderers here offered no comfort. They'd all sold their souls to the devil, it was just that some were more aware of it than others, and some were even proud of the fact.

Someone farther back began playing a mouth organ, a wistful little tune. Bruno gazed out of the window at the dark, undulating landscapes; it'd begun snowing, just a little. The snatch of memory returned – him and Joseph building snowmen and having snowball fights. Joe always won, of course; he was older and bigger and stronger and more determined. And that was it – in a microcosm. Joe, the determined one, rose so fast and so far, stayed at home, while little brother, poor old Bruno, was sent to war, cannon fodder for the Führer, his survival immaterial as long as he did his bit. Well, he'd done that and more, much more.

The train drew to a stop at a station. Bruno wiped the condensation from the window with his sleeve and peered out. His mood lifted immediately. He knew this place; this was the last stop before his. A few of the men alighted, gathering their things, and stumbling out, mumbling their goodbyes and good lucks and 'see you soons'. There was a little more room now. Indeed, the seat opposite him was now empty. One of the men would soon take it.

'Excuse me,' came a voice, a female voice, from behind

him. A woman? Here? 'So sorry, excuse me.'

She came into Bruno's view, a whoosh of a dress, the scent of sweet perfume, a smell so overpowering in its purity, its cleanliness, it took his breath away. He watched, goggle-eyed, as she reached up to place her suitcase in the rack above. He'd offer to help but he couldn't move; he'd only make a fool of himself. Anyway, she looked more than capable. Her suitcase in place, she gathered the seams of her dress and sat down. He stared at her as one might a painting, incredulous at her sudden appearance. Did she not know there were a couple of carriages at the front reserved for civilians? These carriages were only for military personnel. What was she doing here? Still, what did it matter? She was like a rose in a field of nettles, a lone star shining bright in a sky of black, an oasis of lushness in a barren desert, a shaking flower in a storm. She was beautiful. She, like him, had the blondest hair; she had gentle blue eyes, long, delicate fingers. But the poor thing, she wore her self-consciousness like a cloak, aware of everyone looking at her, no, not looking, but bedazzled by her. She sported a rather large bruise on the side of her face. He wondered how she got that. He longed to stroke her face, to feel the softness of her pale skin, to see if it was real. The men around him all had skins of leather, turned black by the ravages of an unrelenting sun during summer and the hell of the Russian winter. Still, no one talked, the mouth organist had ceased playing, but everyone was awake now, spellbound by this woman who'd accidentally wandered onto the wrong carriage.

He longed to speak to her, simply to hear a female voice speaking in his native tongue, to listen to a gentle voice, one that didn't shout, that didn't threaten, that wasn't full of hate.

Half an hour or so later, the train slowed down again, and this, at last, after so long, was Bruno's stop! The thought of being home injected him with renewed energy. After so much lethargy, his veins surged with life. Grabbing his haversack, he barged his way to the nearest carriage door far earlier than necessary, tripping over outstretched feet, being sworn at, such was his eagerness to be the first to jump off. Waiting at the carriage door, he leant down to view the passing countryside as the train slowed. Yes, there was that barn he and Joe trespassed in when they were kids, the field that was great for tobogganing every winter, already half white from the season's first flurry of snow. The station came into view, the old church spire behind it, still standing proud. If only there was someone to greet him but there'd be no one. Between Russia and here, there simply hadn't been time to write.

The train was coming to a halt when he realised she was behind him, getting off at the same stop. That smell of her perfume that somehow symbolised peace. How could such a simple, sweet odour smell like heaven? Because for two years, he'd only ever smelled cordite, burning wood, shit and death. He risked glancing back, and flashed her the merest hint of a smile. He received one in return and he had to look away.

The train stopped. He opened the carriage door. He threw down his haversack onto the platform and, ignoring the steps, jumped down after it. Many times over the two years his heart had pumped with fear or hatred, but now it pounded from pure joy. He remembered the little ticket hall with its turret, the beech tree to one side. He looked round for the station cat but sadly she wasn't to be seen. Oh, to be back, to be back.

Grinning, he turned to the young woman who, negotiating the steps with her swirly dress and suitcase, appeared a little tottery. 'Can I help?' he said, offering his hand. She was about to take it when he noticed his palm and his mitten were black with grime. She saw it too and hesitated just a fraction. He saw the crease in her eyes. Quickly, he withdrew his hand. 'I'm sorry,' he said, wiping his hand on the seat of his trousers. And he was sorry, more than sorry, mortified.

'Don't be silly,' she said in a gentle, reassuring voice.

She descended the steps. Only a few others had alighted at this station, the platform was near deserted.

'I think I may have got on the wrong carriage.'

He wanted to say she couldn't have been more welcome, but he feared it'd come out wrong or that it might appear suggestive in some way, so he said nothing and smiled in, he hoped, a sympathetic way. 'I think you were quite a welcome distraction though. Not that I mean…'

She laughed. 'It's all right, I know what you mean. It looks like an attractive town, this. Do you live here?'

'Yes, about a five-minute walk down that street,' he said, pointing the way. 'And you? I don't recognise you.'

'Just visiting.'

He was about to respond when a voice cut through. 'Fraulein Schiffer?'

Bruno stepped away a yard as a tall, officious-looking woman appeared out of nowhere heading for the young woman. 'Are you Hannah Schiffer? How do you do?' she said to her in a brisk voice. 'I'm Frau Sterne. This way, please.' The woman called Sterne hadn't noticed him; it was as if he were invisible. She took Fraulein Schiffer by the elbow and brusquely led her away. Fraulein Schiffer glanced over her shoulder and threw him an apologetic smile.

Bruno's joy was complete.

Chapter 23

The train made painfully slow progress, stopping every half an hour or so for extended amounts of time. Hannah looked at her watch; they were already an hour late and on this, an hour's journey. Not that she cared; she was in no hurry at all but it wasn't comfortable, such was the squash of soldiers on the train. So crowded, she'd removed her coat. Someone helped her place it next to her suitcase on the rack above. She seemed to be the only female on board. She tried not to look at them, tried keeping her focus on the passing countryside, but her morbid curiosity was proving too hard to control. These men, boys, were wrecked. She'd seen men go off to war; their uniforms clean, their eyes sparkling. She'd expected the return to be more sombre but this shocked her. Most seemed to have an injury, an arm in a sling, a bandage around the head, but it was more than the visible wounds. As one, they all looked so haggard, their faces drawn. Their eyes told their own story. And the stench – she'd never smelt anything so fetid, so vile. But it wouldn't do to cover her nose so she forced herself to bear it. They all watched her, unabashedly staring in total hush. Her presence had silenced them all. She was self-conscious of her every movement. Yet, she knew they watched her, fixated on her, not out of desire or sexual craving, but merely for her femininity. More so since, having been stripped of her Maidens' uniform, she wore a long, flowing dress patterned with a motif of daisies, topped with a hat with bow. She was every man's sister, daughter, mother. She was their first sighting of normality after God knows what. She was home; she was safety. It brought tears to her eyes. And she felt safe with these men. She couldn't imagine a single one of them slapping her so hard, she saw stars. The man opposite, especially, had a kind, if sorrowful, face. She wondered what he did before war had swept him in its path.

The Gestapo officers had bundled her into Angela's office and questioned her. She readily admitted giving the knife to the Slav, as they called him. They wanted to know why.

'Because I feared Herr Müller was going to kill him, and I knew he should remain alive to answer for the attack on Ella.'

'But you said Herr Müller's son attacked your friend.'

'Yes, he did. I wanted Jan to defend himself. It's not right that a good, upstanding Maiden should be attacked by a boy in uniform.'

And that, she realised later, had saved her. It appealed to their sense of logic and decency. Hannah was ordered to remain in the home. Ella confessed; Hans had his knuckles rapped and told not to do it again. The following day, a woman called Witte came to the home specifically to see Hannah. Their interview lasted all of two minutes. Hannah said nothing but this Witte woman seemed pleased. She told Hannah that the following day she should catch the midday train from the village to the town fifty kilometres west, south-west of Stuttgart, where she'd be met. She was to wear her civilian clothes. She parted with the chilling words, 'We can make use of you.'

So, the following day, the bent old man, with a large feather in his hat, who'd given her a lift on her arrival here, now took her the opposite way. She perched on the trap, shivering, as the pony snorted.

And now, two hours later, the train finally drew to a halt. The haggard soldiers watched silently as she retrieved her coat and suitcase, and edged her way out. She wanted to say something, to welcome them home, to say thank you, but her nerve failed her.

It was a relief to step off the train. The first flakes of snow were falling. The man seated opposite her on the train was getting off too. They exchanged words, and she was taken aback by the gentleness of his tone, his manner. It was nice, after all this time, to speak to someone who wasn't judging her. She was wondering how to prolong the conversation when she heard her name being called out. She turned to see a tall, smartly dressed woman bearing down on her. 'Are you Hannah Schiffer? How do you do? I'm Frau Sterne. This way, please.'

Frau Sterne led her to another pony and trap. They rode in silence. Hannah wanted to ask what was happening, where she was being taken but held her tongue. The snow was falling heavier now; it'd soon settle.

Twenty minutes later, they passed beneath a gatehouse and trotted up a long muddy track, looming pine trees either side. They arrived at what looked like a hotel, a majestic if imposing complex with jagged roofs, balconies and tall chimneys. Frau Sterne confirmed its status; it was indeed once a hotel. 'But now, it serves a far more important function.'

And that is? But Hannah remained silent.

Frau Sterne took Hannah inside. The lobby was wonderfully warm and infused with an amber glow of several standard lamps. Hannah admired the red leather armchairs and the large, ornate fireplace. She'd never seen such luxury. But no time for that: Frau Sterne led Hannah upstairs to the second floor, down a long, carpeted corridor and to her room. 'Get settled,' she said. 'Someone will come to see you shortly.' Hannah wondered how long this new room was to be home. It was certainly much nicer and better furnished than her previous room.

'Do you smoke?' asked Frau Sterne.

'Yes,' said Hannah, immediately regretting telling her the truth.

Sterne held out her hand. Hannah pretended not to understand. 'Come on, hand them over.'

'I've not–'

'Hand them over now.'

Damn it. Hannah handed over her last packet of cigarettes.

Frau Sterne made to leave but then paused at the door. Pushing the door to, she said, 'One word of advice, Fraulein Schiffer. During your stay with us, remember always obey orders and never question why. Follow my advice and you'll be fine.'

'Thank you, Frau.'

'You'll be called down shortly for your initial assessment with the doctor.'

'Doctor? Why do I need a doctor?'

'What did I just tell you, Fraulein Schiffer? Is your memory so poor? Never. Question. Why.'

*

The room was not like your typical doctor surgery, it was more like an office, a plush one at that, a leather armchair, an old writing desk with curved legs and an inlay of green leather, framed certificates, and paintings of hunting scenes and woodland either side of the ubiquitous portrait of the Führer.

But in the corner, a couch covered with a white sheet with a curtain pulled back on its rail. The doctor, a man in his sixties, thought Hannah, with a pince-nez, introduced himself as Dr Heinkel and the large-bosomed nurse as Nurse Lowitz. 'Take a seat,' said the doctor. 'Please, I want you to feel comfortable. Now, I need to ask you some questions, some maybe of a rather... personal nature. I'm sure you understand. Nurse Lowitz will be taking notes.'

Nurse Lowitz flashed her a smile.

Hannah was desperate to say she didn't understand; she didn't understand one bit, but when she opened her mouth, Dr Heinkel raised his hand.

'Now, Fraulein, you've recently turned eighteen. Correct?'

'Yes, sir.'

'I understand you smoke.'

'Yes, Doctor.'

'You don't smoke any more. Smoking here is strictly forbidden.' He paused to allow the instruction to sink in. 'You were, until...' He focused on his notes. 'Oh, it says the day before yesterday. So you were, until just a couple of days ago, a Maidens leader but now you are not.'

Hannah wasn't sure whether he was asking her a question.

'That is some bruise you have on the side of your face. I won't ask how that came about. In terms of past behaviour, et cetera, we like our girls to start here with a clean slate. We can look over little indiscretions here and there, misjudgements, that sort of thing. Racial hygiene, however, is another matter. Racial hygiene is non-negotiable. Your Maidens' senior has sent me your record and I'm pleased to see you are one hundred per cent Aryan going back as far as the records show. Not a whiff of Jew.'

'No, sir, not a whiff.'

'Strange, however, that neither of your parents are party members.'

Hannah sensed a distinct rise in temperature.

'Why is that?' he asked.

Because my father always said he'd rather be dead than kowtow to that bastard in the Reichstag. 'My father still played his part in advancing the cause of National Socialism, sir, and still does.'

Nurse Lowitz scribbled on her notepad while the doctor tweaked his moustache.

'Now, Fraulein, you need to know about the set-up here. First of all, you are not allowed to leave the premises nor receive any communication or any visitors. Indeed, you'll have no contact with the outside world. Don't even try; security is tight. Secondly, you and half a dozen other young women will be staying in the west wing of the home – at least to begin with. The east wing has been sealed off. It is entirely forbidden territory to you until the time we see fit for you to transfer there. We have locked all doors between the two wings.'

'I don't understand.'

'It's not for you to understand, simply to obey.'

Hannah nodded. 'So I'm not allowed in the east wing.'

'Correct. Now, let's proceed with your examination. Open your mouth, please. Wider, please.'

The doctor shone a light down her throat, in her eyes and down her ears while muttering to himself. Switching his torch off, he asked, 'Would you mind taking your clothes off, down to your underwear.'

Hannah glanced from the doctor to the nurse and back again. 'Now? Here?'

'Well, I certainly don't mean outside in the snow.'

Nurse Lowitz put down her notebook. 'What are you waiting for? Do as the doctor says.'

Never question why.

Dr Heinkel went to stand at the window, his hands behind his back, watching the snowstorm. Nurse Lowitz raised her eyebrows at her as if to say *Get on with it*. Hannah took a deep breath and untied her shoelaces, removing her shoes and socks. She removed her cardigan. Her heart quickened a notch with each item. She untied the sash to her dress, pulled it down over her shoulders but then paused. Nurse Lowitz said, 'The doctor hasn't got all day, you know.' She let the dress fall to the floor and gingerly stepped out of it. She gathered it up and placed it on the back of a chair. She stood trembling slightly in the centre of the room, her hands clasped in front of her. Fortunately, the doctor remained at the window.

'Arms up,' said the nurse, who then proceeded to measure her bust, hips and waist with a cold, metallic tape measure, jotting down Hannah's measurements in her notebook. 'Good. Now, if you could lie on the couch: there's a good girl.'

Hannah lay down, her hands crossed over her breasts.

'The doctor will examine you now.'

'What?'

'Please remove your knickers.'

'But… but why?'

'Do as we say. Now, will you remove them or shall I?'

She lay there, exposed, shivering, her legs pinned tightly together.

The doctor came away from the window and stood beside the couch, his shadow falling over her. 'When did your last monthly end?'

'I'm sorry?' Did she hear him correctly? Had he really asked her that?

'I think you heard the doctor,' said Nurse Lowitz. 'Well?'

'I-I d-don't know. About a week ago, I suppose. Er, yes,

l... last T-Tuesday. But why?'

'Asking questions again, Fraulein? I am the one who asks the questions here. Now, tell me. Are you a virgin?'

Now, the temperature shot up. Hannah was fully aware that she'd turned bright red. 'Y-yes, sir.'

'Hmm. Now, open your legs.'

'What? No, surely not, please.'

Nurse Lowitz came into view. 'Now, do as the doctor says and get it over and done with. That's it, open your legs. No, wider. Please, stop being silly. Now, much wider, Fraulein. That's it. Wider still.'

Chapter 24

Bruno surveyed the town centre. Everything seemed intact. No English bombs had fallen here; nothing had changed. Thank the Lord for that. It wasn't too far a walk from the railway station to the outskirts of the village where, along a narrowing track, lay his parents' home. For a man used to trekking for hours on end, across the unending Russian steppes, day after day after day, this was nothing. So, why, Bruno wondered, was every step painful? He'd come to the end of a long journey, one that started early autumn in 1941, and had taken him to places he never imagined could exist. And now he was back. His shoulder ached, the cold making it worse somehow. He thought about the woman on the train, Fraulein Schiffer. He wondered where she was going. It was obvious she didn't know the woman who came to meet her, had obviously never been here before. What would bring a young woman like that out to this backwater just as the snows fell? When would she see home again?

It was four o'clock, dark within the hour. Bruno had come to the familiar curve in the road, a stone wall, a solitary elm tree behind it, lonesome and now naked without its leaves. At the end of this bend was his home. He shifted the weight of his haversack and picked up his pace. He saw the little cottage, smoke coming from the chimney and stopped. The haversack slipped from his grasp. The cottage had a long, sloping thatched roof that came so far down, one could touch it, whitewashed walls, which, by the looks of it, had been recently redone, and at the front, a large window.

He picked up his haversack, which now felt heavier than ever, and walked the last few yards, his eyes fixed on his home, on that window. For so long he'd dreamt of this moment, and here he was at long last… back home.

The front door opened. He held his breath – it was his mother, wearing her apron, carrying a small bucket. She hadn't seen him, lost in her own world. He stopped and watched her as she dropped potato peelings on the compost to the side of the house. He smiled. Some things didn't change. But, he thought, she looked thinner, a little older, and a little frailer. She was about to return indoors when he called out her name. She whipped round and on seeing her youngest son dropped the bucket. She crumpled, bit her knuckle. 'Mama, don't cry, it's all right, it's OK now.'

She almost fell against him. He wrapped his arms around her. She was so thin; there was nothing left of her. 'Is it really you, Bruno? Is it really you?'

'Yes, Mama, it's really me.'

'Oh, Bruno, Bruno, oh my.'

He stroked her hair. 'Come,' he said. 'Let's go in.'

He sat in the comfortable armchair, his mother opposite. She simply sat and stared at him, her eyes tinged red, shaking her head and repeating his name.

'Your shoulder's hurt.'

'Yes.'

'Does it give you pain?'

'Sometimes. I was lucky.'

'Lucky?'

121

'Believe me.'

'How long are you back?'

'Until it gets better.'

'Do you have to go back?'

'Yes.'

'Oh, Bruno.'

'I know.'

'You look well, considering.'

'I know.'

'Is it as bad as some say?'

'It's hell.'

'But you can hold your head high.'

'No, I can't.'

'Your father would have been so proud.'

'No, not if he knew.'

'But…'

'You don't want to hear.'

'I'll leave you to rest.'

Bruno watched his mother buzz around him, offering him tea, something to eat, to run a bath. He could barely make sense of her; she spoke so fast, so animated. 'Why don't you have a bath while I rustle up something to eat. You could have a shave, perhaps.'

'Tell me, how is Joseph?'

'Oh, he's got himself married. Would you believe it? He'll be passing by any minute. He likes to visit every now and then.'

'Married? My brother? Good God, who's the poor girl?'

'A not-so-young woman called Clara. A tough bird, I can tell you. Not that I ever see her. She doesn't come here and Joseph's as good as told me I'm not so welcome to his. So don't expect to see her anytime soon.'

'And, er, is he still the village's proud Nazi mayor?'

She sighed. 'Yes, he is. Nothing's changed.'

'And the business?'

His mother sighed. 'Not good. Who has money now to buy shoes? Best not to mention it.'

Bruno tried to get up but even rising up from the armchair was too much, and he decided to close his eyes – just for a few moments. It was so nice to be home, to see his mother again. The house was lovely and warm, and he felt so tired, so damn tired.

Bruno was aware of the front door closing, of boots on linoleum, of a loud, familiar voice. He had no idea how long he'd been asleep for. He opened his eyes just at the point his brother came in, unbuttoning his coat.

'Well, bugger me, our very own hero returns.'

Bruno rose from the comfort of the armchair, still slightly groggy. 'Joe, hello. Congratulations are in order, I hear.'

'What? Oh yes. Thanks. Well, it's good to see you, brother. I'd embrace you but…'

'It's fine. I know I stink to high hell. I'm about to have a…'

'Yes, I would. Not to put too fine a point on it but you smell like shit.'

'Yeah. Well. Yeah. I'll go and… and run that bath.'

Half an hour later, by the time Bruno had finished his bath and changed into clothes he hadn't worn for over two years, dinner was ready. He was starving. The three of them sat down at the table together. 'What is this, Mama? Pork? Where do you get meat these days?'

She tapped her nose. 'There are advantages of having such a powerful son, you know, Bruno.'

Joseph brushed it aside. 'It's just a matter of knowing where to go.'

'So where did you meet Clara?'

'She's a friend of a party comrade of mine.'

'When do I get to meet her?'

'She's going away for a while. Her parents live in Stuttgart.'

They ate in silence as Bruno savoured a proper meal, the first for such a long, long time, closing his eyes and enjoying the sensation of every mouthful, the warmth inside his stomach.

He finished and realised he'd bolted his food, that his mother and brother still had a long way to go. 'Oh, I'm sorry. I seem to have forgotten my manners.'

'You were hungry; it's understandable.'

After a while, his mother asked, 'Do you want to talk about it?'

'Maybe, but not yet.'

Why, he wondered, had he said 'maybe'. Because it wasn't true; he didn't want to talk about it or even think about it, now or ever again. But his brother would force him to talk, would want to know every detail. Bruno still couldn't work out after all this time, why the wrong brother went to war.

*

A memory. Bruno is about seven, his brother fifteen. A warm summer's day, late afternoon, the shadows long. Together they watched a group of five boys Bruno's age racing snails. In itself, racing snails lacks excitement but the boys were laying bets, play fighting and making a lot of noise, and their joy was infectious. The five snails had been lined up rather disorderedly and trying to put them in a straight line was causing much hilarity. Bruno and Joseph were on an errand, and Joe was in a rush to get home, something to do with a girl. The boys invited Bruno to join in; he just needed to find his own snail first. Joe, Bruno knew, was under strict instructions not to leave Bruno to wander alone. Bruno begged Joe to allow him to play. Joe said no. Bruno pleaded some more. Then, in a show of defiance, Bruno told his brother he refused to return home with him, he *was* going to stay and that was that. Joe's response was swift and brutal. He stamped his boot hard on each shell.

Bruno learnt all there was to know about his brother that day; that Joseph was hard, that he was used to getting what he wanted and was prepared to do anything to get his way, even if it meant stamping on and smashing shells. Even now, all these years later, Bruno could hear the sharp crackle as each shell yielded under his brother's boot, could see the shocked expressions on the boys' faces. Over the years, he got to know all five boys and sort of became friends with them. But he was never able to truly give his friendship to them, that underlying sense of shame held him back. Three of those boys were dead now, another a prisoner of war in the Odessa somewhere, and the fourth living at home being spoon-fed by his parents, a man trapped in an infant's body. Such is war. So, yes, he, Bruno Spitzweg, was lucky. His brother luckier still. He was a Nazi. And Bruno hated him for it. The world had been blown apart by his beliefs, millions killed or maimed, countless lives ruined, yet Joseph, his blinkered brother, still believed.

Their mother had gone out, hoping to buy vegetables at the weekly market. Bruno's brother unexpectedly appeared. It was the first time since Bruno's return that the two brothers found themselves alone. Joseph stood at the writing desk, flipping through files, his back to Bruno.

'Did Mother mention that my business has folded?'

'She may have mentioned it in passing.'

'Yeah, well. I'm not too worried. Once victory is ours, I'll simply start up again. People always need shoes. At least in peacetime. You must be getting bored, Bruno,' he said over his shoulder. 'Sitting here all day with nothing to do.'

'Better than the alternative.' He lit a cigarette and blew out a plume of smoke that caught the morning wintry light coming through the window. 'How's it going with the party work?'

'Ah, busy as ever. Busier, in fact.'

'That's good.'

'Yeah. Aha, here it is.' Joseph tucked the file under his arm and made to leave but stopped in front of his brother. 'We make a good team, don't you think? You fighting for the Führer on the front, me fighting the good cause at the back. There's still a lot of work to be done, Bruno, a long way to go.'

'Before what, Joe? Before Hitler's killed us all?'

Joseph narrowed his eyes. 'You've been through a lot, Bruno. You're not well; anyone can see that. So I'll let it slide this time.' He stepped forward. 'But if I ever hear you say something like that ever again, I'll have you shot as a traitor. Loyalty trumps blood. Don't you forget it.'

'Don't let me keep you, Joseph.'

'Heil Hitler.'

Bruno's body shook with the thump of the front door. He lifted his hand to smoke his cigarette but found his hand shaking so much he couldn't manoeuvre it. And somewhere, deep in the recesses of his brain, he heard the sharp crackle of five snail shells being broken.

Chapter 25

The days and weeks passed, and Hannah found it difficult to understand what was meant to be happening to her and why. Firstly, nothing was happening to her. They kept her locked up in the west wing of the home along with several other women of her age in luxurious surroundings. They each had a room, and very lovely rooms, too, not unlike her previous home, which looked over large expanses of lawn now covered in snow. They lived in a gorgeous house that was until 1941 a hotel of good reputation. The dining room boasted a large photograph of Kaiser Wilhelm II and his wife, Princess Augusta, who stayed one night here in 1911.

They had plenty to eat; they could have baths and had use of a swimming pool and a huge library to choose books from. There was a war on, for goodness sake; food was rationed; people weren't meant to live like this. And yet they were. The other girls were equally nonplussed. They weren't allowed access to the radio. They were entirely cut off from the world. It was as if they'd entered an entirely new existence, totally devoid of what was happening out there in the real world. She was even beginning to get over her craving for cigarettes.

Hannah found the other girls difficult to talk to, had little in common with them. Perhaps because she was the only city girl among them, a little more *cosmopolitan* as her father used to say. The nurses who came and went were even more vacuous. So much so, Hannah began looking forward to seeing Nurse

Lowitz; she may have had the bedside manner of a dragon but at least she could talk to her.

On about the fourth day, when Hannah couldn't bear the lack of information, she cornered Nurse Lowitz. 'Nurse, you look very nice today.'

Nurse Lowitz didn't miss a beat. 'What is it you want, Hannah?'

'Please, Nurse, tell me why I'm here.'

'We'll let you know when the time is right.'

'And when will that be?'

'Not long now.'

'But I... just tell me, Nurse. I was sent here because... well, as a punishment because–'

'No, Hannah, you weren't sent here as a punishment. You were sent here because it was felt you could better serve the Fatherland and the Führer here.'

'But I'm not *doing* anything.'

'You will.'

'But–'

'Enough now. No more questions. Now, have you had a good breakfast?'

And so Hannah spent most of her days lounging on a sofa in the communal lounge, reading books, going for the occasional swim and eating. Oftentimes, she found her mind replaying her conversation with the handsome corporal she'd met at the railway station. He said he lived nearby. How she'd love to bump into him again.

'I think they're fattening us up,' she said to the other women.

'I know what's going to happen to us,' said one of them, a pretty dark-haired girl called Lena. 'I 'eard they're gonna send us to the Eastern Front where we have to entertain the soldiers, well, the officers.'

'What do you mean *entertain*?' asked Hannah.

'You know, sing and dance for them, that sort of thing.'

'I can't sing to save my life. Are you sure?'

'That's what I 'eard.'

'Perhaps,' said another woman, Erika, 'they're gonna experiment on us.'

'How?' asked Lena. 'In what way?'

'I dunno.'

'No,' said Hannah. 'Don't be silly. Who would *experiment* on us? What sort of people would do *that*?'

Hannah didn't believe any of it for a second. But she had to find out. She remembered Angela's key cupboard in her office at the old home. Surely they'd have something similar here. She'd already worked out that the old hotel was indeed divided into two, with a corridor on each of the four floors linking the two wings. Finding the key to the ground floor door would be too risky, too busy. But if she could find the key to the third-floor door…

She also worked out that Nurse Lowitz's office was on the other side of the kitchen, a place totally inaccessible to the 'residents', as they were called, not prisoners, which she would have thought a more apt label. The kitchen was locked at night but open all daytime – and also busy all daytime. She began watching the nursing staff and taking note of their routines. They ate their evening meal together soon after the residents at seven. No better time. She strode into the kitchen, deciding assertiveness was the best policy. Sure enough, she was stopped and questioned. 'It's OK' she said. 'Nurse Lowitz asked me to fetch Lena's file.' Using Nurse Lowitz's name was enough to quash further questions. Her office, though small, was tidy; everything filed away, everything in its place. And, yes, sure enough, just like Angela, a key box all neatly arranged. And there it was: *3rd Fl. corridor.* Perfect. She slipped the key into her pocket.

She walked calmly back through the kitchen, shaking her head. 'Couldn't find it. I'll come back later.' No one took any notice. She checked the landing, could hear the nurses enjoying their evening meal. She walked up the three flights of stairs to the top floor, fearing that catching the lift might draw attention. She found the top floor in the dark. She had to turn a light on, couldn't see otherwise. She should've brought a torch but then, from where? Where did they keep torches? And, yes, there down the landing, was a door, obviously a temporary one that had only recently been installed, a cheap, nasty-looking thing when everything else was so grand. She was almost there now, and she'd know why they were keeping her and the others here, against their will. She took the key, her fingers now trembling with anticipation, eager to know what exactly lay on the other side in the east wing. She slotted the key into the keyhole, her heartbeat fizzing with excitement, and turned. She heard the satisfying turn of the Chubb lock. She held her breath. *Knowledge is power*, she thought. 'Good evening, Fraulein Schiffer,' said the booming voice behind her while, at the same moment, a heavy hand landed on her shoulder.

Chapter 26

Hannah lay on her bed. Then, finally, she got up, paced the length of her room, sat at the window for a while watching the snow fall, then returned to her bed. She was desperate to step outside, to breathe in the fresh air, to enjoy the freedom. She'd eaten her lunch in her room, was escorted to the bathroom and back, and that was the highlight of the day. She'd been locked up in her second-floor room for five days now. This was her punishment: total isolation, solitary confinement in luxury. But the luxury, the soft bed and the breathtaking view, made it no less torturous. No books, no radio, no company. She even missed Lena and the other girls and their inane chatter. They'd even confiscated the clock, so she had no idea what time it was except by the extent of daylight outside. They'd not allowed her out for a wash, simply to use the toilet. And when there was no one to escort her to the toilet, they left her a bucket to piss in.

All she could do was think. And she thought of Jan; she thought of little Greta, and how they had both suffered, and she thought of her parents. Part of her wanted to hate Greta for having given her away but she couldn't. The girl was as much a victim as she. Her father had died fighting for the Führer, a hero's death. What shit. What good was a hero's death when you're eleven years old and all you want is to have your daddy. He'd never be there for her future birthdays, the Christmases to come. He wouldn't be there to give her away on her wedding day; he wouldn't be there to be a grandfather to her children. Not even a grave to visit, a grave to stand over and talk to, to say hi, to say thank you, to say I love you.

Her own father had been right. He had hated the Nazis from day one, and he hated them later, still, when hating them could have you arrested. Her poor father, with his quaint beliefs in free speech and democracy. When everyone has a say, no one has power. Isn't that what the Nazis believed? And her poor mother who spent her life shushing her husband, terrified his anger and sense of righteousness might bring them all down. Her mother, the true backbone of their small family. Only now, stuck in her padded cell, did she appreciate just how strong her outwardly fragile mother was.

And then there was Jan. Jan, whose real name she didn't know, would never know, a Pole, a man of great dignity who, somewhere, had a wife and a daughter waiting for him, hoping, praying, that he was well and surviving. They would never know what happened to him. Even years from now, when the world was finally at peace, when the Nazis were finally defeated, they would still not know how, when and where their husband and father died. She hated the fact she didn't know his real name; it felt wrong somehow, like a final insult, that in the moment of his death, she didn't know the name that he had been christened with.

For the first few days, cooped up in this former hotel, she almost laughed that this was the extent of her 'punishment'. Perhaps they'd made a mistake, that instead of punishing her, they'd accidentally got her file mixed up with someone else's and sent her to this place of luxury to relax and enjoy herself. She knew now this was no mistake – the Nazis rarely made mistakes. It was part of the bigger plan, something she'd been incapable of appreciating at first, let alone seeing. For now, after weeks here, and days in this solitary confinement, she knew she was theirs, truly and utterly theirs. Not through pain, not through physical torture, but through a subtler and far more effective means – the submission of her will. Hannah knew she was broken, mentally, physically and, most crucially, spiritually. From a higher plane, she could see what they'd done to her and almost admired their patience and skill, their manipulation of the mind. For she knew she'd do anything for them now. Absolutely anything. She paced her room, her cell, at a total loss, unable to think any more, desperate to see a face, anyone, someone to talk to, any form of interaction.

Another day or two passed. Her body clock had lost all meaning. She slept odd times, sometimes for just a few minutes, sometimes, when she was lucky, for hours at a time. Other times she felt energized when outside it was pitch black, and she paced up and down, unable to find an outlet for her energy, frantic for a release. Her disorientation was complete.

So when, after several days, Nurse Lowitz unexpectedly appeared in her room, Hannah fell onto her, weeping then howling with relief at seeing a familiar face.

Nurse Lowitz held her close to her bosom, stroking Hannah's sodden and now greasy hair. 'It's OK, my dear, it's OK. You let it out. That's it, let it all out. Good girl.'

'I'm so so sorry, Nurse, I'm so…'

'It's OK now, I know, I know. I'm sorry we had to do this to you, but we had to make you understand.'

Hannah could hardly speak. 'I'm sorry,' she spluttered.

'Yes, but why are you sorry, Hannah? Why? Tell me why you're sorry. Come on, take a deep breath and tell me.'

The nurse's gentle hand stroking her hand was the most delicious, warmest sensation she'd ever experienced. 'I'm sorry I tried to find out what's in the east wing.'

'Good girl. But your curiosity was merely emblematic of a greater malaise. You're not like the other girls, Hannah. You're far cleverer than the others, so your curiosity was to be expected. We knew you'd doubt us but you have no need to. We only want what's best for the Fatherland, the Führer, and for you. You understand this now?'

'Yes, yes, Nurse, I understand. I'm sorry.'

'You doubted us.' The nurse gripped Hannah that much more tightly, pressing her head firmly against her bosom, so tightly Hannah found it difficult to breathe. 'You doubted us.'

'Yes, yes, I doubted you. I'm sorry.'

Nurse Lowitz loosened her grip a fraction. 'We did this for your own good, Hannah. Do you see now?'

'Yes, I see now, I see. I'm sorry.'

'We think you're ripe now to proceed to the next stage. Would you like that?'

Hannah tried to sniff away the mucus building up in her nose. 'Yes, I would.'

'Would you like to proceed now to the east wing?'

'Yes, yes, yes, I would. I am ready.'

'Are you sure? Because if not, we could leave–'

'No, no, anything but no more. I'm ready, Nurse. Believe me, I'm ready.'

'Good girl,' she said, patting Hannah's back. 'We think you're ready too. So, tomorrow evening, we shall proceed. Would you like that?'

Chapter 27

Hannah woke up. It was light but she had no idea what time it was. She fell back on her pillow unable to find the energy to get up. She remembered Nurse Lowitz coming to her room, talking to her. Had it happened, or had it been a dream? She'd said Hannah was ready to *proceed*. That was the word she used. Proceed. Tonight, she'd said. Tonight. Nurse Lowitz was quite simply the nicest person she'd ever met. Just the *nicest*.

An orderly came and took Hannah to the bathrooms. This time, for the first time since her isolation, they let her have a shower. Oh, the bliss. She stood there, a smile on her lips, eyes closed, as the deliciously warm water cascaded over her. 'You need to wash your hair,' said the orderly. Hannah was happy to do so. Fifteen minutes later, she returned to her room, cleaner than she had been for a long time.

She sat at her window, a towel wrapped turban-like around her hair, watching the clouds drift by, watching a fresh layer of snow form, happy for once, for today was the day. Nurse Lowitz would come and fetch her; she just needed to be patient. They used to have a silly saying when she was at school – today is the first day of the rest of your life. They used to say it all the time, a little ritual of a greeting. But today she actually believed it was true. Today really was the first day of the rest of her life.

Her ears pricked up whenever she thought she could hear footsteps outside on the landing. Surely, this time. Surely, this time. Daylight was fading, night drawing in. The snow, whiter and crisper than ever, gave the world a new brilliance, one that dazzled her eyes, awed her by both its purity and its harshness. The orderly brought Hannah her meal, quite the biggest and nicest since the start of her isolation. 'You'll need to eat it all,' she said.

And then half an hour after finishing her meal, her door opened. And it was her, Nurse Lowitz. Hannah rose unsteadily from her seat. Could this be it?

Nurse Lowitz nodded. 'It's time.'

'Do I… do I need to–'

'No. You can leave everything here. You'll have everything you need in your new room.'

'In the east wing?'

'In the east wing.'

Hannah slipped on her slippers and followed the nurse along the landing, reaching the separating door. This was like being born again, thought Hannah, the transition from one life to a new one, a better one. She waited as Nurse Lowitz unlocked the door. Hannah shook a little, had to force herself not to chew at her fingernails. 'Wait a moment,' said the nurse as she led Hannah from the west to the east. Nurse Lowitz locked the door behind her. Hannah looked around her, expecting things to be different but they weren't, not yet.

'You've eaten?' asked Nurse Lowitz.

'Yes, all of it.'

'Good. So I'll take you to your new room first, then we'll go downstairs and meet the others.'

'Others?'

'Lena and your other friends.'

Hannah swallowed her disappointment.

Nurse Lowitz saw it. 'And then,' she said, 'we'll introduce you to our very special guests.'

Hannah's heart quickened a beat. 'Special guests?'

Nurse Lowitz patted her arm. 'All in good time, dear. All in good time. Here we are, your room.'

Oh, this was different, this was plusher. A double bed, a long mirror above it, a full-length mirror, an octagonal clock, a large wardrobe, an armchair, a standard lamp and a dresser laden with boxes and tubes of make-up.

'You approve, I hope.'

'God, yes, it's… it's lovely. Thank you.'

'Have a look in the wardrobe.'

Hannah put her hand on the doorknob of the wardrobe but paused a moment, relishing the fizz of apprehension. She opened the door and… oh, my. 'Are these…?'

'Yes, Hannah, they are. You can pick and choose to your heart's content.'

Hannah ran her fingers along the rack of dresses, enjoying the tactile deliciousness. There were eight, no, ten dresses here of varying styles and colours, some of thin material, some glittery, some bright, some long, some short. And beneath them, neatly lined up on a rack, were five pair of shoes, some high-heeled, some black, some brown, some patent, some buff.

'They should all fit you,' said Nurse Lowitz. 'And you need to pick one now, for tonight.'

'Tonight?'

'Oh yes, for tonight, Hannah, you will be going to the ball.'

Chapter 28

Bruno's thoughts and dreams often returned to the war in Russia. It wasn't a place he wanted to go to but he had no control over it. And invariably he remembered the girl they called Zoya.

Bruno and his colleagues had heard rumours that it was a young girl slipping through unnoticed and sabotaging their positions. The local population began to revere her as a saviour; her brave deeds were giving them hope. The Germans needed to catch her. This girl's merry band had laid mines on the railways, laid spikes on the road, disrupting their supply lines. They'd set booby traps in the woods nearby. It'd got to the stage the Germans were more frightened of this girl leader than the Russians were of them. She had to be stopped. Her bravery knew no bounds. They had occupied a small village about two hundred kilometres south of Moscow. In itself, a small, insignificant little place, but its location on one of the main arteries towards the capital meant it was of high strategic value. They had to hold on to it, and if for nothing else, they were not prepared to be defeated by a teenage girl.

Bruno and his comrades were asleep one December night, the temperatures touching minus twenty. The lookouts missed her. She slipped in and set fire to a house that had been used by the Germans. She wasn't to know they'd abandoned it just a couple of nights before because it was overrun with vermin. They had to applaud her audacity but this really was too close

138

for comfort. They learnt that the locals called her Zoya. If that was her real name or not, it didn't matter. Zoya she was, and Zoya had to be stopped.

A week went by, nothing else happened. Two weeks. Three. Maybe, they thought, she'd been killed, or sent to another partisan group somewhere else. They began to breathe a little easier.

It was Christmas Eve, nearing midnight, when Bruno, on patrol, went to check the barns at the back of the village. He heard something, saw a shadow. 'Halt,' he called. He gave chase. Now he could see her, a figure in black, sleek like a cat, her footprints in the snow. Bruno's shouting alerted his comrades. He lifted his rifle, slammed its butt against his shoulder, took aim and fired. And missed. Private Gluck emerged from the latrine, buttoning his fly, stamping the snow off his boots, when he too saw her. But too late, she saw him first and shot him with her revolver. Gluck slumped. More soldiers appeared at the far end of the passageway. She had to turn back on herself. She ran straight from where she'd come from, obviously not taking into account that Bruno might still be there. Again, he lifted his rifle. She skidded to a halt; she'd seen him. The two of them locked eyes, a mere ten feet between them. She was so young, her eyes so fierce, a dangerous, feral beauty. Bruno's heart pounded. Physically, she was indeed just a girl, small, fragile. But by gods, those eyes burnt holes in him, the raw hatred pierced him. He knew what they'd do to her, the torture, the indignity, the slow death; they'd pulverize her. She wouldn't stand a chance. He whispered her name, 'Zoya', then pulled the trigger. The shot rang out. The girl collapsed like a puppet cut of its strings. Men appeared from all around. Some slapped him on the back, asked if he was OK, others kicked the corpse. Blood seeped from beneath her, shockingly red against the snow.

The church bells nearby rang out midnight. Someone slapped Bruno on the back and said, 'Merry Christmas, my friend.'

Bruno sat upright in his bed. His body drenched in sweat, his breathing like a steam train. Had he been calling out, he wondered. His little bedside clock showed 4 a.m. He rubbed his eyes, trying to shake her free from his memory, from his dreams. He'd done her a favour. Zoya would have known it too. His officers were furious with him. She would have had valuable information. Why hadn't he just maimed her? Had he really been so freaked by a teenage girl? Frankly, yes. He saw what she was capable of, witnessed her determination. Bravery doesn't need a pair of balls.

Bruno had only been a boy when Adolf Hitler came to power. Joseph, already twenty-one, had long been of a supporter of the National Socialists, albeit a cautious one. But once in power, he embraced the regime with a full heart. He blamed the Jews for all of Germany's misfortunes and truly saw Hitler as a gift from God who would reverse all the nation's humiliations and restore the country to its previous glory.

By the time the war started, Joseph was such an integral part of the local party's machine, they could not afford to lose him. And so Joseph remained behind while Bruno, now of age, was obliged to join up and fight.

A few days earlier, Bruno had been to see the village doctor, who inspected his shoulder and declared himself happy with Bruno's progress. He'd write up a report, he said, and send it to Bruno's regional commanding officer. As he returned to his mother's, he found himself looking round on the off-chance he should see the lovely woman he'd met getting off the train.

Now, Bruno found himself sitting in Colonel's Kiefer's office, being watched over not just by Hitler but a whole array of portraits of the party leadership. The colonel refilled his pipe while skim reading Bruno's notes. 'Hmm. The doctor seems pleased enough with your progress. But that shoulder blade will need time. Are you right handed?'

'Yes, sir.'

'Just as well. Now, what I want to know, Corporal, is why you were shot in the back.' He looked up and straight into Bruno's eyes. 'Were you running away from the enemy?'

'No! No, sir, not at all. It was a sniper, sir. I was… unlucky.'

The colonel flung Bruno's file on the desk. 'So it seems. It also says here that you shot dead a partisan, when capturing her alive would have been far more beneficial.'

'It was her or me, sir.'

'Something doesn't seem right here. You're one slippery character, Corporal. And now I suppose you're sitting on your arse twiddling your thumbs.'

'It wasn't just the wound, sir. I was due some leave. I'd been in Russia for over two years.'

'Oh, my heart bleeds. Do you think the Führer thinks himself entitled to a bit of leave? I know, let's all go on leave. A couple of weeks on the coast to recharge the batteries. What do you think we're running here, Corporal?'

'I'm sorry, sir. I didn't mean any offence.' Bruno's cheeks burned up. Two years of fighting, fearing for one's life, of the cold, the mud, the filth. And this office-bound officer should speak to him like this and question his commitment.

'Yes, well.' The colonel lit his pipe, sucking several times before disappearing behind a vast cloud of blue smoke. He coughed and slapped his chest with his hand. 'As it is, you need not twiddle your thumbs for much longer. I've got a job for you.'

'Sir?'

'Here, take this. It explains everything.' He opened a drawer at his side and flung a brown folder on the table, a cloud of ash blew up from the ashtray. 'And believe me when I say you'll thank me for it. Seriously, Corporal. The job I have for you is simply the best job any sane man could wish for.'

Chapter 29

Nurse Lowitz told Hannah to take her time getting ready; she'd come back to collect her in exactly an hour's time. Hannah needed every minute, choosing what make-up to put on, carefully applying it. This, in itself, provided a joyful experience. The National Socialists frowned on women making themselves up. With this in mind, she decided to keep it subtle; she wouldn't want to scare anyone off. She wished she'd asked Nurse Lowitz what sort of evening it was and how she should present herself. Was it to be a formal dinner? No, surely not, otherwise why the meal earlier? Perhaps a dance? Again, no, because, apart from the doctor on her first day here, she hadn't set eyes on a man for weeks. Nurse Lowitz had mentioned special guests. Would there be any men amongst them? God, she hoped so. It occurred to her how much she missed seeing men. She was an attractive woman; she knew that, and she'd become accustomed to men looking at her, admiring her. And now, when she thought about it, she missed it, cooped up here in this strange place. She wanted to be appreciated again. So what to wear? She held up every dress against herself and considered it in the full-length mirror. She'd wear this one. No, it was too daring. She'd wear this one instead; no, it was too conservative. This one, surely. No, too old for her. And what about shoes? Would this pair go with this dress or that pair with that dress? This was too much. It was like offering a starving man a full banquet when a simple soup would suffice. She tried on all the dresses and shoes in various combinations and in quick succession. She'd almost run out of time. In the end, she settled for the black, shiny shoes and the first dress she'd tried, even if it was a little daring. She opened the drawers inside the wardrobe and, delight of delights, found a couple of stoles. Was this ermine; was this mink? No, probably not. Still, she chose one and stared at the finished article, nodding with satisfaction.

Exactly one hour later, Nurse Lowitz returned. She put her hand to her chest and, tilting her head, smiled. Hannah had never seen the woman smile before. 'My, you look divine, Hannah.'

Hannah curtsied. 'Well, thank you, Nurse Lowitz.'

'That red really suits you, and the purple trim as well. Lovely, Hannah. You'll be a big hit, that's for sure.'

'A big hit with who?'

'You'll see. Now, come, let's meet the others.'

Hannah felt like the proverbial ugly duckling re-emerging as the beautiful swan. Nurse Lowitz was showing more interest in her and greater concern than her own mother ever did. It was a new and marvellous experience, but if only she knew where and what Nurse Lowitz was taking her to and exactly what was expected of her. Together, they caught the lift down to the ground floor. Hannah held her breath trying to calm herself. 'Don't worry,' said the nurse. 'You'll be fine.'

'But where are you taking me?'

The lift doors opened. 'Follow me.'

Hannah was sure that wherever she was going to, Nurse Lowitz wasn't going. She still had her nurses' uniform on. They came to the dining hall. Nurse Lowitz paused at the double doors. 'Tonight, Hannah, your task is as important as any soldier serving on the front line. The soldier knows he's been entrusted with a responsibility towards his fellow men, his nation and the Führer. Your responsibility is no different and no less.'

'I don't understand–'

Nurse Lowitz opened the double doors and, stepping aside, motioned Hannah to go through. The nurse made a discreet exit.

Hannah saw her fellow residents all looking resplendent in their dresses and gowns seated at small round tables dotted around the room. The lights were dimmed, the eye drawn to a huge chandelier glinting, a gentle fire burned in the ornate fireplace. A gentle waltz played in the background. A couple of waiters waited in the wings. Hannah noticed one change the record. The girls all stood on seeing her. 'Hannah, where have you been?' said Lena, hugging her at arms' length. Each girl had a glass of something sparkling and each, for some reason, had their first names typed out and plastered on their bosoms.

'We thought you'd left us,' said one of the other girls.

Erika approached her. 'Here, you'd better put this on,' she said, passing Hannah her own name badge.

'And here, have a glass of this,' said Lena, thrusting a glass of wine, or was it champagne, in Hannah's hand.

'Oh, it's gone right up my nose.' She giggled.

'You're not meant to gulp it down, silly. You're meant to sip it, like this, like a lady.' Lena demonstrated. 'Nice, though, isn't it? You can have as much as you want. It'll help you relax.'

Erika proposed a toast. 'To our Führer,' she said, glass in the air. 'And our futures.'

Hannah took a delicate, ladylike sip.

'And here's to fucking,' shouted Lena. The girls laughed raucously.

'Why… w-why did you say that?' asked Hannah.

'Well, it's what we're here for.'

'What do you mean?'

'What do you mean *what do you mean*? Haven't you been told?'

'Told what?'

The double doors opened. Nurse Lowitz reappeared. 'Ladies! Ladies, please welcome your guests.' She stepped aside and bowed. 'Gentlemen. Do come through, come through, please.'

Chapter 30

They did come through, one after the other, six uniformed supermen. The girls clasped their hands. One giggled; another clapped; another whistled. 'My God, look at them,' said Lena, thrusting out her chest. The men, boys really, were all cut from the same mould – muscular, straight-backed and confident. They all wore the black, shiny uniforms of the SS apart from one, Hannah noticed, the one who came in last. Instead, he wore the uniform of the regular army, a corporal. He caught her eye, a flash of a smile, and she realised with a jolt that she recognised him. 'Good evening, ladies,' said the men in unison. 'Good evening.'

Nurse Lowitz, Hannah noticed, had slipped away. The men moved around the women looking at their name badges on their chests. Hannah's heart skipped a beat as she remembered where she'd seen the man she recognised. She'd seen him on the train; they alighted together. She wondered whether he'd recognised her too. She willed him to come to her. But no, he approached Lena, who didn't look terribly pleased about it.

Instead, another approached. 'Aha,' he said in a booming voice. 'You are Fraulein Hannah.' He offered his hand. She took it and he drew her hand to his lips and kissed it. Hannah shuddered at the touch and had to stop herself from snatching her hand away. 'Lieutenant Felix Brosch,' he said. 'Delighted to meet you.'

Lieutenant Felix Brosch had surprisingly soft hands for such a square-shaped man. A square head on a square body, like a set of building blocks. 'I'm to be your companion for tonight. Shall we sit?' He held out a chair for her, pushing it in slightly as Hannah sat. Equally incongruous was his lopsided smile; he smiled a lot, thought Hannah, but his eyes remained stony.

A waiter circulated with a gold-coloured tray of wine. Felix grabbed two glasses, gave one to Hannah. He stood abruptly and addressing the room, shouted for a toast. A number of rowdy toasts came in quick succession, after which, Felix sat down, a satisfied look about him. Hannah sipped her drink and watched the handsome man in the army uniform talking or, at least, trying to talk to Lena. He seemed entirely different from the others as if he wasn't part of their gang, an interloper.

'So where were we?' said Felix, returning to his seat and indicating that Hannah should return to hers.

'We are to be companions, apparently.'

'Ah, yes, indeed.' He lit a cigarette. 'Lucky you, hey?'

'Yes, Lieutenant.'

'Hey, hey, less of the lieutenant. Please call me Felix, at least for tonight.'

'Can I have one of those… Felix?'

'I'm sorry? One of what?'

'A cigarette.'

'You what?' He laughed out loud, throwing his head back. 'You are feisty. I like that. But no, you bloody can't. You were joking, I hope.'

She forced a chuckle. 'Yes, of course.' Pause. 'Felix.'

He took a deep drag of his cigarette and watched the resultant cloud of smoke dissipate. Glancing over, Hannah noticed Lena already talking animatedly to her partner, her hands flapping like the wings of a bird.

'So, Hannah Schiffer, no doubt you'll want to know all about me, that sort of thing.'

'Yes, for sure,' she managed to say without missing a beat.

And so the lieutenant spoke about himself. Hannah tried to listen and nodded in what she hoped were appropriate places. He told her about his upbringing and how impoverished his parents had been until the day Hitler took over. And they, as with the rest of the nation, owed the man such a debt of gratitude. He topped up her drink. 'You are beautiful, you know.'

'Thank you.'

'So tell me... what about your parents. What do they do?'

Hannah watched one of the waiters throw a log on the fire.

'Well?'

She described her parents as generically as possible, hoping to pass the baton of conversation back to him as soon as possible. He took it, describing his own parents in detail and his work in the SS. An hour passed. Everywhere, around the room, couples engaged in similar conversations, lots of polite laughter. Hannah's lieutenant didn't say anything that made her laugh but she pasted a smile.

Hannah noticed Lena's partner get to his feet, heard him say, 'Won't be long.' As he passed behind Lieutenant Brosch, he looked straight at her and used his eyes to say something. To follow him?

'Excuse me, Felix.'

'What?' he said, not attempting to hide his irritation.

'I'm so sorry but if you'd excuse me, I need to...'

'Powder your nose?'

'Ah yes, very funny, that's right.'

She tried to maintain a dignified pace as she walked out of the room, through the double doors. She heard a whistle down the corridor. It was him. He beckoned her over. Upon reaching him, he pulled her into a small dark room. She went to put the light on but he stopped her.

'You remember me,' he said, more as a statement than a question. She could make out the pained expression in his eyes. 'Have you been in this place since that day I saw you?'

'Yes.'

'Are you OK here?'

'I suppose it could be worse. How are you? Are you better now? You look…' He looked what? He looked handsome but vulnerable. He looked like someone who already knew too much about life. 'You look well.'

'I feel better. I've…' He looked away. 'I've thought of you – a lot.'

'Me too,' she said. 'I've thought of you a lot too.'

He laughed softly. 'Oh, it wasn't just me, then. I don't even know your name.'

They exchanged names and he said, 'Well, it's lovely to meet you again, Hannah.'

He said it with such warmth, such sincerity. 'Thank you.'

'Look, you know why we're here, don't you? It's just that you looked so uncomfortable in there.'

'To be companions for you and your friends for the night.'

He looked hard at her. He looked frightened now. 'They're not my friends, Hannah. I don't know them. All I know is that you don't mess with them.'

The door swung open. 'No, you bloody don't mess with us.'

Hannah cried out. 'Lieutenant?'

He'd come with two of his colleagues, their presence

filling up the small room. 'I wondered why you were taking so long. And you, Sunny Jim, you've left your lovely companion looking awkward as hell. Not really polite that, is it, old man? A bit bloody rude, if you ask me.'

'We're just going back,' said Bruno.

'Oh no you don't.' His two comrades took a step forward. 'Hannah,' said Felix, 'please return to the dining hall.'

'I'd—'

'We'll be with you shortly.'

She looked at Bruno and he nodded.

She stepped out into the corridor. The door was firmly closed behind her.

Chapter 31

For a split moment, Bruno feared he was drowning, or was he standing under a waterfall? He opened his eyes and two bulky figures hovered above him. 'Up you get,' growled one. Bruno wiped the water from his eyes, shook his head, trying to rid himself of his grogginess. He noticed one of the men was holding a bucket. It all came back to him.

'What time is it?' he asked, finding his voice.

'Time you were going. Now, get up.'

His shoulder throbbed. He tried to get up as ordered, but it was harder than he thought. One of the men yanked him up, a hand under each armpit. Bruno gritted his teeth, determined not to show these men the pain he was in.

Standing, he found his balance. He was still in the small room that, earlier, he'd pulled in the woman he'd met. What was her name? Hannah, that was it. Hannah. He stretched his shoulder. 'Where's Hannah?' he asked.

'Never you mind.'

'What about Lena?'

'Come on, we're going.'

'Where?'

'Home.'

'But I was told–'

'Tough. You missed out there. Change of plan. Hurry up.'

They almost dragged him down the corridor, across the grand entrance hall with its two-tone tiles, and out through the front door, down the stone steps, where they deposited him on the gravelled drive. 'My hat,' he said. And there it was, tossed through the air, landing a few feet behind him. The two figures stood at the doorway, the light from within making silhouettes of them.

'Go on, sod off outta here.'

They closed the door behind them. Bruno heard the heavy clunk of a key being turned and bolts slammed home. He found himself alone and blinking away the outline of light still flashing on his retina. It was only then he realised that they hadn't given him his coat, and he was shivering from the drenching of cold water. He debated whether to ask them for his coat but decided against it. And so with his arms wrapped across his chest, he began the long walk home. He tried to will away the cold. After all, he'd just come back from Russia; he knew the meaning of cold. The world had turned white but only on a superficial level. One scrape of one's boot and one could soon see the colour of the grass or the road beneath. This wasn't like the snow in Russia. There, the snow was so deep and so compacted, one truly felt closer to God, three or four, perhaps six whole feet closer. This was nothing; this cold was nothing. So why were his teeth chattering, actually chattering?

He knew for the rest of his life that snow would always remind him of her. Zoya. Her blood seeping into the snow, the shock of the vivid red dissolving on the pure white, turning a strange colour of pink. They crucified her. The platoon commander's idea. They fashioned a cross from two beams, took her body and with several nails attached it to the cross. They planted the cross at the main entrance to the village with a sign hung around her neck. *This is what we do to those who oppose us.* This is what we do. Stupid thing was, it backfired, just as

Bruno had predicted to himself but lacked the nerve to say out loud. By making her into a Christ-like martyr, that was exactly what she became. People from miles came to pay their respects at the cross, Zoya's cross. With temperatures often reaching minus twenty-five, even minus thirty, the corpse froze, so it didn't decompose. It simply remained there, life-like, regal somehow, a point of pilgrimage. Even in death, Zoya had the last word.

And now this, quite the most bizarre evening. What were Colonel Kiefer's words? *The job I have for you is simply the best job any sane man could wish for.* The brown folder contained just the one sheet of paper – to report at a specific time on this date at the former hotel and report to one Dr Heinkel. Dr Heinkel welcomed him into his office, shaking him by his hand and offering him a seat and a cigar. The job, the doctor said, was usually one reserved for the SS. He'd arranged everything with the colonel when one of the SS men had taken ill, and there were no others available at such short notice. But Bruno's name had come to the doctor's attention via the mayor—in other words, Bruno's brother, Joseph.

'Yes, I guess that would explain it, then,' said Bruno.

'What do you mean?'

Bruno cursed his stupidity; one does not ever criticise a mayor, even if that mayor was your brother. 'Oh, nothing. Nothing at all, just a little sibling banter, you know.'

The doctor laughed politely but narrowed his eyes. 'How is your shoulder?' he asked as if wanting to move on quickly.

'Oh, still sore, you know, but getting better.'

'Good. That's good to hear. No doubt, you'll be keen to get back into the thick of it as soon as possible.'

'Yes, yes, absolutely.'

'But, as I'm sure you aware, there are a myriad ways in

which we can contribute, and this is one, albeit a rather novel one.'

'Hmm.'

'Your racial ancestry is beyond reproach, and as an experienced and long-serving non-commissioned officer in the Führer's army, you fit the bill.'

'Thank you.'

'Yes. So each SS officer is assigned one girl with whom he should procreate.'

'Right.'

'And the name of your partner, Corporal Spitzweg, is…' He checked his sheet of paper. 'One Lena Clarin.'

That was the day before yesterday. But it hadn't quite worked out. As soon as he entered the room, he recognised the woman from the train, was bedazzled by her strange, detached beauty, her mournfulness, the darkness that lay behind her eyes. He remembered every word of their conversation in the railway station, the way she spoke, a lightness that was at odds with the way she looked at him. He'd been entranced by her, like a rabbit caught in headlights. It was one of those moments, one of those meetings, you never wanted to end. Over the next few days, the memory of her became the only thing capable of allowing him to forget the other woman who, so briefly, had made such an impact on his life – Zoya. So to see her in her gorgeous red dress looking like something out of a Tolstoy living room, her face made-up, her hair full of life, it took his breath away. But instead he'd been ordered to couple up with a girl called Lena. Lena was your typical German girl so consumed by Nazi ideology, and so imbued by it, she'd lost her own sense of identity before it'd had a chance to properly take shape. She talked about wonderful futures, sacrifices and glory, and spouted statistics as fact and proof. She was nervous, poor girl, as indeed he was too, but his concentration was shot at, painfully aware that the woman from the train was there, just a few feet away speaking to one of the SS thugs. He could tell that Lena was equally disappointed to be landed with him. After all, he was a dowdy corporal wearing the dowdy uniform of the Wehrmacht. What was he compared to a proper officer in a shiny, black SS uniform, with sleeked-back hair and perfectly shaped fingernails? The fact that Lieutenant Felix Brosch had done nothing during the war but terrorise local doubters and Jews, while he, Bruno, had truly fought, was immaterial. Who was he to vocally pour scorn on a member of Himmler's beloved SS? Lena kept glancing over at the handsome lieutenant while Bruno's attention was drawn, magnet-like, to the lieutenant's companion for the night, the woman from the train. And she also looked uncomfortable. Perhaps he was misreading it, but no, her discomfort would be obvious to anyone with a heart, which perhaps explained why the good lieutenant was so oblivious.

Unable to bear it any more, Bruno excused himself from the delightful, if distracted, Lena, and pretended he needed to use the facilities. Passing behind the SS lieutenant, he stole a glance at her and knew immediately from the way she caught his eye that she also recognised him. Instinctively, he used his eyes to plead with her to follow him. The briefest widening of her eyes told him she understood.

He stepped out into the corridor, relieved that no one was there to ask if he needed any help. He tried opening a door down an adjacent corridor only to find it locked. But its neighbour was not. He stepped inside to find a small, darkened room, perfect, he thought, to speak to her. He waited, looking down the corridor, hoping he wasn't wrong, hoping she'd appear. She did. The vision of her, in her flowing dress, her pure beauty, hit him in his heart. He whistled and caught her attention.

He pulled her into the small, dark room. She went to put the light on but he stopped her.

She was even more beautiful close up, a beauty untainted by vanity. They spoke quickly, both aware, perhaps, that time was against them. He didn't feel as if he could simply launch into warning her; he needed to work out whether she knew already, whether she was a willing accomplice in this ridiculous scheme. He realised they didn't even know each other's first names. He soon clocked that she was unaware of what was expected of her. She assumed he was connected to the SS men out there, that they were comrades or friends. God forbid. 'They're not my friends, Hannah. I don't know them. All I know is that you don't mess with them.'

As soon as he'd said it, the door swung open and there, in front of him, snorting like a bull, was the lieutenant, flanked by two of his comrades. 'No, you bloody don't mess with us.' He told Hannah to return to the party, but when Bruno tried to follow her, the SS men stopped him. They waited until Hannah had gone. Making sure no one else was around, Lieutenant Brosch jabbed him in the chest. 'So who are you anyway?'

'I've just come back from fighting in Russia.'

'Oh, right, so you're a war hero. Can't see what a beauty like Hannah Schiffer would see in a streak of piss like you.'

'I'm not staying to listen to this.' He tried to push by them, but the lieutenant's two men seized his arms. He tried to shake them off. Their grip tightened. The lieutenant's fist smashed into his stomach, doubling him over. He fell to the ground, spluttering, fighting for breath. The two men pulled him back up, held him up. Bruno opened his eyes to see the lieutenant's fist coming at him like a steam train, the sensation of being hit on the side of his face by a sledgehammer.

How long he'd lain there on the hard floor, out cold, he didn't know. The two hotel orderlies had woken him up with a bucketful of cold water and chucked him out. But now at last, he was home.

His mother was there to greet him. 'Bruno, what's happened to your face? Where's your coat? Why are you wet? Oh, my, you're shivering.'

Joseph came through from the kitchen. 'Why you back so early?'

Through clattering teeth, Bruno asked, 'Why did you put my name forward?'

'Come on,' said his mother. 'Take this shirt off; you'll catch your death in this. Joseph, go run a bath, will you?'

'Why, Joseph?' Bruno shouted at his brother's retreating figure.

Joseph stopped. 'Because you need to be doing something useful while you're here.'

'What?'

'You'd better not have let me down; you'd better not have disgraced yourself and our name.'

Chapter 32

Lena was on her as soon as Hannah returned to the dining hall. 'Where is he? What have you done to him?'

'I… The man I was with, he wanted to have a word with him.'

'And half the others too. You weren't meant to do that.'

'Do what?'

'Steal him.'

Hannah laughed.

'It's not funny, you know. We're all allocated. You can't just pick and choose. Oh look, they're back.'

Three men, not four, walked back in, the lieutenant leading the way, his chest inflated, his expression stony. Felix's comrades rejoined their partners. Felix, on seeing Hannah, broke into a wide grin. 'Ah, now where were we?' He scooped up a glass of wine and drained half of it in one go. 'Good stuff, this. They're spoiling us. I think it's almost time.'

'Where's Bruno, Lieutenant?' asked Lena.

'Felix, please.' He bowed. 'I'm sorry to say Bruno, that's his name, yes? I'm sorry to say that your companion is feeling unwell all of a sudden. He asked me to convey his apologies, but he's had to go home.'

'Oh?' said Lena. 'He seemed all right a minute ago.'

Felix shrugged. 'As I say, he's most sorry.'

'Well, that's inconvenient. So I'm going to be left here like a lemon?'

'You could join us, Fraulein, and be a gooseberry instead.'

'This is not funny, Lieutenant. I'll be accused of not doing my duty.'

'I shall vouch for you; don't you worry.'

Lena huffed. She hoisted up her dress and, shooting daggers at Hannah, stormed straight out of the room.

Felix and Hannah watched her go. 'What a drama queen,' said Felix.

'And I need to go check on Bruno.'

But before she had time to move, Felix swung his arm around her waist and pulled her back. 'Oh no you don't. Like he said, he's had to go home. I saw him leave.'

'Let me go. I don't believe you.'

'Here's our big chief nurse.'

Nurse Lowitz stood at the double doors, a wide smile on her face. She clapped her hands, drawing everyone's attention. 'Ladies and gentlemen, I see you're all getting on famously. That's wonderful to see because the time has come. I wish you all the very best of luck. Gentlemen, I know you've been told but a reminder, if I may. These young women are the future mothers of Germany. Treat them with respect.' She paused, allowing her words to sink in while Hannah reached out for the back of a chair, trying to steady herself. She wasn't hearing this; this could not be real. 'Thank you, gentlemen. Now ladies, if you could escort your companions to your room.'

One by one the couples left, hand in hand, nervous smiles all around. Felix offered Hannah his hand, an expectant smile on his face. She shook her head, took a step back.

He tilted his head; she knew what he was saying, knew what he expected of her. 'You really don't understand, do you? We have to go to your room now and have sex. You and me, we have to make a baby, a perfect Aryan baby for the

Fatherland, to play our part in improving the racial purity of this nation. And I'm telling you, my darling, I'm *aching* to play my part, so if you don't mind…'

She tried calming her breath, placed her hand against her chest.

Nurse Lowitz approached. 'Anything wrong here?' she asked breezily.

'I won't do it. You can't make me.'

Nurse Lowitz seized Hannah by the elbow. 'Excuse me a moment, Lieutenant.' She led her to one side. 'What did I say earlier?' she said, talking quickly through the side of her mouth. 'About a soldier's responsibility? And your responsibility being just as important?'

Hannah was desperate to have the nurse on her side. 'I didn't think you meant *now*, tonight. I can't, Nurse, please, not like this.'

'Why? Isn't the lieutenant good enough for you?'

'It's not that. It's not right.'

'Doing our duty, yes, your *duty*, for the Führer is not right? Is that what you're saying?'

'I can't. I can't just…' Don't cry, she told herself. Don't cry. 'I've never done it before.'

'I know that. You told us, and that makes it all the better, Hannah. Think of your sacrifice for such a noble cause – the future, our future, *your* future.'

'What is it, Fraulein?'

'Ah, Lieutenant. Give me just another moment and we'll have this sorted out.'

'No, I heard. Precious miss here thinks she's too good for us,' he said, jabbing himself in the chest. 'The pride of Germany and we're still not good enough for her.' He threw his glass into the fireplace where it shattered. 'Damn it all; I'll not stand here wasting my time.' Now it was his turn to take Hannah by the elbow. He flung her into a chair and leant over her. Hannah shrunk down, waiting for the slap, bracing herself. He thrust his face towards her. 'All you have to do is open your legs,' he seethed, spraying her with his spittle. 'Not that difficult.' He swung his hand back, ready to strike. Hannah, letting out a little cry, flinched. But he stayed his hand. Instead, he leant even closer, the smell of wine on his breath engulfing her, and said, 'You'll pay for this, you stupid bitch.'

Chapter 33
January 2002

I wait until ten o'clock on the Sunday morning before phoning Tessa. I thought there'd be no point ringing before – it was a Saturday and she's a student. I'm dying to know how her dinner date with Tom went last night. I ring but there's no answer. I leave a message. 'Hi, Tess darling. Just seeing how it went last night. Hope you're OK. Speak soon.'

I busy myself with household chores. Tessa's date isn't the only reason I'm on edge. Having received 'my' Tom's message on Friends Reunited, I wrote back saying I'd be delighted to meet up. Now I await his response. I logged in numerous times since but nothing yet. Each time I'm both disappointed and relieved. Disappointed because, obviously, I'd love to see Tom again after all these years, forty-two years, to be precise. And relieved because it seems too momentous. Tom occupies a big space in my childhood memories; that's where he belongs, and perhaps, I think, that's where he should stay. What if we did meet and we don't get on? I imagine us sitting in a restaurant or in a pub catching up then having nothing to say to each other. That would spoil my memory of him, would tarnish his special place in my heart. I couldn't bear that. What if he's developed into a really nasty or arrogant person? What if he thinks I have? Forty-two years. It's half a lifetime, perhaps more. People change in so many different ways.

Having loaded the washing machine, having mopped the

kitchen floor, having done numerous other tedious tasks, I'm ready to try again. First, I try Friends Reunited. Tabby jumps up on my lap while I wait. Still nothing. Hmm. Surely, Tom would have answered by now. Perhaps, he's having second thoughts; perhaps, he, too, realises he'd rather have me as a 1950s teenager and not see me again. I stand up and Tabby falls to the floor.

So then, pacing the living room, I'm ready to try Tessa again. I'm about to punch in her name when my mobile rings, making me jump.

I see Barry's name on the screen. I'm tempted to ignore it but no, I don't, and tap the little green button.

'Liz? It's me, Barry.'

'Barry, I do know your voice and you do know, don't you, your name comes up on my phone whenever you ring me?'

'Yeah, sure. Shelley taught me.'

'Well?'

'Oh yeah, so listen, I know it's short notice, but how about you and me going to Germany for two nights from next Tuesday?'

Oh, that is short notice. My mind tumbles through the possibilities, the potential hurdles. I can't think of any. Work is slack at the moment; I'd easily get the time off – even at such short notice. I just wasn't ready to face it so soon. This is not the Barry I know and love, *used* to love. I'm not even sure it's me talking when I say yes, why not. Next week would work for me.

But there is surely a fly in this particular ointment. 'Barry, what does your *girlfriend* think of you gallivanting to Germany with me?' I say the word 'girlfriend' with gleeful animosity. I know he can hear the righteous resentment in my voice.

'Ah, don't worry about Shelley,' he says. 'I'm the one who

wears the trousers around here.'

I have to stifle a laugh. 'Yes, Barry, if you say so.'

'So I'll book the tickets, yes?'

'Yes, Barry, that'd be great. Thank you.'

I breathe out. Am I really ready to face Germany? No, I'm not but equally I know I never will be. I'm grateful to my husband. Now, that's a sentence I haven't said in a long, long time.

I don't want to think about it too much, at least not yet, so to take my mind off it, I try Tessa's mobile again. It's eleven o'clock now. It rings several times, and I'm wondering whether to leave another message, when she answers.

'Tessa, love, it's Mum. You OK to talk?'

'Yeah, yeah, sure.' She doesn't sound it. She sounds as if she's just woken up.

'I can ring back if you like.'

'No, it's fine.'

'So tell me. I'm dying to know; how did it go last night?'

'Oh yeah, it was lovely. I had a great time.'

'Good.' Was that it? 'Nice food? Nice company?'

'Yeah, both.' I hear her yawn.

'Good, good. So, erm, do you think you'll be seeing each other again?'

'Yeah, probably. Definitely.'

'Oh, that is good.' I feel as if this conversation has already run its course. 'Well, look, darling, I can see you're tired, so I'll leave you be. Call me when you're ready.'

'Yeah, sure.'

It's then I hear a cough, a loud rasping cough, a *male* cough. 'Is that...? Tess?'

'Mum, I've gotta go. Speak soon. Love you. Bye.'

The phone goes dead.

I clench my eyes shut and put my head into my hands. Oh, Tess, Tess, Tess... Not on a first date. You're too young; you're still a little girl. Damn it, Tess. I just hope to God she was careful, that *he* was careful. Oh God, I remember the girls when I was young that slept too readily with their boyfriends. Word always got around. I remember a girl called Amanda Blyth. Lost her virginity at fifteen, had slept with half the town by the time she was eighteen, at least that was the rumour. All the boys liked her for the wrong reasons, and all the girls thought poorly of her. She got pregnant by the time she was twenty. The boys lost interest, especially the boy who made her pregnant, and the girls pitied her. I so don't want my daughter to be Amanda Blyth. You stupid girl, Tess, you stupid girl.

I try Friends Reunited again. This time without trepidation. Frankly, I don't care any more whether Tom gets back to me or not. Somehow the moment's gone. I wait for the connection and idly wonder whatever happened to Amanda Blyth. I log back into the site and, oh my, this time there's a message for me. It has to be Tom; who else would message me? I click through to the inbox and yes, sure enough, it's from Thomas Fletcher.

My heart ramps up a notch as I click on his message. Not only does he agree to meeting up, he's suggested a place (nearby) and a date and time – tomorrow evening. Tomorrow? Is he serious? I can't just meet *tomorrow*. It's too soon; I need time to prepare myself. It's like Barry and Germany all over again. Where did this reluctance to *do* anything creep in? I never used to be like this. But then I think, why not? Why not tomorrow? 'Yeah, sod it,' I say aloud.

I realise my fingers are trembling as I write back. *Great. See you tomorrow, Tom. Look forward to it*. I hesitate a second, the cursor hovering over the send button. I've had forty-two years to prepare for this: why wait another day? If my daughter can sleep with her date after just one night, then I can go out for dinner with a man I've loved for almost half a century.

I click send.

Chapter 34

I decided I need a new outfit if… one, I was meeting Tom for dinner, and two, if I was going to Germany with my former husband. So today I went into the town's shopping centre. I'd lost a lot of weight since I found out about Barry's affair, and I needed an upgrade for my wardrobe, a big upgrade. Who needs one of these slimming clubs? I have found a far easier solution – find out that your husband is sleeping with a woman twenty years younger than yourself and is prepared to leave you, your daughter, the cat and his home and everything he's worked for for the last twenty-plus years in order to live with this bint, this slip of a girl. You're guaranteed to shed the pounds, believe me.

So I find myself in the shopping centre on a Saturday afternoon and wonder why it's so darn busy. Still, I have a lot on my mind, but I need to do this. So much is whirling around my mind, I don't know whether I'm coming or going. I have so much to worry about, I don't know what to worry about first – going to Germany with my ex-husband to try and find out about my earliest years, my mother finally dropping clues about what exactly happened in Germany at the end of the war, meeting up with Tom, my first love, after forty-two years, or the fact that my only daughter is sleeping with a boy she's known for all of five minutes.

I see the mums shopping with their daughters and try to push away the envy. The centre has only recently opened. It's huge, with several floors, escalators, polished floors, covered with a glass dome of a roof, a glass lift that moves with frightening speed, and large Triffid-like plants.

They call it retail therapy and one can see why. Having been in and out of several stores, tried on numerous shoes, skirts and blouses and bought far too much, I'm wiped out, in need of tea yet strangely elated. Laden like a pack mule, I head for a coffee shop on the ground floor. It's packed; people are almost fighting for half a spare table to sit at. I see all the exhausted-looking men, the short-tempered women, the fractious children. Robbie Williams is playing on the loudspeakers. But where can I sit? I'd kill for a cup of tea and a large slab of cake.

I hear a familiar voice calling out my name. I turn round and see her sitting down at a table, a boy either side. 'Oh, hi, Shelley,' I say in my best *how lovely to see you* voice.

Her boys, Dylan and Jake, say hello politely. I will say this for Shelley, she's doing a fine job bringing up her boys. No sign, however, of Barry.

'Do you wanna join us?'

Oh dear, what to say?

'To be honest,' she says, 'we're just going.'

Oh, that's all right, then. I drop all my bags either side of a little wicker-back chair and plop down.

'You've been busy,' says Shelley.

'Yes. I did need a few little items, you know.'

'Yeah.'

'No Barry today?'

'He's buying a pair of boating shoes.' She laughs. 'Not that he's planning on going boating.'

'Just the style.' Again, I'm impressed – I don't think I'd ever have got Barry into a place like this.

169

'In fact, we should go. I said we'd meet him on the hour. Right, boys, you ready?'

She bends down to pick something off the floor and her necklace hangs down from her top. It's *that* necklace, the necklace I thought was mine but never was; and an inexplicable desire to hurt her rises within me. Swallow it down, Liz; you're better than this. 'So I hope you don't mind me taking Barry away from you next week.' Obviously, I'm not.

'Eh?'

'Our little jaunt to Germany together. It's so kind of him to offer to accompany me. I'm sure he's told you all about it.'

'Oh, yeah, yeah. Of course, no probs.' Her neck flushes red, I swear there's fire coming from her eyes. 'Come on, boys, let's go.'

'Nice seeing you again, Shelley.'

'Yeah, and you, Liz.'

I watch them leave, gathering their bags. She can't wait to get away. 'Tell Barry not to forget his passport.'

She doesn't answer. I sit there, and I know I'm grinning from ear to ear like the spiteful witch I am, and it feels great.

*

After two hours, I'm almost ready. I could not decide what to wear, oh, the dilemma. In the end, I've opted for an off-the-shoulder dark green, A-line dress that falls just below the knee, which comes with a wide belt. It has a definite 1950s vibe to it, appropriate, I think. I finish it off with the bumblebee brooch Barry gave me for Christmas the year I was expecting the notorious necklace. I look great, though, if I say so myself. A fair bit of make-up but subtle; mustn't overdo it at my age.

I'm about ready. I check my purse, my phone, my keys.

I've left some food out for Tabby in case she ever deems herself ready to return home. Right then, all set. The doorbell rings. Blast. Now? Really?

It's Barry. He barges in, not so much as a hello.

But the time I saunter in my heels back through the living room, he's already sprawled on the armchair, running his fingers through his hair. 'Look, Liz, I can't come with you to Germany any more. I'm really sorry.'

'What? Why not? Barry, you said.'

He puts his hands up in surrender. 'I know, I know.'

'Well? Why not?'

He sighs. 'Shelley found out, didn't she?'

'What do you mean she found out? Didn't you just tell her in the first place?'

'Well, yes, I meant to. I just sorta forgot to mention it, you know. So today she found out, God knows how, and she went ballistic. I mean, Christ.'

Poor Barry; he does look rather shell-shocked. 'So that's it? You're not coming.'

He shakes his head. 'I'm sorry, Liz.'

'So much for being the one who wears the trousers.'

That cuts, I can tell. 'Yeah, well.'

'You've taken a risk coming here to tell me. Couldn't you have just phoned?'

'Nah, that'd be riskier. She checks my phone.'

'Oh, does she? How wicked.'

'Anyway, I wanted to tell you to your face.'

'Most gallant.'

He looks at his watch. 'I'd better go. Gotta take the boys ice skating. I said I was popping out to get paper for the printer. I'll say they've run out.' He drags himself out of the armchair and, straightening himself, looks at me for the first

171

time. He steps back. 'Whoa, you look…'

'Yes?'

His mouth moves like a fish on dry land. 'You look… well, gorgeous. Wow, Liz. Hang on, you going out?'

'Well, I don't tend to dress up for an evening by myself watching the telly. So, yes, I'm going out.'

'Looking like that?'

I laugh. 'I'm not your teenage daughter, Barry.'

His eyes narrow. 'You're wearing my brooch. Where are you going? Are you… Hey, you're not meeting a fella, are you?'

'Actually, I am, not that it's any of your business.'

His mouth hangs open, his eyes blaze. 'No, hang on a minute. What about Tessa?'

I shake my head in confusion. 'What about Tessa?'

'Well, you can't just…'

'Yes, Barry? What can't I?'

'Who is he, then, this fella?'

I don't answer; I just look at him.

'Oh, right. OK, then.' His shoulders slump.

'I think you'd better go, Barry. You don't want to be late for ice skating, do you?'

'No, you're right.' He checks his watch again. Then looks at me from head to toe. 'I'm sorry about…'

'About…?'

'About Germany.'

'It's OK, Barry, I'll cope.'

'Yeah. Sure.'

Chapter 35

It is a lovely restaurant; Tom's chosen well: low-ceilinged, interior brick walls with archways, low-hanging globe lights, parquet flooring and islands of red carpet. I see this all from the foyer as the maître d' checks for Tom's name. 'Yes, he has arrived, madam.'

Yes, he has. I see him at a corner table, scanning the menu. My heart flips. I approach and, sensing me, he looks up. He stands, a nervous smile on his face, his hand extended. I take his hand, and peck him on the cheek. 'You look lovely,' he says. 'The years have been kind to you.'

'And you, Tom.' He has a thin, well-groomed beard, prominent crows' feet, his hair, entirely grey, is short and neat, and his face exudes kindness. But I don't think if I saw him passing in the street I would have recognised him.

We sit, and I congratulate him on choosing such a lovely restaurant. 'The wonders of the internet,' he says, waving his hands about. We mention the parking, the weather, today's specials on the blackboard. We say how lovely it is to see one another; forty-two years, such a long time.

'I was overjoyed when I saw your message on Friends Reunited,' he says.

'Like you say, the wonders of the internet.'

A waitress with dyed red hair asks us if we're ready to order, and we haven't even begun looking at the menus yet. She leaves us and we discuss whether we want a starter as well as a mains, or whether to save ourselves for the dessert. Our waitress returns and we order.

So now we can talk. But where to start. We start at the point we last saw one another, the day Tom left.

'It didn't really work out in Kent. I don't know the details, but Dad didn't like the job, or they didn't like him. Either way, he gave it up and took on something with less salary than we had here. So, in the end, it was a pointless move. It took its toll and my parents divorced. I was rather miserable most of the time.'

The food comes. A beef lasagne for Tom, a vegetarian roulade for me. We skipped the starters. We have a small glass of red wine each.

We talk about school, the names we remembered, especially Cerys Atkins. 'How could we forget Cerys Atkins?' he says.

'She had the hots for you,' I say. But then most girls did. He blushes.

I tell him about how my mother sold Dad's café and then the house, how we downsized, as we say now, and I, too, was 'rather miserable most of the time.' Tom likes talking about my father, but there again, my father had that effect on people. They liked him. Even now, forty-two years on, Tom still wanted to talk about him. 'I wasn't so keen on his brother though.'

'My Uncle Bill? Dad's brother-in-law. No.'

'A bit creepy.'

'Yeah, very creepy. I'm sure Dad knew just how creepy, but in those days what could you do?'

We talk more about those long, lost days. I relax as I eat and sip my wine. He's easy to talk to, as easy as ever. I'm enjoying myself. I could talk to him all night.

It's not until desserts that we move on to our current lives. He tells me about his work as a freelance graphic designer, how he likes the flexibility of it and not having to answer to the same boss day in, day out. 'Are you married, Liz? Children?'

'Separated.' I tuck into my crème brûlée as I tell Tom about Barry, how we met on the day of the Queen's silver jubilee in 1977. I tell him about Tessa, university, etc. 'And you, Tom? Are you married?'

'Also separated.'

'Oh, I'm sorry. Married life is never easy, is it?'

'No. We were together twenty years. And in the end, you know what it's like, you grow apart, and acknowledging it, recognising that fact, is one of the hardest things ever. There were no children, so that made things a little easier. So it means we have no contact whatsoever.'

'Not sure whether that's a good thing or not.'

He takes a sip of water. 'No.'

He doesn't mention her name. I don't ask. 'So why did you return here?'

'I never truly felt at home in Kent. After my dad remarried and Mum died, and after the separation, I thought, there's nothing holding me here any more. I'll return home. Because this *is* home for me, always has been.'

I absorb this statement, and we finish our desserts in silence. 'That was delicious,' I say.

'Mine too. You haven't been here before, then?'

We talk about restaurants, food, films we've seen, CDs we've bought. Time passes quickly.

'How's your mother?' he asks. 'She must be…'

'Eighty-six.' I tell him about the dementia, the care home. I even tell him about the Elvis impersonator. He listens

175

carefully, half smiling, attentive. I feel his kindness. I could tell him anything, everything, and he'd listen without judging, prepared to accept me for who I am, not what someone else wants me to be. Here, with Tom, I am Elizabeth Marsh again, not someone's wife, or a mother, a daughter, but a woman. And so I tell him about the German certificate with the swastika I found, about my mother meeting the man I believed was my biological father in Germany in 1943, about my need to know more about this certificate and what it means.

'So what's written on this certificate?'

'The number fifty, a couple of signatures and an address of a hotel, at least that's what it is now, and the date, December 1944.'

'I speak German.'

'You do?'

He laughs. '*Ja ich spreche gut deutsch.*'

'I only speak the few words I've picked up from my mother but not enough to hold a proper conversation – unless it involves robins.'

'Robins?'

'I'm going to Germany next week. I'm going to visit this address and see what I can find. It'll be a waste of time, I'm sure, but…'

'It's something you have to do.'

'Yes, exactly. Barry was going to come with me, but his new woman found out and she went ballistic, according to Barry. He came round earlier to tell me this, his tail between his legs. So, Tom, if you want to come with me, you'd be most welcome.'

'What days?'

'Tuesday and Wednesday nights. Back home Thursday.'

'OK.'

'What? No, I wasn't being serious. I mean…'

'But I will come, seriously, if you'd like me to.'

'But… it's very short notice. What about your work?'

'I'm freelance, remember? I could come in the official capacity as your translator.'

'You really are being serious.'

He tilts his head to the side and smiles. 'Absolutely.'

Chapter 36
December 1956

It's Christmas Day! We had a tree decorated with baubles and candles and we had a Yule log, and on the mantelpiece, hiding the figurines, our small display of Christmas cards. I looked through and read all of them. They all seemed to be from Dad's relatives or his friends, none from Mum's and certainly none from Germany. I wanted to ask her why, but there was no way I had the courage to do that.

We even had visitors – Dad's sister and brother-in-law, my Aunt Vera and Uncle Bill. Aunt Vera arrived with a cooked turkey. It was simply a matter of doing the potatoes and vegetables, she said, and reheating the turkey. We could eat like kings again this year – everyone up and down the country could, now that rationing was finished.

The menfolk and I went to church. I sat between my father and uncle. Uncle Bill sang so loudly and horribly, I found myself shrinking into myself. I sidled up towards Dad. I didn't like Uncle Bill too much. I didn't like his huge moustache or the way he always winked whenever he spoke to me. Afterwards, Dad and Uncle Bill sent me on home while they went to the pub. Back home, I found Mum and Vera in the kitchen. I was itching for Dad and my uncle to come home because then we could open our presents.

Finally, they did come home, stinking of beer and fags. It was time.

I spent as much of the day as I could in my bedroom after

that. I got a jumper. I got a silly doll. I got a Frisbee, and I got a pogo stick. How old do they think I am? I didn't want any of these things. I wanted a TV set, a record player and lots of records to play. And then we had Christmas dinner and no one spoke to me. I might as well have been a ghost, so I don't think anyone noticed when, after dinner, I disappeared to my room. I lay on my bed, my hands behind my head and stared at James Dean. I could hear them talking and shouting and enjoying themselves downstairs. I wondered whether my mother would be having her 'one cigarette of the year' about now. She usually did.

I'd almost dozed off when I heard the clump, clump, clump of my father's footsteps on the stairs. He knocked on my door and didn't come in until I'd said enter. But it wasn't Dad, it was Uncle Bill. I sat up and crossed my legs. He glanced down so I pulled my dress lower, to cover my knees.

'Hey, Lizzie, what you doing up here all on your tod?'

'I think I've eaten too much, Uncle Bill. I don't feel too well.'

'Oh dear. I think we've all eaten too much to be honest. So how it's going at school?'

'It's all right.'

'Got yourself a boyfriend yet?'

'No.'

'What? A pretty lass like you? I don't believe it. I thought you'd have all the boys chasing after you.' He put his hand on my knee. A shot of tension gripped me. 'Don't worry, your time will come.'

'Thanks, Uncle Bill,' I said, aware of the small quiver in my voice with his clammy hand resting on my knee. I was desperate for him to remove it, desperate for him to leave me alone.

'You're a good girl; I've always said so. I have lots of nieces now, well, four of them, but I want you to know you're by far my favourite, Lizzie.' He grinned at me and I wasn't sure how to respond.

He was too busy grinning at me to hear my dad coming up the stairs. I wanted to shout out, *In here, Dad, in here.* Luckily, I didn't have to. Dad came in. Uncle Bill's hand left my knee as if he'd been electrocuted. I couldn't understand why I was so happy to see my father. 'Ah, there you are, Bill,' he said. 'We were beginning to wonder what happened to you.'

Uncle Bill reddened a little. 'Oh, you know, just having a little chat with Lizzie here.'

'Oh, I'm sorry to interrupt but Vera wants you. No idea why but I think you should go; there's a good chap.'

'Right you are, Arnold; better be off, then. Mustn't keep her waiting. Still puzzles me why we call them the gentler sex. Nice talking to you, Lizzie. Remember what I said.' He scurried off, rodent-like, closing the door behind him. Dad took his place on the bed.

'You OK, love?'

He said it so nicely, so kindly, that I had to swallow down my tears.

'Life can be hard sometimes, can't it? Look, work is going well at the moment. If it keeps going, I'll be able to save up enough for one of these television sets.'

'Really?'

'I know it's what you really want. I'm sorry about…'

'It's OK, Dad.' And I meant it now. It was all right now.

'I got you another small present but… but it's too young for you again. I'm sorry, my love, you're growing up so fast that I can't keep up. I promise I'll try harder.'

I loved my dad then. I always did, but at that moment, I

wanted to throw my arms around him. Instead, I asked, 'What's the other present?'

'Tickets!' he said, beaming. 'But it's for the panto, so if you don't–'

'No, that's great, Dad. That'd be brilliant.'

He was right; I *was* too old for the pantomime, but right then I'd have gone anywhere with him.

Chapter 37

The pantomime was two days after Boxing Day. Just Dad and me, Mum didn't want to come. Not that I minded; in fact, I preferred it when it was just Dad and me. So off we went to the local theatre to see *Cinderella*. We walked. I kept my head down, pulled my scarf up and wore a woolly hat pulled down as far as I could. 'Heck, love,' said Dad. 'It's not *that* cold.'

'Oh, but Dad, it is.' But he was right – it wasn't cold at all; I just didn't want to be recognised walking down the street and going into the Theatre Royal to see the panto. Luckily, we got there without being spotted. Dad bought us a big bag of marshmallows we could share and found us our seats.

'This should be a laugh,' he said, rubbing his hands.

'Yes,' I replied, trying my best to sound enthusiastic.

'Here, have a marshmallow.'

The theatre was packed, lots of children with their parents but they were all that much younger than I. Still, it's the thought that counts, I said to myself, using one of Mum's oft-repeated phrases. The lights dimmed and the curtain went up. And so we began.

*

I've never laughed so much. Dad, too, throwing his head back with laughter. Tears streamed down our faces, we laughed so hard. Dad kept slapping his knee with delight. An hour and a half later, it finished. The actors took numerous curtain calls.

Dad and I clapped as if our lives depended on it. And then it was over.

'Told ya, didn't I?' said Dad, blowing his nose.

'Yeah, it was funny, really funny. Thanks, Dad.'

He sighed with satisfaction. 'You see, I don't always get things wrong.'

We sat in silence for a while, while people around us gathered their coats and their bags and shuffled along the rows of seats.

'Really enjoyed that,' said Dad, tapping a cigarette out from his packet. 'Those ugly sisters, weren't they great? Funniest thing ever that. That bit where the red-haired one tripped over, oh my, that was so good.'

'Yeah, it was good.'

He slapped me hard on the knee. 'I know it wasn't the same as getting our own TV, but one day, once I've saved up some…'

'Thanks, Dad.'

'Good, good. That's good. Well, it's nice to have a chat once in a while, doesn't do no good keeping it all bottled up. So how about we finish the day off at the chippie? Would you like that?'

'Yeah, yeah, that'd be great.' To be honest, I would have preferred to have gone home. I felt we'd pushed the father-daughter bit enough for one day. But I could never resist a fish and chips dinner.

We came out into the foyer to find lots of people milling about, all in high spirits, lots of noise. Dad looked happy. His chest seemed to inflate as if he was pleased our trip out had been such a success. 'I'll just pop to the loo, love. You wait here a minute.'

And off he popped. I looked around and, yes, I was right.

As far as children went, I was by far the oldest. I saw a small girl leaning against one of the pillars crying while her mother, on her knees, struggled to get the girl's coat on her, a big blue bulky thing with large toggles. Thank God no one was here from school to recognise me. I was buttoning up my coat, still chortling at some of the jokes and the ugly sisters' mishaps when I heard my name being called.

I looked up. 'Oh, Tom! Hi.' Oh, shit, I didn't want Tom seeing me here, but wait, if *he* was here, then surely it was OK for *me* to be here.

'You been to see the panto?' he asked.

'Yes. You?'

'Absolutely.'

'Good, weren't it?'

'It's all right. I only came because it was a Christmas treat for my sister.' He pointed behind him at the little girl leaning against the pillar. Her mum, his mum, was now trying to insert the little girl's hands into her mittens.

'Yeah, me too. My little sister too.' Why in the hell did I say that?

He looked round. 'Where is she, then?'

'Oh, gone to the loo.' I smiled, hoping it'd cover my little fib.

My dad returned. 'You all set to go, then, love?' He saw Tom. 'Oh, I'm sorry, didn't realise–'

'This is Tom, Dad. He's in my year at school.'

'How do you do, Tom. Enjoy the show?'

This wasn't good. Dad might expose my lie. I had to steer him away as quickly as possible.

'Yeah, thanks, Mr Marsh. It was funny.'

Dad liked that, I could tell, the way Tom immediately addressed him as Mister. 'Wasn't it just? Haven't laughed like that in years. That bit where—'

'We should go, Dad, before the chippie gets too busy.'

'You might be right. Goodbye, Tom. Nice to meet you.'

'Yeah, you too, Mr Marsh.'

'See you back at school, Tom. Bye.'

Dad had already turned to leave when Tom asked, 'Hang on, don't forget your sister.'

Dad heard. 'Eh?'

'Come on, Dad, we need to go.'

I'd managed to push Dad away. I glanced back at Tom. 'She's very independent,' I mouthed.

Luckily, he was distracted by his mother and his sister.

We'd reached the exit, our progress hampered by so many mums and dads and their kids. I looked back, hoping to see Tom again. I did. We locked eyes across the crowded foyer and he smiled and waved at me.

I left the Theatre Royal floating on a cloud of happiness.

Chapter 38

It was a freezing cold Monday morning in January; first day back at school. I woke up, and the novelty of waking up and not feeling dread hadn't worn off yet. Since that day when Tom came to my rescue, Cerys Atkins and friends have left me alone. Maybe they'd found someone new to pick on, I don't know. A few girls even speak to me now. It's the best feeling – being *normal*.

I hadn't spoken to Tom since the pantomime. I saw him occasionally, usually talking to a pretty girl or larking around with his friends. I wished I could speak to him myself but I couldn't, wouldn't know how to, wouldn't know what to say. I still remembered the look of hurt on his face when I dismissed his help that day. If I could take those words back, I would.

On the first Saturday of the New Year, I went to ballet as normal and afterwards headed to the café via the town park. A low mist gave the park an eerie atmosphere; the grass was sodden. I could see Mr Watts and Rory as I passed, but this time they weren't playing football but standing next to the large elm tree in the centre of the park looking up. Mr Watts was shouting up. 'You're almost there, son. Can you reach it?'

Rory saw me and beckoned me over. 'You all right, Rory?'

'Nah, got my ball stuck in the tree.'

Just as he said it, the orange ball dropped out of the tree and bounced next to Rory. 'Yeah!' He ran after it.

'Thanks, Tom,' said Mr Watts.

Tom? I peered up into the canopy of the tree, and sure enough, sitting on a branch looking pleased with himself was Tom Fletcher.

'Hi, Tom,' I called up.

'Who's that? Oh, hi, Liz.'

'Tom's our knight in shining armour,' said Mr Watts.

'Yes, he's good at that.'

'You all right up there, Tom?'

'Absolutely, just coming down.'

We watched as Tom edged along the branch towards the trunk of the tree, trying to keep his balance.

'Careful how you go, son.'

'It's more difficult getting down,' said Tom.

Rory ran after his ball squealing in delight.

Tom was clambering down the tree. He stopped, gripping on for dear life, and glanced down.

'I reckon you could jump from there,' said Mr Watts.

Tom hesitated, weighing up whether he could or not. In the end, he did. I grimaced as he hit the ground. He lost his footing on the wet grass and fell heavily. The still air was shattered by Tom screeching. Mr Watts ran over. 'Oh, Christ, Tom.'

Tom sat up, holding his left hand up, his eyes creased up with pain, his face shockingly white. My knees went to jelly. His hand had gone all limp and hung at an odd angle, almost back to front. He clasped his bent wrist with his other hand and rocked, clenching his teeth, trying not to cry out.

'Oh, heck, that looks serious, son.'

'You OK, Tom?'

'No,' he said, still gritting his teeth. 'It really hurts.'

Luckily, Mr Watts took control. 'That hand don't look

good. I reckon we need to get you to hospital, son. Liz, would you take Rory home while I take Tom to hospital?' He gave me his address. It wasn't far, just the other side of the park. 'Come on, son, put your arm around me. That's it.'

With Mr Watts' help, Tom pulled himself up. He didn't look well. He'd really gone as white as a ghost, and his wrist had already turned a vivid colour of black and purple.

'How will you get to the hospital, Mr Watts?'

'There's a bus that goes direct. Bus stop is just there. That's it, son. We'd better get this checked out. Rory, you go home now with Liz here, you got that?'

'Yes, Dad.'

'Oh, Liz. Might be an idea to tell Tom's folks where he is. D'you know where he lives?'

Tom spluttered out his address. Now I had two addresses to remember. I repeated them in my head.

'Can you remember all that?'

'I think so, Mr Watts.'

'You're a good lass. Come on, son, let's get going.'

Rory picked up his ball and came and stood next to me. We watched his dad and Tom walk across the park towards the bus stop. 'What's that?' said Rory. I looked to where he was pointing to, and sure enough, there was something red and metallic lying on the grass. I went to pick it up but Rory, dropping his ball, beat me to it, and I didn't think it'd look good to fight him for it. 'It's a penknife,' said Rory, holding it up in triumph. 'It must be Tom's; I'll go after him.'

'No! No, don't Rory.'

'He's only over there,' he said, pointing unnecessarily. 'I can catch him easy.'

'No, it's not that, it's just that... erm, they d-don't allow knives in hospitals, that's all.'

Rory seemed to consider this and, to my relief, accepted it. He inspected the knife. It had the Swiss flag on it. 'Cor, I wish I had one like this.'

'If you give it to me, I can give it to Tom's mum.' I held out my hand and he looked at it, then back to the knife, unwilling to surrender it to me. 'I'll make sure she knows it was you who found it.'

That did the trick. He handed it over.

'Right,' I said. 'Let's get you home first.'

Twenty minutes later, I arrived at Tom's, having dropped Rory at his house and telling his mum what had happened. I was astonished at Tom's house. They had their own driveway and even a car! A khaki-green Austin A30 with white-walled tyres and headlamps so big, they looked like happy eyes. We could never afford a car, let alone a happy one. Tom's house was much bigger, much nicer than ours. Proper big windows with nice lace-net curtains, and a bay at the front, not like our pokey house and its tiny windows. I'd never thought there was anything wrong with our house until this moment, but standing at the end of the driveway, I experienced a pang of jealousy; why couldn't we live in a house like this? I bet they didn't have an outside loo with a horseshoe nailed to the door. I bet they had a television set.

I rang the bell. I recognised Tom's mother from the pantomime. She seemed really nice and smiled sweetly, a smile that soon disappeared as I told her the story. She seemed panicked however much I told her that it wasn't that serious. I had Tom's penknife in my coat pocket and was about to hand it over when I thought, No, hold on to it. It could prove useful. Tom's mother slammed the door on me without even a thank you. I didn't think she was so nice after all. But at least I still had the penknife.

Chapter 39

I left it two days, didn't want to appear over keen or overly concerned. Tom was off school. Everyone knew why because the teachers knew and they told one of the kids who told someone else, and soon our whole year knew – Tom was off school because he'd been hit while protecting a kid from bullies. Tom was a hero – and now everyone knew it. I didn't want them knowing it; I wanted to keep that all to myself, but I couldn't bring myself to tell people what really had happened. So today, Wednesday, I took the penknife to school with me but made sure it was properly hidden at the bottom of my satchel.

Today, I handed in my Christmas holiday homework – an essay on the women suffragettes and how they got the vote. It made me seethe how women were denied the vote until 1918, and even then only women thirty and over could vote and only if they owned a house. 'Quite right too,' Dad said.

'Dad!' I wasn't sure if he was joking. I think he was by the way he hid behind his newspaper. I just saw this little cloud of smoke drift up.

They allowed women of twenty-one to vote from 1928. That means I'm going to have to wait nine years. Anyway, I handed in my essay to Mrs Barrett, our history teacher, and perhaps my favourite teacher. She never shouts, but we all listen, and she always looks nice in colourful dresses.

So, after school, after handing in my essay, I didn't go

home but went to Tom's house instead.

Mrs Fletcher answered again. It took her a second to recognise me. 'Oh, it's Liz, isn't it? I think I owe you an apology, closing the door on you like that the other day.'

I didn't expect that and I blushed. 'It's OK.'

'I think I was in a panic. I'm sorry.'

'Tom dropped this.' I held out the penknife.

'Oh, is that his?'

'Rory found it.'

'Who?'

'Erm…'

'I don't recognise it but I can give it to Tom if you want.' My hand withdrew a fraction. She saw it and understood. 'Why don't you come in?'

I stepped into the warmth of her hallway and had to stop myself from gasping. The polished floor, the huge plant, the huge gold-framed mirror. The smell of cooking drifted through, something sweet reminding me I was hungry. I spied a room to the side and another farther on, and a wide staircase. Such a far cry from the pokey little place that I called home.

Mrs Fletcher whispered, 'Would you mind taking your shoes off?'

'What?' Why would I – oh, it was *that* sort of house. I removed my shoes. Satisfied, Mrs Fletcher sidled past me. 'Tom? Tom, you have a visitor, darling.'

Darling? She called him darling? I heard a grunt, not a welcoming one, and I glanced back at the front door.

Mrs Fletcher beckoned me into what I guessed they called their living room. 'Do come through, Liz.'

Her gentle voice drew me along. Tom was lying across a orange-coloured settee, his wrist in a plaster cast. 'Can I get you a drink, Liz? Orangeade, maybe?'

'Hmm? Oh, no, thank you.'

'I'll leave you to it, then.'

'Wow,' said Tom. 'It's you. That's a turn up for the books. Hello.'

'Hi.' I stood next to the door, taking in the space of the room, the brick fireplace, the rose-patterned curtains, the thick turquoise carpet, I could see why Mrs Fletcher wanted me to remove my shoes. And best of all, they had their very own television set. 'How are you?'

'Fine. Sit down, take the weight off.' He motioned to a matching orange armchair, big and squashy. I sunk into it.

'You've got a nice house.'

'Is it? Suppose.'

'You've got a TV.'

'Have we? Oh yeah, didn't notice that before.'

'Hey? But it's just...' Damn, I'm such an idiot. I was burning up. 'How's the arm?'

'You already asked that.'

'Sorry.'

'It's fine. Doctor reckons I'll need to keep the cast on for a month to six weeks. As you can see, no one's signed it yet.'

I opened my mouth to say I'd sign it for him. I'd be the first, but something held me back.

'Oh, I almost forgot. You dropped this.'

'That's not mine.'

'Oh. I thought...'

'It's nice though. Chuck it over.'

I passed it over, not trusting myself to throw it properly. He inspected it, weighed it in his hand, his good hand, and pulled each one of the blades out. 'Nice. Very nice.'

'You could keep it.'

'It's not mine to keep.'

'No. Sorry.'

'Suppose we'll never find whose it is so maybe I could.'

We sat in awkward silence for a while. 'I oughta go,' I said.

'How's school?'

'Oh! There's a hundred different stories about what happened to you.'

He sat up. 'Is there?'

'God, yeah.' And I told him some of the variations I'd heard doing the rounds, exaggerating here and there for effect.

Tom listened, smiling and shaking his head. 'Oh my God, that's so funny. People will believe anything. Doctor said I could go back to school next week.'

'That's good.'

'Yeah, absolutely. Guess so. So, tell me, how's that little sister of yours, the one who can take herself off to the loo by herself?'

Now I truly burned up. 'Oh God.'

He chortled. 'You're funny. You really are. My sister's also called Elizabeth. Elizabeth Mary Fletcher.'

'She has a middle name? I don't. I'm plain old Elizabeth Marsh. I wish I had a middle name. So did you enjoy the panto?'

'Yeah, it was really good.' He started impersonating the ugly sisters, remembering several of their jokes, and I found myself laughing with abandon, such was the relief.

'You have a nice house, much nicer than…' I stopped, conscious that I didn't want to appear disloyal to my father. 'And you have a TV.'

He looked at his watch. 'Oh, it's almost time for *Dixon of Dock Green*. You wanna stay and watch it?'

'Really? You wouldn't mind?'

'Absolutely.' I noticed how Tom liked saying *absolutely*. 'I wouldn't be asking if I did. Yeah, stay, if you're allowed to. Mum won't mind. She'll bring us some biscuits if we ask nicely. Would you like that?'

I nodded fearing that if I said something, I'd gush and look stupid, because right there, right then, there was nothing on earth I'd rather do than watch *Dixon of Dock Green*, whatever that was, with Tom Fletcher.

Chapter 40
January 1944

Dr Heinkel invited Hannah to sit down. She did as told, conscious of her every movement. Nurse Lowitz sat on a chair in the corner while the doctor perched himself on the side of his desk, looming above Hannah. She tried to catch Nurse Lowitz's eye, hoping to elicit a hint of sympathy. The nurse, lifting her chin, looked away. Hannah waited for what felt like an age while the doctor polished his pince-nez. He held them up to the window and squinted. Satisfied, at last, he placed them back on.

'You are a disappointment to me, Fraulein Schiffer. A huge disappointment.' He stood with a sigh as if moving caused him some effort, and went to the window. Facing out, his hands behind his back, he continued. 'You made a disgrace of yourself at the evacuees home, and for that alone, you could have ended up in a concentration camp.'

Concentration camp. The words echoed inside Hannah's head.

'But the powers that be saw something in you. They said you were still young, still naïve, and that you should be given a second chance. After all, why waste a potentially useful member of society because of one foolish mistake? You're too beautiful, too full of life, to be thrown to the wolves. So what to do with a naïve, beautiful young woman of perfect childbearing age? Why, make her bear children, of course.'

Now, he spun round. 'Think about it, Fraulein,' he said, his voice rising. 'Women your age are working fourteen hours a day in factories, or eighteen hours a day as nurses. These are loyal women, worthy women. But because of your beauty, you were spared such rigours. Despite your earlier foolhardiness, you were sent to us to live in luxury, to be pampered, to eat well, certainly better than anyone else your age in these trying times of war. We looked after you; Nurse Lowitz especially. Even when you broke the rules and went snooping around, we still looked after you.' He paused. Removing his pince-nez, he rubbed his eyes.

'Now, I heard what you said – that you couldn't do it. And you know, I understand, Hannah. I do, really.'

A little flutter of hope seeped through Hannah as she sat stock still, her fingers gripping the sides of the chair.

'In ordinary times,' said Dr Heinkel, 'you would meet a young man, fall in love, get married and *then* have babies. But in ordinary times, Hannah, we wouldn't put a rifle in a young man's hands, tell him to point it at that man over there, to fire that rifle and kill that man. And yet that's exactly what we do ask – a million times a day. Think about it, Hannah. What we're asking of you is far less drastic than what we ask a whole generation of men right now. It's my fault; I should have explained it to you before. I made an assumption, and I apologise for that. So let me tell you: this programme of producing perfect Aryan babies, the result of a union between the most perfect specimens of German manhood and the most perfect specimens of German womanhood, comes from the top, devised by Heinrich Himmler, no less, and fully endorsed by the Führer himself. You are perfect mother material, and so it is your duty to procreate for the sake of our nation and our race's survival. Do you understand now,

Hannah?'

Hannah did understand but, thinking of the vile Lieutenant Brosch and his leering face, she still couldn't bring herself to acknowledge it.

'Hannah?' said Nurse Lowitz. 'The doctor's asked you a question. Do you understand?'

'Yes,' she said as quietly as possible. 'I understand.'

Dr Heinkel returned to his position on the edge of his desk. 'Good. That is good.' He blew out his cheeks. 'You see, Himmler takes a great interest in our work. You know, for the lucky women who give birth on the seventh of October, his birthday, he will stand as the baby's godfather. Can you imagine such a thing? What an honour! But if last night's unfortunate episode were to get back to him, it wouldn't look good – for any of us.'

He rounded the table and sat down at his seat. Hannah stole a glance at Nurse Lowitz. The nurse sucked in a cheek, a hint of sympathy. Hannah knew the doctor was right – they were all part of this, all answerable to the highest of powers.

Dr Heinkel steepled his fingers and stared at her intently. 'We're going to give you one more chance, Hannah. But, hear me now, this is it. You *have* to do your duty. If you fail us this time, I'll have no option but to transfer you to a concentration camp.'

The doctor paused and Hannah realised he was expecting a response. 'Yes, sir.'

'Now, I've spoken to Lieutenant Brosch and–'

'No, please, not him,' she said more hurriedly than she meant.

Nurse Lowitz spoke. 'I don't think you're in a position to dictate your terms, young lady.'

Dr Heinkel held up his hand. 'No, let her speak. If not

Lieutenant Brosch, then who, Hannah? Who?'

'If you're really forcing me to do this, then…'

'Yes?'

'I'd like the father to be Bruno.'

'Bruno? Bruno who?'

'I don't know his surname.'

'I do,' said Nurse Lowitz. 'Bruno Spitzweg. He's the wounded army corporal who we drafted in at the last minute as a replacement.'

'Ah yes, of course.' The doctor's eyes seemed to sparkle at the thought that a solution was at hand. 'A fine-looking man. I have no problem with that. It shall be arranged.'

His relief was palpable. And so was hers, and for a moment, Hannah allowed herself a small smile.

Chapter 41

Dinner had finished, the places cleared and re-laid in preparation for breakfast the following day. Hannah sat alone, waiting. The fire, although dying, still maintained its warmth. She went to the huge window that overlooked the grounds. More snow had fallen, the branches of the trees, weighted down by snow, shone silver under the light of the moon, throwing long shadows over the white expanse of grass. The stars appeared particularly bright tonight. The world seemed so still, so quiet. Incredible to think it was at war. She heard the doors open behind her. Then silence. She sensed his presence. She held her breath a moment. She heard him approach and stand next to her. She detected a hint of alcohol. Had he been drinking in order to fortify himself?

'Hi,' he said.

'Hello.'

Neither looked at each other. Not yet. They stood together, gazing out.

'Did you walk?' she asked.

'Yes. It's, er, fairly cold out there.'

'Yes.'

'But beautiful.'

'I wish I could walk freely and feel the cold and breathe the fresh air.'

Hannah was consoled somehow that he appeared as uneasy about this as her. They both took a seat, sitting opposite each other across a round table.

'What happened to your face?'

'I fell.'

'I see.' She scraped her fingernail at a faint stain on the tablecloth. 'Bruno, can I ask you something?'

'Of course.'

'Have you… have you ever killed someone?'

His eyes flicked sideways, a slight knotting of his brow.

'I'm sorry,' she said. 'I shouldn't have asked.'

'No, it's fine.' He ran his fingers through his hair. 'I have, yes.'

'How did it…'

'Make me feel?'

'Yes.'

He didn't answer for a while, and she could see his mind reaching back, grappling with a memory that made his eyes darken. 'You don't think about it at first, too full of adrenaline, I guess. Then afterwards, you try and justify it; it's war after all. I was under orders; I had no choice. And all of that's true. You just hope that when your day comes, God will appreciate all that, take it into account. I want Him to know I'm not a bad man by nature, only by circumstance.'

'I'm sure He knows that.'

'I hope so.' He tapped his finger against the table. 'Hannah, you know why I'm here.'

'Yes, I do.'

'I'm sorry.'

'Don't be. Like you said, it's war. We're under orders; we have no choice. There're a lot worse things. I know that now.'

'It doesn't make it right though.'

'I chose you.'

He blushed. 'You did? Oh. Thank you. I'm honoured.'

She laughed. 'Bruno, you're about to have sex with me, no need to sound so polite.'

'This is ridiculous; I've honestly faced the enemy and felt less nervous than this.'

She patted his arm and realised they hadn't even touched yet.

'I need to ask you a favour,' he said. He leant forward and lowered his voice. 'Do you have a portrait of the Führer in your room?'

'Of course. I pray to him every night.'

'Do you?' She pulled a face. 'Oh, I thought you were being serious for a minute there. Anyway, when we, you know… can we turn it around so that it's facing the wall?'

She tried to laugh.

'Oh,' he said. 'Take this.' He handed her a slip of paper. 'It's got my address on it. Keep it safe. You might need it one day; you never know.'

'It'll be OK, you know.'

'Yes, I know that now.'

'Shall we go?'

'Yes.' He stood up and offered Hannah his arm.

'Why, thank you, dear sir.'

Chapter 42
May 1944

Hannah, Lena and Erika spent most of their time closeted together, day after day. They sat and sewed. They read and talked over endless cups of black tea. After four months, Lena was the only one of the three whose stomach had begun to show. Nurse Lowitz kept a vigilant eye on them, making sure they were OK, that they coped with their bouts of morning sickness. She regulated their diets and made sure they all had plenty of sleep. They each went to see Dr Heinkel on a regular basis, where he listened to their hearts, checked their blood pressure and reported back on their urine tests. The other girls had been sent home. They had four attempts at conceiving and failed. They were of no use to the doctor and the home. Thus Hannah and her two friends were now the sole occupants of the east wing. They'd heard that several new girls had recently been installed into the west wing. It'd soon be their turn.

They knew things were going badly for the nation, that Germany was being squeezed on both sides, East and West, but they'd been banned from listening to the wireless for fear the unending bad news might affect their mental health and thus endanger their precious cargoes. Lena was always the most upbeat of the three. 'I've heard that the Führer's been working on a new secret weapon, something we've never seen before. And once it's ready, it will destroy the English and those Yanks and those beastly Russians.'

'Well, I wish he'd hurry up,' said Erika. 'So what are you sewing now?'

'This? Booties, of course, look.' Lena held them up.

'Oh, they're so sweet. You are clever, Lena.'

'My mother taught me.'

They fell silent. Hannah remembered the days, so long ago, when she went shopping with her mother. From clothes shop to clothes shop, trying on dress after dress, top after top. 'Are we enjoying ourselves, darling?' her mother would ask, and Hannah would nod her head and force a smile. 'Don't tell your father,' her mother would say, and she'd buy Hannah pastries thick with cream in order to buy her silence. Father worked hard, worried about money. They could afford the occasional luxury, he'd say, but as Hannah soon found, her mother's definition of occasional differed from her husband's. But it all stopped, occasional or otherwise, that day in 1933 when men like her father, Social Democrats, feared for their lives. They never went shopping again, her mother and her. Hannah had always had a distant relationship with her mother. She didn't have any siblings, and she always half suspected that her birth was a mistake. Her mother had never loomed much in her mind but now, after all this time, Hannah longed to see her. She had so many questions to ask. Lena and Erika were no good, knowing as little as she, and Nurse Lowitz and Dr Heinkel countered her questions with evasive answers and aloofness. Her mother had experienced pregnancy, had given birth, had known its pains and joys. But her mother didn't even know her daughter was pregnant, that she was just a few months from becoming a grandmother.

And where was Bruno? None of the women had seen the men who'd impregnated them. Lena and Erika seemed not to care but Hannah did – very much. She'd only met him three times, and she found herself reliving each occasion with as much detail as possible. She remembered closing her bedroom door and, having turned the painting round, facing the man as he twisted his hat in his hands. She knew nothing about love and nor did he, she found. How strange, she thought as they stood in that bedroom, slightly cold, that this twenty-three-year-old man knew all about killing but nothing about loving. She took his hand and kissed his palm, pressed it against her cheek. 'We're here now,' she whispered. 'Just you and me. There's nothing to worry about. Just you and me, Bruno. Kiss me.'

Afterwards, as she lay on the bed, the sheet draped over her, she wondered why, physically, something was not quite right. It'd all been so brief. The Great Mystery had been unlocked, and the thing that lay behind the door was more mouse than lion. Bruno offered her a cigarette. Grateful, she took one and lit it. But whatever the experience, one thing she did know was that her feelings for Bruno had changed – no, more than changed – transformed. They sat on the bed, both smoking, unsure of what to say.

'Wasn't so bad,' she said, conscious she should have said something more encouraging.

'No.' He puffed at the dog end of his cigarette. 'Listen, Hannah…'

'You don't have to say it, Bruno.'

'No, maybe not.'

It was still only ten in the evening. They fell asleep in each other's arms. When they awoke in the early hours, they made love a second time. And this time, it was different, perhaps what it was meant to be. Afterwards, she felt warm inside and out, her heart caressed and comforted by a sense of contentment she hadn't felt for as long as she could remember.

Bruno, too, had changed as if he'd shed his outer shell and allowed her to see the real man inside. They were, for that brief amount of time, without past, without future, without war, just the two of them, joyfully suspended. She longed for Bruno to stay, to keep her warm, to keep the war at bay. Instead, he got dressed, and she watched him in silence, the sheet wrapped around her breasts. He scraped the hoarfrost from the inside of the window and looked outside into the dawn gloom.

'I'm sorry I have to leave like this. I'll come back to see you.'

She nodded her acceptance, not trusting herself enough to speak.

He leant down to kiss her, hesitated a moment, then kissed her on the cheek, on her lips.

He paused at the door and his attempt to smile came out more like a grimace. And then he was gone. Hannah stared at the door willing him to come back if only for a few seconds. She could hear creaks and bangs coming from within the house. The world was slowly waking up.

And now after four months, Bruno still hadn't been to visit her. She couldn't understand it. *I'll come back to see you.* But he hadn't come back. She'd waited for him, desperate to see him, to hold him again. He'd done his job, and the result, apparently, was floating and growing within her. Did he not want to know? Did he care so little for her? She thought they'd made a connection in their short time together, an understanding, maybe something even deeper. But the days passed, one by one, and she'd have done anything to see him striding up the drive leading to the house. Anything. She found herself lying in bed, saying his name aloud, caressing the memory of him, dying to hear the sound of his voice. She'd wake up persuading herself that she hadn't known him long enough to form such feelings for him, and she almost believed herself. But then the longing returned. But as the days turned into weeks, her feelings for him began slowly to morph into something else. Resentment. Annoyance. How dare he cast her aside so brusquely? Duty or no duty, she was still a person, a woman with emotion, a woman deserving of respect. How dare he?

Chapter 43

Bruno had been to see an army doctor. The man clapped him on the back and informed Bruno that he was fit to return to duty. Bruno tried to accept this news with good cheer. 'I know what you're thinking, Corporal. And I'll admit, you could do with another couple of weeks, just to be on the safe side. But the situation, as it is, dictates the need for urgency. We need every man we can get.'

'It's getting desperate.'

'Heck, no, I wouldn't say it was that bad. The final victory will still be ours.'

'Yes, I know that. I appreciate that. Thank you, Doctor.'

'So I'll phone through to the regiment and make an appointment for you to see the colonel tomorrow at ten. I imagine he'll have you packed off back to the front in no time. Meanwhile, I suggest, Corporal, you enjoy the rest of today off. Good day to you.'

Bruno walked home in the warm mid-morning sun in a stunned vacuum, unaware of anything around him. He knew that he had, in effect, just been handed his death certificate. His regiment had been wiped out, most of the men killed, wounded, or, worst of all, taken prisoner. The situation in Russia and indeed on every front was awful. If they sent him back to Russia, he'd never come back alive. No one believed in the final victory any more but it took a brave or foolhardy man to say so. The only true believers now were the fanatics.

Unfortunately, his brother was one of them.

He had to see Hannah. He was desperate to see her. And today was his last chance. He'd not stopped thinking of her. This very morning, before going to see the doctor, he'd been shaving in front of the bathroom mirror when he stopped, razor in hand, and said aloud, 'I think I love her.' The sound of his own voice, the words he'd said, took him by surprise. Had he really just said that out loud? He stared at his reflection, wondering if it was true – did he love her? He'd only met her three times, but he'd certainly never felt like this about anyone; no woman had ever obsessed him like this before. Except maybe the woman they called Zoya.

By the time he arrived back at the hotel, he'd been walking for over an hour. Once he'd decided he wanted to see Hannah, he bypassed home and came straight here. He knocked on the door and asked to see her. An orderly led him through a maze of ground-floor corridors and asked him to wait outside an office while he knocked and went inside. Presently, the orderly came back to him and told him to go through, and he found himself once again in front of Dr Heinkel.

'Before we proceed,' said the doctor, 'I've asked my second-in-command to join us. Do take a seat.' They waited in awkward silence. After a while the doctor, feeling perhaps he should say something, said. 'So I imagine you're chomping at the bit to get back to where the real action is, hey?'

'Yes, sir.'

'Tell me, what's it like out there, fighting the good fight in the wild frontiers of Russia?'

'It's hard, sir, but we believe in the justice of our cause, and we fight nobly, happy to die, if necessary, for the Führer.'

'Yes, Corporal, quite so and my name is Father Christmas. Ah, here she is.' A Rubenesque woman appeared, her hair tied tightly back, thin bloodless lips, dark eyes. Bruno stood. 'This is Nurse Lowitz. You would've met before?'

'Indeed,' said the nurse. 'Do sit, Corporal Spitzweg.'

'So, Corporal Spitzweg, what brings you here today?'

'I'd like to see Hannah, please.'

'Hannah Schiffer?'

'Yes.'

'No, most certainly not,' said the nurse.

The doctor's face creased as if he didn't understand. 'Why on earth would you want to see her?'

'Because... because we... you know.'

'Corporal Spitzweg.' He sighed as if what he was about to say was beneath him somehow or so obvious that it shouldn't need explaining. 'You and Fraulein Schiffer fulfilled a duty. We are grateful. However, it was a purely biological duty, not an emotional one. If your union should ultimately prove unsuccessful, then she'll be introduced to a new partner–'

'What? No, that can't be.'

'I beg your pardon? What do you think we're running here? It's not a marriage service.'

'I want to see her.'

'No.' The doctor put his hand up. 'I thought you knew how we operated here.'

'And if she has the baby?'

'Then if all is well, she'll nurse it for the first six to eight weeks of its life.'

'And then...'

'And then,' said Nurse Lowitz, 'the baby is handed over to an Aryan couple.'

Bruno tried to speak but found it hard to process this. The doctor and nurse watched him with some amusement: amused, perhaps, at the extent of his naïveté. 'Does... I mean, is Hannah happy with this?'

'Whether she's happy or not is frankly immaterial.'

'But I don't understand. What couple?'

'A *deserving* couple, a couple who haven't been blessed with a child and now wish to raise an adopted child as their own.'

Bruno shot to his feet. 'No, this can't be right. I demand to see her.'

He heard Nurse Lowitz's sharp intake of breath. 'You're in no position to demand anything.'

'Please, sit down, Corporal,' said the doctor. 'I'm sorry that you've formed some sort of attachment to Fraulein Schiffer. She is indeed a very attractive girl, can't say I blame you. And, granted, it's a risk this sort of venture entails but you're to have no more to do with her.'

'But she could be carrying my baby.'

'Enough now. Your sperm has created a baby for the Fatherland, but it is not and never will be your child in any way. You have to understand.'

'I can adopt it.'

'Don't be silly,' said the nurse.

'Are you married?'

'I want to marry Hannah.'

Nurse Lowitz failed to stifle a laugh. The doctor reddened. 'OK, I think this meeting has come to an end.'

'I'm being serious, sir–'

'You're not married, and you're not even a party member.'

'I've done more for this country than my brother and half the bloody Nazis who stay at home and shine their buttons every day.'

'Enough! How dare you speak like that. Who do you think you are?'

'We should report him, Doctor.'

'If he's not out of this door in two seconds, I will do.'

Bruno made for the door. 'I'll find her myself.'

'You'll have a hard time,' shouted the doctor.

Bruno paused at the door. 'Why's that?'

'She's done her work here. She's been moved to a different facility.' He finished the sentence with a small smile of evident satisfaction.

Bruno absorbed this, realising he'd never see her again, not today, not ever. He tried to frame a final parting, a stinging rebuke of some sort. Instead, he quietly closed the office door behind him to find the orderly waiting for him. Meekly, he followed the man back to the entrance, out of the door and outside. It'd been the second time in a matter of days he'd been dumped outside this former hotel. Last time, he'd been manhandled out. But this, this was so much worse.

Chapter 44
October 1944

Hannah never realised such pain could exist. Each contraction threatened to rip her in two, taking her breath away, causing her to sweat and scream the foulest words and not care. Nurse Lowitz took her hand. Hannah dug her nails into the nurse's skin, hoping to cause her as much pain as possible, to try and diminish her own. The midwife urged her to push, told her 'not too long now' numerous times and 'almost there, almost there'. Hannah hated her, hated Nurse Lowitz, hated everyone and everything. The pain stretched endlessly, no end in sight, nothing else, just the agony becoming the only tangible thing in her existence, threatening to engulf her entirely. Then when she tried to talk during the little islands of painlessness, it simply came out as a grunt, a guttural cavewoman. Her hair stuck to her head, her fringe to her forehead; her gown was soaked and filthy. Right now, in this pain, death seemed the better option.

'OK, this is almost it, Hannah. You're doing well.'

'Stop saying that.'

She turned her frightened gaze to Nurse Lowitz. 'I want my mother,' she growled. 'I want Bruno.'

'We don't know where your mother is; you know that, dear.'

'I want Bruno. I need him here now, right now, please.'

'Bruno has played his part, dear; it's down to us now. Keep

going, Hannah; you're so close now.'

She could sense it coming again – another contraction. She started whimpering, fearing it, fearing the fresh, frightful pain it was about to unleash. She tried to brace herself but found herself too weak to do so. The intense stretching of her flesh between her legs caused her to howl, but this time, beneath the horror of the pain, there was something else, a force of some sort, something hard, something tangible, something alive.

Chapter 45

The colonel was delighted to see Bruno, congratulating him on getting better so soon as if Bruno had willed himself better. He told Bruno he'd be sent back to the Russian front on the next transport out, Friday, two days time. He'd said it with such enthusiasm, as if parting with the best news, and waited with anticipation for Bruno to express his gratitude that his time kicking around at home was finally at an end.

Bruno told his mother. She pulled at her handkerchief like a set of worry beads and tried her best not to cry in front of him. Rather bizarrely, thought Bruno later, she seemed to castigate him for not getting himself properly wounded. If only he'd got a leg blown off, he wouldn't have to go back at all. Joseph was happy for him. 'Don't look so worried, little brother. Hitler has launched his new bombs.' Bruno had heard. Capable of flying almost six thousand kilometres per hour and causing untold damage, initial tests had proved positive. 'Just a matter of time now,' said Joseph, 'and we'll be churning them out faster than sausages.'

'How's your wife, Joe? I've yet to meet her.'

'Still in Stuttgart,' came the curt reply.

Bruno wandered into town, his collar turned up against the autumn chill. Swastikas still hung from almost every house and across the streets. But they looked tired now, limp from months of weather. He watched an army jeep speed by. Part of him was tempted to stand in its way, to try and get himself properly injured. The prospect of facing a firing squad at home seemed preferable to returning to Russia just at the point their winter was starting. He sat on a bench beneath an elm tree in the centre of the square and watched as a number of old farmers emerged from the tavern at midday, joking with one another. A couple of mothers passed, pushing their prams. He could hear them talk about the rigours of breastfeeding and forever having to wash nappies. He wondered whether Hannah had given birth to her baby, *their* baby. It must be time. The two women stopped near him and cooed into the prams, pulling faces and making comforting little noises at their babies. He wanted to join them and peer down at their babies and also make funny little noises. He wondered what sex his baby was, or would be; he wondered whether Hannah had given their baby a name. Did she know the baby would soon be taken from her? She must know, must've known from the minute she volunteered to step into that dreadful home. But these women, the two mothers here, they wouldn't give up their babies. They'd fight to the death. It was too unnatural – the idea that a woman should carry a foetus for nine months, give birth to it, nurture the child for his or her first six to eight weeks, then simply allow someone like that dreadful doctor come and *take it away* and give it to another woman. The two women kissed each other and went their separate ways, pushing their prams. And there, walking by just beyond them was someone he recognised.

He almost fell over himself in his eagerness to speak to her. 'Hello,' he called out. 'Hello there.' He couldn't remember her name. 'Hello!'

Now she stopped, realising the man yelling was in fact yelling at her. She stepped back, shielding her eyes against the sun as he approached, a worried look on her face.

'Hi, I'm sorry but…' He stopped in front of her. 'Do you recognise me?'

She shook her head, glanced round as if looking for someone who might help.

'I recognise you. You were…' He wasn't sure how to say this. No one knew what went on in that home, and he was sure she wouldn't want to talk about it. 'I was , erm… at the old hotel a few weeks back.'

Her eyes widened. 'Good for you, now if you'll excuse me.'

He didn't mean to, but in his panic, he grabbed her by the sleeve of her coat.

'Get your hands off me, else I'll scream the place down.'

'Please, I just want to ask you a question, one question, that's it.' Slow down, he thought, you're frightening her. 'Please.'

'What is it?'

'Do you know where they sent Hannah? Hannah Schiffer?'

'Hannah?' He saw her casting her mind back. 'Oh God, that little prude. She was one of the ones that got knocked up, lucky cow. They didn't send her anywhere; she's still there.'

'What? Are you sure? I mean, I was told…'

'Told what? I'm tellin' you. I went back the day before yesterday and I saw her feeding her baby for meself.'

'Feeding her baby?'

'Yeah. Now, sod off, will ya?'

'Yes, sure. Sure. Thank you.'

He watched her scurry away, swinging her empty shopping bag. They'd lied to him, of course they had. The doctor had lied. She was still there, with her baby, *their* baby. He had to see the baby, and like the two women with their prams, he'd fight to the death to see his baby.

Chapter 46

Hannah hovered in that sweet hinterland between wakefulness and sleep, little Helga nestled on her bosom, smacking her lips in that warm, drunken post-feed delirium. She'd thought of the name herself. For the first day or so, Dr Heinkel referred to her as *Fünfzig*, Fifty, the fiftieth baby born at the centre. 'How's our special little *Fünfzig* doing today?'

'I'm calling her Helga, Doctor.'

'Helga? Yes, that's nice, very nice. Helga.'

Almost two months old now, and already Hannah could hardly envisage her life before Helga. She hadn't realised until Helga had come along exactly how empty and directionless her life had been. She'd been drifting, pushed from shore to shore by circumstances beyond her control, not able to control her own destiny. She cared for no one, least of all herself. And no one cared for her. Her father, perhaps, her mother maybe a little. Still, it pained her that her parents had no idea their only daughter had brought their grandchild into the world. Her father, especially, would be delighted. But there was no way she was leaving the sanctuary of the home. Not now. She was allowed to listen to the wireless now. Dr Heinkel had authorised it, so she knew how perilous the situation was. It wasn't difficult to read between the lines. The need for sacrifice, total war, to fight to the last breath. These weren't the words of a nation on the cusp of victory; these were the last defiant utterances of a nation on its knees.

Berlin was no longer a city but a jungle of rubble. Desolation, destruction and death. As were Hamburg, Cologne, Stuttgart and so many more, towns large and small. But here, deep in the southwest of the country, nestled beneath the pine trees in an old hotel, Hannah and Helga were safe. She'd bore a child for her Führer and she was proud of that. The irony wasn't lost on her. While most people were losing their faith, she, Hannah Schiffer, had belatedly perhaps seen the light. She was going to stay in this hotel for as long as possible, their little safe haven, tucked away and forgotten. Here, mother and baby were well cared for, had a wonderful diet. The nurses came and made sure Hannah ate properly, in order for her to be able to feed Helga properly. They weighed the baby on a regular basis, took her temperature. Where else would she and the baby receive this amount of care and love?

Hannah still thought of Bruno. Nurse Lowitz had told her he'd gone back to war, such was his recovery and eagerness. And she was proud of that and had told Helga this several times. 'Your daddy is a hero, little one. And once our Führer delivers his new super weapons, we will win this war and Daddy will come back to us. And he will look at you and will love you as much as I do, and he'll never leave us again.'

She usually fell asleep dreaming of their life together, the three of them. Perhaps a little farm, a few hens and a couple of dairy cows, perhaps somewhere farther east, once the mighty German military had finally conquered the land that was by rights theirs to own. And Hannah would give Helga a little brother or sister. They'd live simply but happily. No bombs, no talk of orderly retreats, just peace and gratitude, and a future of security. She didn't want Helga growing up in a city as she had done, forever in the shadow of one's mother and her vanity. Helga was the centre of her world, not a being who existed in its periphery. This child would always know the meaning of love. After so long drifting through life and not knowing her place in the world, this tiny little bundle had come along and changed everything, simply everything, and Hannah could not have been happier.

Chapter 47
December 1944

Hannah had just fed Helga. Both mother and child lay on her bed, propped up by several pillows and savoured the post-feed glow of satisfaction. Hannah stroked Helga's downy cheek and sang her a little song. With Helga falling asleep against her breast, she moved to the window as she did every time, simply to gaze outside and watch various delivery men come and go. Helga was coming up to her seventh week birthday. In that time, Hannah had done virtually nothing, seen no one except the staff, and thought of nothing. Yet, strangely, the time had raced by. She was grateful she had so much care. Out there, in the real world, mothers with newborns still had to deal with the comings and goings of life – preparing meals for their husbands, shopping, mending clothes, washing, knitting little outfits and so on and so forth. And that was just in normal times. Now, with the war and the lack of essentials, those tasks were a hundredfold harder, the lack of food a constant worry. And it was essential that she, as a mother to a baby, ate well for both their sakes. So she was happy. She was grateful.

Dr Heinkel came to check on her occasionally. During the first week or two, he came daily, sometimes twice a day. The fact he only came to see her every three days or so was in itself a good sign. It meant he was pleased with both her and Helga's progress. They were both healthy, nothing to concern him. Nurse Lowitz, on the other hand, was forever popping in.

She'd fuss over them both, coo over little Helga and tell Hannah what a beautiful girl she had. The woman had become like a mother to her, far more caring than her own mother. Her parents had always been so loving with one another; they still doted on each other. Very sweet. But somehow, her mother's love stopped there. She couldn't imagine her mother pouring out her love for Hannah as a baby as Hannah did now for Helga.

The only time Nurse Lowitz had showed any antagonism was when Hannah had mentioned Bruno. 'Can I see Bruno?' she'd asked in all innocence.

Nurse Lowitz looked at her aghast as if Hannah had just uttered the most terrible blasphemy. 'No you may not,' she'd said, almost stamping her feet.

'But–'

'No, there's no buts about it. He's done his bit, and I've been told he's since returned to his regiment. He is no more this child's father than you are her mother. Remember what the doctor told you.'

'Duty.'

'Yes, exactly. We all do our duty; it's more imperative now than ever. So don't get all sentimental over a man who did no more than donate his sperm. That's all it was, Hannah.'

'Yes, Nurse.'

'Now, has Helga had a bath today?'

And with that, Nurse Lowitz left Hannah to her thoughts. Nurse Lowitz was right – Helga needed a bath. She liked it when Nurse Lowitz called her by her name. It made her feel special somehow, wanted, cared for. She still didn't know Nurse Lowitz's first name and she wished she did, for then she would feel as if they were on an equal footing somehow. Still, in the scheme of things, it didn't matter so much.

It was only later that the nurse's words puzzled her: *He is no more this child's father than you are her mother.* Why did she say that? How odd. Of course I'm her mother, she thought, squeezing Helga that little bit tighter. Who else could be?

'What a silly woman,' she said to Helga, jigging the baby on her knees.

There was a steady stream of delivery men coming to the home today. Food deliveries, the laundry, medical supplies, the cleaners finishing their shifts. But who was that lurking at the end of the drive, darting in and out of the trees? It looked like… but it couldn't be. She went to the window, almost pressing her face against it. He'd gone back to his regiment, Nurse Lowitz had said and Nurse Lowitz wouldn't lie. But it so looked like him. Oh, but it *was* him, she realised with a tug at her heart, it was Bruno. She rapped excitedly at the window. But he was too far away to hear. She fumbled with the window lock but couldn't do it with just the one hand. She carried Helga to her crib and placed her down. She skipped back to the window but where was he? Bruno? Where are you, Bruno? Where have you gone? She squinted, peering left and right, but he was nowhere to be seen. He'd come back for her, she was sure. But why the stealth? Where had he been all this time? No matter; the main thing was that he was here now. She went to the mirror and brushed her hair. Perhaps she should change into a prettier dress? She so wanted to look nice for him.

Chapter 48

This was it, the day Clara Spitzweg had been waiting for years. She was to be a mother. It didn't seem real. She woke early, Joseph, her husband, still asleep, and dressed in the dress she'd mentally put aside for when the day came. And today, at long last, was that day. She admired herself in the full-length bedroom mirror, caught in the early hazy sun. The dress, orangey-red with little white dots, fitted her perfectly. She shook with excitement, clenched her fists with glee. She attached a small swastika pin on the collar. Perfect. She glided down the stairs and decided to have an early breakfast. They said she'd failed in her patriotic duty to have a baby. She'd been accused of putting self before state. Not any more. She sliced up some ham, her hands shaking. To think by the time she returned home this very afternoon, she'd be a mother. She wasn't a particularly religious person, but there had been the odd occasion when she felt the need to stop and thank Him. The day the nation appointed Adolf Hitler as their chancellor, the day the war broke out and now this, the best of all.

Now, this really was it – she'd never have to have sex with her husband ever again. If truth be told, she only married him because she needed a child. She tolerated the sex for so long because she had to. Now, with this new solution, there'd be no more waiting for the right time to have sex in order to conceive and trying to eat the right foods. No more listening to the wives of her husband's stupid acquaintances who said you had to have sex in *this* position or *that* position if you wanted to get pregnant. No more waiting, praying that her period wouldn't come, fearful every time she went to the toilet. No more sitting on the toilet bowl watching the swirl of blood in the water beneath her and despairing that it would ever happen. No more visiting that stupid Dr Weber and taking his idiotic advice and listening to his nonsensical reasons why his advice hadn't worked. No more listening to his crackpot theories as to why she and Joseph couldn't get pregnant. They'd smoked too much, drank too much, didn't do enough exercise.

But she'd forever be grateful to Dr Weber for putting her in contact with Dr Heinkel. She and Joseph went to see this Dr Heinkel in his office at the back of what was the Hotel Cavalier. She remembered her heart speeding up on hearing his opening words: 'I think I can offer you both a solution.'

She laughed on remembering Joseph's immediate response on hearing the doctor's proposal. 'You've got to be bloody joking. Another woman's child? What sort of solution is that?'

'Not so hasty, Herr Spitzweg, please. Let me explain. It's a programme that this and many other centres are actively engaged in. We have Himmler, no less, to thank. We call it *Lebensborn*, the Spring of Life. The idea is that young women procreate with virile young men of pure Aryan blood and give birth to perfect Aryan babies. But the women are single and too young to be trusted to bring the children up in the way we regard as proper. Therefore, the babies are donated to politically minded devotees of the party, couples like your good selves. Himmler sees it as a way of safeguarding our future, ensuring that we create a band of racially perfect supermen and women who will one day lead this nation, taking over when the time is right. It is the duty of these young women and men to create these babies and then the duty of patriotic couples to bring them up to be the leaders of tomorrow.'

Once Joseph understood, he shook his head in wonderment, and Clara could see him warming to the idea. And Clara loved the idea too. No more pointless sex, not having to subject her body to the demands of pregnancy, assuming she ever got pregnant and now that she was nearing thirty, she feared for the worse. And no more having to face people's silent criticism. It wouldn't matter so much if they were ordinary citizens, but Joseph was the mayor. People expected more of him, of them as a couple.

'Do you have a preference which sex you want?'

'A girl,' said Joseph firmly.

Dr Heinkel raised his eyebrows. Clara guessed most self-respecting Nazis would prefer a boy but she knew why. As a boy himself, her husband had had to be the babysitter to his younger brother, Bruno. Many a time he wanted to go out and play with his own friends but no, his mother insisted he stay and look after Bruno. He'd always wanted a girl. Herself, she didn't mind. Well, she did mind – she wanted a boy but as her husband took no notice of her opinion, a girl it would have to be. Frankly, she'd be happy, more than happy, either way.

'Well then,' said the doctor. 'There are various forms to be filled in. We'd need to double check your ancestry—'

'You what? My ancestry? I'm the bloody mayor of this town; I am one hundred per cent Aryan, thank you very much. You do not need to check me out on my ancestry. Nor my wife, I can guarantee. Do you think I look like the sort of man who'd marry a Gypsy or… or something?'

The doctor hesitated. 'Maybe, but…' He removed his

pince-nez. 'Actually, you're right. My apologies. We'll take your ancestry as a given.'

Joseph nodded in a *should think so too* gesture.

'How long will it take, this adoption process?' asked Clara, pleased at asking a question of her own.

'Not too long. A week or so to identify the right mother, and we process new girls at quite a regular pace. Then, of course, however long it takes for her to get pregnant. Not that it should take too long. The boys we recruit are like walking stud horses.'

Clara sensed her husband bristle at that, the unintended comparison to his own virility, or lack of it.

'Plus, naturally, the term of pregnancy. Then it's official policy that the girls should breastfeed their newborns for the first few weeks.'

'Why?'

'We feel the mother's own milk gives the infant all the necessary nutrients so important in those first few vital weeks. Again, it is official policy that you should never meet either the biological mother or father to the child we give you. There's nothing I can do about that.'

'Fine by me,' said Joseph. 'Wouldn't want to anyway.'

Clara agreed with that. She couldn't bear the thought of meeting the real mother.

'So,' said Joseph, 'all told, we're talking about a year.'

'God willing, yes.'

'God willing,' repeated Clara.

And indeed, that was all a year ago. Ten days later, Dr Heinkel telephoned to inform Clara that they had found a perfect young girl willing to bear her a child and a young man from the SS prepared to impregnate her. Clara replaced the receiver and told herself she was excited. But the news brought it home that there was a woman nearby capable of doing what she had always failed to do, to do the one natural thing on this earth that she, as a woman, was meant to do. Joseph, when he came home, took the news in his stride as if she'd just told him she'd managed to procure a leg of lamb for dinner.

Not long after, she'd received a second call from Dr Heinkel. The chosen girl was pregnant on the first time of asking. Now, all she had to do was wait – and pretend. She had to pretend to be pregnant, wearing flowing, billowing dresses, and, at the point she should have been showing, disappearing. She went to her parents' place in Stuttgart, and was happy to do so, happy to escape her husband and his cloying mother

And now, today, finally, the wait and the pretending were over.

Chapter 49

Bruno lurked between the trees. He had to find Hannah, had to see his baby. In two days time he'd be on a train heading back to the Russian front. This was his last chance. He simply had to see them both.

He watched as various delivery people came and went. Some went straight to the main entrance at the front but a few, he noticed, went round the side of the building. And that, he decided, was his best option. Pulling down his brimmed hat, he jogged along the drive. He thought he could see figures inside the hallway. He picked up speed and made it to the side just as a couple of nurses came out. He followed the path. The path took him around the side and to the back of the hotel where he saw a number of wooden cubicles. These, he realised, housed all the huge bins, from which came an obnoxious smell of rotting food. He heard a noise, a shuffle, and pinned himself against a wall. It was just a cat. It stopped and considered him for a moment as if knowing this strange man was not supposed to be there. A woman in a brown overall appeared, carrying an empty wicker basket. The cat slunk away. The woman shouted something over her shoulder and laughed at the response. Bruno waited for her to pass then approached one of several back doors. The first one was wide open and led to the kitchens. Various staff in white overalls were inside, shouting good-naturedly at each other. He darted past. The second door with a small *Verboten* poster was locked but not the third one. It led straight into a large, stale-smelling storage room of some sort. A pile of chairs had been stacked up to one side, next to a table upside down on top of another, its four legs pointing upwards. Bruno crept through, his shoes crunching on shards of a broken glass. Easing the far door open, he stepped out into a corridor. Looking down towards the left, he could see the beginning of a staircase, not the grand main staircase, but a smaller one for the staff.

Bruno stopped at the bottom of the staircase. The enormity of what he was about to do hit him. He knew he'd never wanted anything in his life as much as he did right at this moment – the desire to see his child was, he realised, consuming him. Yes, he hated the way the child was conceived, hated the way he and Hannah had been manipulated and coerced. But it had happened, and in the process he'd been introduced to the most gorgeous, kindest woman he'd ever met and she had borne him his child. The staff here had stopped him before; they weren't going to stop him this time.

*

Joseph had told Clara her orangey-red dress with little white dots was inappropriate for what they were about to do. And he liked her wide-brimmed summer hat even less. He'd been waiting downstairs for her when she descended the stairs as if floating. 'We're going to adopt a baby,' he said. 'Not going to a dance. Now, go change into something less…'

'Yes, Joseph? Less what?'

'Showy.'

Clara was not going to let her husband spoil the day she'd waited so long for. This was her day, her special day. 'No, I shall not go change.'

He huffed but made no further attempt. Joseph wore his full mayoral uniform with its golden epaulettes, the gold leaf collar, his billowy jodhpurs, his peaked hat with gold braiding and the Nazi eagle. They got into their new car, an Opel Kadett. It may have been new but Clara knew Joseph hated it. Their previous car, and Joseph's most treasured possession, an Opel Admiral, was black with white-walled tyres. But it had been requisitioned by someone farther up the food chain, a mayor in a nearby and much bigger town. Now saddled with this tiny two-door thing, it rankled Joseph every time he had to drive it. He lit a cigarette and passed it to her, then lit his own. He turned the ignition but didn't drive. 'So,' he said after a while, 'you're sure about this?

'Yes, of course. Why aren't you?'

'Yeah, absolutely. It's just now that the moment's come, it all feels a little strange.'

'It's our patriotic duty, remember? Christ, Joseph, you've spent the last ten years telling people to do their *patriotic duty*. I reckon it's probably our turn now.'

He took a last drag of his cigarette then threw it out of the window. He took off the handbrake and they were off.

Her husband may have been having second thoughts but not her, not Clara. She'd never been so sure of anything in her life. She'd been brought up an only child and had had a lonely childhood. She had always found making friends difficult. She was considered 'snooty' or affected or aloof, any number of foul words. But it was her lack of self-confidence that made her appear remote, and the apparent aloofness that exacerbated the situation. Two years back, she met Joseph. The very things that seem to put other people off appealed to him. Neither ever admitted they were lonely, but he was just as lonely as she. His uniform, which gave him such confidence and kudos, alienated people. She understood that. How can you trust a man who can have you carted off to a concentration camp with the click of his fingers? They married. Not out of love. But because they hoped life would be easier. It was. And she married because she hoped for the one person who could, after all these years, show her a degree of affection – a baby.

Joseph drove slowly. Clara suspected he'd happily drive the rest of his life if it meant not having to arrive. But it wasn't a long drive and soon the old hotel came into view. The clouds parted, and Clara had to bite on her knuckle to try to contain her excitement.

*

Hannah didn't know what to do, whether to go in search of Bruno or stay put in the hope that he remembered where her room was. She looked at Helga fast asleep in her crib, a thumb jammed into her mouth, her head turned to one side. She couldn't bring herself to pick her up and possibly wake her. So she remained, pacing the length of her room, waiting, waiting. She heard footsteps out on the landing, but it wasn't Bruno. She knew those footsteps, and there were others too. Nurse Lowitz knocked on her door and entered without waiting for a response.

Hannah would have greeted her with a hello or a Heil Hitler but the greeting died on her lips. They crowded into her room, Nurse Lowitz, Dr Heinkel and, behind them, two of the male orderlies, all of them wearing their white cloaks. One of the doctor's trouser legs had caught in his sock. The silence stretched. Something was wrong. Hannah could sense it vibrating through the air. The hard look in Nurse Lowitz's and the doctor's eyes. Had they found Bruno?

Her fingers twitched. She scratched at them. 'Is there s-something wrong?' she asked.

The doctor nodded at Nurse Lowitz. The nurse stepped over to the crib and looked down at Helga. Normally, whenever she did this, she'd smile and say something soothing. But her face remained stony. Some deep instinct told Hannah what was happening. It took a nanosecond for the frightening reality to hit. She knew. The nurse leant down, her arms reaching down. Hannah noticed a chain escape her blouse and fall from her neck, dangling, the gold catching the glint of sunlight. Hannah, her every nerve end on fire, made to stop her but she couldn't move as if being sucked back into a whirlpool. Hands were holding her back, two, three pairs of hands gripping her arms, pulling them back. Hannah screamed. 'Noooo.' Nurse Lowitz scooped the baby, the movement happening both quickly and, at the same time, as if it were taking place in slow motion. The baby cried, no gentle mewl this, but a full-lunged bellow. Nurse Lowitz held her tightly against her chest. Hannah struggled, tried biting at the hands holding her back. The veins in her neck bulged as she screamed for her baby, screamed as she'd never heard anyone scream before. She kicked at the doctor and the two orderlies. Her slippers flew off. Her vision blurred as she saw the hazy figure of the nurse carry Helga away, out of the room. 'No, no, noooo.' Mucus poured down from her nose, over her mouth. The sharp needle pricked her in her upper arm. She saw the needle in the doctor's hand. How long did she have before it took effect, before she fell asleep? Already, she sensed herself going down, her strength deserting her. Her head weighed heavily, too much for her neck to hold up. Her legs gave way as if made from straw. The orderlies guided her to her bed. She noticed the crack in one of the orderly's watch face. 'No,

233

no.' She wasn't screaming any more, her throat on fire, red raw, her voice rapidly fading. She could hear the doctor's soothing voice as if it were a thousand miles away. She was dying, she was convinced, slipping away from this world to the next. They'd taken her baby and now they were murdering her. She didn't care. It didn't matter any more. They could do what they liked with her, she didn't care.

*

Clara rose to her feet when she heard a firm set of footsteps approaching the doctor's office. 'I think this is it,' she said, her eyes focused on the door. Joseph stood also, his chin high, his hands held in front of him.

Yes, she thought, this was definitely it, the moment had come. The door opened and in came Nurse Lowitz carrying a little bundle wrapped in a thick blanket. 'Frau Spitzweg, Herr Spitzweg,' she said, a large smile on her face. 'Please say hello to your daughter.' She turned the bundle around.

Clara's hand went to her mouth. She let out a little shriek before the tears started rolling down her cheeks. 'Can I... can I hold her?'

'Of course,' said the nurse. 'She's *your* child now.' The nurse passed the baby to Clara. Clara took her, fearing she might drop her. She looked into the baby's scrunched-up eyes, her face red as could be, and for the first time in her life she knew the meaning of love. 'Oh my God, she's so... so perfect. Look, Joseph, look.'

Joseph nodded, unable to speak. She could see that he, too, was overwhelmed by it all.

'Why don't you both sit down,' said the nurse. 'It's too big a moment to be on your feet,'

'Oh, look at her.' Clara couldn't take her eyes from the

baby, transfixed by the little miracle in her arms. 'She's got your eyes, Joseph.'

Joseph opened his mouth but, evidently thinking better of it, maintained his silence.

Clara was vaguely aware of another presence in the room. She looked up to find Dr Heinkel beaming down at her. 'All in good order, I hope?'

'Oh, yes, Doctor. She's simply perfect.'

'Isn't she just?' The doctor sat down at his desk and slid a piece of card across his desk. 'If I could ask you both to sign this certificate, and then it's all official.'

Joseph signed the certificate. Clara signed. The doctor dated it – 1 December 1944.

'What does the number fifty mean?' asked Joseph.

'Your baby is the fiftieth to be adopted from our centre. We're very proud to have reached this milestone.'

'And what's her name?'

'Her name? Why, that's for you to decide. Many parents like to call the girls Gudrun, after Himmler's daughter, but there's no obligation. Or you could name her after your mother, Herr Spitzweg, or yours, Frau Spitzweg?'

But Clara was no longer listening. The baby was wide awake now. Her eyes swept left to right then looked up and seemed momentarily surprised at seeing Clara grinning down at her. Then, a moment later, she began to cry. 'Oh dear, oh dear,' said Clara, jiggling the baby up and down.

'Not so rigorous, Fraulein,' said Nurse Lowitz.

'Don't tell me what to do,' snapped Clara. The baby's crying intensified, the noise jabbing in her brain like a stick. 'Why won't she stop?'

'She's hungry,' said the doctor. 'We've prepared some formula made from evaporated milk for you. Nurse Lowitz, would you mind.'

Clara took the proffered bottle and gently eased the teat into the baby's mouth. But the baby shook the head from side to side, refusing to take the bottle. 'Oh, for goodness' sake,' said Clara. She tried again, conscious of how flustered she was, the colour rising in her cheeks.

'Don't worry,' said Nurse Lowitz. 'She'll calm down soon enough.'

'She'd better,' said Clara. 'Here, Joseph, you take her a while.'

*

Bruno had heard the screaming. It stopped him in his tracks. He imagined everyone within a five-mile radius would have heard it. He'd reached the top floor but it was coming from the floor below. Quickly, he ran back down the stairs. Glancing left and right along the corridor, he saw the retreating figure of Nurse Lowitz, the nurse he'd met, the one who, along with the doctor, had lied about Hannah's whereabouts. He could still hear the woman crying, a cry the like he hadn't heard since Russia, a cry streaked with raw emotion, with primeval desperation. He had to stop and catch his breath, propped up against the corridor wall as he tried to bat away the flashes of memory that came unbidden to his mind. He had to keep going. He followed the cry until he reached a door, slightly ajar.

It was her. She was lying on the bed, a man on either side. One was dabbing a solution to her arm with a pad of cotton. They saw him. One of them jumped up. 'Who the hell are you?'

'Dr Klum,' he said, the first name to come to mind. 'Visiting to see how you do things here.'

236

'Apologies, sir, Heil Hitler.'

'Heil Hitler. So this patient's just given up her baby, I presume?'

'Sir. She took it badly. The sedative's just kicking in.'

'Dr Heinkel's got an issue downstairs. Told me to order you back to his office.'

The two men looked at each other.

'Well, go on, then. Don't keep him waiting.'

'Yes, sir.'

He closed the door behind them. He rushed to Hannah's side. 'Hannah, Hannah? Can you hear me.'

She looked at him, her eyes wild like a tigress but now glazing over. She saw him, recognised him. 'They took her away, Bruno.' Her words were so slurred he had difficulty making them out. 'They took our baby away. Took her away, took her…'

'Where did they take her, Hannah? Hannah, where did they…' It was no use; the sedative had kicked in.

He heard the sound of a car revving up outside. Something made him leave Hannah's side and check. He saw a car, a small Opel, its driver's door open, Dr Heinkel standing at the door talking to the driver. Nurse Lowitz appeared carrying a small blanket, the sort you'd give a baby? Bruno had never run so fast. He took the stairs two at a time, jumping the last few. He pounded across the landing to the next set of stairs. He charged down, pushing an orderly out of the way, jumped again the last three steps. Ground floor. He made for the main entrance, zigzagging around a couple of nurses. He raced through the foyer and outside only to see the car reaching the end of the drive, Dr Heinkel and Nurse Lowitz watching the car depart as if they were saying goodbye to much-loved relatives. He sprinted past them. The car was still progressing slowly as it crunched over the gravelled drive. He heard the doctor and nurse shouting at him, telling him to stop. He kept going, pushing himself on, gaining on the car. He could see the silhouettes of the couple, the man, driving, wearing a peaked hat, the woman wearing a fashionable hat. The car stopped at the end of the drive, its indicator flashing right. The driver checked left, right, left, right. Bruno screamed at them to stop. He was so close now, so close to be within almost touching distance. The road was clear. The car eased out to the right. For a moment, he saw the car mirror, saw the gold braiding on the driver's hat. But a cloud of exhaust fumes obscured his view. Bruno lost his footing, his ankle buckling beneath him. He shrieked as he crashed to the ground in a heap. The car pulled away, its occupants oblivious to him.

The sudden torrent of tears clouded his vision. He clasped his hands around his ankle, but it was the ripping pain in his heart that made him scream to the heavens. He heard footsteps running up towards him. He glanced back. It was the two orderlies he saw in Hannah's room. Beyond them, he could make out the doctor and the nurse shouting, their arms gesticulating. He knew what was coming next. He curled up and braced himself as the first boot smashed into his stomach.

PART THREE

Chapter 50
January 2002

I can't quite believe this is happening. I am on an aeroplane flying to Germany, sitting next to Tom Fletcher. A month ago Tom had been part of my childhood as lost to me as skipping ropes or pogo sticks. Yet now he is sitting next to me reading a novel by Anthony Trollope and working his way through a packet of dry roasted peanuts. I have to pinch myself, for I have reclaimed a small part of my past, and now he's here, helping me reclaim the rest of it. I'm a little embarrassed reading my Bridget Jones. Tom, I have come to realise, is a cultured, intelligent man. He's travelled half the world, experienced the sort of things I've only ever seen on TV documentaries, quotes Shakespeare and knows his Monet from his Manet. I think of my Barry and I can't help but chuckle. Barry hasn't read a novel since Harold Robbins, and he only read that for the rude bits, and wouldn't know a work of art if it bit him on the bottom. Tom isn't short of a bob or two either. One can tell by the way he dresses, the watch he wears, his beautiful shoes. But for his culture and his wealth, he is still a humble man, which, frankly, I find most attractive.

Once my workplace had OK'd me taking leave at such short notice, I felt obliged somehow to tell Barry and Tessa where I was going. I still can't explain why. If Barry decided to bugger off for a couple of days, would he tell me and vaguely hope to receive my blessing? Of course not, but I did. First, I rang Tessa. Our conversation was a two-way mirror of awkwardness and guilt. We were both hiding the fact we had a 'Tom' in our lives. 'So is he your boyfriend, this Tom?' I ask.

'No,' came the indignant reply. 'Actually, yes. I don't know. It doesn't work like that, Mum.'

'Well, surely he is or he isn't.'

'Not necessarily; that's so old fashioned, Mum, this idea of ownership.'

I try to silence my groan. 'But is he treating you nicely?'

'Mum, can we change the record?'

'I'm just concerned for you, darling.'

'Well, let's just say I'm not using you and Dad as role models.'

'Tessa!'

'I'm sorry, I didn't mean that but…'

'I know, darling. It's not been easy on you.'

'Bloody right it hasn't, Mum. You know, when you're a kid, you never think your mum and dad might split up one day. You just think it's Mum and Dad; they're always gonna be there.'

'I know that feeling, Tess. I'm sorry.'

'I know it wasn't your fault, Mum. Anyway, how are you?'

'Me? Hmm, I'm well, thanks. In fact, I'm going to Germany for a couple of days,' I said breezily.

'What for?' Just two words, but loaded with so much negativity.

Barry said exactly the same. Neither said, 'Oh, how nice' or 'Lucky you.'

'What, by yourself?' they both asked as if I was breaking some law.

I could have lied at this point, almost did, but why should I, damn it. 'No, I'm going with a friend, actually,' I said, my voice an octave higher than normal.

Of course, they both assumed my friend was female. When I nonchalantly added, 'His name is Tom,' I got exactly what I expected. They would have been less outraged if I'd told them I'd been arrested for exposing myself in the park.

'What will Dad say?' asked Tessa.

'Frankly, it's none of his business,' I replied.

'What will Tessa say?' asked Barry. *Ditto.*

'You can't be serious,' said Barry.

'Why not?'

'Because… because it's not right, that's why.'

And you running off with Shelley and breaking my heart and messing me up and destroying everything I'd worked towards, that was *right*, was it, you hypocritical bastard?

'You OK, Liz?' asks Tom.

'Oh yes, fine, thank you. Just something I forgot to do at work.' I fan myself with the aeroplane's in-flight magazine. 'How's the book?'

'Very good. Have you ever read Trollope?'

'Yes, oh yes. I loved *Mayor of Casterbridge*.'

'Wasn't that Hardy?'

'Yes. Absolutely. Hardy. As in Laurel and.'

He laughs. 'Oh, Liz, you haven't changed one bit.'

*

We catch a taxi from the airport to our hotel in Weinberg, a small town in Baden-Württemberg. Tom pays.

Once Tom had committed himself to joining me on my "little jaunt", as Barry called it, he insisted on booking the hotel. I'd researched a budget hotel on the internet and had been on the point of booking two rooms when Tom took over. So now I find myself in the foyer of Hotel Mirabell, quite the plushest hotel, with uniformed staff at the reception, shag-pile carpets, chandeliers and bellboys. Tom speaks to the receptionist in German; he speaks back to Tom in English. We're shown to our adjacent rooms, and I collapse on the huge, squashy bed.

As we drove up in the taxi, Tom said he would pay for the hotel, the food, everything. 'I'll put it against my expenses,' he said, tapping his nose. I wanted to refuse and insist on paying my share, but he had, in effect, priced me out of my range. There was no way I could afford a hotel like this, so I had no choice but to humbly accept and offer my gratitude.

An hour later, we meet downstairs for dinner. It's all so lovely and classy and formal. I don't want this; it's too much. Still, Tom has a way about him that makes everything seem natural and easy. The menu is written in German, so Tom has to translate for me. But that's OK. Thank God he's here. I can't help but think of Barry. We'd never come to a place like this, even at home. Barry would be too intimidated. Tom and I spend much of the evening talking again about our shared past.

We're waiting for our desserts when he asks, 'So what do you hope to find out from tomorrow, Liz?'

I lean back and try to think; it's such a big question. 'I want to know what my mother was doing at the end of the war. I want to know how she met my father, both my biological one and my *real* dad.'

'Your father never told you?'

I sigh. 'He would have told me everything, I know because he once hinted I was almost ready. But then…'

'Yes.'

'So I used to ask my mother. How did you end up in England? What was your life like in Germany? What were my

German grandparents like? What was my *German* father like? She refused point blank to say anything. I had a right to know, still do, but she refused. After she moved to the care home, I went through all her things and that small piece of card was the only thing I found. Why did she keep that one thing? Was it an oversight or is it important somehow? Tom, if this leads to nothing, I'll be so embarrassed–'

'No, don't be, please don't be. It's just so wonderful to see you again. After we left for Kent, I missed you so much.'

'I've still got your letters, all three of them.'

'Yes, well.'

'I know. It was never going to be the same.'

'No. But you know, I never forgot you. I often used to wonder how you were getting on, if you were happy, whether you settled down.'

'Nor me, Tom. I never forgot you either.'

Two hours later, we retire for the night. We catch the lift up to the fourth floor and head for our respective rooms. We stand outside our doors, fumbling with our keys when the words, unplanned, unrehearsed, tumble out of me. 'Do you want to come in for a nightcap?'

'Erm…' In those couple of seconds, my heart somersaults several times; I'm desperate for Tom to say yes, at the same time knowing I don't want him to, not yet, not yet. 'Do you mind if I don't?'

'No, no, that's fine.'

'It's been a long day and–'

'Yes, I agree. I know. It's fine.'

'Really?'

'Really.'

He nods. 'Sleep well, then, Liz.'

'And you, Tom, and you.'

Chapter 51

We all want to know where we come from, don't we? It's an intrinsic part of us. For those who know where they're from, whose lives are built on solid foundations, it's not something to think about. But for those of us who have lived all their lives with a sense of... *unknowing*, it magnifies as one gets older. You reach a point when you know something is missing, and you become obsessed with that missing piece of the jigsaw. It's as if one needs a complete sense of one's past before you can move forward. Perhaps, if Barry hadn't left me, perhaps, if Tessa hadn't left home, I might not have felt this way. I found myself increasingly drawn to my past, and the questions that had always remained unanswered. Today I woke up in this huge bed, in this plush hotel room, and I knew I was on the cusp of unlocking the secrets of my past. All the roads of my life had led me to this single point, my moment of reckoning. For good or ill, I had to know the truth of who I was.

Tom has asked reception about the address on my mother's certificate, the Hotel Cavalier. It's out of town, they say, about fifteen minutes by car. They book him a taxi. And now we sit in the taxi.

'How you feeling, Liz?' Tom asks as the car leaves the grounds of Hotel Mirabell.

I think for a few moments before I answer. 'I feel as if I'm on the edge of a volcano and if I'm not careful, I might fall over.'

He squeezes my hand, and I'm so pleased that Tom, of all people, is here with me. Yet, part of me wishes Barry, my husband, was here with me. Yes, Barry lacks Tom's sophistication, but he is still, technically, my husband, and it surprises me how much I miss him.

The town of Weinberg is achingly beautiful despite the steady drizzle. The car rattles through the cobblestone alleyways, and it's as if we've been transported back to some sort of medieval idyll. The timbered houses with gabled roofs and shuttered windows, painted in pastel colours, are breathtaking. Every window, it seems, sports a display of flowers. The taxi cruises along a winding road running parallel to a wide river, and up upon a hill on the other side, we see a castle with tall turrets that looks as if it belongs in a fairy tale. Leaving the town, we pass through an expanse of pine forests and a lake of shimmering beauty. I am privileged to experience such beauty. Tom smiles at me, and I feel like such an innocent.

The car draws up at Hotel Cavalier, a stunning sandstone building with low sloping roofs of red tiles and large windows. Tom asks the taxi driver to wait.

'This is it,' says Tom.

'Yes.' I need to control my quaking emotions.

We walk quickly across the driveway wanting to get out of the rain; it's too short a walk to bother with our umbrellas, which the hotel reception kindly lent us for the day. We enter the cool interior, a vast expanse of polished floors and potted plants. Tom approaches reception where a man and a woman stand ready to help. I hold back and admire the statues of Venus-like women, the arched wall, the huge lights. Is this really the address on that certificate in my pocket? Tom and I know we cannot show this slip of paper to anyone here, not with the swastika so prominent. We need to tread carefully. There is something strange about this place; I can sense it. It's vast yet soulless. It has the same plushness as the hotel we're staying in, the same sense of luxury, but it's empty somehow, devoid of any heart. There is a melancholy that seems to seep from its walls, its very fabric. I don't like it, and I have to resist the urge to leave.

Tom speaks to a ghoul-like man at reception. '*Guten tag.* Sorry, but do you speak English? My friend here doesn't speak German.'

'Yes, sir,' says the man in English. 'I am happy to speak English. How can I help?'

'We're from England and…' Tom hesitates. I know why; we are already entering delicate territory.

I step forward. 'I'm trying to trace my family history. I'm hoping you can help. My… my mother was German, *is* German, and I think she may have stayed here during the war.'

'The war?' His face reddens a little.

'Yes.' I stop myself from apologising.

'I wouldn't know anything about that.' I can see him stiffening a little. 'If you could excuse me a minute…'

He disappears. The female receptionist throws me a sympathetic look and I'm grateful for it. 'Are you from England?' she asks.

'Yes. Your town here, it's beautiful.'

'Thank you. We like it. We have many football fans here. They are not happy when your England beat us.'

'Yes. My husband was very happy.'

'Yes, I can imagine; it is not often Germany lose by so much.'

The woman turns her attention back to her work, tapping on her computer keyboard. Tom has drifted back a little and is flipping through a newspaper. I think of home, not wanting to be here, wishing I were back at home, not the lonesome home as I now know it but the happy home of yesteryear. It's like a memory that belongs to someone else.

The ghoul-like receptionist returns at last. Tom leaves his newspaper on a table. I am already at the desk but the receptionist speaks to Tom in German. I watch as Tom nods. He thanks the man. Turning to me, he says, 'It appears no one here knows anything. But he's given us an address of the town's local history archive. Apparently, it's just a block away from our hotel, so that's where we need to go.'

'OK.' I look around me. Part of me is happy to leave this cavernous place and as quickly as possible, but part of me would like to stay and explore, to look around and view its rooms, its corridors. It's all a little odd, this desire to leave yet the need to know it better, to unearth its secrets.

'Liz? Liz, shall we go?'

'Tom?'

'Yes?'

'Don't leave me.'

He takes my hand. 'It's OK, Liz, I'm here; I won't let you go.'

I fight back the tears. 'You promise?'

His hand squeezes mine. 'I promise,' he says.

And I believe him; Tom won't let me down; he's come this far with me, followed me all this way on no more than a whim; Tom won't let me down.

Chapter 52

The town's archive shares a red-bricked municipal building with the library. It's barely a five-minute walk from our hotel and is perhaps the only ugly building in the whole town. The fresh-faced library assistant phones through to the archive department then asks us to follow her. We take the lift and go down one floor where she deposits Tom and me at a desk. We thank her and wait. The room is small; the walls are lined with shelves full of old-looking books and box files, hundreds of them. On one wall, above the shelves, is a framed rectangular medieval map of the town, dated, according to the decorative legend, 1679. Behind the high counter is a catalogue drawer. I pick up a photo album off the counter and flip through pages of postcards, mostly black and white. After a while, a middle-aged man with a goatee appears, reading a sheet of paper. He looks surprised to see us. '*Ja? Kann ich helfen?*' His tone is far from helpful.

Tom speaks to him in German. The man's expression gives nothing away. While Tom is explaining, a second man appears, this one much younger, a fair-haired man with large, round spectacles. His name, according to his name badge, is F Schmidt.

Tom turns to me. 'Show him your certificate, Liz.'

I am strangely reluctant to do so but I've come this far. And so I pass the card to the archivist. He frowns on seeing the swastika. Mr Schmidt peers over his boss's shoulder.

The archivist looks up at me. 'Where did you find this?' he asks in English.

I wilt a little at his harsh tone. 'I found it among my mother's possessions. She's German.'

'Is she alive?'

'What difference does that make?' says Tom.

'She is still alive, yes,' I say.

'In that case, I suggest you ask her.'

The man named Schmidt slinks away. The archivist passes me back the card.

'Can't you help at all?'

'It's just a random number, a date and the address of the Hotel Cavalier, which your husband says you've already visited. No, I can't help.'

'Hang on,' says Tom. 'You must know what that hotel was used for during the war.'

'Yes, it was used as a nursing home for wounded soldiers. If you want to know more, I suggest you go back there and speak to someone more senior, perhaps.'

'Do you have any photos of that time?' I ask.

'Yes. They are in our files. If you like to see them, you can make an appointment. We have space on Friday afternoon, after lunch.'

I look around me. There isn't another soul here, and by Friday I'd be back home. 'It doesn't matter.'

The man looks at us. Deciding we're not going to say anything else, he bows his head and says good day.

'That's us dismissed,' says Tom as we head back up the lift.

'I'm sorry, Tom. I could've just phoned and been told that.'

'No, you needed to see what this hotel looks like for

yourself. I can understand.'

The lift doors open. We step inside the library and hover near the automatic doors. 'What do we do now?'

'You know, it might not be a bad idea and do what he suggests. We just talked to the first person we saw at the hotel. We should try harder.'

The automatic doors whoosh open, and a woman walks in followed by about ten small, preschool-aged children walking in pairs and holding hands. Another two women bring up the rear. The children's excitable chatter lightens the atmosphere. The teachers shush them and say good morning to us. As they pass, I see the archivist leave the building, his collar turned up. I nudge Tom in the arm. Tom shakes his head. We're about to leave when I realise I've left my umbrella downstairs in the archive. 'Wouldn't do to lose the hotel's umbrella,' I say.

'I'll wait here,' says Tom.

I rush back down the stairs. At least I won't have to face the grumpy archivist. Instead, I see his fair-haired assistant, Mr F Schmidt. 'You forgot your umbrella,' he says in English, handing it over the counter to me.

I thank him.

'I'm sorry about my boss,' he says. 'He's very good at his job but not when it comes to anything to do with the war or the Nazis. Can I see that card of yours?'

I pass it to him.

He scrutinises it. 'Can I take a photocopy of this?'

'Sure.'

A minute later he returns and hands me back my card. 'Don't tell my boss, but I'll see what I can find. Can you write your mobile number here? And your name.'

'Yes, of course. Thank you for this.'

'I can't promise I'll find anything but I try for you.'

I return upstairs, and the sound of small children singing the German equivalent of 'The Wheels on the Bus' fills the library. I find Tom flipping through a book on graphic design, tapping his foot and humming along. It stops me short; it is such an endearing image, and I adore him for it.

Chapter 53

Tom and I spend the rest of the morning exploring the town, looking in its many shops and having a *kartoffelsalat*, a German potato salad, for lunch. I insist on paying. It'll probably be the only thing I can afford. After lunch, we have a look in the museum of ceramics, a local speciality, apparently. I check my phone on a regular basis, desperate to hear from Mr Schmidt, the archivist's assistant. We peer at all the exhibits in glass cabinets, all helpfully labelled in English as well as German. I find Tom smirking. 'What is it?' I ask. 'Oh my.' It's a large vase from, I think, ancient Greece, depicting the silhouette of a man, an athlete, with an unrealistically large and banana-shaped phallus. Tom may be an intelligent and cultured man, but he still sniggers like a teenager on seeing a huge cock. I shake my head and he apologises but still sniggering to himself.

Halfway through our museum visit, my mobile does ring but it's not Mr Schmidt, it's Barry.

'Hang on a minute, Barry.' I mouth Tom an apology who's still grinning about the Greek vase. I step outside to take the call, sheltering under the awning of a fruit and veg stall. 'OK, I can talk now.' I see the stallholder, standing at the entrance, rocking on his feet, his hands deep in the pockets of his striped apron.

'All right, Liz? Just wondering if you're having a nice time.'

'No, you're not, Barry. I can tell by your voice. What's happened? Is it Tess? Is she OK?'

'Yeah, yeah, no probs. Tess is fine. Not that I've spoken to her.'

'So what is it, then? Be quick. I'm expecting a call any moment.'

'Oh, right, nice to feel wanted. OK, so listen. It's only for a couple of days, and I promise I'll be gone by the time you get back, but I'm staying at yours.'

'What? What for?'

'I thought I could keep Tabby company.'

'Barry.'

'OK, truth is me and Shelley had a bit of a falling out. I mean, it's nothing serious.'

'Nothing serious but you had to move out.'

'Yeah, well.'

'Barry, this is not on. When you buggered off, it wasn't so you could have two homes on the go. You can't just wander back in whenever you feel like it.'

'It's more than that, Liz. I mean it was quite a big argument.'

'You said it was nothing serious a moment ago.'

'Nothing that can't be mended. When did you say you'd be back?'

'Late tomorrow, and I don't want to come home and find you there. I want you gone, Barry. And this time, once you've locked the door, you post the keys back through the letterbox. You've got that?'

He doesn't answer.

'Barry, I said—'

'Yeah, yeah, I heard you, Liz. I heard you loud and clear. Thanks.'

He says it so pathetically, that for a second, a nanosecond, I almost relent. But I don't. I mustn't.

'I've gotta go.'

'Yeah, sure, you don't want to keep Tim waiting.'

'Tom, not Tim. And you're right, I don't.' I slam the phone down – at least, metaphorically. It's not the same on a mobile. The stallholder catches my eye. He quickly turns away. I think he could tell I was some sort of mad foreigner and not the sort of woman to mess with.

As soon as I return the phone to my pocket, it rings again. This time it's a local number. I blow out my cheeks. It can only be Mr Schmidt.

'Hi. Elizabeth?' he says. 'It's Franz here. Can we talk now?' Ah yes, Mr *F* Schmidt. I thank him for calling me, and yes, I have all the time in the world.

'Apparently, the Hotel Cavalier *was* used as a home for wounded soldiers but only at the beginning of the war, and then it turned into a *Lebensborn* centre.'

'A what?'

'*Lebensborn*. It's, erm… It was a horrible experiment that the Nazis did. They housed Aryan girls and brought in Aryan men, usually SS, who slept with them and made them pregnant. Once the children were born, the doctors stole the babies and gave them to *deserving* couples.' I can hear the air quotes around the word 'deserving'.

'My God.'

'Yes. That number you had, number fifty – it refers to the fiftieth baby adopted from that place, on the date it was adopted, the first of December 1944. That's not you, is it, Elizabeth?'

'No. I was born that October but who knows?'

'And I know who that baby was given to.'

My heart quickens a beat. 'You do?'

'Yes, I have the name and the address, and I think the man

still lives there. He used to own a large shoe company but he's retired now and still very rich. If he can't help you, then I'm afraid there are no other avenues.'

'It's our only chance.'

'Yes.'

'Oh, Franz, thank you. You've been so helpful.' I grapple for a pen in my handbag and an old train ticket. 'OK, I'm ready.'

Tom appears in front of me. 'You OK?' he mouths.

I nod my head. 'OK, I got it. Thank you so much.'

'Good luck, Elizabeth.'

His tone catches me, and I smile. 'Tom, that was the young archivist. We've got an address to go to.'

'Excellent! Let us go, then.'

Chapter 54

Once again, Tom asks the taxi driver to wait for us. The taxi driver steps out of his car and, lighting a cigarette, tells us to take our time. We get out at the granite gateposts and walk up the drive, avoiding the puddles. At least it's stopped raining, but the clouds still look ominous. We see the house. It's not huge but it has class. Thatched roofs, balconies, little church-like windows in the gables, a large conservatory to the side. Is there someone sitting in there? The ground-floor windows are surrounded by wisteria, now past their best. 'Liz, I didn't want to ask you in front of the taxi driver, but you're saying the man who lives in this house is the man who, along with his wife, adopted the baby born in that nursing home on the first of December, 1944?'

'That's what Franz told me. He used to be a big shot round here. He ran a business that sold shoes and became very rich as a result. His son runs it now. Or sons, I forget what Franz said.' I stopped, needing to catch my breath. 'The question is, is he linked in some way to my mother?'

Tom put his hands on my shoulders. 'Liz, he might not. Your mother might just have worked at this place and nothing more, no connection at all. Your mother might have picked up the piece of card along the way to use as a bookmark or something. You have to be prepared for disappointment.'

'I know; you're right. Listen, Tom, whatever happens here, you know I'll always be grateful to you for this.'

'Here's looking at you, kid. Come on, let's go. By the way, did I hear your husband call you? Is everything OK back home?'

'Oh yes. Yes, everything's just fine.'

Tom knocks on the huge door using the clapper on the lion head door knocker. A plump woman in an apron answers the door. Tom speaks to her in German, apologising for arriving unannounced and asking if we could see the man of the house, Herr Spitzweg.

They have a conversation but I can tell from the woman's tone that it's not looking promising. I hear Tom say the words *Großbritannien*, Great Britain and *bitte* several times, please. He's putting on his best English gentleman act, which he does so well, and I can see her weakening under his charm offensive. She half closes the door on him and retreats back into the house. 'The housekeeper said she'd asked, but he doesn't usually accept visitors. I had to persuade her we're not press.'

'What would I do without you, Tom?'

'Well, let's see if it works first. Nice house, isn't it?'

We wait for an age. I take my phone from my pocket and put it on silent. Finally, the housekeeper returns and speaks to Tom. He smiles and thanks her. Result!

'We're in,' he says to me. 'Five minutes only. After you, Liz.'

We follow the woman down a corridor 'decorated' with numerous deer and stag heads on the walls watching us with their beady, glass eyes. She ushers us into the conservatory where we are immediately set upon by a couple of dachshunds. An elderly man in a wheelchair shouts at the dogs. 'Good afternoon. I'm told you are from England. Would you like me to speak English?'

He has a long, thin face, the odd liver spot, and half-moon

259

glasses. He sits with a blanket, covered in white dog hairs, over his legs, a book face down open on his lap. Next to him a little round table with spindly legs and a cup and saucer. 'You're staying in the Hotel Mirabell, I hear. A fine choice. Now, I'd offer you tea but you won't be staying long enough to warrant it.'

One of the dogs approaches me, sniffing.

'Shoo her away, Frau... I'm sorry, I've already forgotten your name.'

'Swingle. Elizabeth Swingle. And this is my friend, Tom Fletcher.'

'So you're not journalists, pedlars, salesmen, politicians, window cleaners, Christians, blackmailers or charity workers?'

'No, sir. None of those things.'

'That's a start, I suppose.'

He places a bookmark in his book and puts it on the table next to him. Perhaps Tom is right, perhaps my mother simply picked up a random card that happened to have the name of that weird maternity home and used it as a bookmark. Perhaps I really had come here on a wild goose chase.

Herr Spitzweg makes a show of looking at his watch. 'I should point out that you've already used up forty per cent of your allocated time, so I suggest you don't waste a second more. What is it you want?'

Tom speaks first. 'We apologise for calling on you like this, sir, but my friend here is trying to trace her mother's origins.'

'German, was she? Is she?'

'She is.' I will my hand to stop shaking as I lean over and pass him the certificate. 'I understand, sir, that you adopted a baby during the war as part of the *Lebensborn* project.'

'What did you...' His eyes widen as he reads the card. His

arm shoots out straight as he hands me it back. 'What is this? Who gave you this?'

'I found it amongst my mother's possessions.'

'Your mother? What's her name?'

'Barbara Marsh. Her maiden name was Lüpertz.' He blanches. He knew my mother; it's written all over him. 'Herr Spitzweg, I was hoping–'

'Stop. I don't want to hear another word from you.'

Tom tries. 'Sir, if–'

'Nor you. Now leave. Leave immediately before I call the police. How dare you come into my home brandishing this… this revolting nonsense.'

I have to try one more time. 'Please don't be angry, sir, if you–'

'Oh, but I am angry. I don't care if you have come all this way from England or Timbuktu for that matter, just get out.'

There's a presence behind me. It's Herr Spitzweg's housekeeper, her arms folded, her expression grim, like a bouncer in a nightclub.

Tom and I get to our feet. We thank him anyway. He doesn't respond, only calls for his dogs that both come running and jump up onto his blanket. The housekeeper shows us to the front door and slams it shut behind us. Tom and I stand there, thoroughly ejected.

'He knew my mother.'

'Yes, I thought so too.'

'What do we do now, Tom? The archivist said this was our only avenue.'

'Come on, let's get back to the hotel. We'll think of something, Liz. Let's not give up yet.'

Chapter 55

I lie on my bed in my hotel room, and I am exhausted. Tom and I are meeting downstairs in two hours' time. He's booked us a table at a swanky-looking restaurant in town. What an afternoon. I'd never met a man like Herr Spitzweg. He may have been ancient, but what a force of personality. I pity all those who worked under him over the years. I've had my share of bosses, but Herr Spitzweg would have been in a different league. Afterwards, Tom and I did go back to the former maternity home and Tom asked, then demanded, to speak to the manager, or manageress, as it turned out. It didn't do us any good. She merely repeated the line about the place being used as a home for wounded soldiers. She knew nothing about it being a centre for the Nazis' *Lebensborn* project. At least, she claimed she knew nothing. She was lying; I was certain of it. Tom and I had come up against a brick wall. No one wanted to talk about what went on there during the last years of the war. And now I don't know where to go next. I don't care any more. I just want to go home. I want to get drunk.

My mobile rings. It'd better not be Barry. I scramble across the bed and grab my phone from the bedside table. It isn't Barry.

'Hiya, darling. How goes it?'

'Hi, Mum.'

I hear the catch in her voice. 'What is it, Tess? What's wrong?'

She doesn't say anything, but I can hear her breath on the other end of the line, and I know she's trying to contain herself. I sit up. 'Tess? Speak to me.'

'I wanna come home.'

'Well, of course you can, darling. I'll be back tomorrow early afternoon. Why don't you catch a train down and I'll pay for your fare if you like.'

I hear her sigh. 'No, I mean... I mean for good.'

'For good?' My insides tighten. 'I... I don't understand. What do you mean, for good? I thought you liked it there.'

'I hate it, Mum. I don't like the course; I don't like the city.'

'I thought you said you'd bonded with some of the girls.'

'No, everyone seems so much younger than me.'

'Well, you did insist on taking so many years out.' Shit, why did I say that?

'Oh, great, thanks, Mum.'

'OK, sorry about that. I didn't mean to... But surely–'

'No, I bloody hate it here.'

'But what about... Are you still with Tom?'

'No. He dumped me.'

'Oh, darling, well, that's probably it. You're upset about that, that's all. And that's souring everything else. Once–'

'No, Mum. You're not listening. It's not about Tom. I couldn't give a shit about him. I really do hate it here.'

'So, that's it, then. You want to jack it all in? It's been, what, four months, and you're already giving up?'

'What? I can't believe I'm hearing this.'

'You'll stay to the end of the year, at least. Then we'll consider your options. You are not to throw in the towel at the first sign of trouble.'

'You can't order me to stay.'

'I think after paying for five years of your education, then yes, I can and shall have a say.'

'Sod you, Mother.'

'Tessa! Don't...' But she's rung off.

Damn it, damn it. I pace to the window. It's so damn hot in here but I struggle with the latch. What is it with kids today? They're pathetic. Why did I let her take those two years out? It's not even as if she did anything with them, just a stupid low-paid job in a supermarket. I should've been firmer. Barry definitely should've been firmer.

But Barry's always been incapable of standing up to his daughter. For God's sake, it was like having two teenagers sometimes. The times I said to him, 'What side are you on, Barry?'

And he'd smirk and say, 'Lighten up, Liz. Give the kid a chance.' Well, we did. We let her waste those years of her life, and for what? Damn it, I just want to go home even more now, I want to get drunk, and damn it, again, I want to have sex with Tom.

*

I am back at home in East Anglia. Tabby, at least, is pleased to see me back. No one else is. I keep thinking back to our last evening in Germany and every time I let out a loud groan. Tomorrow, I'm going back to work. I'll be pleased to do so, to try and put some distance between now and the most excruciating moment of my life. I would have thought I was too savvy for such experiences but no, apparently not. It appears I'm not too old to make a total tit of myself.

By the time I met Tom in the hotel foyer that second evening, ready to go out, I was already a little tipsy. I'd raided the minibar and drunk a half bottle of red wine. I kissed him on seeing him. 'OK, Tom, let's paint the town red.'

'Hmm, OK, but we might be the oldest swingers in town, Liz.'

'Who cares? Live a little.'

We ate well, although afterwards I couldn't recall a single thing I ate. But I do know we ordered a bottle of house red, and Tom drank barely half a glass while I merrily polished off the rest. And I talked. How I talked. I told Tom things I'd never told anyone before. I told him all about my fractious relationship with my mother. Then having previously told Tom how Barry and I met, I now told him in minute detail how we split up – the necklace, Shelley, the texts, all of it. Looking back, Tom didn't want to hear all this; I was embarrassing him. But the floodgates had been opened, and there was nothing he could do to stem the flow. Poor man.

Towards the end of the meal, I suggested another bottle of wine. 'I don't think that'd be wise,' he said.

'Gee, Tom, listen to yourself. I didn't know you could be so pompous.' But as a compromise, I ordered just the one glass of red, a large glass.

Tom paid for the meal. 'I'll pay you back one day, Tom. Honest to God, I will. I'll save up. I'll win the lottery. I'll pay you back.'

'Let's get you back.'

'What? No. I thought we were going to paint the town red.'

'Come on, give me your arm.'

Tom led me back to Hotel Mirabell. The town really did look like it belonged in a fairy tale, the street lamps illuminating the pastel-coloured houses and reflecting off the cobblestone streets. 'It's so romantic, isn't it, Tom?'

He escorted me to my hotel room, unlocked the door, and

guided me to my bed. I patted the bed and made him sit next to me. 'It's been so nice seeing you again, Tom. So nice.'

'And you, Liz.'

'Look, you know I fancied you like mad when we were kids and, you know what, Tom, I still do.'

'Liz, please.'

'No, hang on a minute. Let me have my say. Look, we're both adults; we're both single, and we know each other like no one else—'

'Liz…'

'No, no interrupting,' I said, my finger on my lips, shushing him. I took his hand. 'Tom, sleep with me tonight.'

He snatched his hand away as if I'd burnt him. 'For Pete's sake, Liz, you say we know each other like no one else, so how in the hell have you not cottoned on to the fact that I'm gay.'

Chapter 56
January 2002

Hannah wanted to get up. She had no desire to stay in bed any longer. But she couldn't – it'd spoil the occasion. The bedroom door was ajar and she could hear Bruno clumping around downstairs. She plumped up her pillows and sat upright. Freddy, her cocker spaniel, lay on the bed with her, wagging his tail whenever she talked to him or mentioned his name. 'I think we're the same age now, Freddy. We're both seventy-five.' Finally, she heard Bruno slowly coming up the stairs. He pushed the bedroom door open with his spare foot.

'Here we are, my love.' He came in carrying her breakfast tray. 'Happy birthday, darling. You don't look a day over seventy-four.'

'Hey!'

He placed the tray on Hannah's lap and, leaning down, kissed her on the cheek. 'But you're still beautiful to me.'

'Thank you, you old charmer. So what have we here? Oo, scrambled eggs on toast, tomatoes and ham! And tea. Bruno, you're spoiling me.'

'Enjoy it. I'll be back in a moment.'

Hannah had almost finished her birthday breakfast, sharing the ham with Freddy, when Bruno reappeared bearing an old-fashioned wicker basket laden with presents.

'It's such a shame the girls couldn't be here,' she said.

'I know.'

'What did Zoya say she was doing?'

She knew she'd asked before, perhaps several times, and Bruno had told her.

'She's at a conference,' he said. 'The future of Western Europe, post nine-eleven.'

'Ah yes, that was it.' She shook her head. She knew her memory was going. She knew it would only get worse. 'And Claudia, she's not due back from Australia for another month.'

'New Zealand, that's right. Now, how about opening your presents? Then, after you're dressed, we'll head over to Joseph's. He's expecting us about eleven.'

'Yes, that'll be nice. Thank you, darling.' She patted Freddy and looked down at her small pile of cards and presents. 'Now, where to start?'

*

Frau Horch, Joseph's housekeeper, let them in. Hannah and Bruno found Joseph in his conservatory as always. His dachshunds jumped up and rushed over to greet them.

'Aha, here comes the birthday girl,' said Joseph. 'I'd get up but…'

'It's fine,' said Hannah. She leant down and kissed her brother-in-law on the cheek. He looked tired today, she thought, more so than usual. She must remember to ask Frau Horch whether she'd noticed anything and whether he'd been taking all his medicines.

'You look radiant, Hannah, my dear.'

'Oh, Joseph, you're as bad as your brother.'

He reached over to the little table next to him. 'Here,' he said, proffering his present. 'Happy birthday.'

'Why, thank you, Joseph.'

She and Bruno sat down. She opened the present. 'Oh,

Joseph, thank you, my favourite perfume. How did you know?' she asked, shooting her husband a quick look.

'A little birdie told me.' He grimaced, his hand clutched his chest, his whole body tensing.

Bruno rose from his chair. 'Joseph, you all right?'

Joseph, his eyes clenched shut, waved him away. Slowly, the pain receded. He took a number of deep breaths and allowed a small smile to lighten his face. 'It's fine,' he said breathlessly. 'Give me a moment.'

Hannah stroked the dachshunds. Frau Horch appeared, pushing a trolley bearing cups and saucers and a coffee pot. She wished Hannah a happy birthday. They waited politely as she poured, handing each of them their coffee. She tucked in Joseph's blanket. He thanked her. By the time she'd left, Joseph had recovered.

'How's it going, then?' asked Bruno.

'Not so good today, to be honest. I had visitors yesterday, and it shook me up a little.'

'Visitors? Who?'

He manoeuvred his wheelchair so he was looking directly at Hannah and Bruno. 'There's something I need to tell you both. We need to talk about the past.'

Hannah shook her head. 'I'd rather we didn't.'

'I've lived this last half century with an uncertainty so strong it's blighted my life. Yes, I know, I'm being melodramatic, I'm old and senile, so I'm allowed to be melodramatic. This visit I had yesterday – it was like the last piece of a jigsaw being inserted. Everything clicked into place. There's something you need to know. You will hate me but I have no choice.'

'Must you?'

'Yes, I'm afraid so. It is time.'

Chapter 57
January 1959

"Praise my soul, the king of heaven, to his feet thy tribute bring. Ransomed, healed, restored, forgiven, evermore his praises sing."

It was perhaps my favourite hymn, and I sang it loudly and proudly but certainly not as loud as Mr Parker, our headmaster, Pick-Your-Nose Parker, who managed to sing with gusto while keeping an eye on us over his half-moon glasses. We always had assembly on Friday mornings in the imposing school hall with its wooden walls decorated with panels depicting former house captains, their names shining in gold letters. In the corner, we had a special panel listing former pupils who had fallen in the two world wars. Assembly consisted of prayers, hymns, speeches, news, notices, communal tellings-off, the usual stuff.

'Praise My Soul' finished and we all sat. Cerys Atkins sat right behind me. I could feel her presence, her friends either side of her. I knew Tom was sitting in my row some twelve places to my left, not that I'd counted or anything.

We bowed our heads as Mr Parker recited the Lord's Prayer.

Our Father, which art in heaven, Hallowed be thy name.

I thanked God for Tom breaking his wrist. If he hadn't, and if Rory hadn't found Tom's penknife, which wasn't actually his, I'd never have called on him, and we wouldn't now be best of friends. Well, as best of friends as one can be when one of us is a girl and the other… isn't. That day in his house, we watched *Dixon of Dock Green*, which scared me horribly, and as Tom had said, his mum brought us orangeade and biscuits, ones with a layer of cream in them, and talked like we'd known each other all our lives. And when his mum popped in, they talked to each other like… it took a while to work out, but like they were *equals*. I used their toilet simply to have a pee in a proper, warm toilet, not sitting outside on a stone-cold toilet seat shivering in a freezing outhouse with a corrugated roof. As I left, Mrs Fletcher said it was nice meeting me and I was welcome to return anytime, and I could tell she meant it, and a wave of warmth rushed through me.

Give us our daily bread. And forgive us our trespasses, as we forgive those who trespass against us.

I walked home and part of me was happy, part sad. I was happy because I really liked Tom. He was easy to talk to, unlike any boy I'd ever spoken to, in fact, unlike *anyone* I'd ever spoken to, and we were friends now. But, happy though I was, a little cloud of despondency followed me home. Yes, I was jealous that they lived in a nice house, that they had an inside toilet, that they had biscuits with cream in the middle and, most of all, that they had a television. But it was more than that, much more. It was the way Tom's mum spoke to him – as if she actually *liked* him. My mum never spoke to me unless it was to tell me to do something or to tell me I'd done something wrong – again. She never spoke to me with a smile on her face, with a kind voice. Dad did, for sure, but never Mum. How lovely it would be to have a mother like Mrs Fletcher.

And lead us not into temptation, but deliver us from evil:

I was worried, though, about seeing Tom back at school.

I feared he'd ignore me. I walked through the school gates the day he was due back from his injury and saw him almost immediately. He was with his friends, standing in a circle, their cold breaths dancing in front of them, rubbing their hands against the cold – boys, for some inexplicable reason, eschewed gloves. I could hear Tom telling his friends what really had happened when he broke his wrist. I wanted to say hello to him but I couldn't; he had to say it first. He saw me, and cool as you like, he simply waved and called over, 'Hi, Liz, you all right?' like it was the most natural thing in the world. I waved back. 'Yeah, fine, thanks.' And I was fine because Tom hadn't ignored me: he really was my friend now.

For thine is the kingdom, the power, and the glory, Forever and ever.

'Amen,' we all said in perfect unison. Mr Parker waited for utter silence. The last shuffle of bottoms on seats, the last coughs faded away. Silence was absolute.

Hooking his thumbs into his waistcoat, Mr Parker congratulated us on all completing the Christmas holiday assignment – on the role of the women suffragettes, then invited Mrs Barrett, our history teacher, to take over. Now, Mr Parker had the loudest voice known to man. People in the next village could hear Mr Parker at assembly, but Mrs Barrett spoke like a mouse, and unless, like me, you were in the front rows, no one could hear her.

She shuffled onto the stage, head down, clutching a large sheet of card. 'Thank you, Headmaster. Welcome back, children, and may 1959 bring much joy to you.' Her fingers toyed with the string that held her glasses. 'Now, we received some tremendous essays on the women suffragettes. We all know now how important they were and how much they did to advance an equal society.' She glanced over at the headmaster. 'Yes, well, thank you for putting so much work and enthusiasm into your essays. As you know, I had to choose one as the best of all. Now, mark my words, it was an almost impossible task because there were so many worthy of the certificate. I really didn't want to choose one above the others but still…' She muttered something so quietly that even those of us in the front rows missed it. 'So the person who won the Women's Suffragettes Essay Prize is…'

She paused for effect. Mr Parker cleared his throat: this melodrama wasn't to his liking.

'Elizabeth Marsh.'

Oh, shit, that's me.

The school hall erupted into deafening applause. There were shouts and cheers and stamping of feet – it was mayhem. People clapped me on the back and called out my name. I went up and collected my certificate with tears in my eyes and thanked my parents for their love and support. At least, that's how I remembered it that night as I fell asleep. In truth, the announcement was met by utter silence, although someone a few rows back coughed. I jutted forward as Cerys, behind me, kicked my chair. I went redder than a strawberry and honestly would have quite happily died there and then. Then, from the silence, came a single enthusiastic clap of hands. I didn't dare look but I reckoned it came from twelve seats to my left. Someone else joined in, then another and another, until soon, it became almost respectable. I rose from my seat and feeling as if someone had put clay in my shoes, stumbled along the row of seats, down the aisle and up the steps leading to the stage. The silence had returned, and I tried to walk as softly as possible, hating my noisy shoes.

Mrs Barrett half smiled, half grimaced as she shook my clammy hand and gave me my certificate. 'Well done, Elizabeth. Good work.'

I managed to mumble, 'Thank you, miss.'

I returned to my seat as fast as I could without looking like an even bigger idiot than I already felt. 'Yes, well done, girly swat,' said Cerys behind me.

Mr Pick-Your-Nose Parker returned to centre stage as Mrs Barrett scurried back to her seat on the side. 'Congratulations, Elizabeth Marsh. A fine achievement, I'm sure. Now, time for our next hymn. Please rise to sing 'Immortal, Invisible, God Only Wise.'

Chapter 58

I put the certificate in my satchel, careful not to damage it in any way. I didn't even look at it, didn't want anyone seeing me look at it. The day passed and I tried to forget about it, although I wasn't allowed to. Several girls 'congratulated' me, although I don't think a single one meant it. Not a single boy mentioned it. As I was leaving, I heard footsteps running behind me. It was Tom. 'Hi,' he said. 'I'll walk you home.'

A tingle of joy caressed me. I tried not to show it. 'Isn't it out of your way?'

'Nah, only a bit.'

I looked around for Cerys or her friend Becky or any of the others but sadly couldn't see them. Still, I walked out of school that afternoon half a foot taller than when I went in.

'Well done on the certificate. Your parents will be pleased.'

'Yeah. But going up onto that stage was so embarrassing.'

'Yeah, I guess it would be. It's not right, though, is it? To be embarrassed by something like that.'

'You going home to watch *Dixon of Dock Green*?'

'Not sure it's on tonight, but there'll be something else. Wanna come round?'

'Yeah! Oh, no, wait. Shit, I can't. I said I'd help my dad in the café after school today.'

'That's all right; we'll go there instead.'

We? He just said it as if it were the most natural thing in

275

the world. 'Yeah, sure. Great stuff.'

So we walked briskly towards the café. But, as we approached, Tom slowed down.

'You all right?' I asked him.

'Liz, there's something I have to tell you.' He stopped and, looking down at the pavement, kicked at a stone. 'We're moving away in a few months.'

'What do you mean?'

'My dad's got a new job; it's a promotion, I think. But it means we have to move south, somewhere in Kent.'

My mind seemed to cloud over for a moment. 'Truly?'

'Yeah.' He looked at me and my heart contracted. 'I'm sorry, Liz.'

'When?'

'Not for a long while. There's a lot to organise, apparently. October time, I think.'

'I don't want you to leave.' My voice sounded so fragile somehow.

'I know. Nor do I.'

Dad's café was never particularly busy late afternoons, but he still needed help when Betty was off. And today was such a day. We walked into a fug of smoke although there were only a couple of customers in, one nursing a mug of tea, the other chomping through a bacon sandwich, a little spillage of ketchup on his chin. I saw my dad's café through Tom's eyes, seeing it as if for the first time: the yellow walls, the long benches painted green, the large mirrors, the red-and-white oil tablecloths, and I thought, yeah, it looked good. My dad had done a fine job doing up the place. Dad greeted me cheerily. Clocking Tom, he stubbed out his cigarette and asked, 'Who's this, then?'

'We met at the panto, Mr Marsh,' said Tom, holding out

his hand.

Where did he learn this stuff, to behave like this?

'Ah, yes, of course. Well, you can give us a hand, if you like.'

'Absolutely.'

'Dad, can I show you something first?' I pulled the certificate from my satchel and passed it to him. He took it. I noticed Tom slink away a little as if not wanting to encroach on this. I watched Dad as his eyes scanned left to right. 'Whoa, this is wonderful. The top essay award awarded to Miss Elizabeth Marsh. That's you. Oh, love, come here.' I was standing at his side when his bearlike arm wrapped itself around my shoulder, and he pulled me in and planted a big kiss on the side of my head. 'I'm very proud of you, love. Good girl.'

'Thanks, Dad.'

'This was about those women, wasn't it?'

'The suffragettes, yes, Dad.'

'Well, I'm sure they'd be very proud of you as well. We'll have to show this to your mum; she'll be thrilled.'

I returned the certificate to my bag. 'What do you want us to do, Dad?'

*

Two hours later, Dad and me were back at home. He'd given Tom and I three shillings each for our efforts. We were both delighted, Tom, especially, because he hadn't been expecting it. Then Dad gave me an extra shilling for being 'such a clever girl'.

'Hey, Babs, come and see what our clever girl got today.'

My mum came through from the kitchen. 'What's all this fuss? What is it?'

'Go on, then, love, show her.'

I waited as Mum wiped her hands on her apron then passed her the certificate. 'Yes, very nice.' She passed it back to me. 'Now, Arnold, did you remember to get the bread, as I asked you?'

'No, hang on a minute, Barbara. This is more than nice; this is great. Liz beat hundreds of other kids in her year to get this. Show a bit more…'

'What, Arnold? What is it you'd have me do? A little dance, maybe?'

'I don't know. Christ's sake, Barbara.'

'It's OK,' I said.

'I know,' said Dad. 'I'll frame it, and we can put it on the wall.'

'Don't worry about it, Dad.'

He shot a look at my mother. 'Liz could end up going to university if she keeps–'

'University? She's a girl, Arnold. Don't be silly.'

'I'm going to my room.'

'No, don't, Liz. Your mum doesn't mean it; she's just tired, aren't you, Babs?'

'It don't matter, Dad.' I looked at my mother, and she had the decency to at least look a little contrite. 'It don't matter.'

'I need to get dinner ready.'

I waited until I was sure Mum was out of earshot. 'Dad, how did you meet Mum?'

He sighed and ran his fingers through his hair. 'One day soon, love, I'll tell you everything.'

'Can't you just tell me now?'

'No. We need to be alone. Anyway, I think we should wait until you're a little older.'

And right, then, it really didn't matter. What did matter

was that Tom was moving away. Lying on my bed, gazing at James Dean, the enormity hit me. Tom was my best friend, my only friend. How would I survive without him?

Chapter 59
January 1945

Hannah hadn't moved in what felt like weeks; it'd probably been only a couple of days. Her arms lay heavily either side of her on the bed, her head even heavier. They'd locked the window, locked the door; they'd imprisoned her. Occasionally, someone would escort her to the bathrooms and kept close to her for fear she might try to run away in her nightgown or do mischief to herself. As if she had the strength. Most of the time her mind remained in a state of passive emptiness. Once in a while, someone brought her a tray of food. That same person would return later to take the tray away again, not commenting on the fact that Hannah hadn't touched a thing. The thought of food left her nauseous. She knew the weight was falling off her, knew she was becoming weaker by the day. It didn't matter, her sense of self-preservation had evaporated, leaving her without caring whether she lived or died.

She gazed at the sky from her bed, watched the shifting shapes of the clouds, a flock of birds soaring by, perhaps a bird of prey banking. When she did think about it, it was too difficult to process it as a whole. Instead, an image would come to her: the glint of Nurse Lowitz's gold chain, the crack in the orderly's watch face, the doctor's trouser leg caught up in his sock. She couldn't allow herself to think about Helga. It was too much, too difficult. Even a fleeting thought of her baby caused her breasts to ache as they swelled with her milk. Milk that had no purpose now, no purpose at all. She remembered dreaming about Bruno. It was strange, she thought, that her desire for the man was so intense that in the midst of it she'd conjured him up, dreaming he'd come to her, had taken her hand and stroked it. She wished he'd come back to her; she longed to see him; she ached for him. She ached for her baby.

There were moments when Hannah didn't know whether she was awake or dreaming. She often dreamt of the other girls, Lena, in particular. They still had their babies, and she couldn't understand why. She'd wake up and ponder the question for a while. Perhaps she had done something to displease the staff. Perhaps her body wasn't feeding Helga sufficiently. Perhaps they thought she'd make a terrible mother, like her own mother. But how did they know about her mother. Sometimes, in her dreams, voices would come and go, one moment clear, the next hazy, voices of people she knew – her mother, Bruno, Dr Heinkel, Nurse Lowitz.

A couple days before, she was awoken by a shaft of intense light shining in her eye. First one eye, then the other. The light snapped off but its glare remained on her retinas, blinding her. She heard their voices. 'She needs to go now. She's taking up a bed and valuable resources.'

'But where, Doctor? Like I said, we can't just throw her on a train and pack her off. She's too weak still.'

'Why are you so sentimental about it? She's no good to us now, so as far as I'm concerned she's not our problem any more.'

'Give me a few days. I might be able to sort something out.'

The doctor didn't respond immediately. After a while, he said, 'You have until the end of the week.'

Hannah knew she had to stir herself. If they simply threw her out, with nowhere to go, no money in her pocket, she'd starve. She began to eat, she got dressed and was allowed out into the dining hall, where she sat and talked with several of the other girls, most of whom she hadn't met before. Some had babies. The first time, on seeing the babies, or smelling them, she had to flee the room. She sat at the bottom of the stairs, quivering, fighting back the tears. It was a fight she lost, and she sat there, her head in her hands, while the tears streamed, crying so hard, her body shook.

She hadn't cried since.

Now that she'd begun eating, her appetite returned with a vengeance, and she found herself capable of eating and eating. She was allowed now to wander the gardens. Oh, the joy of such simple pleasures, to breathe in the air, to hear the birds. On the second occasion, she saw Lena pushing a pram. Hannah's first instinct was to hide but she stopped herself. She had no reason to hide. Lena greeted her warmly.

The two women sat on a bench. 'They can't hear us here,' said Lena.

'You've still got your baby?'

'Yes.' She jigged the pram. 'I'm leaving tomorrow.'

'With the baby?'

'They didn't want him.'

'They didn't… Why?'

'Look at him.'

Hannah didn't want to look at him, frightened of what he might provoke in her. But Lena urged her. So she stood and peered down at the sleeping child, sucking furiously on his thumb.

'Can't you see?'

'See what?'

'Look, for Christ's sake, Hannah, look.'

'I'm looking. I don't see anything except a… a b-beautiful

little boy.'

Lena stood up next to her. 'Seriously? You don't see it?' Her voice was shaking now.

'He's gorgeous, Lena.'

'They didn't want him because... because of the harelip. They called him deformed, unsuitable for their purposes. As if he was just...'

'I know, I know.' Hannah looked more closely, and yes, she could see it now, the telltale line that ran from his upper lip to the side of his nose. 'It hardly shows.'

'You're just saying that.'

'No, Lena.'

Lena tried to hold on, tried biting her knuckle and looking away. But it didn't work, the tears sprang to her eyes. 'Thank you, Hannah.' She hugged her. 'Thank you.'

'Just think, just because they saw something that no one else will, you get to keep your baby.'

Lena pulled away and with a stuttering smile, wiped her eyes with the back of her hand. 'Yes, I know.'

'What's his name?'

'George, after my father.'

George began stirring, a little whimper of a cry. Lena picked him up. 'I can't believe I came to this awful place voluntarily. How stupid. I'm sorry you had to lose yours.'

Hannah swallowed. 'Thank you.'

Chapter 60

Hannah felt as if she'd been away from the outside world half her life. It'd been over a year since she first arrived on the train from Berlin. And things had changed, one could feel it in the air. Before, people still had a degree of optimism. The nation had suffered some setbacks; it was still reeling from the defeat in Stalingrad, but one had the sense that these were temporary setbacks, and we'd soon be back on the road to victory. Not any more. You could see it in people's faces. People looked drawn now, sullen and fearful. No one looked each other in the eye.

Turning the corner from the main square into one of the several side streets, she let out a small cry on seeing several buildings destroyed, a pile of rubble. This funny little town she'd never heard of before coming here had finally fallen victim to the English devils in their aeroplanes. A few people, men and women and children, were passing bricks from one to another, like a long chain. The production line stopped as one on seeing her. And she knew she stood out in her clean floral dress and her straw hat with its bow. One of the men whistled at her. Her cheeks burned. 'Wanna give us a hand, miss?' shouted another.

'I need to… No, I've got to find this address,' she said, waving a piece of paper. 'Could you help?'

A number of men rushed over, eager to help, while the women shook their heads and waited with their hands on their hips. Hannah received precise instructions. She thanked them. 'I was always told they'd never bomb this place, that it was too small.'

'Nah,' said one of the men with dust on his cap and in his beard. 'It was one of them bombers going back home. They was just lightening their load and this,' he said with a sweep of his hand, 'is the result.'

'Oh.'

The man nodded. 'Good luck finding your address, miss.'

Hannah stood outside Bruno's house. It looked worse for wear but still attractive with its timber frame and low sloping roof and high chimney. Although the paint looked fresh, the windows were dirty, a couple cracked. Nurse Lowitz had no issue with her leaving the home now and going out into the community alone. There was no need to keep Hannah wrapped in cotton wool any more, not now that she was no longer considered 'useful'. So she and Lena had left together. Lena was heading home and told Hannah that she could always stay with her, George and her mother.

She realised now that what she'd thought had been a dream was not. Bruno really had appeared that dreadful day; he truly had been there. He'd held her hand and comforted her as she drifted off. She remembered now also seeing him minutes earlier creeping around the gardens of the home. He had not gone back to war; he was here. They'd lied to her.

She remained standing outside, too fearful to approach and knock on the door. What if, despite everything, Bruno refused to see her, turned her away? Their relationship was a uniquely weird one after all. What if he wanted no more to do with it? She wouldn't blame him. She'd feel the same if it wasn't for the inconvenient fact that she had fallen in love with him. And she needed him, desperately so. They'd stolen their baby; she wouldn't be able to bear it if he turned his back on her; she couldn't lose both of them. She *needed* Bruno to help her keep the memory of her daughter alive. She needed someone to tell her that things would be OK, and that together they could face anything. She couldn't do it alone.

She rang the bell but realised it wasn't working. Instead, she knocked gently on the door. Then, on hearing no response, she knocked harder. She waited three, four minutes, knocking a couple times more. No one at home. She wondered what to do. Perhaps return to the home, collect her few belongings and traipse to Lena's house, hoping her offer was genuine.

But as she turned to leave, a car drew up, a small green Opel. It parked right outside the house. A man jumped out. Hannah's heart recoiled at the site of him. The man was dressed in full uniform, a Nazi to the core. 'Heil Hitler,' he called. 'Can I help you?'

'Heil Hitler.'

The man held the car door as an older woman emerged from the back of the car. Hannah could see also another woman, a younger one, sitting in the passenger seat, a baby wrapped in a blanket on her lap.

'Well?' said the man.

'I'm sorry, I think I must have the wrong house.'

The older woman walked towards the house, a headscarf covering her hair. 'Who are you looking for, dear?'

'A friend of mine.'

'And does this friend of yours have a name?'

She didn't want to say it, not in front of the Nazi, but the woman was waiting. 'Bruno. Bruno Spitzweg.'

Her face lit up. 'That's my son.' She stepped forward and offered her hand. 'And what brings a beauty like you visiting my son?'

Hannah blushed, partly from the compliment, partly because she didn't know how to answer.

The Nazi saved her. 'He's not here. He's in hospital.'

'Is he?' cried Hannah, unable to hide her concern. 'Is there... Is he ill?'

'He's fine.' Turning to the older woman, he said, 'You OK, then, Mother?'

'I'd invite you in...' She motioned her head towards the woman in the car.

Sure enough, the woman opened the car door and shouted at the Nazi. 'Hurry up, Joseph, Elizabeth needs a feed.'

'Elizabeth?' said Hannah to herself. 'That's a nice name.' She wanted to approach the woman, say hello to the baby. Seeing Lena's baby earlier had not upset her in the way she'd anticipated. Could she do it again?

'All right, I'm coming,' shouted the man.

Hannah jumped back. Without another word, the Nazi got into the car and sped off.

'So you're friends with my son?' said the man's mother, retrieving her house key from her handbag.

'Yes. Yes, I am. Is he sick?'

'He, er, got into a fight, the silly boy, and came off the worse for wear. But he's fine now. He's coming home tomorrow morning.'

'A fight? Oh. Well, do you mind sending him my...'

'Your?'

'Best wishes.'

She opened the door. 'Why don't you come back and see him for yourself. Come back this same time tomorrow. I'm sure he'd be delighted to receive a visitor, and such a pretty one at that.'

'Yes, I will. I'll come back tomorrow. Thank you.'

Chapter 61

Hannah had a fractious night, unable to sit still, to eat, to think properly. She'd found Bruno's home; she was seeing him later that day. She'd met his mother, his brother and, presumably, his sister-in-law and even seen a glimpse of Bruno's niece, Elizabeth. She'd be drawn just that little bit closer into his world. She hoped he was OK. He must have been beaten horribly to end up in hospital for a whole week. This was to be her last night in the home. Nurse Lowitz had found a hostel she could go to. Hannah packed her things, not that it took long, and sat on her bed, admiring the view from her window one last time.

She tried to persuade herself that she wanted to go home, to see her parents. But she knew she didn't. She'd learnt so much in the last year and come to know what she always half suspected that her mother was a self-centred, vain woman. She knew she'd inherited her mother's good looks but she hoped that was all she'd inherited. Did she have goodness in her heart? Was that something one could judge oneself? She'd tried to help the Polish man, Jan. She didn't do it for any other reason than she knew he was a victim and she'd tried to help. She was the victim now, and she needed help, not her mother's help, which would always be loaded with a degree of the self, but Bruno's help. She needed his help, and she yearned for his love and to give him her love. Helga had filled her heart with love and they'd taken her away, but the love still remained, brimming over within her, and it needed an active conduit. The world was so full of hate; she'd seen it too many times. Love had become a precious commodity. It had to be protected, had to be treasured. *Oh, Bruno, I beg you, when I come to you, please don't turn me away.*

So for the second time in so many days, Hannah stood outside Bruno's house. If she'd found it difficult yesterday, this was a hundredfold harder. Perhaps it'd be better to turn away and run. Not knowing would be preferable to knowing the worst. She had a choice now: to sleep at the hostel as suggested by Nurse Lowitz or turn up at Lena's. Either appealed more than having to face this. But she had to do it. She'd regret it for the rest of her life if she didn't. Her legs like lead, she walked the final few steps and knocked on the door.

Her anxiety was eased a little on being greeted by Bruno's mother's smiling face.

'Are you sure this is OK?' asked Hannah.

'Oh, yes, yes. He's a bit sore still but he's fine now. He'll be getting up soon, so why don't you sneak up and see him now? I, er, I haven't told him about you. I thought I'd leave it to you, thought it'd make a nice surprise for him.'

'Well, a surprise, yes, but I'm not sure about nice.'

She put her hand on Hannah's sleeve. 'He'll be delighted; don't you worry, my dear.'

Hannah puffed out her cheeks.

'By the way, my name's Edith.'

'Edith, thank you. I'm Hannah.'

'Nice to meet you, then, Hannah. Go on, then. Last door on the right.'

She quietly ascended the stairs, her hand on the banister. The landing carpet was frayed at the edges, the window at the end smeared. But she liked the house; it had a sense of welcoming about it, like being drawn into an embrace. Last door on the right. She knocked gently.

'Come in,' said the quizzical-sounding voice within.

Hannah held her breath, her hand on the door handle. She stepped in, momentarily dazzled by the bright sun streaming through the window.

She paused and looked at him. Neither said a word. He looked pale, his eyes dark. He'd grown the beginnings of a beard. But he was still just as handsome. His cheekbones now more prominent merely added to his allure.

'Hannah? Is it really you?'

'Hello, Bruno.'

She could see the confusion in his eyes. 'I never thought I'd see you again.' He eased himself up, grimaced at a brief shot of pain, and propped himself up against his pillow. 'Have you come to say goodbye?' he asked, his voice brittle.

She stepped across the room, treading carefully, quietly. She sat on the edge of his bed. She didn't ask. She knew now she didn't need to. 'No, I haven't come to say goodbye. I've come to stay. And I'm never leaving you again.'

He looked intently at her, his eyes wide open as if not quite understanding. The air stilled between them. Outside a cockerel crowed. Bruno reached out for her hand, his own hand trembling a little. She took it. And as he stroked her hand, the tears rolled down his face.

Chapter 62
March 1945

The Americans are coming! The Americans are coming! People whispered it between themselves, but only to those they absolutely trusted. The Soviets were near Berlin, another couple of weeks and the capital would be theirs. To the ordinary person it seemed madness that the nation's leaders continued to resist. The war was lost, had been for months, so what was the point of wasting so many more lives for a lost cause? But no one dared say these things aloud, not with people like Joseph still about, the fanatics, people who still believed that victory could be snatched from the jaws of defeat. To be heard saying such blasphemous things could have you in front of a kangaroo court and shot dead sixty seconds later. But it seemed to Hannah and Bruno that even Joseph knew the end was in sight. Over the previous week, he'd changed, become a lot quieter, not so vocal in his support of the Führer's infallibility.

'I'm still not having that man as a witness,' said Bruno for the umpteenth time, but this time to his mother who was about to carry a basketful of wet washing to hang outside.

'That man being your brother, Bruno?' said Edith.

'Can you imagine years down the line, people will look at our wedding photos and there's this giant of a bloke to the side of us wearing full Nazi regalia?'

Hannah stifled a laugh.

'It's not funny, Hannah,' he said, trying not to laugh himself.

'No, darling, it's not. But your mother's right, he's first and foremost your brother.'

Edith placed her basket on the table and took a chair opposite Bruno. 'There's something you ought to know, Bruno.'

'Oh boy, this sounds serious.'

'Who do you think kept you from returning to duty for as long as possible?'

'My army doctor, of course.'

'And don't you think he might have been influenced along the way?'

Bruno was about to speak but stopped open-mouthed. 'Are you saying…'

She rose to her feet. 'I'm not saying nothing.'

'Anything not nothing,' said Bruno under his breath as his mother collected her laundry basket.

Hannah thumped him in the arm. 'Now's not the time to correct your mother's grammar.'

'My God, she might be right. Perhaps it was my brother.'

'You can't really ask him.'

'No.'

Hannah still frequently thought back three months, the day that changed her life for the better, the day she visited Bruno in his bed. She knew it would forever remain her most treasured memory. She climbed into the bed with him and lay with her head against his chest, listening to the rapid beat of his heart.

'I tried to stop them, you know, Hannah.'

'I know you did.'

'I saw them get in their car from your bedroom window

and I ran down to try and catch them. I got outside just as they were pulling away. I still ran, almost caught them. But I fell, and I watched them drive away with my child in the car, a child I've never seen. And these men from the home caught up with me and kicked the shit out of me. I woke up in the hospital next to all these wounded soldiers, and I knew I'd never see you or Helga again.'

'At least you were wrong on one account.'

'Yes. And I'm so glad. It's the best thing that's ever happened to me.'

'Yes. Me too.'

They lay silent for a while. The cockerel resumed his crowing with much gusto. Hannah could hear Edith thumping around downstairs, and she felt she could fall asleep on Bruno's chest with the largest smile on her face. She hated the thought of those orderlies hurting him.

'Those men in the home were horrible.'

'If I ever see them again I shall shake them by the hand and thank them.'

'What?'

'If they hadn't put me in hospital, I'd be back in Russia by now, and probably dead. And I wouldn't have been here, and you would never have found me.'

Over the months to follow she found this to be a trait of Bruno's, to always search for the best in people, whatever the situation. Even Joseph. He hated that his brother was still a Nazi, but otherwise… Joseph had suffered too. Clara had left him, taking with her the baby. No one knew where, or why, least of all Joseph. He seemed to take it in his stride, far better than his mother who cried about having lost her only granddaughter.

Once Hannah asked Edith what Clara was like. 'A nasty,

scheming *zimtzicker*,' was Edith's considered assessment, a bitch. 'I only met her a couple of times. She never wanted to come here, too drab for her. Only wanted to be seen in that big home of his. And she stopped Joseph from inviting me to theirs. She never loved Joseph. It was simply a marriage of convenience – for both of them. But once his business went under and then they sacked him as mayor and took away his car, for the second time, mind you, that was it, she was off. Didn't matter that she had a baby, my grandchild for God's sake, she was off. She's one of these people who only ever thinks of themselves, Hannah. The world is full of them, unfortunately.'

'Yes,' she said. 'I've met a few.'

Hannah had been living with Bruno and his mother for a month or so when one mid-morning Sunday, Bruno and Hannah went for a walk through the woods. It was the sort of day when it was still cold in the shade however warm it was under the sun. They sat in a clearing next to a stream that at that particular point pooled to make a small bulge of water. They sat, their arms around their knees. Bruno looked up at the sun and squinted.

'Do you ever think of her?' she asked.

'There isn't a minute that goes by when I don't think of her.'

She loved him even more for that.

A pair of starlings settled on a low-lying branch on the other side of the stream. They clocked the pair of humans sitting on the bank on the other side and together flew off. 'It just feels so wrong that I should have a daughter not so far from here being looked after by a man and a woman who aren't her parents. It's so unfair I never got to hold her or see her.' He turned to face her. 'I've not told you this before,

Hannah, but sometimes I get so angry I feel like taking a gun and shooting that bloody Dr Heinkel to smithereens. I've not liked to ask you before, but what was she like, my daughter?'

'Oh. She… she smacked her lips a lot whenever I'd fed her; she liked hearing my voice, especially when I sang to her, and…'

'Yes?'

'Oh, Bruno, she was the most beautiful human you've ever met.'

'More beautiful than her mother? I find that hard to believe.'

'Dear me, well, as beautiful, then.'

He took her hand and kissed it. 'Hannah, will you marry me?'

'Oh, Bruno. Yes. One hundred per cent yes.'

'Ought you not think about it first?'

'Perhaps you're right; I should.' She counted to ten in her head while he threw a couple of pebbles into the stream and watched the ripples. 'OK, I've given it a lot of thought and, yes, I still want to marry you.'

'Oh wow, oh–'

'No, wait, wait, Bruno,' she said, putting her hands up to fend him off. 'On one condition.'

'And what's that?'

'That we have lots and lots and lots of children.'

'Oh my word, my darling. There's nothing I would like better. At least ten!'

'Oh? Heck, Bruno. I was perhaps thinking of four or, at the very most, five.'

'Three, four, five, however many we feel like.'

'However many we can afford.'

'I'll work with Joseph. We'll rebuild his business after the war, and we'll make a huge success of it and become disgustingly rich and vulgar, and we can buy each other silly presents.'

'What? You and Joseph?'

'No, you silly turkey, you and me. And we'll have lots of pampered children and… and…'

'And?'

'And we'll teach them that actually money's not that important but peace is, the ability to listen and understand each other so that they never make the same terrible, terrible mistakes we have made.'

The two starlings reappeared on the same branch.

She put her arm around him. 'I love you, Bruno.'

'And I love you, Hannah, and I love you, Helga, wherever you may be.'

Chapter 63

The first of March 1945. The day Hannah and Bruno married. A smaller wedding could not be imagined. They had hesitated; it seemed wrong to marry when the country was in its death throes. People still talked of the Americans, their God-given saviours. Everyone thanked the Gods they lived in the western half of Germany and that it really would be the Americans, or perhaps the Canadians or the British, that would come and accept their surrender. They pitied their co-nationalists living in the eastern half of the country, expecting the revenging Soviets any day. Hannah knew Bruno had fought in Russia and knew, without having to ask, that he'd witnessed some terrible things. She only hoped he'd witnessed them and didn't perpetuate them. She couldn't imagine how; he was far too decent a soul to do such things. But then what did she know about war, about how it can change a man, turn him from saint to beast. Occasionally, she'd watched him as he thrashed about in his sleep and a couple times now she heard him mutter a name. Zoya. Always the same name. Zoya. She wanted to ask but knew she couldn't. She vowed to herself never to ask her future husband who Zoya was and what she did to give him such terrible nightmares.

And so the morning of the wedding came round. Hannah hadn't seen Joseph for weeks; he rarely came to his mother's house, too worried about looters to leave his big house two kilometres farther out of town. At least, that's what he said.

He wasn't the confident man he was when she first met him. Bruno thought it was because of Clara and the baby leaving him. Hannah didn't like to say she disagreed. It was because Joseph had lost his place in the world. For so long, he'd been the Nazi mayor proudly strutting about in his uniform, respected and feared in equal measure. With each passing day, people were more vocal in their hatred for the Nazis and for what they'd done to the country. Joseph's fall as the town's top Nazi was spectacular. Bruno hadn't seen him for a while, too, and Edith certainly hadn't.

'I'm so sorry I haven't anything better to wear,' said Edith, wearing a rather drab and shapeless brown dress.

'It's fine,' said Hannah.

'You look gorgeous in that dress. It fits you perfectly.'

'Thank you.' Yes, she thought it did. She had to wear it because, like her future mother-in-law, she had nothing else but she hated it. It was the dress she wore the night where, had he had the chance, the SS lieutenant would've fucked her and impregnated her with his foul, Nazi seed. She promised herself that as soon as she was able, she'd burn it. It felt such an insult to be marrying Bruno in it. He would have seen her in it that night. She just hoped he wouldn't remember.

'Are you all right, Hannah?' said Edith. 'Did I say something wrong?'

'What? No, no, not at all. I was just… just thinking.'

'No time to think, you're getting married today.' Edith took Hannah's hand. 'Hannah, my dear, I want you to know I'm so thrilled you're marrying my son. He's such a kind man, and you're a lovely young woman, and I know you'll make each other very happy.'

'Oh, Edith, don't; you'll make me cry.'

'I wanted you to know.'

'Thank you. Thank you so much.'

A week earlier, Edith had asked Hannah whether she had a ring to give Bruno. She did not. The fact had been worrying her. Where would she find a jewellers now? 'Hold out your hand,' said Edith. Hannah did as told, and her future mother-in-law placed a gold band on her palm. 'It belonged to my husband.'

'No, no, Edith. I couldn't–'

'Yes you can.' Edith curled Hannah's fingers over the ring and squeezed her fist. 'Yes, you will.'

'But–'

'Shush, child. Nothing would give me greater pleasure than to see my husband's ring on my son's finger. It is yours to give him. You do that and I'll be a very happy woman.'

Now, a week later, the two women held hands and smiled at each other. They tried to ignore the fact that outside it was thundering with rain. Bruno had spent the night with a friend, a wounded soldier he'd met in hospital. He was to be one of the two witnesses and Bruno's best man, while Joseph was acting as the second witness. Joseph now appeared, making both women jump.

'Joseph, what are you wearing?'

'Hello to you, Mother.' He kissed them both. 'No choice, I'm afraid.'

Hannah had expected him to dress in his full Nazi regalia, but instead he'd turned up in the most drab, ill-fitting army-like uniform, and one drenched in rain.

'Can I have a word with you?' he said to his mother.

'I'll go,' said Hannah. 'Leave you to it.'

'No,' said Joseph. 'I want you to hear this too. I've told Bruno already.'

'What is it, Joe?' Hannah had never heard Edith refer to

her son as Joe. Somehow, it sounded wrong.

The three of them sat down. Joseph played with a ring on his small finger. 'I am now officially a recruit of the Volkssturm.'

'The what?' said Edith.

'Oh, Mother, where have you been? It's the new army we've set up.'

'Army? You, Joseph? But you're far too old.'

'That's it. It's because we're desperate. It's made up of small boys and older men, like me. I'm only thirty-three. There are many much older than me.'

'But you... you don't know anything about fighting. You've never even held a rifle. Have you had any training?'

'A couple of weeks.'

'A couple of weeks? Oh my God, it must be bad. You'll be slaughtered, all of you. Lambs to the slaughter. The maniacs.'

'Mother, I insist–'

'No! Stop right there, Joseph. For years now I've listened to your Nazi claptrap. I will not tolerate it any more, not in *my* house. And stop referring to *them* as if we're part of them and they part of us. They arrested and effectively killed my husband. They almost killed one of my sons and now the other is facing a certain death sentence. And I have to consider myself one of the lucky ones. Do you want to fight for this... this?'

'Volkssturm. Of course I do, it's my duty. I'm going straight to Berlin–'

'Berlin? Oh my God. So they expect a middle-aged man like you with absolutely no experience to defend our capital against the highly trained and ruthless Red Army, do they?'

'Since you put it like that, it does seem rather optimistic.'

'Oh, Joseph. Oh, my poor boy.'

'Anyway, as I was saying, I have to go straight after the ceremony; that's why I'm wearing this uniform.'

'And that's the best they can rustle up for you? A former mayor?'

'Yes.'

Edith checked her watch. 'Come on, then. We better go. This beautiful young lady is about to be married.'

Joseph looked at her, the first time since he arrived. 'You look lovely, Hannah.'

The way he said it, with such pathos, hurt her. She, with her future beckoning, while he, poor Joseph, was condemned to die for the system he'd stoutly championed for so long. There was a certain justice in it somewhere, but right now, looking at the forlorn figure sitting in front of her, she failed to find it.

Chapter 64

Hannah and Bruno's mother waited just inside at the church door. She could see Bruno at the far end of the aisle, waiting with his brother, his friend from the hospital and the vicar. A couple of villagers had come, old women in headscarves. Outside, the rain had stopped and the March sun shone weakly but inside, the church felt frosty, still gripped by the winter cold. Banners hung from the sides of the aisles, alternating between the cross and the swastika. But no music, no confetti, no bridesmaids. But Hannah hardly noticed; so focused on the handsome man waiting for her. There was to be no wedding banquet afterwards, no party, no honeymoon. She didn't care.

'I've got the ring,' said Edith.

Hannah smiled. 'Thank you.'

'Pleasure's all mine.'

'Not the best time to get married.' No one knew they were getting married, and it was best that way. The Allied bombers were killing thousands every day all across the country. She feared that getting married now, in the midst of the misery, might be considered inappropriate, tactless even.

'Maybe not. It's such a shame your parents aren't here.'

Not really, thought Hannah. Neither of them would have approved of Bruno, especially her mother. She was marrying a corporal; they would have expected so much more. She could hear her mother's slightly affronted tone in her head.

Edith squeezed her hand. 'But the main thing is that you

love each other and that you make each other happy.'

'Yes.' Her mother would never have said that; she wouldn't have been capable of thinking up a sentence like that, a sentence that focused on the recipient and not herself.

The vicar waved at them.

'I think that's our signal,' said Edith.

A flutter of excitement tickled Hannah's insides. She took Edith's arm and together, slowly and in time with one another, they walked the length of the aisle, Hannah conscious that she couldn't stop grinning.

Bruno turned on hearing her approach and broke out in an equally broad smile. Bruno was wearing a pinstriped suit, dark brown, thin lapels. Hannah knew she should acknowledge Bruno's brother and his friend, but she couldn't take her eyes off Bruno and the way his love for her radiated from him. No one had ever made her feel this way; it was making her giddy.

The vicar cleared his throat. Now, finally, Hannah took her eyes away from her husband-to-be to face the vicar. A round-faced man with large, rimless spectacles, the vicar wore a shiny Nazi pin on his cassock. She nodded a hello at Joseph and at Bruno's friend, whose name she still didn't know. He had an arm in a sling, a surprisingly white and clean one.

'Welcome,' said the vicar in a voice that seemed to imply the opposite. 'We are gathered here today…'

Soon the moment of truth came, the exchanging of rings. She held out her hand and Bruno repeated the vicar's words. 'With this ring…' Hannah's face flushed on seeing the ring, the gold so bright to be almost yellow, a small but glossy red ruby nestled on top. She glanced up at Edith and Hannah knew – it'd been hers. The vicar turned to her. Edith passed Hannah her husband's ring. Bruno held out his hand now and

Hannah slipped the ring on. Did he recognise it? She wasn't sure.

'I now pronounce you man and wife.'

Man and wife. Bruno pulled her in and kissed her hard on the lips. Hannah laughed. Man and wife. The words reverberated in Hannah's head. She'd done it; she'd actually done it! In these most difficult of times, she'd fallen in love and knew that she'd met the man she wanted to spend the rest of her life with. It didn't seem real; she was still floating too high. She was still smiling as they signed the registers.

'Well,' said the vicar, now looking a little more relaxed, 'that was my first wedding for a long while. I'm so sorry, but I don't have any more copies of *Mein Kampf* to give you.'

'I'm sorry?' said Hannah.

'We're meant to present every marrying couple with a copy. I'm sorry.'

'It's OK, Vicar, thank you anyway. I'm sure we'll…'

'Cope,' said Bruno.

'Yes, cope.'

Together, Hannah and Bruno walked down the aisle, their tiny party behind them. The two old women in headscarves stopped talking as they passed but didn't smile. They stepped outside into the cool sun and Hannah breathed in the fresh air.

The vicar congratulated them and then excused himself, heading back into the church, his cassock flapping behind him.

Joseph, Bruno's mother and his friend offered their congratulations and shook Bruno's hand and kissed Hannah.

'I recognise that dress,' said Bruno.

'Oh, possibly.'

'It was…' He stopped himself. She gave him a lopsided grin. He reached for her hand. 'I'm sorry.'

'It's fine.'

He smiled warmly at her. 'You look lovely.'

'And you, my love.'

'I've prepared a little food,' said Edith. 'Not much, of course, but if…'

Bruno's friend spoke for the first time, only to excuse himself, saying he had to get back to see a doctor.

'Nice chap,' said Bruno. 'Don't suppose I'll ever see him again though.'

Even Joseph appeared flustered. 'Look, I'm sorry about this but I have to go too,' he said. 'Have to report for duty. Today's the day.'

'Of course,' said Bruno. 'Thanks, Joe.'

The two men hugged and remained in each other's embrace for a while.

Joseph was a changed man now. Hannah didn't know whether it was Clara leaving or because he'd been forced into signing up for the old-man's army, perhaps both, but he appeared diminished now, older than before.

'Bruno,' he said, his eyes glistening.

'You don't have to say it, Joe. Come back when it's all over and we'll start again. We'll make a go of it, and soon every gentleman for miles around will be wearing your shoes. One day, it'll happen, you'll see.'

'Yeah. Perhaps. Listen, you were right, Bruno; you were always right. I was wrong. I shall live the rest of my life knowing I was wrong.'

'It doesn't matter now.'

'I'm sorry. I want you to know that.'

Bruno nodded.

Joseph turned to his mother. He leant down and hugged her while she whispered something in his ear. He bowed his head, then, pulling away, wiped his eyes.

'I shall pray for you, Joseph. I shall pray every day until the day you come back to us.'

Joseph stopped in front of his brother and Hannah. 'You make a lovely couple. You'll be very happy together. I know it.'

They watched him leave. The man who once represented the future of the nation now bowed and defeated. They continued watching him, silent and grave, until he turned the corner and disappeared from view.

Edith, perhaps sensing the happy couple needed a few minutes alone, excused herself and returned to the house.

'Well, not your usual wedding,' said Bruno. 'I'm sorry.'

'Don't be silly; I'd have married you no matter what.'

'What a shame he'd run out of *Mein Kampf*s.'

'Tragic. It's ruined my day.'

He laughed as he wrapped his arms around her. 'Did you feel her presence?'

'Helga's? Yes, of course. My own little ghost; *our* little ghost.'

'We'll find her one day. You know that, don't you, Hannah. However long it takes, we'll find her.'

'Yes,' she said. 'I know. You're right; we will. We'll find her.'

Chapter 65
October 1959

We'd got our television set, just as Dad promised, and I loved it. Unless I was working at the café, I'd come home and watch TV after school with a plate of bread and chocolate and an apple. Sometimes, Tom would come over, but I preferred it when I went to his. It was nice to get away from my mother for a while. We were so close now, Tom and me, like brother and sister. We liked the same TV programmes, laughed at the same jokes, and spent as much time together as possible. But not at school where we tended to avoid each other. We'd say 'hi' if we bumped into one another, but that was it. He often joined me at Dad's café, helping with the washing up and taking orders. Dad liked having him around, I could tell.

Dad was happy – he'd got permission from the council to put a couple of tables and chairs outside the café, and now that the weather had improved, it certainly brought in some new customers.

Life was on the up. But, of course, it wasn't really. Tom was leaving. Every day that passed brought it a day closer. I tried not to think about it, and we never talked about it. Except one day, he told me they had a date now – the ninth of October, the day after the general election. They were moving to a town in Kent called Maidstone. I knew he was dreading it, too, the new boy in a new school and all that. I told him he'd be OK. Boys always gravitated towards Tom. There was something about him that drew people to him. They *wanted* to be his friend. But *our* friendship was different, and it made me feel special, and the thought of losing him left me distraught. I tried to push it to the back of my mind. It was too difficult to think about.

Dad was despondent about the election. He wanted Labour to win, but, he said, they stood no chance. We'd have to put up with that 'lilly-white useless Harold Macmillan for God knows how long. I was only fifteen but after my essay on the suffragettes, it interested me. I knew my interest helped me forget that Tom was leaving. There were election posters everywhere, people coming to our house trying to persuade Mum and Dad to vote this way or that. Mum refused to speak to any of them. I didn't like to tell Dad that Tom's dad would be voting for Macmillan.

The third day of October, the Saturday before the election, Tom and I worked in the café until after lunch when Dad gave us a couple of shillings each and told us to run off and enjoy the sunshine. But he asked us if we would return at four to help him finish up for the day. Of course, we said yes. Not only would it mean another shilling each, but we'd get to eat the leftover doughnuts. Who could resist? And, Tom and I both knew, it'd be our last day together working for my dad.

Afterwards, we went back to Tom's and I hated it – everything was in boxes. The house even sounded different. Mrs Fletcher was rushing around, looking flustered. I didn't stay long. I felt in the way even though Mrs Fletcher was as nice as ever. I didn't want to remember Tom's house like this. As I left, I looked around the living room, especially the television, and I knew I'd never see it again.

I went home and did my maths homework then watched some TV. Time passed. It was ten to four and I had to head back to the café. It took fifteen minutes to walk there so I knew I'd be late. He may have been my dad, but I didn't like being late. And I knew Tom would be there on time. So I rushed along, the autumn sun fading slightly, casting long shadows. I saw the front page of a discarded newspaper on the pavement, Harold Macmillan's serious face peering up at me; I saw two seagulls fighting over a chicken bone; I saw a woman's poodle squat; I saw a girl of about eight pushing her little brother on a tricycle. I saw a man with long sideburns sitting at a bus shelter rolling a cigarette. Perhaps aware of me looking at him, he glanced up and we locked eyes for no more than a second. I passed on. I saw two girls, older than me, sitting on a bench together, reading a glossy magazine and laughing. I saw an elderly gentleman stroking a ginger cat that was perched on the top of a wall. I even saw Cerys Atkins from a distance and we waved at each other. All these things I vividly remember, small things not normally worth remembering, but each and every one of them is indelibly implanted in my memory, like small markers on the way to catastrophe.

I approached the café, knowing I was late, rushing, sweating. I saw the large white vehicle outside the café. I slowed down and squinted, shielding my eyes against the fading sun. An ambulance, both its back doors open. Why was it there? Was someone poorly? Perhaps one of Dad's bacon sandwiches had made someone ill. The thought made me chortle. I saw Tom, his hair dishevelled, his arms folded, one hand clasped against his mouth. A chill shot through me. A number of customers milled about at the café entrance and Betty too. I heard someone shouting, a man. 'Make way, make way.' A man in a black uniform and peaked cap. A stretcher, the person on it entirely covered by a blanket. A second man at the other end of the stretcher. Who is that on the stretcher? Tom stepped back, giving them room. I hurried on, but it's as if I was trudging through treacle.

'Dad? Daddy?'

Tom heard me. But he didn't move, looked incapable of it. The men slammed the ambulance doors shut. The slamming doors pounded in my head. They ran round to the front. Tom was shaking his head. I am running now, my vision obscured by tears. The ambulance jerked into life. But no bell. Didn't they always ring their bell?

'Tom, Tom, what's happening? Is it Dad?'

The ambulance eased away from the pavement and onto the road.

'Tom?'

Somehow I was in his arms. 'He just collapsed, Liz. Just collapsed.'

The ambulance drove off but in no apparent hurry.

'I don't understand. Is he OK?'

Tom stepped back from me, the better to look at me. His hands clasped my arms. 'Liz, he's dead. I'm sorry. Your dad, he's dead.'

Chapter 66

Time warped following my father's funeral. The days merged into one, a never-ending drudge of routine and nothingness. I walked around as if wearing blinkers. Everything beyond my immediate vision was simply a blur: voices, faces, passers-by on the streets. I couldn't think of the past and didn't dare think of the future. I wanted to be upset and sad. I wanted to be angry, but I felt nothing, aware of nothing except a deep void within me.

My father died of a heart attack. Too many cigarettes, the doctors said. He was only fifty. Everyone at school knew Dad had died, at least everyone in my year. The teachers treated me with kid gloves. The kids either ignored me or didn't know how to speak to me. Tom came round a couple of times, but he was often away – spending days in his future home in Kent and his future school. Cerys Atkins hugged me and said she was sorry. I almost fainted with the shock. Mr King, my form tutor, took me to one side and said he was sorry to hear about my dad. If there was anything he or the school could do… He said if I needed a few more days at home, I could. I couldn't think of anything worse. School provided a respite away from my mother. We'd never been close but now, following Dad's death, we drifted even further apart. After he died, I waited for my mother to reach out for me. I couldn't begin to imagine what form it'd take but I desperately needed her. But she said nothing. Nothing at all. It was almost if Dad hadn't died, just gone away for a few days. We never spoke unless we had to. There were hardly any photos of Dad, and the ones we had were old and grainy. And I knew Mum would never voluntarily speak of him.

I enjoyed the funeral, strangely. Harold Macmillan had won the election. Dad wouldn't have been pleased about that! I was happy for Dad that so many people turned up, including many of his café regulars. Also, a number of men in dark blue blazers, berets and medal ribbons. They were, apparently, former comrades of my dad's from his army days. A couple of them spoke to me: 'Your father was a fine man and a fine soldier.' I did wonder, if they liked Dad so much, why I'd never seen them before.

Mum hated every moment of the funeral, I could tell. She looked like a kitten in a dogs' home. I could see her shrinking away from the ex-soldiers, hiding behind my Uncle Bill and Aunt Vera.

It rained all day, a non-stop drizzle, the clouds forebodingly dark. Perfect weather, I thought, for a funeral. We stood, heads bowed under black umbrellas, our shiny shoes squishing into the wet grass, as the vicar conducted the service.

Mum wore black, naturally, but with a veil I'd never seen before that rather suited her. Somehow, with mother shirking her responsibilities, I became the chief mourner: a role I enjoyed.

The vicar recited the mournful words and I stared down at Daddy's coffin. It didn't seem real – was it really my father down there in that horrible box? How could it be? He was my dad, for God's sake; dads don't die, not at fifty. I loved him so much, and I couldn't even begin to imagine a life without him. He'd been there, every day, part of my little world, its centrepiece. Dad was my rock. It'd taken his death for me to realise it. I could hear his cheerful voice, his laugh, see his wide grin and sparkling eyes, the way he called me 'love'. Why was this happening, why? I didn't understand. Who'd make me laugh now. Who'd make me feel loved and warm inside? Instead of warmth, my insides ached as if a stone was resting in the pit of my stomach. Tom had told me Dad half fell against the counter in his café, clutching at his heart. He let out a little cry before slumping to the floor. I was haunted by the thought of that cry. What went through his mind those final few moments? Did he know? Was he frightened? I realised my hands were trembling, that I couldn't catch my breath. Why, Dad? Why did you have to leave me? I shall never forget you, how could I? I shall miss you so much, so very much.

Tom and his mum came and both hugged me. I couldn't speak. Mrs Fletcher even held my hand for a while. Aunt Vera hugged me; a lot of people hugged me. I was loved and cared for. But not my mother. She never hugged me or touched me in any way.

At the end of the funeral as people started drifting away, Tom came up to me. I knew what he was going to say, I'd been avoiding it all day, but now the moment had come. We stood opposite each other on the grass, a few feet away from Dad's open grave.

'You're leaving now.'

'Yes.'

'It feels strange – I lose my dad and now…'

'I know.'

'It'll be weird without you.'

'I'll write.'

'Will you?'

'If you want me to.'

'I guess.'

'It'll be weird not seeing you.'

'Yeah, I know. Hope your dad's job goes well.'

'Thanks.'

'And you, you'll be fine. You always are.'

'Perhaps.'

We stood in silence while around us, people were saying goodbye to each other, wishing each other well, what a grand man my dad was. Time stretched, a gentle wind rustled the leaves of the trees nearby. I could see Tom's mother waiting for him in the distance.

'You'd better go.'

'It's difficult.'

'Go now, please.'

'I'll miss you. I'll miss your dad.'

'I'll miss you too.'

'Goodbye, Liz.'

'Yeah.' I swallowed hard. 'Bye, Tom. Goodbye.'

I watched him join his mother. She placed her arm around his shoulder and gently led him away. I looked up at the sky, at the fast-moving clouds, at a solitary bird banking. I watched a distant vapour trail slowly evaporating. No sign of the plane though. It must've disappeared behind the clouds. I looked back down and Tom and his mother had gone. All that was left were the imprints of his shoes on the wet grass.

Chapter 67

About a month after the funeral, I returned home from school to find two bulging suitcases in our hallway. Perhaps Mum was moving out. Then I could go live with the Fletchers and move down to Kent with them. What a wonderful thought. But curious as I was by the sight of the suitcases, I was distracted by the sounds of voices, men's voices, coming from the living room. I went through to find two men in dark suits sitting at the living room table with my mother sat opposite them. Both men said hello to me, but I could tell from Mum's expression that my presence wasn't welcome. So I went through to the kitchen to get my bread, chocolate and apple. I hoped the men would be gone soon because I wanted to watch *Blue Peter* on television. I could hear what they were saying now, and it sounded as if they were indeed finishing. 'I think we're done here. Thank you for your time, Mrs Marsh. We'll go back to the office and start preparing the paperwork. We'll give you a ring once everything's ready.' I could hear the scraping of chairs, of briefcases clicking shut. 'No need to see us out.' Having heard the front door slam shut, I returned to the living room.

'Who were they?' I asked, sniffing the faint trace of their aftershave.

'They want to buy the café from me.'

'They want to… What? You can't do that! Dad spent years–'

'And how do you propose I live? On your dad's war pension? No, we need the money. It's decided. Now, I need to make dinner.' She stopped at the kitchen door. 'Oh, I might as well let you know, we may need to take in a lodger too.'

'A lodger? Here?'

She shrugged. 'We need the money. And I need to make space that's why I'm taking your father's clothes to the charity shop.'

'Dad's clothes?'

'I've packed them up already.'

'No, not…' I didn't know what to say. I could hear Mum clattering around in the kitchen. I crept out into the hallway. I opened both suitcases.

My heart pummelled so hard, it hurt – it actually hurt. The familiar jumpers, a scarf, and the shirts he wore, all neatly folded. I kneeled down and lifted them out one by one. Dad was not one to buy new clothes so I knew them all of old. The piles of checkered shirts – Dad liked his checkered shirts – the one cardigan Aunt Vera bought him for Christmas the year before last, his many jumpers. And with each one, an image jumped out at me: Dad taking me to school when I was much younger, Dad watching me at ballet, Dad at the café welcoming me whenever I went to see him there, Dad at the panto, Dad smiling when I showed him my certificate. Mum had washed them all, yet when I pressed Dad's favourite green jumper to my nose, I could still smell him. It had two red stripes across the chest. His smell was so strong. He came back to me in an instant. He felt so real. I was touching him. He was here, now. The smell brought back his voice, that deep, soothing voice he had, the way he always called me 'love'. I couldn't understand how she could do this. Did he mean so little to her? My father, my wonderful dad. She wasn't taking this jumper, not the green one with the red stripes. I buried my head into the green jumper and let the tears come.

Chapter 68
March 2002

My mother has died. Mrs Hale, the manager of the care home, rang me the day after I returned from Germany. The news left me numb. Not sad, particularly, although that came later. Just numb as if my soul had been weighted down.

The funeral is a pathetic affair. There are just two of us in attendance, me and Mrs Hale, plus the crematorium employee conducting the dismal service. Two people. And frankly, given a choice, one of us would prefer not to be here. I wondered how it worked – you live eighty-seven years on this planet, and only two people show up to your funeral. I was genuinely sorry for her. But did I feel much sorrow? I did in a way if I tried hard enough. I'd felt such resentment for most of my life that I had such a cold, unloving woman for a mother. But I realise now, standing here in front of her coffin, that resentment was the wrong emotion. She deserved my pity, not my resentment. Where had this bitterness come from? Ultimately, I tell myself, it wasn't her fault. She was a product of her time, perhaps, a young woman in a nation ravaged by our bombs. Perhaps she was the product of her upbringing, but that's something I never knew about, another of those many things she simply refused to talk about. Perhaps it was because she'd outlived most of her friends. But, of course, that's just fanciful thinking because, in truth, Mother never had any friends, never did. She spurned anyone who came within five feet of her, anyone who showed the slightest interest in her.

The woman from the crematorium gives a short speech based on the few facts I'd given her about my mother and the life she'd lived. The rest of it is made up of generic platitudes that could apply to anyone who ever lived and died. She talks of love, but love is the one thing that remained alien to my mother throughout her life, at least my part in it. Love was an unnecessary emotion.

I can't help but contrast today to my father's funeral so long ago. I remembered the pride I felt that so many people turned up, that he was held in such esteem that they made the effort. And often, in the past, I wonder how such a loving, caring man as my father ended up with my mother. What did he see in her that no one else did; what part of her made this man think to himself, 'I want to spend the rest of my life with this woman'. I will never understand.

The moment has come. 'Abide With Me' rattles out from the speakers as my mother's coffin glides along the rollers and slowly disappears behind the curtain into the fiery hell that lies beyond. What a sad, sad life, you poor woman.

Barry would have been here had I told him but I hadn't. He never liked my mother. He tried his best but, to be fair, she never showed him any affection. 'She's a difficult person to like, your mother,' was his damning assessment years ago, soon after we'd married. And he wasn't wrong, I think, as the coffin disappears into the abyss. She was exactly that. And I had to live with that all my childhood.

I shake the crematorium woman's hand and thank her. I thank Mrs Hale for coming, knowing she can't wait to leave, and a part of me wants to scream.

I knew my mother had a story to tell me, about her life during the war, about my earliest years, that part of me that still, to this day, feels incomplete. But she never did tell me. She kept her secrets to herself her whole bloody life, and now she'd taken them with her to the grave, and I will never know. I want to weep.

*

Spring is on its way. The days are gradually becoming warmer and longer. Today, a Sunday, I go for a walk in the local forest and stand gazing at the blankets of snowdrops everywhere. Snowdrops always make me think of the park in Waverley. How, when we thought no one was looking, we'd pick a bunch and give them to our mothers. And our mothers would put them in a little glass with water and put it on the sideboard or in the centre of the dining table. Today I think I was the only person either without a dog or all alone. I envy the young couples, their children splashing in the puddles, muddying their wellington boots. I envy the older couples and their easy companionship. I envy how all these people will return home after their walks and with rosy cheeks and clean lungs share a pot of tea and a cake. I envy all the things couples do and take for granted, the pleasure of mundane routines. I envy the simple to and fro of conversation between people who love one another. I often will not speak to another human being from the time I leave work on Friday evening to my return on Monday morning. Often, I will go to the local shop to buy a newspaper I know I won't read simply to have another person to talk to, to pass comment on the weather, however briefly.

It's been two months since my ill-fated trip to Germany and I think about it every day. In my lighter moments, I can laugh about it; how could I have managed to alienate the three people who mean the most to me in the space of just forty-eight hours? It really was quite incredible. I did indeed return home and find Barry's key on my doormat. I hurried through to the kitchen expecting, hoping, to find a note for me, perhaps a folded slip of paper propped up against the kettle. There wasn't. I know he is back with Shelley, that whatever disagreement they had has been patched up. I hope he's OK, that they're OK, and it surprises me how sincerely I mean that. He was my husband for twenty-two years, after all, and I still care for him, worry for him when I think he's unhappy.

And Tessa, still miserable at university but enduring it because I'd insisted. I phone her, but her mobile always goes straight to voicemail. I've long given up leaving messages, because I know now she won't respond. It's her way of punishing me, and it's working. I long to hear her voice. The thought of her so far away from home and unhappy renders me miserable. I still can't fathom how it happened – two telephone conversations while I was in Germany, and I messed them both up spectacularly. If I had been at home, I might have handled them differently. It was because I was in Germany, far from home and temporarily divorced from the minutiae of everyday life and feeling under the strain of my mission that I dealt with them both so brusquely and hurt them both so much.

And then there's Tom. Looking back on it, he was right. The signs were there; I just failed to see them. The partner he never mentioned by name, the way he never showed any interest in me despite finding ourselves alone for two whole days. It wasn't just the fact that he'd told me he was gay that causes me to groan, it was my reaction. My only excuse was that I had drunk the best part of two bottles of red wine, and after our meeting with Herr Spitzweg and the way he spoke to me, I was still feeling shell shocked and bruised. But nothing justifies the way I looked at Tom, who was now on his feet and running his fingers through his hair. Then, to my utter shame, I laughed. 'Sod off, you're not gay; don't be daft.'

He looked as if I'd just shot him. He shook his head in disbelief. 'No, you sod off, Liz. Why shouldn't I be?'

'Because… because…' I started to cry. 'Because I don't want you to be, Tom. Because I thought…'

'I'm sorry, Liz, you thought wrong.'

And with that, he left me.

The following day, we breakfasted at different times and then returned home together. We hardly spoke a word. We caught a train from Heathrow back to East Anglia and sat side by side in total silence. From the train station we shared a taxi. The driver dropped Tom off first. He insisted on paying and I so resented it but couldn't work out why. As the driver retrieved Tom's suitcase from the boot, I got out of the car. 'Tom, thanks for… you know, everything.'

He stopped and looked at me, and my memory took me back to that last day I saw him forty-two years previous, the day of my father's funeral. I felt wretched then. I felt wretched now. We'd come full circle. I willed him to come to me, to put his arms around me, to say goodbye, that it didn't matter, to leave me with a peck on the cheek. Instead, he nodded, turned and walked away. 'I'm so sorry about last night,' I said. But he was already too far away; he didn't hear me. I could have said it again, louder, but I didn't.

I haven't heard from him since.

For the second time in my life, Tom has left me. I so needed him then. I so need him now. I'd lost Barry and Tom had lost his partner. We could have been a comfort to one another. We could have been friends for life – if I hadn't hurt him so with my careless, tactless words.

I'd gone to Germany to find my past. I didn't find it. I

failed. Instead, I lost my present and my future. I'd never been so adrift.

And, you know, when I'm at my lowest, when I hate myself the most, when even Tabby can't console me, it's not Tom I miss, nor Barry, and not even my precious daughter. It's my father. The gentlest, kindest, most loyal soul that ever did live, who shouldn't have died so young. And I miss him so much still that it hurts in my chest. I'm fifty-seven years old now. I'm already seven years older than my father when he died. Even at the time, I knew he'd died young but one doesn't truly appreciate how young fifty is when one is only fifteen. Even after all this time, I still miss him. He was such a kind man, a gentle soul. I mourn for all the years he should have had, the years he missed out on. He would've been in his early seventies when Tessa was born. He would have made a fabulous grandfather, just as he was such a lovely father. Life can be so unfair. I'll spend an evening trying to recapture him, every memory I possess of him, his voice, his smell, the way he laughed. And if I try really hard, if I really concentrate, I swear I can feel his presence beside me, and it brings such happiness that I drown in the joy of it. And then he is gone, and I'm left, all alone again, destroyed.

Chapter 69
April 2002

Today, another Sunday, I return to the shopping centre. I need another fresh round of clothes, I'd lost so much weight of late. I see the boys first, Dylan and Jake, coming out of a sports shop, each carrying a small plastic bag bearing the shop's name. 'Oh, hi, Auntie Liz.'

'Hello, boys. You've been shopping?'

The song 'Freedom' by Wham rings out across the centre.

They tell me what they'd bought. Their mum had given them five pounds each and told them they could spend it as they wished. They were just going back now to meet her. Shelley, they said, was in the Body Shop, the shop with "all those funny smells." It hit me how fond I was of these two boys; they really were like nephews to me, borne out of the weirdest dynamic, but still.

'Well, say hello to your mum from me.'

Then I hear her voice calling their names. She comes over, smiling, happy to see them again, despite having been apart for no more than ten minutes. And then she notices me. 'Oh, Liz. I didn't see you there. You all right?'

'Yeah, yeah, absolutely.' I hold up my shopping bags. 'Retail therapy again.'

She laughs politely. I hear her name being called out, a man's voice. 'Hold up, Shell.'

She turns towards him and I know straight away that this

man with long sideburns is no passing acquaintance; this man who called her 'Shell' means something to her. 'Thought I lost you there. Hello, boys. Got what you wanted?'

He doesn't notice me. Shelley takes me to one side. 'You do know, don't you?'

I shake my head.

'Barry's left me.'

The way she says it, the anguish in her voice, I almost say how sorry I am. But I don't; she'd obviously moved on quickly enough. So why are there tears in her eyes?

'About a month ago.'

'I didn't know.'

'I thought I'd found my man, Liz. I still don't know what I did wrong.'

I hear the man and the boys talking. 'You sure they're the right size, Jake?'

'Think so, Uncle Sid.'

Uncle?

Shelley sees me listening. 'Sid – my brother.'

'Oh, I see.'

Culture Club's 'Karma Chameleon' is playing now.

'Have you seen him, Liz?'

'Barry? No, not for a couple months now. He hasn't even phoned. What happened, Shelley? Actually, you don't have–'

'I don't know. We had a falling-out but then we were OK again but…' She's crying now. 'He just walked out, Liz. Just walked out and left. Why would he do that, Liz. Why?'

People are walking around us, cutting through us, Boy George is singing, and this woman who had stolen my husband is standing in front of me with tears streaming down her cheeks. I see the glint of silver around her neck, the necklace chain. And I try not to, try so hard, but in no time, I am crying too. And in slow motion, almost, we drop our shopping bags and stepping towards each other, hug one another. I hold on to her and I realise I mean it. I want to offer her comfort and want her comfort in return. We have much in common, namely a wastrel of a man called Barry, a wastrel but a man we both love in our own stupid ways.

When, finally, we draw apart, I see her brother looking at us. He nods at me as if thanking me.

Shelley finds a tissue and wipes her eyes. 'I'm sorry, Liz.'

'It's OK.' And I mean it. At that moment, I truly mean it.

'I know why he left me though. He was missing you too much.'

'No, that's not true, Shelley. I know he loved you.' Was I really saying this?

She grips my arm with surprising force. 'I love him, Christ knows I do. But in the end, I couldn't compete with you and your daughter.'

I don't know what to say. Sid comes and gently takes her by the hand and leads her away. 'So then, boys and girls,' he says loudly. 'Who fancies a burger?'

His proposal is met with great enthusiasm. I watch them saunter away, the four of them. Sid puts his arm around Jake, the younger of the two. Shelley glances at me over her shoulder, and the way she looks at me, with such sorrow in her eyes, I would do anything for her at this moment. Dylan, now taller than his mother, takes one of her bags then does something that almost makes me cry again. He takes his mother's hand, not as a small boy might, but as a man, a man offering his mother his support.

*

A couple of days later, a Tuesday, I return home tired from

work and make myself another microwave meal. While it was heating, I try ringing Tessa again. Again, it goes to voicemail. It is automated, so I don't even have the pleasure of hearing my daughter's voice. This time I leave a message. 'Hi, Tessa. Are you OK, darling? Please ring me back. I'm worried about you. You haven't heard from your father by any chance? I've not heard from either of you for so long.' I pause, not sure how to finish, 'Please call me, darling. I love you.' I catch my breath. 'I love you so much.'

The microwave beeps. Fish pie. I am beginning to worry about my dependency on these easy but nutritionally poor dinners. I keep promising myself I'll look after myself better, start eating better, and take more exercise. The occasional Sunday walk in the forest is not enough. I am letting myself go, and my skin has taken on an unhealthy pallor.

Having eaten while watching the evening news, I flip channels and settle on a film starring George Clooney. Tabby, who'd also just finished eating, comes and sits on my lap. My mobile rings. Tabby falls off my lap, such is my eagerness to reach my phone. So certain it's Tessa, I don't even stop to look at the name on the screen. 'Tess, hello. Hello?'

'Hello,' says a man's voice. 'This is not Tess. Tell me, please, is this the right number for Mrs Swingle?'

I vaguely recognise the accented voice. A little tremor passes through me. 'Yes. Who is this?'

'Ah, Mrs Swingle. I hope I am not I disturbing you. Is it all right—'

'Yes, yes, it's fine. Who is this?'

'We met recently when you came to see me in Germany. My name is Spitzweg, Joseph Spitzweg.'

Chapter 70

My telephone conversation with Joseph Spitzweg certainly energised me but with an energy without outlet. I had the physical energy but lacked the ability to concentrate. I make mistakes at work, but I do accept an invitation to an after-work drink one evening. Working in such a large office invariably means it's someone's birthday, and I'm always invited but always decline. This time, much to everyone's surprise, especially mine, not only do I accept, I am the life and soul. I hold forth. I tell stories. I make my colleagues laugh. One young woman, Helen, accompanies me to the ladies. 'Blimey, Liz,' she says as we pucker our lips at the mirror, 'you're a dark horse.'

I haven't drunk as much since my last evening with Tom, but tonight, with Joseph Spitzweg's words ringing in my ears, I toss back glass after glass of cheap red wine as if my life depends on it.

I catch a taxi home and collapse on the settee, drunk but happy. I apologise to Tabby for having got back so late and give her a little extra food by way of compensation, which she promptly ignores, deciding to go back outside instead.

Had I made a fool of myself tonight in front of all my work colleagues? Probably. Did I care? Nope. Having tried to seduce a gay man, I've set a fairly high bar in terms of making a tit of myself; I'd really have to pull the stops out to reach such dizzying heights of foolishness again. I still haven't spoken to Tom since our return from Germany. I should have emailed him and said something but I couldn't bring myself to do so. But now, following Herr Spitzweg's phone call, I surely have the excuse to contact him again. It's still only half eleven, not so late; he'd still be up. Having accompanied me to Germany and been invested in my search, he had the right to know. But should I? I'm a little drunk, I know that, and look what happened last time I spoke to Tom when inebriated. I retrieve my mobile from my handbag and, switching it on, I see that I have three missed calls from Barry. Three! But no messages. I haven't spoken to Barry either since my time in Germany, and the conversation I had with Shelley in the shopping centre still plays on my mind. I'll phone him back tomorrow, I decide.

But the pull of three missed calls is too strong so I ring him back. He answers straight away. 'Barry, you OK?'

'Yep, fine.'

'Really? So why all the calls?'

'Oh, I just wanted to see how you were. You're still my wife– just about.'

'I saw Shelley last week. She told me.'

'Ah, right.'

He doesn't seem to want to talk about it. Instead, I ask, 'So where you staying at the moment?'

'Well, I was in a bedsit for a while but I couldn't afford it for long so I'm dossing down in a hostel right now. You know, until things improve.'

'A hostel? Jeez, Barry.'

'Yeah, I know. How the mighty have fallen.'

'To be fair, you weren't that high in the first place. Oh, Barry, how did it come to this?'

There's a pause, and I think he'd taken my rhetorical

question as a proper question. 'Because I was a dick,' he says after a while.

I can't help but laugh. It was such an absurd comment, yet it seems to sum it up perfectly. We don't know what else to say, but neither of us seems willing to say goodbye. So, totally unplanned, I say, 'Look, do you want to meet for coffee? Meet me at Berty's café tomorrow at eleven. Can you do that?'

I hear the sigh of relief in his voice. 'Sure, I can do that. I look forward to it.'

I turn off the phone, and I think, yeah, I look forward to it too.

*

Bertie's café is a riot of primary colours – red tables, blue walls, several bright green potted plants that loom as high as an adult. Barry is already there sitting at an empty table, when I arrive five minutes late. He's grown a beard, and it rather suits him. Less so the heavy lines around his eyes or the faint line of grey on his shirt collar. We order a coffee and a pastry each and pass comment on the café and the traffic. After a while, he says, 'Liz there's something I have to tell you. I was gonna to tell you last night on the phone but it's too big.'

'Shit, what's happened?'

'It's Tessa… she's pregnant.'

'Oh shit, no. Oh my God. She phoned you about this?'

'We speak every other day.'

I didn't expect that. It hurts a little.

'She'd been poorly and missing loads of lectures, so she was really behind and stressing about it. Then she found out she's pregnant.'

'Oh God. I didn't know any of this.' And what sort of mother did that make me? 'How far gone?'

331

'Four months.'

I make a quick calculation. 'So we're talking... November.'

'She said you'd had a bit of a falling out.'

'Yes.' I deflate. Was this history repeating itself, an echo of my past? A daughter unable to speak to her mother, dependent upon her father? Is this how I made my mother feel? 'My God. I have to go see her.'

'She'd like that. She needs you now, Liz.'

'I know.' I scrunch up a napkin. 'I know. I've been so wrapped up in... no, it's no excuse. I am officially a shit mother.'

'And I've been a shit husband, so...'

'What went wrong with Shelley?'

He blows out his cheeks. 'I wasn't the man she was expecting, I guess. She was looking for a substitute for the husband who died a couple years back.'

'Oh, I didn't know that. Those poor boys. Poor Shelley.'

'Yeah. Thing is, she never stopped talking about him and...'

'And?'

He spoons an extra spoonful of sugar into his coffee. 'And I guess I never stopped talking about you.'

'Oh, Barry. No fool like an old fool.' I finish my pastry. 'So what's it like, this hostel?'

'Not so different from the Ritz, to be honest.'

'Hmm. That's good.' I wipe my fingers on the scrunched napkin.

'I'm going back to Germany next week, Tuesday.'

Now it's Barry's turn to deflate. He flicks a crumb of pastry across the table. I watch it settle. 'You going with that Tim fellow again?'

'Tom, not Tim. No. Not this time. In fact, I was hoping you'd come with me.'

'Me?'

'Unless, that is, you have other plans. I'll pay your way, if that's an issue.'

'Seriously?'

'Yes, what I'm doing out there is important to me, really important. And I'd like you to be there for me. Would you do that?'

'I'd love to, Liz. Thank you.' He wipes at something in his eye, a bit of dust, perhaps. 'But what's it about? Why is it so important?'

So I tell him why I went to Germany in the first place, and I relate the conversation I had with Herr Spitzweg.

Chapter 71

I'd replayed my conversation with Herr Spitzweg constantly.

'Mrs Swingle, I have thought a lot about you since your visit. I'm aware I may have been harsh with you both, and I want to apologise for that. The only excuse I can offer is that I was having one of my bad days. You see, Mrs Swingle, I have cancer of the kidney. It will kill me. I'll be lucky to see the New Year. There are new, special treatments they can offer but I have refused. I am eighty-nine years old now. I have no need to live any longer. I've had my time. Some days are better than others. The thing I've learnt is that death focuses the mind. Funnily enough, I'd learnt that lesson before, during the war, but that was many years ago and I had forgotten it. I have what I think you call in English a skeleton in my cupboard. I need to address that now, while I'm still fit enough to do so. I may not have much time. Time is the one luxury I now lack. This is what I had been thinking about when you and your friend came to see me that day. After you'd gone, I realised that you are part of my story. I knew from the certificate you showed me. I have something very important to tell you, Mrs Swingle, something I need to tell you and my sister-in-law. It affects you all. It is not something I can say down a telephone line. I would like to invite you and your companion to return to my home, where you shall meet members of my family. I will pay for your flights, your accommodation, everything. I will pass you over now to my housekeeper, and she can discuss the practicalities with you. Thank you, Mrs Swingle.'

*

I told Tessa not to meet me at the train station, that I would come straight to her halls of residence. I didn't want her tiring herself out unnecessarily. I catch a taxi from the station to the university. The taxi driver tries to engage me with his cheerful banter. He asks me what brings me to Leeds. I can't tell him I'm seeing my now-pregnant daughter for the first time in months and that I was shaking with nerves. I give him an unnecessarily large tip. A student holds the door for me as I approach the halls. I thank her.

When I saw Tessa's halls back in September, it seemed clean and fresh. Now, popping my head into the shared kitchen on the ground floor, it looks shabby and dirty and so cluttered. Three young women sit around a table sharing a cigarette despite the No Smoking sign, giggling and all talking at the same time. I can't deny there's a certain buzz about the place. I walk up to the second floor. Room 208. I knock on the door and, squeezing my hands together, wait.

I'm not sure what to expect, a whoop of joy perhaps, or a show of sullenness. I didn't expect her to burst into tears on seeing me. I put my arm around her and guide her towards her bed. We both sit down, holding hands.

'I'm sorry, Mum.'

I stroke her hair. 'No, Tess, don't be. It's me that's sorry.'

'But I've messed up big time, haven't I?'

'We can get through this.'

'I only slept with him a couple of times. I didn't think…'

'It doesn't matter now.'

'I'm sorry about Granny.'

'Yeah.'

'I wanted to come down for the funeral, honestly, but I felt so sick, I–'

'Tess, it's fine, really.'

She sniffs and blows her nose into a tissue. 'Do you want a cup of tea?'

'I never say no to a cup of tea.'

She makes the tea in her room and brings it to me in a chipped mug featuring Leeds Art Gallery. 'No biscuits, sorry.'

'You OK for money, Tess?'

'Yeah, just about it.'

'Because if–'

'No, really, it's fine, Mum.'

We sip our tea. I know what I want to ask, have to ask, and she's my daughter, so it shouldn't be that difficult. But for now the words refuse to come. Instead, after a while, I ask, 'Are you still in touch with this Tom?'

I can tell she doesn't like the way I refer to him as 'This Tom.'

'No. And I know what you're thinking; it makes me sound like such a slapper.'

'No, no, darling, of course not.' But, you know, a tiny, tiny bit of me is thinking exactly that and I sense my neck turning red.

'Shall we go out for lunch?' I ask breezily.

She shakes her head. 'I still can't eat at the moment. Anything I eat, I throw up.'

So much for that idea.

'Mum, I want to keep it.'

'OK.' So I didn't have to ask her; she simply told me. And it hits me there, sitting in this tiny room on the suburbs of Leeds that I'm going to be a grandmother. 'Whoa,' I say as the realisation hits home.

'What?' she says, irritated. 'What's that supposed to mean?'

'I'm going to be a grandmother. How exciting.'

She throws me a look. She knows I'm lying.

'How are you and Dad?'

I was dreading this question but I can't lie. 'Not good.'

'You're still divorcing?'

'Looks like it.'

'Christ.'

'You OK, darling?'

'Stop calling me that. Of course I'm not OK. I'm pregnant. I'm gonna be a single mum. I've messed up college, and my bloody parents are divorcing at the very moment I need them both to be there for me.'

I cup my hands around my Leeds Art Gallery mug of tea and I feel like shit.

Chapter 72

Frau Horch, Herr Spitzweg's housekeeper met us at the airport at two in the afternoon and drove us to the Hotel Mirabell. She said she'd return to fetch us at seven. I had the feeling when she said seven, she meant *seven*, not a minute before, not a minute after. The main receptionist at the hotel greeted me back like an old friend. There was a slight twitch of the jaw muscle when he saw that I'd brought a different man with me this time. But he covered it quickly. Everyone in the hotel, it seemed, spoke English so the fact that neither Barry nor me spoke any German didn't matter. Frau Horch had, on my request, booked separate rooms for us. If Barry was disappointed, he didn't show it. This time, I was very much in charge, and it made me wonder how I'd let Tom take control last time. Yes, he spoke German, but it was my mission after all. Yet, if Tom suggested *this* restaurant for lunch, *this* bar for a drink, it was less a suggestion than a decision. Perhaps he sensed I was in a vulnerable state. Not any more. I'd returned to Germany a new woman, able to take control of my life. Barry agreed with my suggestion that as soon as we got back, we'd drive up to Leeds and go see Tessa together. I was going to claim my daughter back. But first I had the small matter of claiming back my childhood.

I gave Barry a guided tour of the town even taking him to the ceramics museum. He also giggled on seeing the Greek vase with its generously endowed athlete. Men – they're all the same. I imagined the glee with which the artist painted this. But I doubt that even he – for I assumed it'd be a 'he' – would for a moment think it'd still be raising a giggle several thousand years later! We had lunch. Barry ate like a horse while I nibbled at a salad, too nervous about what lay in store for me. He knew I was distracted, fretful, but instead of asking if I was OK every five minutes, as Tom had done, he let me be, and I was grateful for that.

We returned to the hotel at five. I slept for forty minutes and then showered and got ready. Frau Horch had warned me in advance that although not a formal occasion, I should dress smartly. And so I opted for a dress I bought the day I last saw Shelley – a dark green dress, with a low back and crossed over at the front. I applied my make-up, but not too much, I hope.

I'm ready a whole twenty minutes early, a first, I can imagine Barry saying. I knock on his door a couple of minutes to seven. He's wearing a white suit. A *white suit*, for hell's sake, the very height of fashion in 1978. I despair, but it's too late to do anything now; I'll just have to accept it. 'You look lovely,' he says. I can't bring myself to return the compliment.

We step into the foyer at one minute past seven and sure enough, Frau Horch is waiting for us, looking a little put out. She says nothing beyond what needs to be said. Barry and I are cowed into silence by her brusque efficiency. It is no more than a ten-minute drive to Herr Spitzweg's home. Frau Horch shows us through to the living room. It's so tastefully furnished, wing chairs, ceiling-high bookcases full of red-bound books, but also the largest TV I've ever seen and, next to it, a cabinet full of DVDs. 'Herr Spitzweg will be with you shortly,' says the housekeeper. She doesn't hang around long enough to hear my thank you.

The DVDs are surprisingly Hollywood, films starring

Bruce Willis, John Travolta, Meryl Streep. Nothing in German.

'Quite some gaff, this,' says Barry.

'Please, Barry, don't use expressions like that in front of our host.'

'Listen to you. Weren't you the one that always said be true to yourself and all that?'

'You'll change your tune when you meet him.'

'No I won't. I don't change my spots for anyone, from king to pauper,' he says, jabbing himself with his thumb. 'What you see is what you get.'

'Ah, my guests have arrived. Good evening.' We hadn't heard him come in and turn to see Herr Spitzweg glide across the living room in his wheelchair.

Barry clicks his heels, bows his head and says, 'Good evening, Mr Spitzweg.'

I almost have to bite into a handkerchief to stop myself from laughing.

Herr Spitzweg says, 'I have to say, you're not the gentleman I was expecting.'

'Herr Spitzweg,' I say, stepping forward. 'This is my husband, Barry. The man you met, the gentleman, was, is, a friend of mine. Oh, he, er, sends his best wishes.'

'Kind of him, for sure. Well, Elizabeth, Barry...' He turns to each of us as he says our names. He's wearing a dark blue jacket, a yellow tie and chinos with razor-sharp creases. 'Welcome to my home. Thank you for coming all this way to see me. And please, you must call me Joseph.'

'It's a lovely ga– house you have here, Mr Spitzweg, Joseph.'

'Thank you.' Herr Spitzweg, Joseph, uses this opportunity to tell us his backstory. He'd started his shoe business pre-war but, unsurprisingly, it died a death during the war. He spent several years in a Russian prisoner-of-war camp, only returning home in 1950, five years after the end of the war. Reunited with his brother, Bruno, they relaunched the business. It slowly gained momentum and by the late seventies had boomed, making the brothers very rich in the process. I glance over at Barry. During the 1970s, Barry had been a milkman, a school caretaker and, after marrying me, an assistant in a hardware store. What different lives we lead. But, he was, I must acknowledge, an estate agent for a short while. While Herr Spitzweg is talking, Frau Horch returns with some delectable-looking nibbles. 'Care for some champagne?'

We certainly did.

Frau Horch pours Barry and me a glass of champagne each but not for, I notice, her boss. He sees me noticing. He pats his breast pocket. 'Medicine.'

Of course.

'Elizabeth, did you bring that certificate?'

I pass it to him and he stares at it for some time, and I realise in the two months since I first saw him, he does look frailer, his eye sockets more obvious, his cheekbones more pronounced.

Joseph glides his wheelchair until he is directly opposite me, very close. The moment has come. I flush all of a sudden, my palms turn clammy. He leans forward from his wheelchair. 'Elizabeth, did you stop to wonder how I obtained your telephone number?'

No, the thought never occurred to me.

'Two weeks ago, I had a visitor. He sat in the same chair as you now, and he pleaded with me to speak to you. He said you are a very special woman, and although you could never be together, he loved you more than anyone he's ever loved. You know who I mean.'

'He said that?'

'Yes, he did, Elizabeth. He said it twice, once in English and, I think, just in case, he repeated it in German. Maybe he thought I was senile.'

'Oh, Tom, you daft bugger.'

'Elizabeth, you need to be brave now.'

Barry rises to his feet.

'No,' says Joseph. 'Please not now.' Barry sits back down meekly. Joseph turns towards me again. 'Elizabeth has come a long way seeking the truth. She is ready and she's strong enough. She was from the minute she was born.'

Joseph spins his wheelchair to face Barry. 'Barry, I would like to speak to your wife alone now. Would you mind?'

I can see the male pride dented. 'Well, actually…'

'It's fine,' I say.

'You sure, Liz?'

'Yes.' I look at Herr Spitzweg. 'Yes, I am.'

Herr Spitzweg presses on a mobile buzzer and seconds later, Frau Horch reappears. Barry is led away like an errant schoolchild, his head down, dragging his feet. Again, I have to stop myself from laughing.

The door closes.

'What… do you mean from the minute I was born?'

We lock eyes, and after a few moments I realise he's beginning to cry. It's just this elderly, dying gentleman and me. Everything else has ceased to exist. I am completely in his thrall as if hypnotised.

'Joseph, whatever it is, please… please tell me.'

'I will. But first, I want you to know, Elizabeth, that I am truly sorry.'

'For what? Tell me.'

'Listen now, listen.' He retrieves a handkerchief from his

342

inside pocket and dabs his eyes. 'I was married for forty years. My dear wife died five years ago. We had three lovely sons. Now, I would never tell them this, and I never told my wife, so you're the first to know, Elizabeth; I was desperate for a girl. You see, I was married before. But only for a few months. My first wife disappeared towards the end of the war, a time when it was easy to disappear. When I returned from Russia in 1950, I searched for her. But I never found her. I thought perhaps she was dead. Tens of thousands of German civilians died in those last few months and weeks. But you see, I wasn't really looking for her, I never loved her, or she me. But I wanted to put right a wrong, and return the baby, that she and I illegally adopted, back to its rightful parents.'

'Oh my God.'

'I never did find the baby, and even if I had, I didn't know who her real parents were. But, in the end, some fifty years later, that child found me. Yes, Elizabeth. That baby was you. And my wife…'

'My mother in England?'

'Yes.'

'How… how did you know?'

'Elizabeth, you said your mother's name was Barbara Marsh and that her maiden name was Lüpertz. My first wife's name was Clara Barbara Lüpertz. The signatures on your certificate: mine and hers.'

'But that's not my date of birth, I was born two months earlier.'

'The date on the certificate is the date we adopted you.'

'Adopted?'

He looks down and pulls on an earlobe. 'Stole you.'

'You were *my dad*, my stepfather?'

'Briefly. I'm sorry. My wife took you away from me. I

343

never forgave her. You were a baby in the ruins of Germany. But you survived and now you are here.'

'And the number? Fifty?'

'You were the fiftieth baby adopted from that centre, a milestone. I never told my brother or sister-in-law that my baby had been adopted by us. Naturally, they assumed that Clara really had given birth. You see, they had lost their baby to adoption, so I thought I was being *sensitive* in not telling them my story. Also, I was ashamed. It was only when you appeared with the certificate that I remembered that number, number fifty. So, the day after you left me, I asked Hannah if the centre where her lost daughter was born had given her baby a number. She, too, had forgotten about the number. Then she remembered her baby was the fiftieth to be born there. And that's when, after all these years, I knew. I'd always suspected but hoped it wasn't true. The baby Clara and I stole was hers and my brother's.'

'You're saying my *real* parents are your brother and his wife?'

'Yes, Elizabeth, I am. Would you like to meet your real parents, Elizabeth?'

The world stops. Joseph's papery features fade in and out of focus. I have to fight for my breath. 'Yes,' I whisper. 'Yes, please.'

He produces his buzzer again and presses the button twice.

'No, stop! You mean… you can't mean now, this minute.'

'You'll never be ready for a moment like this, Elizabeth. It might as well be now.'

'I want Barry.'

'Not yet. You've waited your whole life for this moment, Elizabeth. Now, you have to do it alone.'

With that, he lets go of my hand and spins his wheelchair away from me. 'Don't leave me,' I say quietly as he leaves the room. And so I am alone, in this large, luxurious room, my heart threatening to explode. I try to stand but my knees give way. I force myself up. I have to be standing. And then comes the gentle knock on the door. I don't answer, have no voice in me.

The door inches open. A vision in purple comes in. A small, frail woman, a stranger. I can't see her properly, my vision still blurred. Someone is behind her, an elderly gentleman in a dark blue suit. The woman takes a few tentative steps closer. 'Hello there.' My knees buckle, for there, before me, is my own face reflecting back at me. Older, frailer, wiser, her eyes rimmed red, but I am her, and she is me. My mother, my real in-the-flesh mother. We both hesitate, a few feet apart, and then, like the opening of a sluice, I rush towards her, howling with delight, with anguish, and fall into her arms. And we hug. I hug her, my very own mother, like I'd never hugged anyone before. I breathe in her scent, her essence, and I love her already with a sharp intensity I didn't think possible. I turn and look at my father, my real father, and I see his love for me. He steps forward and places his arms around his wife and me, and I know I never want to let go.

Epilogue
January 2003

I hold Barry's hand as the vicar recites the prayers. We stand, heads bowed, around the font. The vicar, bless her, has to raise her voice in order to compete with Sophie's wailing. Tessa jiggles Sophie in her arms and tries shushing her and kissing her on her downy head. Either side of Tessa are the two young women and the young man she's chosen to be my granddaughter's godparents.

'Good morning and welcome, everyone, to this most special occasion as we baptise Sophie Hannah Swingle, and welcome her into God's family.'

My mother, Hannah, dressed in a fetching pale-blue dress, dabs her eyes, and I experience a surge of affection for her. My father, Bruno, stands next to her. I see him take her hand. I still can't get used to calling this sophisticated and beautiful German woman 'Mum' or, as I sometimes call her, *Mutter*. I fear the effort of coming over from Germany has been too much for them both. Their two daughters, my sisters, look after them every step. I doubt, however, they'll ever make the trip again. No matter, though, because Barry and I fly over frequently to visit. Their home is like a second home to us now. Both daughters live nearby and look after them. Joseph, sadly, lost his battle against cancer. He died in peace, knowing he'd finally put his wrongs to right and knowing that my parents had forgiven him.

Sophie is silent now, her eyes closed, warm and snug against her mother's chest. My mother calls me Helga. It is the name I was born with. I still experience a little tremor of pleasure whenever she calls me it. Barry suggested I make it official, so my name is now Elizabeth Helga Swingle. I've finally got the middle name I've always wanted.

Tessa gave birth in August. Barry and I rushed up to Leeds for the birth and only just made it in time. What an easy birth it proved to be. Sophie Hannah Swingle simply slipped into the world without fuss, and the world was suddenly a better place for her arrival. I hugged my daughter and told her I loved her. Barry drove us back, and halfway home I suggested rather matter-of-factly that he could move back in if he wanted to. He nodded but didn't say anything. I don't think he trusted himself enough to speak.

Sophie is wearing a slightly faded but still beautiful christening gown. It belonged to my mother, used for both her daughters. I loved my sisters as soon as I'd met them, Claudia and Zoya. Between them and Hannah, they told me all about their upbringing, their hobbies, and holidays and schooling. I lapped up every last detail, the childhood that could and should have been mine. They showed me dozens of photographs that chronicled the passing of years within one happy family, happy but for the fact that they knew someone was missing, a family haunted by the fact it wasn't quite complete, haunted by its ghost.

'People of God, will you welcome this child and uphold them in their new life in Christ?'

'With the help of God, we will.'

I still often think of my father, my English father, and I know he loved me as his own flesh and blood, that it never mattered to him that I was another man's child. And my poor mother, always the villain in my mind, was, I've come to realise, as much a victim as any of us.

Barry tracked down my father's regimental history. He'd been in Stuttgart at the very end of the war, a city of rubble, devastated by our bombs. We assume that's where he met a vulnerable young woman carrying a baby and perhaps fell in love with her. Did this woman ever tell him that the baby, me, was not hers? Probably not because I imagine by then I had, in her mind, become *her* baby. I doubt my father ever knew. I knew now that the husband my mother mentioned while in the care home, the one she married in 1943, was not my father but her first husband, Joseph.

The vicar asks Tessa to step forward with the baby. 'Christ claims you as his own. Receive the sign of the cross.' She daubs the sign of the cross upon my granddaughter's brow, and Sophie opens her eyes and gazes up at the vicar as if to say, Why did you do that?

'Sophie Hannah Swingle, I baptise you in the name of the Father, and of the Son, and of the Holy Spirit. Amen.'

A shaft of wintry sunlight cascades through the large, stained-glass window above us. Little pools of colour float on the ancient stone tiles. It's strange: all these years I've had something to cry about and I never did. Now that I have nothing to cry about, I am constantly in tears.

I catch Tom's eye and he winks at me. Standing next to him is Tom's new boyfriend, a tall, deliciously good-looking black man, considerably younger than Tom. Tom is happy and I'm so pleased for him.

The vicar lights a candle. 'Shine as a light in the world to the glory of God.'

It's been a long journey for Tom; it's been a long journey for all of us, especially my real parents. Her daughters have always known they had a sister somewhere, a child stolen from their mother and father, just weeks after the birth. My parents never gave up hope that one day they'd be reunited with their lost daughter. I was that lost daughter. I am lost no more.

THE END

Novels by R.P.G. Colley:

Love and War Series:
The Lost Daughter
The White Venus
Song of Sorrow
The Woman on the Train
The Black Maria
My Brother the Enemy
Anastasia
Elena
The Mist Before Our Eyes
The Darkness We Leave Behind

The Searight Saga:
This Time Tomorrow
The Unforgiving Sea
The Red Oak

The Tales of Little Leaf
Eleven Days in June
Winter in July
Departure in September

**The DI Benedict Paige Crime Series
by JOSHUA BLACK**
And Then She Came Back
The Poison in His Veins
Requiem for a Whistleblower
The Forget-Me-Not Killer
The Canal Boat Killer
A Senseless Killing

https://rupertcolley.com

Made in United States
Troutdale, OR
11/01/2023

14213398R00217